Seminar on Youth

ff

SEMINAR ON YOUTH

Aldo Busi

Translated by Stuart Hood

faber and faber

LONDON · BOSTON

in association with

CARCANET
PRESS LIMITED

First published in Great Britain in 1988
by Carcanet Press Limited, Manchester
This paperback edition first published in 1989
by Faber and Faber Limited
3 Queen Square London WC1N 3AU
Reprinted 1989

Translated from *Seminario sulla Gioventù*,
copyright © 1984 Adelphi edizioni s.p.a. Milan
Translation copyright © 1988 Stuart Hood

Printed in Great Britain by
Richard Clay Ltd, Bungay, Suffolk
All rights reserved

British Library Cataloguing in Publication Data

Busi, Aldo
Seminar on Youth
I. Title   II. Seminario sull gioventù
English
853'.914[F]   PQ4862.U8/

ISBN 0-571-15289-9

17. Himself took our infirmities and bare
    our sicknesses.
                                    A NARRATOR

36. But I say unto you, That every idle word
    that men shall speak, they shall give account
    thereof in the day of judgement.
37. For by thy words thou shalt be justified
    and by thy words thou shalt be condemned.
                                    THE NARRATOR

CONTENTS

BARBINO

What remains of all the pain we thought we suffered when we were young? Nothing – not even a memory. The worst, once it has been experienced, is reduced with time to a slight smile of astonishment – astonishment that we had been so upset by so little, and I too thought things were fatal which then turned out to be lethal only because of the boredom that comes over me when I think of them. In pieces or in one piece, don't we go on living equally split? And the sufferings of times gone by seem to be worlds so distant from us today that it seems improbable that we could have inhabited them in the past.

On Fridays Barbino's mother went off on her bicycle to go to the market, from Vighizzolo to Montichiari, and was away a good two hours – four kilometres there and four back. And the time needed to make a lira. She had a little trade in rabbits which she bred in two jute-covered hutches at the bottom of the garden. Ever since, some ten years before, with one of them – rather with the only one there was and it was an angora, white, very beautiful and plump – she had saved Dolfo, her second son who was dying of pneumonia, all the rabbits had become white, all of the same breed. Her father-in-law said to her then without mincing his words – my father was still away 'at the war' and she and all the others were dependent on old Angelo, who wasn't all that old seeing 'he had his way with everyone's woman' and even with the wives of his sons whether they were away at the war or not – that if children can't pull through by themselves, they let them die, and that if she wanted the money for medicines and the gig to go to the city of Brescia, there was one solution. She had entreated him; Dolfo's little head seemed to droop further every minute. And there was snow. In this respect Angelo was not a violent man – not, that is, with women. He must have looked at her with those blue eyes of his, which were cold and gentle, licking the left side of his moustache, waiting for this daughter-in-law who resisted him to give in. Instead she had called Dario, the biggest of the little boys, and told him 'be a good boy', had explained to him quickly that she was going to be away for a few days, that she didn't know when she would be back and not to say anything – not a word – because otherwise they would come looking for her and not to worry for she had to think of Dolfo, that Dolfo was dying, and to watch if anyone came near the hen-house and to give a whistle if they did because she was putting the white rabbit in the shopping-basket. And to pretend nothing was going on and to bring the rabbit in the basket to behind the shrine by the mill, because she would be waiting there with Dolfo on the bar of the bike in twenty minutes. The cock was nowhere near crowing and no one had noticed anything. Dolfo could not balance on the bar of the bike, perhaps he was really dead already, and before reaching the main road there was a hill more than three kilometres long and then another fifteen to get to Brescia. There had been a frost that night. She had not wept a single tear – she was 'afraid to lose time'. She was away two days and two nights, she had sold the rabbit to none other than a chemist, then he and his wife had insisted that she should stay there, had called a doctor. She had crocheted a table-mat as well by way of thanks. Dolfo had got better and had stayed another month. She had come home. She had been beaten till she was bloody by old Angelo and by her sister-in-law, who claimed ownership of the rabbit. From then on she bred rabbits only to sell them to others and woe betide if anyone mentioned rabbit meat or horse meat to her; she shuddered and vomited. She could not understand how anyone could eat them. They were sacred animals.

When the ragman came round the houses collecting rabbit-skins as well, so that they were taken off the wooden frames where they had been put to dry in the sun, and she heard his rather doleful sing-song of 'old iron, rags, rabbit-skins', she closed the shutters, put her hands over her ears and, tense and motionless, waited, holding her breath, straddling her legs so that all the weight of her body

10

fell on the soles of her feet, as if a sheet of ice or snow had suddenly emerged from underground.

On Fridays, five-year-old Barbino, the third boy – Lucia, the girl so greatly longed for, was newly born and it was Dolfo who looked after her when their mother was at the market – ran and put on her overall, the one she put on when she went into the hen-house with the pig-sty next to it (the pig was for the whole family) or to hoe in the garden, and with the burnt-out head of a match, feeling he had luck on his side, daubed his cheeks with moles and began to sniff under the armpits, and thus got up went out on to the street, dragging a chair behind him and a blanket with an eagle on it. Then he pirouetted on the chair and began to dance. He had filled out the outlines of breasts with balls of old wool and tried to imitate the made-up woman from the inn ten yards away – a woman who had a very strange odour which he was never able to smell even if, when he stood near her, he deliberately sniffed. The women spinning in the miller's byre said that 'Elide has an odour of sin'. He sang a song which was very popular which went 'Ehi mambo, Italian mambo, ehi mambo.' The peasant women stopped with their baskets full of vegetables and the live chickens tied to the handlebars of their bicycles – you could see their knickers and their muscular calves, their tendons were tense and the knee-caps hollowed by exercise on the pedals and only the more fortunate had as a token of their femininity a mole – it was hairy too – near the chin, a hirsute wart of which they were proud and which seemed to send old Angelo, who was no longer living with Barbino's father but with the other daughter-in-law, into ecstasy. They stood watching him, astonished and amused, scratching that facial clitoris of theirs, and perhaps anticipating the pleasure of soon having available a real village idiot, better than any up till now, better than the local barber, better than Scabby-Face, the seasonal swineherd. Behind him just on the edge of the ditch there was a tall plane-tree, a monster of a plane with tangled branches. Barbino danced for it. For all those brown and floury little balls that hung from the hard, gnarled branches and which might be so many testicles slowly cremated by the August heat and ready to fall off for him.

It was difficult to escape from the spell of that animal odour and of those imaginary testicles to whom he offered up in public his most secret and confused pleas – he felt them creeping about among

11

his thoughts and would not have known how to give vent to them otherwise nor indeed been able to do so. He knew however that these pleas were there in his thoughts, like tiny silk-worms, and that he must not knock them down but speed up their transformation if he wished one day to shape the cocoon of the others. He knew that he had to win.

Barbino never liked his mother. This was how things stood at the time of the excremental overall: there is a spectre of a tall thin woman with prominent cheekbones who forces her way into his eyes and leaps into them through the window-pane behind which Barbino watches. Between him (behind the window which looked out on to the ditch) and that woman, on the road, there is his mother close to the lamp-post. The tall skinny woman is naked – her face emaciated, the veins in her neck swollen, two incandescent holes below her forehead, veins which break the smoothness of the brownish skin of the neck, right down to the elbows, to the knees, those thick veins of a peasant woman sent from childhood to hoe in the fields, to scythe and to glean. His mother turns her back to him and is motionless. She makes a defensive gesture with her arm as if to ward off a cart-load of madness which rolls over her, crashes on to her. It is autumn, that is certain, the magnolia has almost finished flowering, those flowers that remain have spadefuls of burnt mud on their petals. Another few months and it will be the turn of the calycanthus. Then there is the blade that flashes out from the great flat hands of this naked woman and his one hope is that the blade will enter his mother's fat flesh; instead the blade remains raised and the other hand seizes the mother's hair, which falls in a cascade from its bun. The mad woman twists it two or three times round her wrist and begins to pull. He hears neither entreaties, nor cries nor any sound of voices. It seems as if they were acting out a scene which *he* has learnt by heart for them except that everything does not go as smoothly as he would like. The blade never falls, it always remains suspended and wavers, plunges down and rises again but always without striking home, bloodied only by the rays of the sun. The naked woman's eyes are those of a rabid cat. He feels that his mother, turning towards him in her attempt to twist out of the grip of the hair twisted round the woman's wrist, catches his indifferent glance, notices perhaps that he is not on her side and, although her son, has

12

not moved to come to her aid; perhaps she has beaten him again shortly before, because after all she has to give vent to her emotions for the cruelty of her existence and Barbino's two bigger brothers no longer suffice and now he enjoys seeing her suffer. Let her suffer then! The mad woman begins to strike her in the teeth with the fist round which she tightly winds the long chestnut hair – it is certainly almost a metre long – there is a gush of blood the colour of periwinkles – everyone has periwinkles among the stones of their courtyards – then his mother begins to slide slowly to the ground as if she were spiralling down an imaginary greasy pole. The mad woman has a waxen face; she looks as if she had been brought there in the Easter procession with breasts that are scarcely outlined and look as if they were dappled like spiders' webs; she throws the knife into the ditch. Barbino feels like going out to collect it from the water and hand it to her and encourage her to strike his mother, who is in a heap on the ground, the ideal position for going straight to the heart, but people are arriving and the scene becomes confused. At these moments his mother seemed human to him. The physical pain and her understandable terror at the knife brandished over her head had relaxed the muscles of her face, which with him were always so cramped by her hardness, her refusal of everything, but so relaxed and resigned and full of hope with his father, the Invaginator. With that undone hair of hers (the way she had to present herself to him in the bedroom and now her shame because everyone had seen how long her hair was – what a disgrace!) and with that suppliant look and above all with her tongue imprisoned by horror (just as it was in the morning when she had to tell him what had to be bought that day) she had become once more the beautiful young woman she had been in her patriarchal family of eleven brothers, four grandparents, two sisters, three aunts, twenty-eight cousins. She, so beautiful and chaste, with the stamina of an indefatigable washerwoman, had been sought in marriage by no less a person than the secretary of the commune of Castenedolo, someone who coud read and write, and then instead ended up with 'that man from the Mill, without even a scrap of land, goodlooking and that's that'. Barbino had never known a caress from his mother; she always had too much to do to get them something to eat, and as for her husband it must by now have been clear to her that he would use his hands only to draw her to him at night with such great tenderness in order to take

13

from her during the day even those few savings laboriously set aside from the eggs, the angora rabbits, the crochet-work. She had it in mind to buy the licence for a business down in the village – an inn. But Barbino did not know this and simply could not forgive her cruelty. The only thing that gave direction to his little terrified soul – poor little soul, poor little soul, Don Paturnia, the priest, always said – and the proud rebellion against everything and everyone that followed from it, were the blows which would rain down on him unexpectedly from her and from Dario and from Dolfo (older than him by ten and seven years) who in their violence were at once similar to and different from his father and whom he had long hated as much as he hated the latter.

He did not run out up along with the other people. He went out at the back of the house, tried to climb the pine-tree, scraped his knee and whistling, as after every momentary failure, began to chase a hen in the courtyard. She had a periwinkle colour in her eyes so intense and dazzling that it brought him to tears and now just imagine my mother stretched out on her bed, with her clothing loosened, her body freed from her brassière, lamenting and telling and retelling the story of what had happened as only she knew how, perhaps vowing vengeance, and beginning to curse the fate of poor people and, my God, let's hope she's not wounded there because she has to suckle Lucia, is her mastitis bleeding? and her two foster-brothers there in the village, more money for the business, the licence, that breast which every so often she still gives Barbino and which is the only part of her body to have a sacred and inviolable life, a piece of capital that is not totally killed off, Maria's munificent breast, the miraculous breast which will produce 840 kilos of milk all precisely recorded by her, ounce by ounce, hour by hour, day after day, month after month, year after year, for decades, and now the bowl of vomit by the pillow, other cronies at the side and end of the bed soaking bits of cloth to make compresses for her, camomile tea, consolation. 'She's mad – you should be sorry for her – she has no man any more': his brothers after nests, green lizards, snakes, their kicks and raps on the head with their knuckles when they come home and say 'It was you that ate it, eh?' and his mother with that excess of saliva at the wrong she has suffered, again! Better to run out into the grass, to dig under the calycanthus to see if the pair of little spectacles has turned into two pairs because he had put the tiny picture of the Madonna and the rosebud there as well so that if the boy who lost them ever came to get them there would be a pair each; but he finds neither the glasses nor the rose, Dario or Dolfo – one or other, for sure – or both. Let her have it, naked woman, hit her harder, hit her.

Barbino is sitting under the lamp; with the white thread he aims at the eyes of the needles; behind him, two steps down beyond the archway, the slaughterman and Elide with the big bosom, whom he imitates with balls of wool when he dances, and on the bench the dismembered donkey still smoking, the buckets with the salted entrails; he passes the needles; the lights are cooking on the charcoal and the mincer whining, the big bottle of wine that goes from hand to hand, cheroots snapped in two, the polenta sizzles on the grid. Old folk coming and going from the room to the wine-bar, jokes, stories, laughter, the feeble light on the whitewashed walls.

'Well done, Barbino, you're good, you're quick. Afterwards I'll give you a tip, eh?' They called him Barbino because he was the brother of Barba (*the beard*) – and Barba, that is Dolfo, doesn't even have one yet. Barbino is all greasy; the needles and the thread are all greasy and sticky. None of the others can see very well and he is used to threading needles because he makes table-mats; one day his mother had given him skeins of green and red cotton and a piece of cloth with on it a drawing of poppies and lilies and said to him: 'Do like this – go forward on the tracing and take a half-stitch back, then I'll make a cushion for us, at least you'll be doing something too. Ah, if only you had been a girl!' and he had begun to embroider, cloth after cloth, table-mat after table-mat beside her – she had no longer resisted the temptation of a chair and with a sigh began to knit for the ladies who wanted 'nice things' in case they had to go to hospital. 'That way,' she said, 'I put the money by for the licence, bless it!' (Barbino had embroidered up to the age of ten as naturally as he went to cut grass for the rabbits or, later in the school holidays, went to the toy-factory to assemble the pieces for the little baskets for the children in the nursery-school; later when there was the hotel and there was a lot of linen to wash, his mother sent him with Lenta (*the slow coach*) to the stream to do the laundry – goodness she's slow! his mother always said – to give her a hand to wring the sheets so that she got a bit of a move on and then would come to see whether

15

he was still there or had slipped off; to push the barrow with the tubs, that was all right, but to get down on his knees at the wash-place with the women, that shamed him to death, but he did it, otherwise he would catch it for some other reason.) Barbino liked embroidering very much and he liked to be with the women when they gathered on the doorsteps at full moon or in the byres, knitting or turning stockings or 'preparing the trousseau'. He liked their chat, so much more interesting than that of the men, and his mother was the uncontested queen of story-telling, making everyone laugh fit to burst; peasant modesty prevented any woman from complaining publicly of her lot and misfortunes had to be kept quiet about or turned to laughter (there had never been a matrimonial crisis or a rape before the coming of television – only at most cuckoldry and 'a little inflammation'). Very soon Barbino got used even to the dirty stories of the older women, stories from the end of the nineteenth century with chases through the maize, atrocious jokes played on the farms on courting lovers to stoke their ardour or their anger at having been made fools of, of gentlemen with waistcoats and merino hats who arrived in carriages and looked at the women too, licking their moustaches; whereas to stay with his brother or with men in general bored him to death, they had nothing to say and if they did he didn't understand because it seemed as if they always started off with an end in mind which only they knew. Men seemed to him conceited donkeys puffed up with anger and interests that had to do with giving or taking, people who could play at cards for hours and hours in the evening not so much to have a conversation but to win, to make someone drunk and get a signature out of him on a piece of paper at the right moment, and so they talked about the cards as cards and no more than cards – the king, the queen, the ace of clubs, the two of spades – without seeing in the symbols any particular plot that might relate the cards they shuffled to the vastness of the world. They were there – on that patch of ground there – and they would never leave their gains and losses. The men talked or winked and that was all, the women talked, were silent, and could choose whether to say things or to interpret them. The men usually played at cards in parties of four: they held their cards tightly in their hands, almost against their chests, and if they were on the table, they covered them with their hands and continued to make grimaces with their mouths, their eyes, or shrugged. When Elide and Rosy turned up their three cards each, the joker and the pack, and played with cards on the table, at every move, which was carefully calculated but apparently secondary to what was really going through their heads at that moment, so that 'the traveller in liqueur candies, you know, the one from Milan who was here last month' was embellished with yet another marvellous detail, and the cards were all face up and the mystery of the fluid which guided the hands with their painted nails was thicker than ever.

And the word-play in dialect! A very simple story told by his mother left the byre with bated breath and yet everyone knew how it ended but they all begged her: 'Maria, what about the one with the parcel of shit that Minazza always put under your oleander tub – come on, tell us the one about what Carolina did that time.' Well, the result of listening all these hours was that a little cottage-industry was born of his embroidery: all three aunts, even those furthest away, had one of his table-mats in exchange for a lira or two, and now he was embroidering them for the neighbours as well. He didn't keep the money. He gave it to his mother, who saw to buying him the skeins of thread (but now of every possible colour) and mats which he went to choose himself from the tobacconist, who had a bit of everything there at Vighizzolo. Barbino knew the chain stitch, the cross stitch and another stitch for dressmaking. One problem which soon faced his mother – and the woman who kept the tobacconist's shop – was to find mats with a single human figure not two or three. There could be as many geese and little trees and cottages as you liked but there hadn't to be more than one dwarf, more than one shepherdess; alongside Little Red Riding Hood he allowed only the good fairy, no granny, no hunter, no mother at the door, if at all then only the long black nose of the Wolf behind a tree, but only to put an end to the arguments. Since there were no human figures on their own, he began to trace them from some little paper or other, especially from one with a funny name *The Victor*, that Dolfo bought (he had begun to work in a carpenter's shop right away, he had already cut two of his fingers; the seminary, his father had said, didn't agree with his health, and he had taken him away; the truth is that he needed someone at home who would go out and earn a bit right away, no question of waiting for him to become a priest, as for Dario there was no way he could stay in a job for more than a month or two and the money was barely enough to keep up the

17

motorcycle and pay for the petrol to go to Ghedi to find 'his idols' said his mother, his uncle Geppe and his grandfather, Angelo; Dolfo did not rebel, then or later; he went to the carpenter's shop, he always brought home his pay, he looked after Lucia, he carved aeroplanes from soft wood and with his pocket-money bought *The Victor* and every so often, in secret, did a Latin translation.) But the finest table-mat at that time was called The Eight Dwarfs – he had traced the seven as usual and then, instead of Snow White, had repeated an extra dwarf. For him eight dwarfs had in some way to represent a single human being.

So from the business of the mats there had come this habit on the farms that when they killed some beast to make sausages, they called in to book him to thread hundreds of needles for sewing up the guts and so it came, by association with the threading of the needles, that there was always some woman who said: 'And when are you going to make me a table-mat, Barbino? and it had better be a nice one!'

In there, through the wide-open door of the inn there is a fair din, then someone begins to play at *morra* – 'it's forbidden, it's forbidden' says Elide every so often; there is a swish of cloaks on the coat-pegs and hands that come and rub themselves over the fire; they have almost finished now, the woman with breasts bursting out comes towards Barbino and says: 'Dance now, eh, and sing Italian mambo' and before he has time to realize what is happening she puts her overall on him, fills out his chest with rags and stands him on the table among the lungs and the heart; she paints his lips with lipstick and shouts: 'Come on, Barbino.' Barbino, who does not understand why everyone is guffawing so loudly begins to wriggle and to sing the mambo song but inside he feels something collapse, a nook which, once brought into the brightness of the light, is demolished: the first in a series. Then he finds himself in the street again with the wooden feeling inside of these gestures made against his will, of that refrain which tumbled from his mouth, fifteen lire in his pocket, a fistful of stuffing in one hand and a little bit of salame in the other, his mother will be pleased even if she turns away her head at seeing that stuffing and that salame; icicles are hanging from the big plane-tree and under the cement bridge the ditch is silenced, the water white in the angora brook; he feels that he will never again be able to dance as before, that *that* was not what he meant, that he was not a puppet, that they had understood something entirely different, that his 'mambo' was not for sale like his table-mats, that the overall ought to remain his and that there was nothing to laugh at like that, that it wasn't like when the puppeteer from Vicenza arrives in front of the church on a Sunday and dresses his puppets and gives them a voice and makes them dance the way people want them to be made to dance. Next day, gritting his teeth with rage – his eyes already have a gleam of hate which was not there before – he puts on his mother's overall again, lays out the army blanket his father had brought back from the war (war! he had passed that in the orderly room too, because 'he had managed to get on the right side of the colonel') and begins to dance. But the song dies in his throat and he can no longer smell anything: the pleasure has vanished, they robbed him of it last night in the inn. Barbino tries again the next day; no one looks at him in astonishment any more, no one will ever again try to understand and thrill with him: they all know about the inn and say: Mad! Mad! Then Barbino stops for ever persevering with that overall which the world has bleached white for ever. And the tears are dry.

He begins to think of other forms that no one can rob him of, which are in a certain sense public without being any less his own. Like playing with Dario's shot-gun, firing real pellets at unwitting children when they are playing bandits but without aiming at them and saying to them: 'You bastard, I missed by a hair's-breadth' and taking them to see the holes in the woodpile or in the walls and seeing them grow pale – even if he knew how many blows Dario would give him the moment they went and told him he had taken his shot-gun. And the tears are tears of anger, of hatred, of impotence.

Or a tableful of fresh pasta newly made by his mother: *tagliatelle* for *pastasciutta* and *tagliatelline* for soup, for certain relatives who had money and who were coming for supper next day because there would be talk of the licence and one had to do things in style. Barbino who gets up at night and reduces them to crumbs. His mother who chases him up into the attic where he went and crouched under the pigeon-hutch and wept when they beat him and him shouting as he fled: 'But it's less effort to chew them!' He gets out through the skylight and lets himself down on to the miller's roof and his mother, who couldn't get through saying: 'You'll get down from there, you'll get down from there!' And after a whole day – there was a

19

mass of people including the relatives there looking, coming and going, and Barbino looking up in the air too to make them angry – he climbs down, that means delivering himself into Dario's hands. His mother beat him so much with the new stick for stirring the polenta that it broke in two, and then – Dario holds him tight in the vice of his fist – started all over again to slap him with her open hand because of the new polenta stick, the new stick! And the tears are a little bit shameless, a little bit justified.

But once he wept for a different and very odd reason. His father had come back late from the village, he had a chocolate sweet in his pocket, maybe it was a liqueur chocolate, he had called him as he slept – everyone said that 'Marcello likes a bit of fun when he's tight' – 'Here,' he had said and had wakened him, in front of him there was a hand with that gleam of red paper and up there, higher, a kind of smile. Dolfo had turned on his side with a howl – he slept lightly like his mother. Barbino had remained there, transfixed, all his little body had become a tumult of unchained hearts; no sooner had the silhouette gone than he felt a wish to shout; then he had got up, had run away up, to the pigeons, and there in the dark had eaten tears and chocolate. But what kind of tears were these?

Barbino lived neither up nor down; attempts had been made to deposit him on the floor of the infant school but he always escaped, he liked air. He had also climbed over the gate of the hospital at Montichiari, which for him was as high as a cathedral spire, and had slipped off home in midwinter the very night they had taken out his tonsils. But after a certain point to cross the dry river or any stretch of grass cost him unspeakable suffering; this fear would ruin all his solitary walks for all the years to come. So that he never saw more than one live snake and that one remained indelibly imprinted on him, and very few others thereafter, perhaps at the zoo, seen and immediately forgotten. This snake belongs to the time of his flight from the hospital and is not seen in its natural setting, something which, since he was used to green lizards and hedgehogs and owls and bats and grasshoppers and crickets, would not have had any effect on him nor the power to set its mark on thousands upon thousands of nights in his life. It is already one with his body when Barbino becomes aware of it. To get in at the back of the house Dario must have forded the canal, then crossed the potato field, then the orchard, then the garden, unless he enlarged the hole in the wire-netting which gives directly on to the road. Now he is standing in the open door, he is all muddy, his face is serious with a sardonic smile lurking in it and his look is frank – impossible to guess what kind of surprise this is. He goes towards the fireplace where Barbino is playing with the little figures from Dolfo's Christmas crib; Dario keeps his hands hidden behind his back and Barbino knows only that he must wait and that there will be no escape, that he will beat him for something he can't even guess at yet. Maybe he will give him a kick or a slap or a blow on the head with his knuckles – although such blows are Dolfo's speciality, learnt from the priests in the seminary – and later he'll tell him why. A darting flash like that of a knife with a flexible blade and the flash disappears into his T-shirt which Dario has pulled open in front with the other hand. Barbino cries 'Dario! Dario!' and lots of little bites wind their way round him from the stomach to the thighs and behind his back and Dario grins, holding his stomach with his hands, and Barbino has more and more difficulty in breathing and first becomes pale and then blue in the face and Dario thrusts his hands into the T-shirt and gropes and chases and grabs and the slimy gleaming thing escapes and re-emerges and disappears again. Stupefied he looks at Dario's fists which are squeezing and phlegmatically crush the head of a snake, the tiny vertical eyes, darting eyes, which gaze at him, protrude a little, until they remain obstinately motionless and are suddenly indistinguishable from the skin.

He walked in the fields, far from the house. In the fields Barbino tried to overcome his terror of snakes – now he saw vipers everywhere, under the pillow, between the sheets (Dario had thrown the snake away into the ditch, had disappeared, and Don Paturnia had given him an injection – he was the only one to have a refrigerator and the serum – just to be sure, even if Dario kept saying it was a water-snake, but no one paid any attention to him and then Don Paturnia had cauterized all the little bites with a red hot iron and Barbino had screamed like a stuck pig). Now every step in the grass or among the rocks had become a challenge.

He knew the countryside round about for miles and miles – so well that not even his brothers, who were as great roamers as he, could ever have known where the finest cherry trees were or the biggest blackberries. He walked and walked – the only time he was prevented was by the barber who clipped dogs: his mother, who used to be all proud of the way she made his hair stand up in a quiff one day said 'You look like a sheep, go to the barber and tell him to give you a real clip and then later I'll come by' and Barbino went without the slightest idea what a good clip meant, in fact he was glad because that way his hairstyle would change – he very much liked his father's, all brushed back, with the brilliantine which made his intensely black hair shine 'like the swells'. That must be what a good clip was. To be brief, such a mess was made of it that on his way back in tears, cursing the barber and his mother, he passed below the village, crossed ditches and fields to reach the house unseen by anyone, from the back. And it was that afternoon when he lost his curls, that he discovered the cat panting. But his misery and his haste to get home to find a cap of some sort to hide his shorn head were too pressing and for that day he, as they say, pushed on. But in the evening, suddenly, while he was still whimpering to his mother because of the trick she had played on him and he was in danger of getting into trouble again, he remembered it. The cat was red, it was panting and swollen, squatting across the bottom of the dry ditch. Next day he ran back to see the kittens: instead the cat was still there, still lying across the ditch, still swollen – but it was no longer panting. Red and green flies and frantic ants. And day after day always a little less: the swelling had gone down, less skin, and the eyes, less sunken than before, further out than the day before. He went there afternoon and evening and in the morning every day thereafter.

'It's waiting for me,' Barbino said to himself, going to his secret appointment with the corpse, which had stopped rotting and was dry by now.

'Where are you off to, curly-head?' the midwife, Rosy, always said to him. 'Take off your cap and let me see!'

'I'm going to get wild irises – will I bring you some too?' No one must know, all the little boys of the parish would have gathered round the carcass to play at Indians or would have thrown it at each other, he would no longer have been able to talk to it in his head in soliloquies swollen with so many unknown queries.

Clouds of flies and insects – beetles, dragonflies – went to and fro over that sort of rabbit skin, tautened like a dried cod by the baking sun. The first day it had seemed to him that someone was pushing to come out or was content to knock desperately. He had never been tempted to defend it from the insects; he sat on the bank and sucked the wild chives, casting a glance at the cat each time he felt he had given substance to an inspiration. Something flashed around in his little shorn head, trying to stuff as many words as possible into the instantaneous parabola of a thought fertilized by the carcass.

Thoughts and sensations interlocked, crumbled away as they rebounded from that stubbled belly, the first and marvellous conjectures about life and death and the source of the contradictions which filled the space between them – both female, both refusing to tell their secret. And Barbino laughed too, gripped by the tension of those riddles which he could not have formulated to anyone, which only he could solve and then only if he let them flow without forcing himself to give them the sense he was capable of giving while leaving to them what he could not grasp.

For days.

Then came the season of the first rainfalls, light at first, and one day at the end of spring there was an impressive storm with hail as well. And next day the tattered cat was not there any more, carried away by a torrent of muddy, unstoppable water.

The midwife who had given him ten lire for the wild irises and then another ten to let her see his shorn head – she was already tortured by baldness herself and had a natural right to see the havoc wrought by the barber and even to know about the story of the cat and the kittens that hadn't come out.

'If you don't want them to die then you oughtn't to let them be born – ah women! what do you mean give life? a lucky cat!' she threw at him. Rosy had never been liked by anyone in the parish but she was the only midwife and a good one. Barbino never forgot these words which began to go round and round in his little head long after he had got his curls back. So there was no trace of the cat any more but there remained the signals between the thing and the thing thought, the connections, the confused relationships between the words, the bald midwife who had pulled him out of his mother (his father had not even wanted to see his son, so great was his disappointment that it was another boy) and who now, with these words, seemed already to be speaking to a dead person or to one of the kittens that hadn't quite been able to force its way out of that

23

womb and the insects which in their turn lived on that carcass, free and unknowing. And the female, the female animal, which gave birth to other animals and caused their death as well, around which the whole world of life and death revolved. And the male animal, which hadn't been there, with the cat that had died alone, the male animal which is always absent from home and arrives only to administer the justice of the stronger, to beat or to punish and to shut the door with the chain behind which the female-mother is waiting, before disappearing once more. But all that faded from Barbino's feelings: what remained was a wonderful, strong intuition – that the cat which had been swept away by the current had been lucky because he had seen it and watched over it, because he had thought about it.

It so happened that Nanda, a little girl a couple of years older than Barbino who lived with her grandparents, who never let her out, one day managed to escape and to be in the byre with him – once she had bought a table-mat and given him a little string of coloured pearls. When the two children managed to meet they immediately took off their pants if they were wearing them and began to rub against each other. Both of them had spied enough through cracks to know almost all about what the grown-ups got up to. Nanda liked one thing a lot – when Barbino kissed her on the mouth and bent down and kissed her between the thighs. Barbino liked to do these things a lot too, he liked strong smells, he sniffed at Lucia's nappies for their smell of ammonia – and Nanda and Resi smelt of salted dried cod down there and he also liked to touch Pierina, only touch her, inside her knickers, because Pierina was too grown up for him, maybe ten or even eleven, and wouldn't play. Nanda was a strange child, not like other little girls, she came from the city, from Biella, her mother had been in these parts working in the rice-fields and her father must have worked in the rice-fields too because he had heard that she was 'a natural child'; no one had ever really seen the father, and the mother, who rarely came to see her, was now on another kind of 'job' which Barbino had never been able to connect with any of all the women's jobs he knew. Nanda was a little apart at the infant school too – in fact she was already of an age to go to real school but they hadn't put her name down because it seemed she was going to have to go away from one day to the next. She didn't play with anyone, didn't shout, didn't get dirty and above all couldn't bear the company of other little girls. Sometimes she took from a pocket two very long earrings which she put on and with these in her ears stood without a word watching the looks of the other children, who were astonished and shy. But out of school, once she had been taken back to her grandparents' by an aunt – all people who worked at the mill – she disappeared from circulation till the next day or for several days on end. The truth is that they considered her a disgrace, something to show only as far as was strictly necessary, so much so that they then took her away from school and tried to take her to Biella and dump her there, but they had to come back because the mother wasn't to be found, and, in short, there was no way of getting rid of Nanda. So they made up their minds to keep her in the house and that everyone loved her, until her mother decided to come and take her away for ever.

She had very short hair – it seemed her aunt had cut her hair that way to humiliate her, to make her feel all the guilt into which the family had been plunged because of her, not to kill off the lice. Nanda had a hard look and you could see that her teeth were never still, clenched in their anger. Barbino went under her window and from below spoke to her, told her to come down, and she said: 'I can't, I can't, but don't go away, stand there' and once she began to let flutter down from the window five and ten lire notes. 'In any case I can't spend them,' she had said and Barbino had gone to buy a stick of liquorice and the lemon for her as well. It was Nanda who taught him those things, 'the dirty games' which you had to do without being seen and without ever telling anyone. Then he had taught them to Resi – but she had run to tell her mother and her mother took Barbino by an ear which almost came off. Nanda had said that you had to shut your eyes and 'never' talk. Barbino obeyed – but his eyes remained wide open. Then it happened that that day, after the affair of the cat in the ditch, Nanda whispered to him 'come on, let's make a baby' and Barbino was seized by panic, pulled up his trousers, she held on to him by his braces, he managed to loosen her hand and nails and fled. But at the byre-door he had looked back: she had opened her teeth and her two bits of clothing had fallen down awkwardly over her front and she had a disgusted expression, he stroked her cheek, she said 'What a bastard', he smiled

25

at her, he wanted her to understand that he did not mean to offend her; then he went to the ditch and kept washing himself with the soap for washing the clothes. In particular he made a lot of foam round his finger – the one that he usually kept on sniffing as long as the smell lasted.

The street-lamps are already pouring down useless dirty light; there are three of them in all from here to the church; it is six o'clock, almost time for the Ave Maria. The son of the tobacconist – 'the shitty bitch, she puts water in the sugar to make it weigh more', my mother cursed her when she came back from shopping – and Barbino are squatting in a field of rotting foliage; every so often a drop of water collected and channelled by the withered leaves falls on their little bottoms. He has brought from home a twist of sugar and half a loaf which are there on the ground on a handkerchief. It is cold, they have goose-flesh.

'Have you done some?' the tobacconist's son whispers arcanely.

'Yes – what about you?'

'Me too, who'll eat it first?' he asks with a quaver in his voice.

'Let's count out' proposes Barbino; he knows a trick by which he always wins the count.

From far off there is the creaking of a cart going back to the steading, the caressing voice of a man saying 'Come on, my beauty, that's today finished too' to his horse; it is almost dark.

'Are you still sure?' asks the tobacconist's son in some perplexity.

'Yes,' Barbino confirms without emotion. 'I don't want to pull out. Come on – let's count out.'

'All right,' the other agrees pulling up his trousers.

'Why are you buttoning yourself up?'

'I'm cold.'

'Leave them down.'

'But why?'

'You might do some more. Come on,' he rattles out the formula. 'You're it. If you want the bread and sugar they're there. Come on, eat it.' And he produces a box of matches from the pockets of his shorts. 'I don't want you playing any tricks'. The little boy's eyes are disconcerted by those of his companion in shitting, he tries a smile then swallows his saliva.

'But why have we to do it?'

26

'Well, are you "it" or not?'

'But I...'

'Get a move on – is this the way you keep your word? why did we come here then?'

'We could have done it at home just as well.'

'What a discovery? because it was coming out – not because we wanted it. What a fuss about a little piece of shit.'

'Maybe – but eating it,' muttered the other; resigned to his fate, he takes a piece of bread and barely dips it.

'No funny business now, put it well in, more – that's right, that's right – well in. A little sugar?'

'No I don't need any,' the boy replied proudly.

'Well done, bitter medicine is good my mum says. And then with that sugar –'

'The medicine, the medicine –'

He has swallowed the mouthful whole and grimaces.

'Disgusting! Now it's your turn!' he says triumphantly, rendered furious by his heroic deed.

The bell rings out the Ave Maria spacing the tremulous strokes with obsessive pauses.

'Let's get out of here – it's time for the procession, the red men are coming to put us in sacks and take us to Rooshia. Quick, let's get out of here.'

'Come on, you eat a bit of mine too, eat it, eat it.' His look is as supplicating as his voice.

'There's no time, hurry up, button yourself.'

Barbino has already rushed out of the field of bushes and behind him the little boy stumbles whining.

'Eat it – just a little.'

In the lane, as they run, there is the obstinate sob of the silence, the wailing turns to panting:

'Yes, yes, this way you'll tell everyone now that I ate your shit –'

'No – Not at all – you have my word of honour –'

'Your word, your word –'

'Look how dark it is, don't you hear the footsteps of the red men? get a move on or look out for yourself. Get on and afterwards I'll give you one of the little pictures Don Paturnia gave me. You know – the one that tells you about the men from Rooshia, eh?'

'Yes, Rooshia, Rooshia. But you haven't eaten mine.'

'Stop whining and tell your mother instead to stop putting water in the sugar.'

Three hours have passed. Barbino makes his way through the expanse of slimy herbage; his teeth are chattering, it is cold; then he crouches in the narrow furrows and opens his eyes wide; he breaks the bread and abundantly keeps the promise made to the tobacconist's son. But no one must know whether he only appears to cheat or cheats to make amends in silence, so as to get used to open treachery without having to give explanations.

The wasted leaves of the maize are all twisted; some heads have crumbled; the peasants have left them there to be consumed by the November frost. There is a clump of oaks. Two sows are crunching clusters of acorns which Scabby-Face knocks down with a long stick. He is huge this herdsman, he must be fifty, he isn't from these parts, he comes and goes, now at one farm now another. Every time a boy goes past he puts his hands on his flies and begins to look as if he wanted to eat him. On other occasions he has made a sign to him but Barbino has pretended not to notice. He has hair that looks like bristles and his face is full of lumps and scars. Barbino arrives, trotting along to get warm; there is steam in the air when you breathe and the droppings of the horses and donkeys are dissolving in the lane. If his mother saw them she would run with the trowel to put them on the geraniums. And with a rush of steps and leaps the imposing figure advances towards him, a pouting smile on his lips which protrude full of pus-filled excrescences, framed by sores that run up till they reach the curve of the jawbones. Barbino draws back in terror; the shepherd stops and squats down and with a finger signals to him to come close: 'Come here, curly-head, come –'

As if he were following the inflections of the hands, which seem to draw towards themselves an invisible thread, length by length, Barbino shakes his head and says no no no and with an eel-like flash begins to run, as fast as he can; behind him the heavy tramping drowns the noise of his steps, which are as breezy and silvery as hair, the air beats its head on the ground beneath his winged feet; there are invariably only a few steps between them, but the man begins to gasp slightly; Barbino seems to slow down but not much although he does not feel the fatigue of his flight at all; he is so trained to run to escape the blows of his family that no one can catch him – not his father nor his mother nor Dolfo – only Dario with his motorbike.

He jumps a ditch, then the one in the next field; the shepherd is climbing out of the first one soaked to the knees. 'Criminal,' he shouts and stares at him from those fifty metres away, his breast rising and falling, with a wry expression that seems another scar on that face dirty with sweat and earth.

'Come here – why are you running? – I won't do anything to you,' he begs, staggering a little.

In the wind that has sprung up he seems to hear the grinding of his teeth, his cavernous breathing. Barbino now feels the need to slow down the pursuit even further. And he stops when, looking round, he sees the giant falling against a plane-tree and rubbing himself on the bark and his big sheep-skin jacket gets caught in the jagged places and loses clumps of hair; his scars have cleared up as if healed; Scabby-Face begins to weep, you can hear his groans; their two glances cross, one exhausted, with no treachery in it any longer or with a treachery that lacks breath, the other searching, defiant, patient. 'Come here, curly-head, come! look how big it is' he says, loosening the string round his big baggy trousers. 'Come here and touch it for me.'

He has three teeth in front in his yellow and black gums and his tears must be burning his sores. And his breath smells of herring and onion.

After that there was no need for chases; he saw him every so often – he was only a half-wit infected by some contagion from being with some animal, nothing special, except that no overseer had taken the trouble to have him seen by a doctor (he slept in the straw along with the pigs). In the end, when Barbino was eight already, and they had moved a couple of times from one inn to another, he let Scabby-Face take him on the bar of his bicycle along the banks of the Chiese. Barbino brought him all the ointments he found at home and obviously some of them must have helped because he was a bit better. The very last time he saw him was in a patch of brushwood on the hill of Santa Margherita one day when a temporary teacher had brought the children here to draw. There was even someone who had a kite and he had one too, made by Dolfo, but it never flew.

He was a hundred metres away, hidden in the forsythia, and he was holding his bicycle with one hand and with the other was busy

29

inside his trousers as usual, but for Barbino it was impossible to satisfy him because by now he was too busy rubbing his elbow on the crotch of the teacher in whose lap he was pretending to be drawing. Suddenly he felt something grow stiff in the crotch whereas the shepherd had never once managed it; and but for the fact that one night when he was crossing the road a car hit him full on and killed him on the spot he would still be there handling himself in vain, happy to have such a patient spectator, addressing words of encouragement to his extremely remote member and asking questions about the mystery of life, which the more you call on it the less it responds, and the more unwittingly you lightly touch it, the more powerfully it shivers and spurts.

His mother, pursuing him with a stick, chased him up into the big room to sleep with Dolfo and shut the door from the outside.

'Make him go to sleep – that way he'll keep out of mischief for a while' she had shouted to Dolfo. They were already living in the village, at the Workingmen's Club, which was sold a year later by his father for the goodwill. Sleeping in the afternoon was something Barbino detested and on other occasions, in other inns, he had lowered himself from the window by tying sheets together; but here he was six metres and more from the ground.

It was very hot and Dolfo, oddly, had more trouble than his little brother in getting to sleep and wouldn't hear of closing the shutters of the two windows.

A blinding yellow light, fine dust, a bed-cover with gold fringes; his footsteps echo and finally the shutters are closed a little; the neigh of a horse approaches up the hill and dies away in the thick feather pillow on which Barbino rests his good ear, that way he doesn't hear anything any more. He must sleep or at least pretend to.

Dolfo seems to be losing patience or to have lost it already and has in his limbs the languor of someone who will never have enough strength to change his position. Barbino follows him from under his half-closed eyelids.

'Watch out – if you don't sleep I'll give you a hammering, right?'

Without hesitation Barbino shams dead. But there's something new in the air, a tension he has not noticed before, even though by now he is used to the fact that when Dolfo is losing consciousness and falling asleep, he begins to grind his teeth. Now he is grinding them, but it is a grating noise that stops as soon as it begins. His ear has risen a little from the pillow. Meanwhile Dolfo gets up again and goes to the windows and closes the shutters altogether; but the other window still lets sufficient light in through the crack for him to make out at each blink of his eyelashes the cobwebs on the beams overhead. Barbino imagines that every so often he gives him a quick glance as if to catch him out and hesitates with that hand of his inside his drawers just as when he went to the window; but then Dolfo seems to forget the brother's presence altogether; he opens his drawers at the top, unbuttons them, stretches out on the bed and very slowly begins to caress his navel, up, towards the chest. His teeth stop rubbing against each other, his jaws grow quiet; his face is flushed with pink and since he keeps his eyes shut Barbino can watch him in peace. He even raises himself an inch or two on his back: a kind of snort from his nostrils and his hand stops suddenly and grasps his cock tightly and his whole body stiffens abruptly, then the muscles relax again and his hand begins to go up and down and the other to caress himself. Then that unexpected panting in the throat and that lament which rises from the bottom of his stomach and the three or four spurts of white spit that finish as so many mother-of-pearl splashes, luminous buttons on his stomach and neck.

Dolfo has got up and taken his handkerchief out of his trouser pocket and dries himself here and there. Then he falls back on his bed and sighs. Now he really sleeps, his teeth grind at full speed, not even the bells could waken him, far less the neighing of the foals on the carts on their way to the slaughter house, or the cries of the knife-grinder and the roar of the motorbikes.

Barbino gets up and looks at his face to catch the mystery of that strange experience of which he has been a witness; the face reveals nothing unusual, it has taken away with it the secret of that dark solitary happiness. He goes to the chair and looks in the handkerchief; it is damp and sticky, just like when you have a cold, no little mother-of-pearl buttons. But he feels he has been part of a magic rite, some-thing very different from the 'dirty games' with Nanda and the contemplation, which had been his gift to the swineherd; and then he is seized by the overwhelming desire to experience in himself that ecstasy – to no avail – until his little cock becomes all red and feels burning and he has to give up. Or at least to rethink this phenomenon of men with milk where they piss instead of in their tits like his mother.

'What do you want, prettly little curly-head?' they were cattle salesmen come to eat tripe and salt cod; the latrine was on the landing.

'It's up there,' Barbino would say and without waiting preceded them. They went into the latrine two or three at a time and took out their cocks and pissed talking about cows. And him, watching them with wide open eyes; up and down that wooden staircase hundreds of times, in Friday's confusion, hoping they would show their cocks, that they would make them spit. But it never happened. And he was tired of waiting, tired of being a little boy.

From the relief teacher's window Barbino, who had recently been confirmed, could see on the other side of the Piazza Garibaldi his mother putting out the intensely white altar linen in the sun, because she washed for the church too (and it was because of this connection that, when the seminary run by the Salesian brothers was closed, they had persuaded her to take into her house Lenta, formerly washerwoman to the holy institution and maid of all work) and then there were the sheets from the bedrooms, jumpers, pants, T-shirts belonging to Lucia, who was already getting a big girl and only wanted to wear skirts, all was so white behind the mass of geraniums, which were a froth of red and pink, and Lenta who came and went with her white uniform and the white head-dress which she wouldn't stop wearing, going about the house, without ever having uttered a single sentence in her whole life – or so they said. Barbino passed his time between Carolina's house and the house of the temporary teacher who now had a class of his own and whom Barbino went to visit every so often after lessons were over. His wife was always very busy with a little spastic girl upstairs in bed and another downstairs in an armchair and a little mongol boy who disappeared into trap-doors for hours. The teacher was a sweet and very handsome man. First of all he gave him a bowl of milk with cocoa and biscuits – Barbino could hardly believe it; in spite of the inn with its board and lodging, at home he had to tighten his belt and here he had all the cocoa, the biscuits, the sugar he wanted. Then the wife, with eyes that were always red, came downstairs, settled the little girl, who had been in bed up to now, in the pram next to the other one in the chair, turned on the brand-new television – they were showing

32

Rin-Tin-Tin – and went about the rooms, lifting up a trapdoor here, opening a bin there, opening cupboards and then went out with the little boy to do some shopping. Barbino stayed alone on the sofa at the back of the room with him, behind the armchair and the pram, where that bundle lay completely motionless. The back of the sofa was very wide and low and one could not see anything. Barbino at once put out his hand to the crotch of the teacher's trousers; he was always already in a state of excitement. Every so often he buttoned himself up, went to his daughters, kissed them on the brow, moved them a little for their circulation, and came back to the sofa without ever saying a word. The two of them looked at each other with wide open eyes. And when his own woman teacher wasn't well – she very often wasn't well, but came to school every so often too, and she liked Barbino very much because when suddenly she began to vomit into the basin and all the children were horrified, he had instinctively gone off with the basin in his hands to empty and rinse it, as if nothing had happened, and if anyone pretended to be queasy and was caught by her holding their noses, he scowled at them as if to say: If you are going to vomit I'll kill you as well – then he was always taken out and put in the male teacher's class. In quarter of an hour Barbino had already convinced everyone that the best thing was to do drawing. He went and sat on the teacher's knees behind the desk.

Now Lenta must have begun to die right in the gateway just after Barbino had turned sharply to the right with the barrow on his way to the stream as he did every Monday. It seems, in fact, that Barbino was the only person to hear a whole sentence uttered by Lenta. The woman behind them – Lenta had her back to her and had just begun to wash all those drawers and jerseys full of Dario's, Dolfo's and Barbino's nocturnal pollutions, and those sheets where the guests had slept in couples – reported that Lenta, before falling into the stream like a stone, had said something but Barbino, on being asked, was always very vague. The sentence, if anybody's, had to remain his. She was leaning with her worn face all screwed up over the stream and was scrubbing away at all those yellowish stains, sighing the while; Barbino was waiting for her to begin on the sheets and meantime was washing the stone in front of her. It would be the last time he went to do the washing with a servant.

Lenta had movements of exhausting slowness but she washed thoroughly. A stone cemented into the little wall said 'Wash well and speak little'. She had in her hands, as a matter of fact, a pair of Barbino's drawers; he felt a shame that was full of pride, he knew what he had done, it had been the first time the night before. Lenta had looked at them more slowly than usual and who knows how much seminarists' intimate linen she felt stretched from ear to ear at that moment.

'Ah, youth, it's a great time for sowing seed,' said the ex-lay sister. It wasn't difficult to pull her to the bank, even if the current was very strong, because the washplace had been built slightly on a slope just before the Bellandelli's mill, and ten metres further on there was an iron grating; beyond that there was the fall with the wheel half in and half out.

BROTHER FOX.
THE MAN WITH THE SQUINT

'But aren't you Barbino, didn't I teach you at Castenedolo?' said
Brother Fox, blocking my way on the pavement outside the metro
at Palais-Royal. Barbino? I felt like answering, who is Barbino?
'Ah, yes.'

At the same instant, giving way easily to this stroke of good
fortune, I eliminated all the Macignas, the Pharaohs, the Jewellers,
the Antiquaries, the Poets, the Publishers in Milan, Lofty from Lille,
and – as I hoped – the Man with the Squint from Fontainebleau. I
did not want even to take into account the first thing that came into
my head on recognizing in the smart rather English gentleman my
ex-teacher of religious studies: that I hadn't gone to his religious
lessons for very long, in fact had stopped going at all, thus sacrificing
the little free film-shows at the oratory, after which he had given
me a bit of a tap with a bit of kindling wood because 'I wasn't sitting
still.' What with all the beatings shared out between people's hands
at home all I needed was to go and get them ecclesiastically. But the
fascination which every successful Catholic arouses in me was
stronger than my fleeting memory of a bruise on the chin – as always,
fascinated by contempt as furious as it was unspoken – I was drawn
towards the *grande bourgeoisie* of the Fathers of the Church, hoping
that all the disgusting memories imprinted on me by that bourgeoisie,
whether petty, middle-of-the-road or overblown would dissolve if
he – from the height of his position in the hierarchy – allowed me
to expose them to him in a natural way, that is to say, from below,
from me to him: beginning with a deacon called Giacomino and

progressing through various monsignors to arrive at the cardinals, the wearers of the purple from Milan's Via Monte Napoleone, where even the public lavatories are so sumptuous that they seem to have been furnished by Pauline Bonaparte.

And now here I am, mute, with one more unpleasant memory: that of this seminarist risen to manager, as dogmatic and deaf as the rest, if not worse. The big bourgeoisie is difficult game to catch or maybe it puts on black masses just so that you can't see them.

With men I always fall into the same trap, am chained to repetition of the same error: did I not fall head over heels in love with the above mentioned Giacomino, the chemist's son, because, even in those days, quoting Cato he said 'one only loves one's peers', philosophizing *a priori* on the impossibility of our friendship; and the immenseness of his benevolence? Did Giacomino not continue to want to see me from eleven at night until the small hours, to stand and talk to me, enjoying my eyes which gleamed with repressed desire, but then taking care not to greet me in broad daylight because my social position 'wasn't up to scratch'? And there was I mad with love, wandering about in the hope of catching a glimpse of him, to get a winked greeting out of him. Then in the long run it is clear that love becomes an enforced masochism, a masochism which does not give pleasure, which despises itself and wants to annul itself, but, my god, how can one manage alone? how can one manage?

Oh idiots, idiots! The one dignified thing Brother Fox could do – seeing he doesn't dream of finding me a job as a paper-shuffler or sticker-on of postage stamps or message-boy or whatever, a job in short which would leave me time to study – would be to give me a kind of Christmas box for all the cold I suffer in the street waiting for him and for all the time spent spying on the movements of the concierge (on his orders) before slipping up the stairs with the little parcel in my hand. I could certainly have spent my time better with my peers, the Arab toilers at the Turkish bath.

I keep asking myself why I go to visit him, what I am doing with him. I am certainly nothing to him, given that power of his to make me feel an object: it could be anyone else in my place or anything else, a dog or a plastic gadget and he would have the same pleasure with the same expenditure of energy. So that this what d'you call it, me, doesn't delude itself that it has a real place in the relationship and doesn't acquire the right to be abandoned.

The rite of defloration almost-for-payment hung over us, it was mythical virginity that freed him from himself – the great protagonist being neither him nor me. Me? I haven't been a virgin for ages, I know how these things are, a hell of a sweat, and then all this – go on! – no! go on! – all concentrated on that arse-hole of his, the arsehole of a seminarist on heat but not too much so; they don't put on much of a show; the little cries, if they make any, they make internally, confessionally, and he didn't have the slightest understanding for me sweating like a horse, reduced to an erection by numbers: not saliva, the cream, yes! that's it! the soft soap!

He would look at me, popping his blue eyes, and there was hatred in his look – he was certainly thinking of a mixture of crucifixes, biblical curses, letters to the Corinthians, imperatives of the psychoanalytical school ('one must try to take him from behind in order to identify oneself with the anal obsession of the West European male') and of the few hundred francs it cost him every so often, a trifle to him. And then I don't do it as a profession, I couldn't, I had asked a favour of him – it's not nice to be without money and without work. In short, I'd have liked to say to him: look, I am twenty-one and you're thirty and more, you have got on by, what shall I say?·selling relics and indulgences, that's it, have cultivated the usual relations with prelates and they have sent you on to the best business schools, I – when I was eight years old, when they put the host in my mouth – began to chew it because they had told me it was a sin even to touch it with your teeth. And perhaps also because, thinking about it now, I couldn't stand the idea that someone claimed to have suffered more than me, which limited *d'emblée* my present and future possibilities of martyrdom. And from then on I too took communion like all the poor children of the village only when the priests gave me a free ticket to go and see Ridolini's comic films.

When I don't feel like going home to the old man with the squint – Brother Fox doesn't let me sleep at his place (he has a woman, he says, who could come at any moment) – I go and sleep on a bench in the Tuileries, now the sharpest frost is past, it won't rain for a while. I really sleep everywhere. According to him 'lucky you, here in Paris to enjoy life!' On the cold snowy nights when I haven't even got out of his charity the price of the metro ticket to get back to Fontainebleau – I am ashamed to ask him for ten francs *again* – I am seized by the fear that when I am stretched out on the bench, the neuralgia of the trigeminal nerve, that deadly thing I got in the army, will stretch itself out beside me. In short: they didn't want to discharge me, I took my stand on article 28, the one about madmen and homosexuals, then the neuralgia got me, in the hospital they didn't believe a thing. But what was I doing in the forces without a lira? a year scrounging fags from the Sardinian shepherds? a year massaging my face?

There is no way of talking to that bastard, Brother Fox. I hardly manage to open my mouth when – zap! – he says: 'Be quiet, please, you're making me tired.' Was I upsetting the ritual, the office of the orifice? At least to be able to say to him: take down from the bedside table the signed photo of Pius XII, the other one of the friar with the stigmata, the other again with the signature of Umberto of Savoy. These six eyes – so watery and shameless – that belong to unbearable mystical and regal voyeurs. And when I attempt to explain away the ebb and flow of my mortified virility he says to me: 'Why don't you get excited?' I'd like to see him in my place. So I caught the ball on the bounce. Probably I began to explain to him why I couldn't get it up in too roundabout a way because he said to me: 'That's too much all at once – I didn't mean you to tell me your life from the moment of conception.' And then I really didn't feel like it any more at all and instead there came anger, the desire to lacerate him internally, to make him suffer. Instead of going to my head the blood all gathered down there; I didn't listen any more, one stroke and we're off, take this and shut up now, I thought. A fine cry, one of the finest I ever heard, a public confession, at last. I interpreted it as applause – I don't know how long it lasted. And with one hand I held his head against the pillow, with the other his arm. Defloration completed, ejaculation accomplished, with a lot of blood on the sheet (my God, I've broken my frenulum) satisfied? I asked him to myself, satisfied? and while he let himself go and stopped wriggling about, I went on buggering him for another ten minutes from force of habit.

Sometimes I write him letters – very sentimental ones – that I don't post. One began like this: 'A page I pen holding my left hand to my nostrils so it can give off the smell of your testicles.' Who would have thought that in Paris I would have met my old mystery-monger and gone to bed with him? I'd like to ask him: how is it that you've freed yourself of homesickness and how is that in my case, I continue to suffer for a place that I couldn't wait to leave? Certainly he with his position could also help me to find a job, a place to live, give me the means to leave my old mythomaniac. But not at all. He says: 'You won't stay in a job, you want to keep on the move, on the move, and I can't compromise myself with a character who flaunts his private life in front of everybody.' I don't know a soul to turn to, a nice stable, gentle soul. With all the meetings in Notre Dame and the orgies in the bushes, there is no one who lets me sleep with them, or better still, lets me really sleep. I am using up all the small savings I had set aside in Lille. Eating is a real problem. The hunger that comes over me! Diabolical! The problem of my hunger in the world. Even the canteen at the Alliance Française has got too expensive for me, the Invaginator always used to say to me: 'What? Still eating?' and he would put the dish out of my reach. And the three days at Cortina d'Ampezzo in the freezing cold. Since then while I can put up with the cold, missing a single meal fills me with anguish. That is to say, it is particularly distressing to be hungry at the same time as one is cold and sleepy. I am afraid of being hungry, that's a fact. The worst thing is that then you even get used to being frightened, and when you experience hunger once more, just at that moment you don't feel the fear, it goes and accumulates in some remote zone of the brain to reappear in the most incredible situations, when you least expect it, when it has nothing to do with hunger. And every time a terrible fear of something occurs to me, I always think it has nothing to do with the matter in hand but with that other fear, bound up with that other hunger. And the fear becomes uncontrollable. Ravenous.

My body is humiliated for a number of reasons – a lump in all my tendons and muscles in general. At the old man's the air has got so thick you could cut it in slices. And here I am, overcome by slight attacks of giddiness, at the *Centre prophylactique*, in the parade of venereal walkers-on offered by the Paris of the poor but tainted, the Paris of the Arab and Turkish and Greek women who come to have themselves given a real clean-out, with their children full of snot, dolls, and plastic machine-guns, and the old natives of the place, Foreign Legion types repatriated with the odd virus which, down there in Algeria, Morocco etc, got along splendidly with the climate and didn't manifest itself and once transplanted here, that is uprooted, there are the glittering pustules on the ears, the hands which become scaly. I am made nervous by all this tranquillity of people waiting for their turn like me, the dirty little ticket in their hands, this almost gay chatter of people who have been under treatment for years and come here on the way from the chemist's and before going to the hairdresser or climbing back on to the rubbish van: the fatalistic comment of a destiny which does not bear anyone a grudge, least of all itself. Well-off Parisians, whether men or women, certainly don't come here – some Brazilian students whom I get into conversation with (a little bit of an orgy, all together, with two young sisters in Montmartre), those Iranians, all so restrained, distant, making anti-imperialist noises (their spiritual head is in Paris, a very devout man, they have shown me a photograph: he is seated; then another; seated there too, it would look like the same one if a fold of his dress on the left knee didn't fall differently). They said he had been here more than ten years. 'Sitting?' I asked. 'Doesn't he ever move about?' 'He's an exile.' And that's that. I know as much as I did when I started. His name is too difficult to remember. But remember one thing: exiles are always seated, they never move about, and they have a sinister look in their eyes. There is a merry band of alcoholics, male and female, who continually have to be called to order. I'd only need to feel like a louse buried alive in a dead litter of dandruff to give myself the illusion of not being like him or him or him again. But it doesn't last. Anyone looking at me is thinking the same about me and my neighbour.

Then there are the fresh drops of gleet, those that have showed up during the night, like mine; some scabs; to the left, near the door, where there is a kind of terrestrial crow's-nest ('Sky! Sky!') someone suspected of lice hovers over an old Portuguese couple. I'll have picked up the discharge at the Rue Poncelet where Francis, the attendant, who is both hunchbacked and lame, likes me, knows that my promiscuity is almost total and that I could turn a gallows into a drawing-room if I am in the mood.

Brother Fox is too inclined to take the world as it is (how is it?) to attach any special importance to those ridiculous adventures of last year, when the terrified bourgeoisie gave all students and workers free rides in their own private cars. In fact, with that flair which distinguishes him, he began to use the metro to get to the office in January or May 1968, such was his terror ('l'ennui') at having to take on board some ill-washed and 'over the top' militant from the University (free!) of Vincennes, where every so often I too go for a walk. He is too wily to fall into the error of first of all having sex with a man and then of constructing for it some sort of justificatory problematic: not a word passes his lips. If he were a graphomaniac and was called St Paul, he would rather swallow his epistles. I feel him bubble with satisfaction, how he enjoys his torpid sense of guilt; he even denies himself the naïvety of recriminations, he would enjoy it less. Not a single fly buzzes over this bed. Absolute silence. In this way he acquires a canonization of the homo, invests it with a 'naturalness' which has never really existed – if not in some Jesuitical mind and in the white spaces between Montherlant's lines. He has the privilege and the power to wipe out the story of the bonfire of dry fennel by getting up and running the water in the bidet.* I hate him for that. I – for the same thing but without his privilege – risked Gaeta, the military prison ('if you don't give over we'll send you there, then you'll be happy, they'll be up your arse from morning to night').

Anyway, our meetings are rare and it is I who provoke them, I who search for him. He says to me: 'I wouldn't like you to make it into a problem – the job's done and that's that.' For him it's easy given the choice of amusements he has – he who passes his weekends invited aboard yachts around Mont-Saint-Michel or riding on the estate of someone called Giscard d'Estaing, a politician, another of his good connections. I'd like to say to him but does he know, this socialist, that you are a hypocrite? But he would reply – he taught spiritual exercises for years then went from high fashion to publishing until he managed to get into a multinational dealing in antibiotics (my God, how often he washes those hands which are always so chapped, always so covered with ointment) – he would say: 'He's someone who knows his way about' or 'That's why he invites me.' His egoism, his sense of reality are so clear and so fenced off from my unreality that I feel like an immaterial mote in his eye. He won't

---

* A reference to the pyres of fennel on which homosexuals were burned under the Inquisition. The burning fennel (*finocchio*) gave off a pungent smoke. Hence the use of the word 'finocchio' for homosexual – *A.B.*

41

waste his energies to get rid of me, twisting a corner of his silk handkerchief to a point: he'll wait for me to melt away of my own accord. Or suffocate me in my excess of oxygen. He never has a doubt, a tiny worry that comes to the surface: infallible taste, a most exclusive circle of acquaintances, the right restaurants ('meeting places' rather, for he takes for granted the roasts and the fresh salmon) and one cashmere pullover after another, dressing-gowns of blue silk with Japanese patterns, socks up to his knees – only Scotch wool – and I who, let's put it this way, throw him my loving hook, am forced to go through the servants' entrance with a stupid parcel in my hand in case the concierge should ask questions. 'Laundry,' I have to reply to her. And he never takes the bait. He has all my childhood at his feet and he is not interested in giving it a hand to pull it up. For example, about how as a child I used to dress up in my mother's overall, the odour of excrement that hypnotized me. I have my own, he answered. I did not know whether he meant childhood, mother or dressing-gown. He had his own and that was that. What is sure is that his mind is caught in the grip of a homo-macho suspender-belt. But did he ever have a calycanthus tree to go to in winter to bury a pair of spectacles with brass frames? Has he ever been there for two winters, eyeless, in the agonizing wait for spring to give the signal for the fantastic excavation to give back their vision to those buried lenses? Has he lived through the tragedy of not finding them any more? If I could tell him these things my prick would perform better.

I don't understand this darkness, this enclosed space, this enforced silence. Is he afraid people will know? Afraid for his career? And why, for once, not invert the fear and make it become fear that they don't know? I feel absurd like a snake that is unhappy with itself and would like to get itself something a little more human, more possible to live with, to find a luminosity to suck it upwards so strongly that it would find the energy to slide along vertically, using its tail as a lever, moistening with its forked tongue this great ungranted favour of an existence resolutely equal to and parallel with all the other vertical existences.

At the Rue Poncelet the circles of Paradise invite one to pollinate rhyming quatrains on the most angelic of effusions of blood. This collective carnality is the essence of the lost medieval civilisation of

Europe, Africa, Asia – but one meets a few Australians or Americans too. One gets such a bellyful of body, of childhood, of democracy, of apolitical innocence in this institution with its first and second class circles that the flesh invents for itself enough spirit to shrug off a possible leakage of matter. No one cares any more – one comes here, one is treated, and one comes back. The syphilitics of the *centre prophy* don't talk about syphilis at all – like everyone else they talk about wages and how to cook a real couscous. How long to cook semolina, where to find good rhubarb. And here I was thinking that all syphilitics killed themselves – but if I should catch it where would I find the stuff for certain gestures? I like life just because I always live it on the sly, because it is never full, because it is a slow business of getting accustomed to the final event, which must be natural: a pot of geraniums on the head after the monologue about your nose, a four-in-hand of horses at walking-pace which barely touches you and kills you on the spot, the coffee which overflows from the coffee-machine when one is taking a nap, jumping into the Seine to save a cat. Only when I am hungry does fear of violent death seize me: Dismembered at the Orangerie / Beheaded at the Slaughter-Houses / Shut up in an Oyster and Served at Maxim's.

Brother Fox has a great fear of germs, he always makes me wash first, and afterwards is in such a hurry to put me out that he doesn't even give me time to go to the bathroom first to piss. It would have been a good idea not to get myself treated, to pretend there was nothing the matter and to let him catch it.

At the Tuileries I drink a lot of water, that's plentiful. To try to sleep I drink more, usually indigestion from drinking water has the power to knock me out. I want an animal lethargy – something so heavy that one can't get up from under it any more – at least not till dawn, because with the first light I can no longer sleep. I envy the countries where black night lasts for whole months. I talked in my sleep, I know, I always have done. On this bench I feel like a cigarette paper, I sleep with only one eye because of the gendarmes (who generally these days shut the other one) but above all because of the people who play tricks on you with lighters. At the *Bella Napoli* – of course they remember me! – they told me to come back in a week.

43

As for the old hypocrite with the mad squint who said to me in Lille: 'But leave this place that stinks of coal and come and live with me, in Paris' and I dithered (Brother Fox, who is in the know *malgré lui* always says to me: 'You should try to be nice to him – a little at least') – they have even cut his telephone wires despite all that money he made out he had. I feel myself suffocating, I hear his insomniac steps near my door, those of an old wild beast and all the nastier for it, a wild beast that doesn't let go its bite, which has lost all notion of impatience. I'm cut off from the world and to get to the metro I have to walk I don't know how many kilometres – and my only decent pair of shoes is in bad shape, my 'tennis' shoes have come all unstuck. And to think that when I hadn't even been here a week to impress me he took me in a fine black car – certainly not his, if one thinks back, a hired car I bet – to visit a 'friend' of his: roads through the woods, snatches of conversation, a lot of mystery, references to lineages, to family trees, to quarterings, impalements and so on then finally – my mouth was hurting from the effort to smile with pleasure – there appears a manor with a marble and cement drawbridge. In it there lived an old man whose skin was quite simply blue, with cataracts, gout and every other illness you can think of. Surrounded by three rather robust and under-age ephebes in an armchair from which he could not move unless lifted. Then they make me leave the room; one of the ephebes accompanies me to see the gallery, full of the scrapings of attics that have been turned over too often. Clearly he had got through everything, what remained was merely a pretext to get five francs out of the curious. I had seven francs in my pocket and seven hundred and twenty at home in my tin trunk where I also keep a jotter full of notes I took in Milan (the other imitation leather one, a gift from Lofty, is full of clothes to take home to my family) and I wasn't at all pleased to go round the corridors after seeing the notice at the entrance with its tariff. There were a lot of ceramics, some fraying surcoats, a scribble – a bull – signed Dalí. The boy sets out the historical background of the family of this ignoble decrepit old man. I ask him to be more frank, I had not understood what *my* old man had come about, did he know anything? He knew nothing precise but *his* was about to sell the estate; who knows, maybe *mine* meant to make an offer: at least that was what he had said on the phone. And these three rent-boys were probably there to guide the crippled hand of *their* old man to make the signature on the contract. But what did that matter to me? I drew a sigh of relief; he was a bit odd and a fantasist but obviously he was still part of *le côté des Guermantes*. Now I, when I gave in my notice to the transport business in Lille and informed him I was about to arrive in Paris, had said to him: No sex, understood? like a stubborn boy with his mind made up to exploit all his grandfather's weaknesses without having to give him so much as a slap. He with that humble voice of his, so artificially human, had said right away: 'That's fine with me, all I want is your company, which I prize – prize a very great deal, – maybe with time...'. In fact I had already thought it all out even before getting on to the train: to get myself organized as soon as possible and find a place to live before that sword of Damocles fell on me from above the dyed hair that hung over a venereal squint. I never talked to him explicitly about money – I took it for granted that he was to give me some, keep me, pay for me to go to the Alliance Française. But the money didn't come. Two days in his company without even getting the fee for the Alliance, a trifle, and the money for the monthly season ticket for the metro, had seemed to me to be an unjust eternity – to have to put up with his drooling attention for all those hours for nothing more than a dinner and a supper. And I was determined not to touch my funds, such as they were. And he says to me on the third day after my veiled request for contributions in return for my 'friend- ship': 'I am expecting a payment of ten thousand francs and today I've forgotten to go to the bank again, would you mind lending me four hundred francs? Two hundred for me, go and enrol at the Alliance with the other two hundred.' Thinking back, he would have gone to hire the official-looking black car with that two hundred francs. But now on the basis of this confidence from the guide I feel joyous, exultant. At the far end we reach a wall full of coloured bits of pottery and he opens his hand: 'Five francs,' he says. It seemed a bit boorish on his part but I didn't want to have arguments, I didn't want to let them see that, with a friend who was about to buy a castle, I was going to haggle over five francs. In fact I gave him all seven. I must have been a bit drunk, going back to schoolroom desks must have made me giddy, life was smiling at me.

Then the old man began to invent excuses, to make mountains out of them, that loan having been written off without indemnifica- tion, I was using up my resources, the sword was coming closer and closer, the pawing of the mangy wild beast at my door, which was closed from the inside, became less and less padded; his voice, wary, urgent, waking me at every hour of the night to ask if I need anything, to say he is watching over me, telling me to sleep well, his treasure. I have great difficulty in containing my hate, my desire to murder. Perhaps his plan is no other than to stoke it, to make it explode, to cultivate day by day his own executioner.

Every so often the old man says I shall have to learn to ride, that I must take swimming lessons to strengthen my arms and back – but never a hint as to how these things are to be paid for. The fact is that in this apartment I began to have problems almost at once – and the business of the castle is off altogether, impossible to learn anything about it. The black car disappeared from circulation immediately after that saunter of a drive. One morning, in the bath, he touched me. I told him that was not the bargain, he begged me to be more understanding, or rather 'accommodating', that he was old, that he was alone and I said to him: 'So I see, so I see'; I told him I was there because he had promised certain things, and what had happened to these things, when would I begin to see something more than always 'tomorrow'? I could have killed him. I masturbated him, holding it with two fingers and turning away my head, putting up with his disgusting caresses on my head, to which every so often he gave a downwards push. When I get really nasty I begin to have tearful tantrums; when I feel myself crushed by the weight of my desire for revenge, I become gentle and like glass, I am prepared to be immolated, fatally: all to distance myself from this hatred which suddenly bursts into flame and flares up and risks overwhelming me, transforming me into Jack the Ripper. Mine is a scientific niceness, so as not to go to prison, through weakness, through philanthropism, for killing someone to do him a favour. So once more I chose official obedience; I was no longer there, I removed myself, it has happened to me before. My savings were almost gone. Now I am completely broke.

On Saturday he went off somewhere or other with a boy whom he introduced perhaps to let me know that my crude presence is no longer desired. I asked him what had happened to my four hundred francs, in front of the boy. 'Oh,' he said, 'I'm sorry, the banks are shut, I'll cash something on the way.' I haven't even a franc and

I haven't eaten since yesterday, the cylinder of gas is finished and Brother Fox is away for his weekend; I cooked some spaghetti two days ago, and now I tell myself I must make them last till Monday.

Up there, on top of the kitchen cupboard, there is a tin of beans, like a hawk lying in wait, and I have no intention of disturbing it. Rather than beans it's better to die of hunger.

I told Brother Fox without beating about the bush as soon as he came back more tanned and more on form than ever, more toned-up, perfumed, massaged etc that I am getting weak, that sometimes I have difficulty in getting excited also because of the food, which is not only 'wrong', as he says, but insufficient. Your little laboratory mouse, I have told him, each time he meets you has probably not swallowed a mouthful for twenty-four hours. I'm sorry, he said, but this isn't *The Bersagliere, Pub Grub Available* and my refrigerator is empty on principle. Besides I am the kind of person who scrounges food. But then, I replied, treat me with more understanding (it was the first time I gave him a whole speech and maybe the last time) is it really possible that you only make love with me because your 'analyst' has advised you to get rid of your fixation and because 'one can never learn enough about the anal obsession in Quevedo'? And how much does he take off you, this fellow, for this great 'analytical' discovery? and what good does it do you to supply *ton derrière* by the tradesmen's entrance and the *ci-devant* by the main door (the usual daughter of some big businessman)? Why don't you try to reverse the roles? and give her the ridiculous parcel of laundry with in it the ghost of a suspender belt for your mental lace panties? He made no comment, he went to the door, opened it, made me a sign with his chin. Not to let myself be seen again. I said to him: 'I don't know how you'll find the courage to keep on seeing *yourself* again.'

Soaked with rain, with the frost in my bones, I get up from the bench and collect my little plastic bag with the grammar and the notebook. They open in an hour – I'll go and sleep on a sofa at the Alliance, in the table-tennis room.

The old mythomaniac with the squinting eyes, veiled by weeping, arrives accompanied by two Arabs, rent-boys, who keep saying to me: 'Open up! open up!' Not fucking likely. I have reinforced the door of the room with the chest, the two chairs and, damn it, he

47

won't want to knock down the door in his own house. I simply must stay inside, somewhere, there has been a terrible frost. In the morning I always go out by the window with my little bag with the books, for fear that they may be lying in wait for me. The old man wants to bend me to his wishes or desires, which are treacly, alluring, indefinable; he finds me interesting, the hatred I nourish for him, nothing else, no one else. I must become his masterpiece, the snake he nurses in his bosom. Perhaps I remind him of someone. I always remind people of someone with whom I have nothing in common. It is I who end up modelling myself on that person, simply because I breathe alongside the person who remembers him. Sometimes I envy the old man the conceit of his desires, for the perseverance he puts into an aim, which in my view is altogether insignificant and disproportionate – like making love with me. His aim is so clear, complete and indestructible, that its inadequacy must be an altogether secondary fact. And he uses only certain means, not others, believes only in these. There is order in his disgusting *vanitas vanitatum* and that order claims as its premise absolute ignorance of the ridiculous nature of the means and the end. And he is order personified in his intrigues, in his cheating, in his avarice – or maybe just poverty. And do these two Arabs mounting guard not cost him anything? you can bet at least enough to fill the sideboard and the refrigerator with food for a week. There isn't even a pickled cucumber, a tube of tomato purée to squeeze on to bread.

Ah, if only I could steal! If only that bastard of a policeman hadn't given me that slap at the market at the age of eight and hadn't made me put down the apple, almost breaking my wrist! What I mean to say is that the poor too can allow themselves a so-called strict upbringing – all you need to do is increase the police forces. And from then on no longer able to pick up anything – only to ask for it or earn it, like cowards and servants. In spite of the policemen who do, yes, make children put down the apple but then go and drink free in all the inns in the village or the parish. Like the carabinieri.

The only object of value in the old man's flat is an arquebus hanging on the wall (with a huge padlock). I could force the padlock and go and sell the arquebus somewhere. But they would want explanations, I'd find myself in the police station within the hour. And I would admit everything, immediately; no, I'd recount the tiniest details. The fascination of having a public is well worth a little prison. But they would let me go at once because they have their hands full of guilty persons who are equally munificent with their guilt. I can't lie; too complicated, it gives me a headache, it forces you to remember everything and in the same form. With the truth, on the other hand, you can change it perpetually, according to your whim: *tout se tient*.

The persons whom, God knows why, I force myself to pretend to love are the only ones I really love.

At the telephone, have dialled Brother Fox's number: what to say to him? in what tone of voice? and how many secretaries shall I have to go through? and how many minutes can I steal of his 'precious time'? Each time, the same story. There is in this comedy – which is so full of obstacles, of meddling by outside parties and of justifications given and not asked for because of mistakes which perhaps no one took the trouble to notice, of gaffes and self-inflicted wounds – something inevitable which goes far beyond any psycho-analytical explanation of masochism. It seems to me that to become a fully rounded hero one must first pass this way: across the set of one's own personality in front of backcloths which give way, amid fluffs and blind doors.

When I think I love someone I at once begin to hate him and to find in him a thousand defects and incompatibilities, perhaps because in this way, through hatred, I manage to make sense even of love which, on its own, would consume itself and would consume me without having given me any knowledge of itself. I do not want to be cut off from the rest of the world as it is at that precise instant when I am walking through it. I do not want to leave anything of any kind in my wake; I want to look behind me and see nothing – either living or dead, woman or man or dog. The world wants me stripped bare and sentimental but I want to give it an attack of vertigo; I cannot bear to be annoyed by heritages which no longer concern me at that precise instant. And hate arrives at exactly the right moment.

When I *love* someone I am inevitably out of work. If I have work I lose it. If I am working I do not love because it is not possible to reconcile the two things; I almost always have to stop working. To stop loving is not possible. Otherwise don't even begin – to work.

It would be no help – neither to the work or to love. Perhaps it is also because the jobs I do are so unfavourable to amours – a working day of more than twelve hours, and always waiter, dishwasher, porter. I find no other jobs, I have not studied. They are jobs that soak you or dry you out or grease you all over or cover love with bruises, cut fingers, painless aerophagias. If I love, then I have to be kept. So when I love someone I become dependent; and since no one keeps you without demanding exorbitant interest, I begin to hate if I am exploited on the pretext that by making myself be kept, it is I who am a scrounger – love practically becomes a job, a black, execrable job.

However, it is always my aim to lose or to keep my balance, I have no intention of saving up or living it up or thinking of the 'future'. And besides what I am doing, according to the person who is about to lift the receiver, is living it up. Never having known anything else – it must naturally be the best. I hate those I love for because of them – and because of the contingencies of unemployment without a lira or a franc or a bed or a roof – in order to repay my debts I have to get involved in a series of such contradictions that I succeed in allowing the rhetoric of their perfect syllogisms to shine in all three facets of the Elect – and no one is disposed to invent a fourth one for my sake. These mental somersaults allow me to save face, where I am concerned, because I put on such a display of leaps and dialectical, glandular and anal pirouettes that really no doubt should exist – admittedly perhaps in a manner that is suspect to Aristotelian mentalities, but I have really earned my crust of bread.

If you bear in mind that I am not drawn to prostitution through egoism, because I am too intent on going about looking for my bit of pleasure and that the pleasure of others doesn't interest me, you will have an idea of this arbitrary and conscious madness, which is exciting in its infinity, impossible to renounce, which above all allows me to get to know a whole lot of odd and contemptible (very *human*) people who always teach me what not to be, what not to become and what is not for me. In short, in this role of part-time vestal virgin I find a proper niche from which to tell myself my own history, which I do not yet know, my future history, without living too much or too little, given that these are people I love/hate and whom I'd like to do without. On the other hand, I know that at the very moment when I could do without them I would no longer live any other human relationship, that I would lose heart in my economic independence and total liberty because it is my greatest and ultimate aspiration, if left to myself, to sleep and at last to get over my longing for it – and that sleep might last for centuries if I don't watch out.

This gives rise to a contest between me and those lovers of bourgeois extraction and ambition: to succeed in a situation so disadvantageous to me, to give them a measure of my hidden power even if it is hidden in activities which are deleterious and self-destructive or 'negative' as they call them. And on the other hand, at the same time, to bring to light the measure of their own insignificance, which is so well armoured in their syllogistic certainties, of which I make use while they use me, of which, in fact, I have a certain need in order to lay the foundations of my edifice, which is programmatically tottering and ruinous. I counterpose my desperately frivolous *cupio dissolvi*, sandwiched between getting together breakfast and supper, to their search for immortality and social security thanks to profit in everything, even in love, or cretinously, in sex. In short, I impose the law of a contractual power without having at my disposal a scrap of it, because they are very strong, they have at their disposal bases which are rock-solid like the dogmas or proverbs of miserly peasants and I am different – I possess only alibis without any credibility, which have the further disadvantage of seeming to be convenient without being so.

I like to pretend to lose on all fronts, to begin with. That forces me to adopt the poses of a beggar in the hope – a vain one – of buying myself first the cashmere and hiding it under the rags, then a pair of woollen gaberdine trousers, a pair of cuff-links, and to slough off my garb as the Unknown Quantity – to him and to myself.

All they manage to see is a hyena jumping out, that is to say another one of themselves, and they miss the boat while they strip me of my 'ill-gotten gains'.

True personalities are those that are invented: there is no greatness where there is not violence to oneself, and no humility is possible unless it is humility in the greatness of not proposing and not pursuing any aim. I have had a hint of *Grandeur* only in certain gloomy, muffled figures in a corner under the bridges. Never anywhere else.

Should I ever succeed in mastering the situation, I would strip myself of my own accord, I would give everything back, and my spoils in their true light would have the task of blinding, of demolishing by irradiation the true essence of the bourgeoisie in all its forms. So as not to lose and not to win, I am led to do many things which 'I don't like', being prepared to experiment with those which disgust me, but voluntarily, before being forced to submit to them from without: to invent a bile to drink to the last drop and then to render oneself immune when one is forced to swallow what the world has mixed for you. I want to shine, I want to be Icarus casting and remodelling himself, not the wings. But my vendetta is very simple: to unmask people, to strip people naked in front of themselves and if possible in front of society, to make them touch the depths of the remote and imperfect beast in them, which has a superstructure made up of any number of 'humane', pious, acquired, accepted, endured, pursued peplums brooded over to the point of being mechanical. My lovers are always more mediocre than me, who am mad and am not and always risk my identity and my story of the moment because, mirroring myself in theirs and renouncing any *naturalness* of my own I can assume another at will, without regret, and so begin to be someone else without laments over identity. I am a movable mirror, I emerge from it when the moment is ripe. Now to be just myself is not enough. People who are all of one piece make me feel slightly disgusted and yet they excite me sexually. They believe in an idea for thirty years, maybe even a political one, they delude themselves into deluding themselves that for forty years they have led a double, treble life and that no one knows this and so on. But they are also the only ones who, perforce, attract me; there's a lot to destroy there, my amusement is assured. My vendettas can take years to come to perfection and to fail, and when they fail I end them. The right time comes for everyone. Now let's see – whose turn might it be? It would always and always be his turn, the turn of the Invaginator. But the matter requires much more time, it must be my finest vendetta, because in his case hatred has been and still is of the finest quality; always able to stand, without tottering, on the highest peaks, without any feeling of vacillation owing to the distance, fearless in the face of winds and tempests and the backfiring of compassion. This is what I shall say to Brother Fox on the telephone: Watch out, I am a hyena that creates its own carrion. Hello? Listen, he says, I have asked you a thousand times not to call me at the office, yes, all right, I promise we shall see each other, I don't know when, call me at home, ciao. And I said 'thank

52

you' to him! As always I don't manage to utter a word – or if a word, never a whole sentence. To say to him: Look out, I'm a vampire, you'll pay for this. Nothing. The speeches I have prepared are smoke when confronted by the peremptoriness of his dry improvisations. Oh to be able to threaten him with blackmail, to hear him become agitated if only down a telephone wire. But that is too high a card; and I am not all that sure that he hasn't already considered it and in a certain sense trumped it. In the end it is always I who say thank you; I say thank you for any reason; it seems to me that I have been done a favour by having things thrown in my face.

Not that I believe in this relationship as something positively different; perhaps all this mechanism set itself in motion when I heard myself being called 'Barbino', perhaps it was because of the Brescian inflection that brought to mind my childhood. It was not a physical attraction but a phonetic one, derived from a certain manner of delivering the downpour of syllables and of drawing out the final vowels in the true manner of Val Camonica.

To go to his place or to go and model at the Beaux Arts (no one has bones that stand out like mine) is the same thing: I simply have to adopt a pose, submit to the interpretations they want to put on me – which have usually nothing to do with me – and wait till it is over. I am a difficult subject to draw, the secretariat at the Alliance scored a bull by sending me there, they call me 'Auschwitz', these shitbags full of thermos-flasks and rolls, always telling me off for moving, saying I never stay still a moment, that I always let my mouth go slack and keep on saying to anyone who has a snack 'Can I have a piece?' these people who live in the communes of the new pink socialism and are making the revolution and don't have a mattress for me because I am a homosexual! As if, faced with a mattress, I could still think of sex. And to adopt a pose continually – just as with Brother Fox – is exhausting, after a couple of hours I feel faint and, after paying for my metro and supper I am skint as usual. And the spring, which is so tardy, is an excess of boredom, the bread left in the cupboard is reinforced concrete, reinforced by two melting slices of salame, my mother's letters all the same – 'it's difficult to keep afloat / my varicose veins / and everyone comes and takes and never gives / put a little money by, you never know' – I burn them without reading them, I open them only to see if there is a bank-note there. I could swear the old man has opened them first and gummed them up again, and I am afraid of dying because never more than when I am exhausted do I have the feeling that life is giving as much to others, to people like Giacomino and Brother Fox, as it is robbing from me, and in desperation I think of all the happiness I will snatch from a future of which I have not the slightest notion. Why does all the water run into the sea? Is the desert not perhaps tired of being desert or perhaps it is more cunning than me and water doesn't interest it? But I am thirsty, if only I could divert some watercourses in a fixed direction. To flee. To London, for example. But to whom? flee from myself or to go to myself? Oh I am as disconsolate as a suckling tugging at a deflated breast.

No chance of work for the moment; at the *Bella Napoli* twenty Italians a day pass through looking for work and the old man enjoys it, he feels me increasingly at his mercy, he enjoys no end giving me vain hopes and taking back every promise, substituting for them each time a bigger and increasingly unrealizable promise. And even the arquebus has disappeared from the wall; my view is that he is even living on the family photographs; it is as if he were preparing a bunker or a final cage to last for ever. But I do not think it is destined for me, even if my long training at playing the victim and my mania for persecution do everything to convince me that it is so. I do not feel important enough to be buried alive like a slave with his Pharaoh, the old man's funereal farsightedness is not directed at others like that of Adel the Egyptian. Squint-eyes is obeying his own impulses as they wander to and fro in the enclosed space of his brain; it is not me he wishes to round up and lock in but himself; otherwise what else is this madness that urges him to transform everything into something stripped, denuded, tomb-like? There is no longer even a chair; every time I come home he has meantime taken something away – sold? – a little picture, the trunk in the room where I sleep, the walnut writing-desk in the drawing-room.

I wander about Fontainebleau got up more or less like a hippy, I feel more credible when I do not resist the temptation to ask children for half a roll if they stray away from their mothers or nurses and experience a diabolical shame. And I even ask a lady in black with a prayer-book in her lap for a telephone token; it is inconceivable that I should be reduced to begging; seeing that for you I am only a forceps in an experiment of yours it would only be fair if you paid me for the work. That you should pay me dearly. Or else shut up about the psychoanalyst, tell me the truth – that you get a lunatic pleasure out of it and then let's call it a day. But you aren't a business-man for nothing, you come from the country like me; you know how to put a proper price on the goods you want to buy. Try to understand once and for all that you are mean and that you can't help it, that you are happy with things as they are; give this starving creature an explanation of some kind, explain to him why you are so afraid of this relationship which you need and which you despise so much. And you too with your mania for giving cast-offs, more ties, a bow-tie! as if I had nothing else in my head but private views and receptions at *l'Humanité*.

Hello? he says. Hello, it's Barbino. And he puts down the phone.

I have collected cast-off ties first all over Italy and then in Lille. That Flemish layabout wrapped in soft flesh began our 'relationship' by presenting me with a white shirt bought in the Galleria in Milan on the day after we met in a place where I used to go trying to bring too many things off at once. A white shirt with cuffs but no cuff-links! When all I wanted, but had not the courage to confess it, was thirty thousand lire to pay my rent and have a good feed – and once we had left the high-class haberdasher's he revealed to me a piece of Milanese folk-lore: a bull inlaid in the paving under the dome of the Galleria. People were queueing up to stand on its balls – Japanese, I think – they say a thing like that brings you luck. Lofty did it before me, joyfully. Then I pressed my heel on the slight hollow in the mosaic of the scrotum and out of politeness, just for a change, spun round. Brother Fox and his presents! I am hungry. Rather Lofty than him. At Croix just outside Lille, after three months of isolation – but how much food there was at the stations of that Via Crucis! what steaks, what abundance in Lofty's refrigerator! Lofty who got down like a sheep with that great fat arse of his covered with a yellowish sheepskin and made me put a silver lead on him and every other day or so he wanted me to 'take him for walkies to do pi-pi' in the flat on the plastic *Begonia semperflorens* and played at being a pig so well that it made my flesh creep and then at being a dog, a griffon, he said, and then, if you please, while it looked as if the long hair were standing out round his buttocks, at being a peacock

55

and, when it was time for the lump of sugar, that is immediately after the whinny, he wanted me to smack him on the buttocks and say: 'Bobò, good old Bobò, would you like a sugar-lump?', after three months of this life at it every other day as if it were a farmyard, very much against his will he found me a job – not such a bad one either; I looked after the rotas of a hundred lorry-drivers, an easy, clean job, a normal working day of ten hours, reasonable wages, Sundays off, so that I went to live in a room of my own in the house of an old lady who looked like the battlemented tower of a castle on which yellow lace had been laid out to dry. She had shown me the bedroom – with four-poster – with the wallpaper coming away from the walls and had said, looking away: 'Faites-moi grâce, pas de dames ici.' Lofty who came and left big packages at the bedroom door for me packed with stuff to eat and essentials: cakes of soap by Roger & Gallet, a pair of opal cuff-links, pyjamas of Flanders linen... Provided I let him do his zoological number at least once more. So he had his work cut out coming and going carrying his lead with its bit in his office brief-case: at my place he never again heard 'Bobò, my darling Bobò'. Today I am rather sorry – he wasn't a pig basically, only another poor dog, who strutted about like a peacock because he too had an orgasm, because he too was 'human'. I had even put on the odd kilo or two.

At that time his habit of thinking of sexuality as a four-legged function disgusted me, whereas now that mania of his fills me with tenderness; a way of expressing oneself like any other, neither better nor worse than that exhausting Yes!-No!-Yes! of Brother Fox or having vaginal intercourse with a woman or taking a vow of chastity, a habit with its own sound sense, its own normative squalor, its own unbridled fantasy, and all of them equally tedious, 'human', 'spontaneous', and I would add 'natural'.

After you have got excited a couple of times and intoxicated yourself with this humanity, spontaneity, naturalness, you smell the musty odour of museums, which is the same everywhere, whether in those of baroque art or those of 'natural history'.

The old man is there looking watery in the drawing-room, which is reduced to a desert with palms for a young Arab who is advancing towards me on all fours under contract. A stubborn odalisque, I have told them both to fuck off and have locked myself in my room

– no chance of their seeing me in action! Yesterday he even took away the mattress so that I have to sleep on the bare netting. The trunk with my things, the tin one with in it my blue trousers and the *Diary* has vanished, I am left only with the artificial leather one with the things for my sister and my nieces and my books. He says he knows nothing about it. He stared at me with a saturnine, watery expression due not only to his glasses, which are pure hydrogen, squint as usual. The Arab calls the old man 'm'sié' and says 'M'sié, it's no use – either I break it down or...' and meantime keeps on fumbling round the door. All laid on to frighten me. But I am not afraid. The Arab is goodlooking all right but they're not ones to wear themselves out for long nor for extravagant demands. 'What do you expect from an arachole? a serenade?' my mother used to say discouragingly. The matter in hand has its own precise ontological value. The old man comes and goes from the window into the garden. I know he can't do anything – too many people in the block, he can't begin to undo the slats of the shutters through which I catch a glimpse of him with that professorial look of a superior person remote from the vulgar weaknesses of this world. Then, from inside, the old man begins to yell, says that I am a miserable petty thief, that he wants me to leave his house at once, that I stole his arquebus. I don't know how I can hold out, not go mad. Just like when at the police station at Montichiari they wanted to make me confess to having stolen 'the jewels' of a dissatisfied *hetaira*, the proprietress of the hotel where I worked by the hour, always sad but never tired of her Swan – every so often she showed me certain prints of erotic mythology and I would say: 'So what?'

The Arab must have gone. I heard them settling up; one of them did not speak in a low voice.

And I passed the night stringing together nightmares in which Brother Fox from behind the grille of a confessional handed out ridiculous things: 'Two hundred aves, two hundred and fifty glorias, three hundred and ten nice gestures to the old man, one thousand requiescats, ego te absolvo.' It is difficult to drag the morning into this place; I went on masturbating so as to wear myself out and to be able to shut all my eyes. There was always one extra that stayed open.

I wait for there to be coming and going on the little pathway of the garden-courtyard, I raise the shutter, throw open the window with the little bag with the grammar already in my hand, run to open the door from the inside, otherwise I won't be able to get in this evening, and with a little jump clear the window-sill. 'Bonjour! Bonjour!' No one replies.

Every time I write to Brother Fox the usual unposted letter I haven't a single thought in my head, that is to say, I feel the insufficiency of all those I have to communicate, the fruit of too great a desire to understand, of psychological investigation. And the best thing is to leave it to the poor in spirit, those who enter the Kingdom of the Post Office, a kingdom one must enter sticking a stamp on to the postcard and where, as the splendid result of that imposition on the intelligence, millions of packets of 'sentiments' are sorted out to rain down – in the form of bucolic bacteria – on as many more million heads exposed to the most incredible social calamities, which are then called (between sender and addressee) 'fate', 'nature', 'humanity'.

You have no choice – either go back to your home in Italy to play the exile sitting and thinking or – just imagine – stay in Paris and learn sex appeal, wrap Brother Fox up in the reddish fur of a desire wonderfully pursued with all the philological rigour of a can-can dancer.

That's easily said! With him everything is so limited, I can count only on *manigances*, the intrigues of a real cat and a cloth mouse in the labyrinth of his stale all-embracing desire for me, spirit skin and bone and stomach, like a whirlpool that sucks in air to expel it – God knows how – in the form of spermatozoa in his well-lubricated intestine, so spoiled by pâté, leg of lamb, creamed vegetables, truffles with cocoa. And I'm supposed to be the greedy one.

Empty and disposable, that's what I am happy to be. Empty like a cast waiting for a ladleful of life but not *this* life – one that there will be, provided I am capable of creating it for myself out of nothing. And disposable like a piece of crude soft clay anxious to reshape itself into a form it does not yet know. To have at its disposal different articulations, joints which are not these and an awareness that goes beyond its own opacity: an awareness capable of forgetting itself.

And there would be no pneumatic voids in Catholic scrotums; women would not renounce medicine to have recourse to the astrologer like him, they would have a mass said as God commands and meantime would set about cooking.

58

With the Alliance Française I am making such progress that in the course of the last two months I have twice been moved up into higher classes. Now it is as if I were in the second year of secondary school. That means that I have acquired the right to take advantage of the invitations which Parisian families of a certain quality extend through the school office to foreign students for an evening in a 'French family'. For dinner! you sit at a table, they told me, and the widow or the bereaved couple or the old maid, in other words, what is left of 'the French family', introduce you to their little dog with its little boots, show you shrunken apartments or deserted parade grounds and then, lo and behold, begin – rich and poor alike – to make every imaginable titbit appear through a little door, which is always the same and always shut, a deluge of gastronomic items presented with some polite phrase like 'a typical dinner'. Not even Pompidou could allow himself to eat so typically once a week.

By now it has happened to me once – but that was an old telegraph operator, a useless specimen of the French Post Office, on pension for ages, and no longer capable of deciding the fate of any aspiring Italian writer who would be happy just to sort them – the letters; one without money, I thought it a good idea to underline, and forced to sleep in the flat of 'an old madman – an immigrant uncle' – at the back of beyond; it was no use and then she glanced at a picture to see if it was crooked – a safe? – and said she had 'a bad attack of migraine.'

This evening will be the second invitation: I am thinking above all of the possibility of finding a job thanks to a little word being put in for me. This evening we shall be received – I, a Spanish girl and a young and extremely dirty Peruvian boy from whom I have nothing to fear – by, as the card says, Mademoiselle Arlette Jarre, Mademoiselle Suzanne Roufer and Mademoiselle Geneviève d'Orian (somebody important?). The flat is near the Bastille. Shall I take them by storm?

If only I could manage to slip out of the clutches of the old madman and from those of Brother Fox as well, which are the ones that, without seeming to, leave the deepest marks on me. I have realized that my caresses had nothing to do with him; I was caressing myself through him and asking myself: When will someone caress me like this? But I went on caressing him, almost to punish him for his blindness and his silence (after the first and last time that I made a speech to him the bargain is that 'if you want to see me, think twice before opening your mouth'); he trembles in his sleep and I am far away from him and his feelings. He is like a boy modelled out of salt, his look is hard even from under his closed eyelids. I make my fingers run over his brow, his lips, his nipples, his testicle (his only one, I have discovered) and I *love* him, I am excited by his way of acting out life, which is as bombastic as it is innocent of *coups de théatre* not foreseen in the script. His *gaffes*, his fluffs are already written in the margin. Everything is there. Perhaps today's Brother Fox is the old madman of the future. He knows his part for tomorrow.

I have been sitting on the steps of the staircase for two hours now – clearly the old man is not back. The key doesn't go in anymore, obviously he has changed the lock. My view is that this idiot has a couple of spare locks which he has gone on alternating all his life according to how his 'platonic friendships' are deteriorating. And the same goes for the furniture which appears and disappears in and out of some underground hiding-place, so as to have the excuse that he is penniless and has to sell everything. I am simply resigned. I shall never see the four hundred francs again; Mademoiselle Arlette Jarre – rabbit with tarragon, pigeon on the spit, chocolate cake, pineapple and cheese! – and Mademoiselle Suzanne, her colleague at the office, and Mademoiselle Geneviève, albino, who if I have understood rightly deals with cattle-breeding for the French government and then, oh yes, looks after international relations as well, in short a rather special kind of lawyer, have said they will see what they can do. From what I understood these three ladies go through life practically together and address each other with 'vous' – and people who say 'vous' to each other in their spare time are the ones who can count on good connections, exactly like Brother Fox – except that he doesn't trust me. Suzanne, who is ten years or so older than Arlette – who is about thirty but looks younger – said to me: 'You will see that everything will turn out for the best' and explained to me why everything will turn out for the best using arguments which left me dumbfounded and it seems incredible to me that anyone could still use them: 'Vous êtes tellement jeune, ça ira très bien,' she said and I listen to her as if under a spell, as if behind the banality of the cliché she were describing the Seven Wonders of the World: 'On pourrait dire à Madame Bonsants,' said

Arlette, looking at Geneviève – the same age as Suzanne – who raises eyebrows without saying anything. A gaffe evidently, even if I cannot interpret it. What I have is a shirt and a pair of blue trousers, provided my suitcase, which has vanished in the hypochondriacal meanders of that paranoid old man, turns up. When things go well everything goes well; today I look in at the *Bella Napoli* for the nth time (I have been to so many other pizzerias without success, but here they know me because of the month I put in last year before Lofty came to take me off to Croix) and they say: 'Stay right here'. How many left-overs of pizzas, chops, fatty bits from steaks – a real blow-out! So I was able to arrive at Mademoiselle Arlette's with a bunch of lily of the valley – exotic early blooms which immediately left me skint but, lucky me!, they paid me in advance for a day's work. From twelve to five, not much of a job, not much pay, but always better than nothing. I'll manage even without the help of Brother Fox, I feel it.

Meantime every quarter of an hour I press the bell for two or three minutes. If he is there he doesn't want to open for me and hopes to keep my stuff. He is really going to suffer for it. In short, he wants to get rid of the victim who refuses to become the executioner.

In fact he was in there. From behind the door he asked: 'Who is it?' as if he didn't know it was me at that time of night. He opened and said: 'Ah bon', I went in without protesting at having to spend half the night on the stairs; besides it was warmer on the stairs than inside. I said I will go (where?) as soon as he lets me have my suitcase back. He said, naturally: 'What suitcase? you have your suitcase in your room.' 'Not that one – the tin trunk.' He shrugged. Behaviour of that kind, in the long run, has one very precise aim – the shedding of blood. There are people like that, always looking for their own assassin, people who should be disposed of legally without a poor innocent killer getting involved. I say nothing; no reaction. That makes him furious, he begins to pop his eyes, to turn pale. The first light of dawn was entering through the slats of the blinds. Apparently they have cut off the electric light too; a candle in his room, one in the corridor. His problems. I am so tired – but happy – that I can't get to sleep. And the heating is off.

I didn't kill my father, so what chance of my killing him? I am so tired I cannot get to sleep. Another letter to Brother Fox, all absolutely identical with the ones I used to write to Giacomino and which I never posted; I write so as not to succumb, that's all, one can't call them letters. I write in the semi-darkness of the Sunday dawn which is so pale, sustained by a painful insomnia. My eyes are burning and I have a headache. I just hope that it is not a fresh attack of neuralgia. You are writing, I say to myself, in order to find an addressee. Or the sender. The only letter I dared to leave for him *brevi manu* a few days ago, he waited till I was there next day to let me find it floating in scraps in the loo.

I have been waiting for Arlette (Mademoiselle Arlette) outside her office because I keep feeling that I did not thank her enough for the dinner and for *their* interest (but I was not insistent on this point, I said it almost in passing), Arlette is a little odd with me, very much on the defensive, that's it; if I say anything to her – I cannot tell whether I am saying shocking things or not, I don't think so, to me they all seem the same – she seems to be petrified with astonishment and yet she's not a little girl. At the height of her alarm she too says 'Ah bon', an acknowledgement uttered without any particular colouring, neutral. But this 'Ah bon' seems to me only a damped echo of a flare of ectoplasm which must erupt in her every so often. It seems to me that she leads a miserable life: home – a one-roomed flat of about forty square metres, a little kitchen and bathroom; office; at the weekend she goes to her parents in the country about eighty kilometres away. Not much – she has no men, that's clear right away – but you can feel that she likes them a lot. After we had been sitting together for a little I felt a very strong little smell coming from her person – my sense of smell is my most highly developed sense, I could write a treatise on smells, discover those not yet catalogued, like the colours of Turner's sunsets with a commentary by Wilde. She is so tiny, Arlette, an odorous little thing. Naturally she wanted to know some things about me: unless she's stupid she must have smelt a rat and if she has taken a fancy to me she will get over it. I am so provincial. She knows nothing about the old man; all she knows is that I want to get away as soon as possible from this 'distant relative' at the back of beyond.

I have noticed one thing: that while it is not possible to talk to Brother Fox, Arlette never seems to tire. After a little she seems to get lost in my words, her upper lip detaches itself from her lower one and from that I read the command to go on, not to stop if possible, not ever to stop. And up to now it seems to me I have said nothing: the weather, the Alliance, ah, to be able to live in Paris and not on the Belgian frontier. The result is that in the end we don't communicate any more; we both go on listening to me. *Merde* if I know what I am getting at. I talk like a mill-wheel – the things said remain half in and half out of the water. Besides she must hear them, my words, because her little eyes, which are as intense as the head of a pin behind her glasses, are never still, they seem to be watching fleas doing a somersault act. This complicity between a vulva and an auditory system fascinates me. Or perhaps she is merely impressed by the fact that there is someone waiting for her at the main door of the block – she seems to come flying down, uncertain whether to shake my hand or to throw her arms round my neck. Women, in general, are marvellous. Suzanne goes into the bar under the office and exclaims: 'What a nice smell of pizza you have about you. Just out of the oven!'

I am afraid that so far as the bank goes (Madame Bonsants, cousin of Suzanne) it will be difficult to get anywhere; I have to produce a diploma of higher education if I want to have any hope of being taken on, otherwise there are no jobs for foreigners. I don't know what to do. I must be the only Italian in the world unable to produce a bogus accountant's diploma. What does it matter? what's the use, seeing that in any case I would be the office-boy? Suzanne is still up in the office, she has to finish a telex. Arlette sips her tomato juice with condiment. Geneviève arrives and seems to have said everything even before she sits down. Never a word too many (she stays, smiles behind her glasses, crosses her very beautiful long legs and her uncertain glance, like that of an angora rabbit with red pupils, seeks to look past one and beyond one and beyond everything else to stop only at the stratosphere). Then Geneviève goes off with Suzanne; Geneviève has smoked a Turkish cigarette with a filter wrapped in a rose petal extracted from a silver cigarette case. You see what it means to have a genius for genetics.

'Arlette, I'd like to be frank with you. You see, I . . .'

'Don't say anything. It's perfectly all right. We'll talk on Monday. Tomorrow I'm going to my parents.' She searches in her purse; hers is a gesture too calm not to have been prepared. 'Here, bring your things. We'll manage, it's a duplicate.'

And she gives me two keys inserted in a little gold knick-knack shaped like a castanet.

DIFFICULT OVERTURES

'The important thing is to have slept two days in a row, dear Arlette, as I have done, while you were in the country at your parents'; certainly it's months since I ate a fowl like this with some flesh on the bones.'

'And I haven't had one so well cooked. I can't understand this business of sleeping – maybe I sleep too much – always alone here – the way I was.'

'In fact, let's make a bargain – I don't want to disturb you any more than is necessary so I'll sleep on the floor, there are plenty of blankets.'

'As you wish. And your suitcases?'

'Oh, there's time.'

Arlette's knife slips on her plate, squeaks in the gravy and a piece of chicken – a drumstick, ends up on the nice red cotton table-cloth.

'Oh that's a fine stain!' I say. 'It looks as if you were scratching like a hen too.'

Arlette gets up, goes to the sink, takes a sponge, rubs, picks up the little piece of celery.

'That's it,' she says. 'Go on.'

'. . .' I begin to say.

Arlette has half shut her mouth, her glasses seem to mist over – only in the centre her two ocular pinheads pierce the glass and light up something which is far behind her and which spans me – unlike Geneviève's gaze – losing itself behind me. Her gaze embraces me. Her understanding half-smile, however, is not directed at me alone: it slides over my back and runs down me and away, reaches other areas of concern of which I am ignorant.

'...'

'Oh that's not important at all. I've told you; your sincerity makes giving it hospitality well worth while,' and finally she smiles that thin, infantile and awkward smile of hers. 'Go on, go on.'

She sits motionless on her damask-covered chair, her little head leaning slightly forward over the small table, takes off her glasses and immediately begins to hold her breath.

'I've never seen the Keystone – what do you call them? – *cons.*'

Now Arlette unwraps the two immense cream caramels which I so much like and breaks – with a certain haste it seems – that kind of immobility which for the last three hours has been relieved only by her stretching her toes in her small shoes. She puts on her glasses again, takes a breath, turns round suddenly and, without moving, holding out the plate, dividing her immobility equally between trunk and bust, sits down again. Her cheeks are glowing with a nice flush and she strikes me as extraordinarily pretty when she isn't smiling; our desires – mine to talk, hers to listen – coincide. I don't even wait for her to tell me to begin.

'Just imagine what a life...'

Arlette shakes her little head, her short dark-blonde hair imparts a wavy motion to the stuffed white canary in the little cage behind her, hanging from the ceiling by a pink string, a present from Geneviève, who is white too.

'...why can't you manage?'

Now she is statuesque. The flush rises up to her cheekbones, goes into the folds at the corner of her eyes, disappears at the tips of her ears and she has once more that ice-cold face which I knew in her when she still only said 'Ah bon.' It feels to me, after that long sleep, that it happened centuries ago. And I go on talking.

I take a breath, perhaps I have let her take my hand but Arlette, above all, must know immediately what game I am playing and in any case after a while I get tired of ineffable language. The explicit is so much more mysterious, it is a kind of safety: to be able to say 'this is the way it went and like this' is a great relief. Maybe none of it is true but meantime something has been dealt with and one can go on from there. If you have someone listening to you. And Arlette is listening, my God, does she listen to me. Arlette drinks me, sucks me, turning from white to red, waving her little head, giving life behind her to something stuffed. It is entirely my turn, it doesn't even occur to me to ask her about herself.

And some days pass – evenings – of perfect listening to me, which acquire a rhythm from mercurial immobility round a perfectly set table, where first-fruits, alimentary eccentricities, *coups de foudre* of gluttony, become 'the typical French dinner'. And Suzanne and Geneviève are busy but it is still too soon for a job. They don't want it to be 'dans la restauration': they have decided unanimously – even Geneviève – that it must be 'a proper job'. Apparently Geneviève said to Suzanne: 'Quel dommage! as soon as possible he must get rid of that smell of capers and brewer's yeast,' but it sounds to me too long a sentence to be true.

Sitting in front of me, Arlette is ready to accept my confidences this evening too. There must be weather of some sort outside. She would put tarragon even in the coffee but I don't say anything to her about the funny sweet taste of the minestrone. She cooks with so much enthusiasm and admits she has everything to learn. She has put on a Spanish record, not really a flamenco: a woman's voice sings: 'Ay, trece, trece de mayo, cuando me encontré contigo.' Above the record-player there are two pairs of castanets, a framed fan with images from bull-fighting. Beyond that in the little one-roomed flat – small for two people – there is no other knick-knack, no significant presence. Nothing to slow down or turn back or speed up the imagination. Apart from the little cage with the little white bird, the canary which mustn't be called that.

'Ah bon,' she says. The sweetbreads, the mushrooms, the chopped ham, the peas escape from her *bouchée de la reine* and even she melts into a smile, but a compact one, as usual.

'. . . it becomes a question of money.'

'Oh one must never talk about money. . . May 1968 reminds me of one thing only. May 1958.'

'El trece?'

'No – nor the first either. The twenty-fifth,' but then she is silent to my great relief. The candle in the two-armed candelabra is burning very low, the wine is finished, the drinking-water from the mains of the Bastille is disgusting, my throat is dry but not terribly dry.

'. . . if I could have told him all this my cock would have worked better too.'

Arlette J., *Jesuisraide*, coughs, that's what they taught her at the nuns': to cough, to look askance, to brush non-existent hair away from her eyes and say:

'You were saying?' but I know she won't hold out much longer, that she will burst out crying or laughing. She gets up, goes to the record-player – there is no television or telephone – puts on the last side of *Norma* and explains to me: 'At this point she says his name,' and she is already preparing herself to listen to something which will move her in the old-fashioned sense of the word, something that will soothe her throbbing and rest her little eyes after the long waking hours we spend together listening to me. But I will not let her off. I want everything to be clear from the beginning, no rebukes later on, no recriminations saying that it is my fault that I *didn't say*.

'Now here's the love-duet. Oh, it's marvellous. There – soon he throws himself on the pyre with her. He discovers he loves her, suddenly that he loves her alone. He has forgotten all the rest. Even the hatred that mingles with his love.'

'I hate opera.'

'I like it a lot. Each time I feel the same emotions.'

'But it's awful.'

I get up and turn on the light on the wall, I snuff out the candle-wick, begin to put the little easy chairs against the wall, to move the table, to prepare my lair for the night. And there, with her in the bathroom, in front of me that shameless lap of goose-feathers, those soft cushions which take centuries to flatten themselves out millimetre by millimetre under my neck. In the morning I arrive at the Alliance with all my bones still creaking in my mind and then, from midday to five, I go back to the *Bella Napoli* to wash dishes and get ready the other room which is used only in the evening. I earn exactly enough for cigarettes and for the little bunches of flowers for Arlette, Suzanne, Geneviève, when at five or half past I go to pick up Arlette and we both rush home in the grip of different overwhelming desires, of spasmodic oral and aural incontinence – shameless, it is – while our presumed friends, if they can be called that, stand there with their little bunches of violets dangling in their hands, watching us run off, benevolent, giving their blessing, arm-in-arm on the pavement behind the import-export company. Are Suzanne and Geneviève happy for us? do they know? do they not know? what is there to know?

At home we pull the curtains at once, turn on the light, set to work with pots and pans, opening and shutting the fridge, running water in the bath, covering ourselves up carefully when one comes out and the other goes in, meanwhile the food is cooking and garlic impregnates the room by itself – to begin with it turned her stomach but she has got used to it.

'There are places for men only. I'd like so much to take you to the Turkish Baths in the Rue Poncelet!..'

'What a crazy idea! and what would I go there for?' she asks, twisting her little mouth which is usually sewn up. And without waiting for an answer she begins to laugh but with her shoulders, without exposing herself: I have always suspected that she has trouble with her teeth.

'.. to be a wall-flower!'

Now Arlette laughs with all her heart, showing her slightly mouse-like teeth, but very white, very close together, and a little very healthy gum. Who knows what happened to her on 25th May 1958.

'.....'

I can't go on pretending not to notice it; I almost always cook with garlic and never reproach her about the tarragon because I know that at a certain point Arlette begins to give off a honey-sweet and heavy smell which becomes more and more sharp and pungent. Her wide-open eyes, reddened like my own by the sleep we are robbing each other of, sometimes stray to the tip of her nose and I know she knows she is stinking, knows that I know, and she cannot let herself be seen to go to the bathroom, cannot allow me to hear all the different jets of water she would have to use, I feel that under the table – it is more and more stained – there is a pressure, a discomfort, a cruel sweat breaking out. This irritates and displeases me, this female friend of mine is not perfectly aseptic. This female friend of mine is a woman through and through.

'And now, if you don't mind, I'd like to go to sleep.'

'Already?' she says, holding back with a slightly perfidious flash of the eyes a yawn which has been lying in ambush for several minutes. 'But it isn't even midnight. I'll make you a coffee.'

'Oh, don't bother, Arlette, aren't you a bit sleepy?'

'I'm not. Go on.'

'.....'

Arlette, totally exhausted, has laid her head on the back of her chair, she half-closes her eyes and scarcely reopens them, perhaps

69

she can no longer even see me, perhaps she is turning over things I don't know about, perhaps she has not even been listening to me. But then the *napoletana* puffs, the smell grows overpowering, it overwhelms and embraces garlic and sweat, she gives a start, shakes herself with a shiver, gets up, busies herself at the stove and then says, lifting up the tin with the sugar-lumps:

'Two? There – there are two. Just.'

She looks at me tenderly, holding out the cup, without relaxing her effort not to appear more short-sighted than she is because of her tired, frayed corneas.

'Tell me. Talk to me. Then you can sleep an hour longer than me in the morning.'

Theoretically yes, but *Jesuisraide* – Iamrigid – in the morning turns on the radio the moment the alarum sounds, very low, but booming treacherously. But above all, opens the curtains and stepping over me goes to the stove, heats up the leftover coffee, no there's none left, makes some fresh, nibbles at three biscuits.

'I wonder if Suzanne will have any news.'

'Oh, what's the hurry, my dear? So I shall expect you at five this evening. Have a good day.'

'Five to half past. Have a good day.'

She leaves ten francs on the table in the corridor, runs away, lightfooted, in one of her nicest dresses of one-tone cotton and a beige coat, displaying in her little white face her drowsy eyes like a trophy to be shown to indifferent Paris. In fact she has not taken the glasses with the plastic frame but the ones with gold wire, with transparent lenses, like a teacher or rather a student who gives herself airs. I go to the window and open it wide. Air, Arlette!

'Here are our two turtle-doves!' exclaims Suzanne, laying her green crocodile-skin bag on the seat at the little table on the bar terrace below the office. The days have got longer. Who knows what Arlette tells them! 'Always talking away together!' She gives Arlette a kiss, the umpteenth (custom says they must brush each other's cheeks at least three times a day), shakes my hand – lets hers fall into mine, as if laying it there, giving me to understand that it has no intention of being a clasp but a maternal caress.

'I'm not inquisitive,' she says, sitting down, 'you can go on. And about his job, don't worry, two or three of us are going over Paris with a toothcomb. The bank isn't the only thing. A pity not to have a diploma, otherwise by now. But you'll see, you'll see. It has never happened to us before to try to get a job for someone who has only pizzerias in his curriculum vitae. We were all so unprepared. But you will see.' She smiles at us maternally. Suzanne is really beautiful, her expression is calm, unshadowed, light pink lipstick on her lips which are full and well-shaped, chestnut hair pulled back very simply, a fine suit of maroon gaberdine, a string of natural pearls, very old ones, violet reflections on her white neck, without wrinkle, adorned with an imperceptible down. In spite of her forty years and more, her mother, eighty years old, still checks the hours she keeps. Suzanne sips her non-alcoholic drink. She and I see Geneviève advancing from the little side street at the bottom of the Faubourg-Saint-Honoré with her dashing gait, her hair very white and shining, the pink blob of her face, her hips caught very tightly in a very close-fitting skirt of bottle-green, a lynx jacket – it is cold even if the horse-chestnuts are covered with buds.

'Well, I leave you to your conspiracies. Oh, darlings, remember – all I'm waiting for is a hint from you to fill up my Tuesdays.' She takes a sip, gets up, kisses Arlette once more, says to the waiter: 'They're my guests, put it on my bill – and, my dear, really, if it's easier for you to come an hour later, please do! Just ourselves. Ah, what it is to be young!' And she runs out with her light step, in her ash-grey shoes with low heels, a slow-motion run which no one could define as such, goes towards Geneviève and both, from the other side of the window, wave to us as they pass by.

'Who would believe that Geneviève has four degrees?' says Arlette, almost absentmindedly, for she never by any chance changes the subject from 'me'. 'One in veterinary science. The first. One in chemistry. Then international law. Then, for fun, philosophy. Shall we go home? Where had we got to?'

'.... "open up, open up", like fuck I will.'

'I don't mind, you know, but other people! Talk less loudly,' says Jesuisraide with a flat voice, laying a hand on my arm, without ceasing to cast glances down the tunnel at the Étoile, under the little rectangle of white-painted tin of the 'Première Classe' and readjusting her glasses charmingly.

'I'm sorry. You know, I speak loudly because I am deaf in one ear.'

71

'Are you afraid you won't hear yourself?' she asks with a sly smile, ever so slightly sly. 'We're lucky we don't have to change. Here it is.'

In spite of it being rush hour there is always room in first-class.

Jesuisraide is ready to burst by now, I'm not sure whether into tears or laughter.

'......'

'How about a spring-onion soup. Look how fresh they are,' she says; we are dropping in at the delicatessen, the baker's, the pastry-cook's, the butcher's, the greengrocer's: inside and out the pieces of the evening's gastronomic puzzle.

'Oh, yes, and if you don't mind, those asparagus.' Something completely out of season, another of my impudent caprices, balm for my vocal chords; and while she's at it, Arlette not only treats them with asparagus, but with strawberries, with avocados, just as before in the patisserie she had treated them with pine-kernels, ricotta and rum, without ever saying these words of rebellion which are always on the tip of her tongue: 'But this is a ridiculous price.' Never.

'... and he who remembers is lost.'

Arlette goes to the record-player and puts on her Spanish songs again, the prophetic 'trece de mayo'. No formalities such as I imagine there would be at Suzanne's Tuesdays; in fact here one has to speak with one's mouth full.

'I have a brain big enough and sufficiently in love with experiments to keep myself in the van of the new happiness, the one that is invented from day to day, the one that is not reshaped on any model of behaviour within easy reach. The happiness, for example, of beginning to consider, to take into account other people's reasons, which are very remote from us, and to see that they are not so very different in their diversity from our own. What do you think?'

'I need a pause to get some rest from these phrases which threaten me somehow.'

'For me too they are real discoveries.'

'But let's listen to Conchita Piquer. Listen, now comes "Como a nadie te he querido". I know a little Spanish – holidays –'

We listen, both of us slipping down over the edge of the easy chairs where we remain with our legs stretched out on the Persian carpet, satiated with food. Arlette has put on a couple of kilos since we have been living together, her cotton dresses hanging heavily on her hips give her a sinuosity which she did not have before. The toe of her shoe lies in quivering immobility a few centimetres from the tip of my right sole, or what is left of it.

Next day in a little Chinese dive not far from the Gare de Lyon – it is the first time we have eaten out: Arlette said 'we must for a while, it is less expensive' – I begin another of my exorcisms which is very close to my heart. Last night she lay down and, for the first time, tossed and turned in the big bed. Then after a while fell asleep without saying goodnight. I said it to her but she did not reply.

'. . . . . and so a competition is born between me and these people –'

'Between you and these men –'

'Yes, in fact they have always all been men –'

'In other words, illusion for illusion, you always win.'

'Exactly. I am invincible. There is nothing I am not prepared to give way to.'

The oriental waiter's bow, as he brings us the umpteenth cup of jasmine tea, is in perfect time with Arlette's suffocated laughter, raising vertebra after vertebra at each joyous gasp of air that came from behind the little hand in front of her mouth.

At home, not even an hour later, without mists from cooking with garlic, with the curtains shut, she begins to assert herself with her odour. She no longer shows any sign of shame. The problematic of the sprays has been dealt with. The fact is that it no longer crosses her mind to have to take countermeasures with ablutions, deodorants – the gardenia which is finished down below and is already all yellow and tomorrow will end up among the rubbish. She sits on the edge of the bed. She has taken off her shoes, she begins to rub her big toes. The nails are painted, I had not noticed it before. Her body is really minute, a little, tired but not disappointed fairy: she has in her possession a tiny magic steel wand which is in no hurry to rust nor fears rusting.

She puts on Viennese waltzes, something which perhaps will have represented for her – between a genuflection and a meditation on 'the temptation of the flesh' – the first notion of sin, picked up by her ears from a balcony, maybe that of the village pharmacist, as she passed in a file with her companions from the Institute going to Sunday mass all with the same little straw hat and blue ribbon.

'. . . .'

73

Arlette looks at me blissfully, the waves of Strauss – great floods – give her myopia a languishing look. Incredibly, she has fallen asleep. I lift the arm from the player, put out the candle, I try to leave everything as it is and try as best I can to settle myself on the floor without disturbing anything.

'Afterwards, please wind up the alarm-clock,' she says in a tiny voice without malice or irony.

'After what?'

'But did you manage to digest it? that pork with honey?... Tell me something, what shall I say, practical now, though I adore your theorizing, I really do –'

'Perhaps, but it's an effort. When you have a stomach ache it's more natural to speculate than to tell stories. How would you like a semiology of bowel movements in general? I am so tired, and I have a sore stomach too. I don't like eating out very much.'

'And how did it all end?' asks Jesuisraide first putting her night-dress on over her skirt and blouse and then slipping everything off underneath. Her tights she slips off once she is under the blankets.

'Goodnight, Arlette.'

No reply.

During the first half of Buñuel's latest film, *The Milky Way*, I say nothing. The stalls are almost empty, there is more going on in the gallery, perhaps because it guarantees pitch darkness. When the lights go up the chewing of gum stops and the sounds of little bubbles exploding that go with it, the prosperous lady goes past who sings: 'Glaces! nougatines! bonbons!' during the intervals. There is great disappointment in some of the rare faces that were expecting a science-fiction film. Arlette notices the gleam in my eye, she makes a sign to the lady whose bosom rests on the vanilla and chocolate ice-cream and buys me an ice, a biscuit, a packet of sweets. The film breaks right at the beginning of the second half. Her gaze, glazed and milky with exhortation, passes from my eyes to my mouth, which opens.

'......'

'Quiet,' shouts an intellectual voice in the centre rows.

'Who cares a damn?' replies another coming to my aid from two rows in front of us.

'..Me???'

'Have you finished all the packet of sweets already?' asks Arlette,

74

without turning her head in my direction, her fine profile with its little upturned nose immersed in the vapours of this way which is neither astral nor cheesy, but merely a stage like so many others in our secret exorcisms.

'No there's one left. Here.'

'Unwrap it for me.'

I take off the paper, embarrassed because the next move now is not to put it in her hand but to raise it to her mouth. Which I do in a flash and add to make it seem less dramatic;

'It's eucalyptus-flavoured.'

'I know.'

'It was written on the cellophane.'

'No, on your breath. You can go on breathing,' she says squeezing my elbow a little, perhaps a little annoyed.

'......'

The silhouette from which rose the voice protesting against the protest gets up, jumps about in the empty places in his row; against the black and white of the screen a dark mass stands out with a few straight hairs in its head, staggers about bumping into the protruding arms. Then the same voice, but very low, says behind us:

'Would you mind talking a little louder? I find if difficult to hear you. Otherwise can I sit in front there? I promise I won't disturb you.'

I look at Arlette, who is terrified; she catches the eager gleam in my irises and immediately I see, smell how excited she is.

'By all means,' she says for me.

'Oh thanks,' and he goes and sits in the seat in front of us; Arlette moves along a place, so do I; now the thin crest of hair is displayed fanwise in an arc of one hundred and sixty degrees and, obliquely, to my left, the first tooth of that comb of hair trembles, implanted in the scalp. On my right, that is where I have the deaf ear, Arlette is and isn't, like my words, like the film.

'......'

From the seat in front of Arlette rises a kind of sexual heavy breathing or groaning. An untimely comment, however you look at it. Without leaning forward, putting my annoyance into my tone of voice, I say: 'You promised not to disturb us. A formal promise. No, don't say anything. Take a leap into the realm of the symbolic. No, be quiet.........:.. Is the syncopated heavy breathing a person makes in the dark of the cinema listening to what others are saying directly proportional to that part of his libido which the eavesdropper himself considers "sinful"? is lust not possible then by the light of the sun? is darkness its premise? does it need to be fertilized by little games of peek-a-boo?, by casting the stone and hiding the hand that threw it, by negating the irrefutable truth and the shameless fetish-isms of what is "prohibited". But it is also thanks to the slimy relationship these people – that is everybody – have with their own animal humours that I am able to master more and more of my desire to make things clear, to turn the mechanism of the world inside out like a glove to see what is inside. And is it possible, the terrified eavesdropper will ask, to enjoy the same pleasure as before? does knowledge not perhaps blunt the edge of sensuality?'

The bloated and amorphous silhouette gets up as if a prey to panic, tries to scuttle away, does not find the opening in the velvet of the exit and while *End* appears on the screen gropes in desperation towards safety and deafness, I shout:

'But I wouldn't dream of it! On the contrary!'

'Let's go, let's go!' exclaims Arlette excitedly.

'God what bores these two are,' comments the 'Silence' behind us as we flee.

Sitting in a crêperie at the Odéon Arlette sinks her teeth with animal greed into the corner of the fan of batter and licks up a drop of raspberry jam which for a moment threatened her V-necked pink jumper of angora wool, which I have not seen before. But I never doubted, if that was the problem, that under the décolleté she had breasts.

'....'

'That's the gospel truth,' says Arlette, leaving me puzzled but free also to order another bilberry pancake. Talking has never stopped me from eating. At home no one ever talked at table. We all kept our eyes fixed on the serving dish to see who would dare to be the first to take a second helping. Hatred darted from the pupils, ranged in a rectangle, and the centre of the table with Sunday's boiled meat.

'I think that precise intuitions,' I go on, 'are only the fruit of a great labour of will and of previous intellectual success: you feel that intuitions are granted you as a gift, but if you don't work at them and if you skip one, let's say, then all those that come later are *inexact*, unauthentic and lead to an inessential existence, full of missing links.

Let's say I had one intuition at a time and gave to each its quota of attention, transformed it each time into meaning I could cash, scooping out a form, its form. There is not a single discarded thing in my existence; everything is terribly logical and centred, calibrated, plastically shaped and brought to a finish and lost to pass on to something else, to the next thing. I mean that *instinctively* – confronted by that overall with its faded little flowers, hanging under the stairs with the demijohn of bleach and the sack of meal for the pigs and the rabbits – when I sank my face for the first time in that dirty but dry piece of cotton and began to sniff at it in ecstasy, to run into the street and to display my pleasure was one and the same thing. It was my contribution to the world, what is true pleasure is shared with the whole world, otherwise it is an orchotomic pleasure, a fine hundred–year–old plane-tree without balls. The smell of that overall was multiplied a hundredfold by the astonished glance of the passers-by and I had an orgasm of pleasure only at the moment when my hedonistic and therefore educative harangue to the crowds began. And I am not exaggerating when I say that I was already, however confusedly, aware that this exhibition would cause me trouble, annoyance and vexation. But evidently that did not worry me; I had to enjoy things to the full and this smell was not so intoxicating if inhaled secretly under the stairs, it became a nasty little smell like the one from the dried seat of one's underpants. To put on that overall meant nothing more nor less than the shudder of a superior kind of sensuality, the one that goes hand in hand with the delight of going naked through the world because *we are naked*.'

Arlette looks at me with a haughty smile. My narrative pauses become less and less frequent and too often I forget that, in all probability, my reflections on these 'ante-facts' – as she calls them – are not 'facts' and she makes me the gift of her polite patience until I have finished. All she loves is the story-line.

Now, if she wanted, she could even take over from me for a little. If she does not, it can only be for one reason; her story must be of the most elementary, sacred-heartish and skimpy and quickly told, one of the kind that needs to settle for a long time in the phonatory apparatus before finding the proper note for the tragedy, the drama 'buried deep in the heart'. I can imagine it all already. The story of the other two Fates cannot be as simple as this, even in terms of words, Suzanne so solid, rotund, so fleetingly happy, no less fleeting

77

than Geneviève, petrified in her albino elegance, majestic, a silent ghost with angora rabbit's eyes. A hieratic genetic sport, a sacred animal. But Arlette lets me go on:

'............'

Arlette is transfixed in front of me, she searches in her bag without taking her eyes off me, some faces round about are vaguely astonished, I must have sung, maybe danced on the chair; she raises her hand which waves her batiste handkerchief and the hand thrusts itself towards my brow, where I now feel the little drops run down to the corners of my mouth, but the hand restrains itself, the elbow hangs limp in the air. She puts the handkerchief into my hand and I smile at her, because hers is an authentic sign of disciplined love; she recognizes in my sweat the fruit of my glands and resists the temptation to make it her own with an unsought gesture of involvement, which I would find profoundly annoying, and allows me to wipe it off myself.

'Believe me,' says Arlette, calling the *garçon* and passing her purse under the table, making sure that everyone sees, 'It's not so urgent to work. And that horrible job in the pizzeria! at this point it seems to me to be merely a whim – that's all. Give it up and let's try instead to produce a bogus Italian diploma. It will take time.'

'Couldn't we force the hand of this Madame Bonsants in the bank instead with the fact that it was you who found a place for her daughter in that English family? You see, Arlette, my problem is not creation – that now comes and goes of its own accord – it is a wage at the end of the month and to live like any man who hasn't great structures to maintain so as to believe he exists more than the others. As an unemployed person, the crowds of dead who threaten my twenty years make me tremble with a psychic disquiet that freezes my limbs. This wouldn't stop you from profiting from my most sincere friendship in order to continue to keep me. You shouldn't worry, Arlette, I have secure reserves, although not inexhaustible ones; to say these things will continue to cause me terrible pain even with a full stomach. It is as if, simply to enter into spiritual communion with you, I was trying to give you some sort of carnal consistency by making you come out of one of my ribs.'

Jesuisraide, radiant, uncontaminated by the slightest deposit of feminism, waves her little hand at a taxi, forgetful of the underground.

78

'Have you ever been up the Eiffel Tower?' asks Arlette as if wanting to change the subject. Sometimes she annoys me! one makes such an effort to escape from the 'village idiot' and the 'genius' and finds oneself once more a medieval court-jester to a pussy. I could pack my things because of a sentence like that if only I knew where to go. Both the suitcases are here now; I am filling one of them with cast-off women's clothing. (Ask in due course for contributions from Suzanne and Geneviève as well. You never know what Lucia would look like in a big lynx jacket.)

'No.'

'Nor I. To think of living so many years or months in Paris and not going up the Tower! You're human, aren't you?'

I accept the thrust with a good grace, all the more since today is Friday and I am accompanying her to the Gare Saint-Lazare. If only it doesn't come into her mind to change programme; she has to go to Mass with her mother and she too needs a rest. Now she no longer has plaits and her hair is too short to discharge all that mass of thoughts which reciprocal insomnia has spread out in her little head where the twenty-fifth mayfly beats its wings.

Alone now on the footboard of the train I notice that she is not a little opalescent coleoptera flitting over the stream that follows its course and thinks, as it mirrors it, 'one coleoptera more or less' but a hard purplish caterpillar which does not slacken its bite when confronted with the nettle and will not do so until it has patiently swallowed leaf after leaf before having even formed an idea of what it is.

Visit to the public lavatory. Mosquito. Another mosquito. Men, naturally. Brother Fox is an excellent teacher to convince me that man *is what he is*, that one cannot and must not do anything for him, that he obeys only his own destiny and that nothing can be done about it. And metamorphoses are rare. A father taking out a kid of three's little prick. That's a lesson I should have learnt from him – this man who is on the side of political violence organized within bureaucratic legality, is impenetrable and decisive for all those who are not in the room with the buttons like him. For him everything is more simple. He can always have recourse to phenomenology and *explain himself*, show that all the bad is not one side. Thank you so much. There are some big and swollen with blood like cherries.

It is like the old man who wanted to have me at all costs, the Aspiring Lord of the Manor, who played Mephistopheles without being able to offer me a little Marguerite. Brother Fox does not want to live or to exist, he wants to make a career and that's all, it is the simplest thing in the world; all you have to do is concentrate on the fact that the ends justify the means, the corpses are included in the price. He says: it's him or me, just like in a bayonet charge. But for him this 'him' – who after all, in the end, is not other than 'him', the perfect copy of himself but coming from the opposite direction – is something completely external, an enemy immediately recognizable and distinguishable, an obstacle or target to be knocked down. I could never be so ingenuous as to offer myself a target which is 'me'; I would desert, and I challenge anyone to call it cowardice. In me there does not exist this need to feel myself alive only because I want to bring someone down; my desire for power is much more far-seeing; it is to acquire a good aim through practice massacres and never to have to fire a single shot. The power to achieve this massacre has to be paid for with one's own blood in order to make it credible to the outside world, where one wishes to reach the point of wielding this power. Mosquito. Look of disapproval. It would be a great failure if I had to descend to putting into practice what it has cost me a lifetime to learn, to vulgarize it in the pitiless defeat of praxis, to 'compete', as they say, with *their* weapons. I want to invent for myself an arsenal of my own and a new one. Adjusting one's aim through years of apprenticeship, concentrating on one target – called 'enemy' – the greatest failure of the intelligence is never to have noticed that, hour after hour, we are becoming that target. Smack! Got away. And that the end exists only as a pretext for giving form to the means, which are an end in themselves and constitute the style.

'I mean to say that if *he* actually believed it was a serenade – him with his small-town Machiavelli act,' I say to my neighbour in the next stall, the only one to appreciate my safari, a very old gentleman with a somewhat rundown martial bearing, 'I smelt all the masked fragrance of the eternal fart. My career is to become "Me", I can no longer be content with anything less.'

'They lay their eggs in there,' this gentleman with his reddish hair says to me, pointing out to me with his gloved hand the ventilator casing up there with its stationary broken fan. 'One ought to put on a veil when one comes here, like with bees.'

'They would no doubt issue them.'

'Belgian?'

'No, Italian. Do you know what it means to become "me"?'

'In military life one sees all kinds.'

'To become "me" means first of all to be exiled, to act so that they chase you from the city, to provoke a confrontation, the challenge to the social contract. In this it seems to me I have been fully satisfied: society is not always prepared to exile the first one to come along: most people, in one way or another, it integrates, offering them semblances of exile, cardboard hair-shirts, foam-rubber thorns, dissipation and acts of disobedience. I, on the contrary, have been gratified in this sense by an exile according to the book, and did not desist until it was given to me in a perfectly official manner – let's just take the discharge from military service: do you think they smiled at me and saw me to the door? do you know how many tit-bits they brought me in the lunatic asylum in Florence to persuade me to give up and that they could play me a dirty trick and make me lose my civic rights? Civic rights! What about the wrongs? But not me – I was unbending. Here's the clause, here's the discharge, I said. And they blackmailed me and blackmailed me but they gave in; they saw that I was one of those rare madmen who if they take the trouble to have an idea or an ideal follow it through to the end. One cannot live for an idea – too easy – if you want to live you must renounce having any. For an idea one dies and that's all, in the old-fashioned way, there, on the spot. An idea cannot be something long drawn-out, it is put into practice immediately. The true hero dies in the end. Those who remain are the philosophers. But there is no comparison, don't you agree? And they understood that I wasn't joking. Are you an ex-officer?'

'Yes, does it show? Oh ballocks. Please excuse me,' says my neighbour and changes stall, going and placing himself next to a little siren of fifteen who is fumbling at his flies and looks at the old soldier with a knowing air and pretends to be having difficulty in releasing the deluge. The old man does not remove his eyes – they are beatific and seraphic – for an instant from the flow which breaks on the foreshore of his mind. The curly-headed adolescent lingers, his legs, which are not parted too widely, bend at the knees a little too often, he puts the fish back among the seaweed. I could have sworn it – one of the crowd of Neapolitans who go the rounds of

81

the pizzerias of the world. My ex-neighbour winks behind the youth's back, lets a visiting-card slip into my hand, whispers: 'When we're young it happens to us all to invent myths about Rimbaud,' and then the two disappear outside. Slap. Slap. One after the other. And let everything be printed clearly, if possible with a red-hot brand. I shall make a collection of labels. I have never undervalued the regenerative capacity of my skin. There is no tattoo that lasts if I don't wish it.

'Ours is always the real leprosy in this twentieth century in Europe and in the whole world, do you realize that?' I ask a slim little piece of arse on my left, with a briefcase under his right arm and an enormous parcel with the name of a boutique on it in the other hand.

'I don't come here to hold a salon like you,' and he goes off in a huff.

But what choice did I have? Either leper or ladies' hairdresser or stylist or butler or, if I had tried harder to be Montale's runabout, journalist or reporter or editor in some publishing house. It seems to me that there really couldn't be a choice of troubles and I went straight to the mark. To be a leper, that was the most difficult career. The usual intuition, prize of other intuitions duly followed through. Smack! Got it. One attracts the other.

'Colonel Jacques Dreyfus – Rue de la Bétonnière 14 – no concierge' followed by telephone number; I slip it into my pocket and already feel myself enveloped in goose-feathers. But I have to go to the *Bella Napoli*, I shall guzzle black olives, artichoke leaves, chopped frank-furter, ripples of mozzarella, as usual I shall clean up the pizza crusts left on the plates. But more out of habit than anything else. I shall make some excuse about tomorrow, for the couple of pennies they give me; no – I'll settle up with them and won't go back. I shall sleep, I shall sleep, I shall sleep.

Society, by exiling me outside the walls, where the witches and prostitutes and theatres are, has kept me alive only in exchange for small but well-paid performances of sexual terrorism so much in fashion now with the *bienpensants*, demanding from me silence or the behaviour of a 'strict' little whore who could never have accumu-lated a minimum of credibility if she had begun to talk. Day and night I steal hours from sleep to distil my global vendetta. Which does not however let slip any little passing vendetta, the aperitive based on gonococci and staphylococci; what drives me to the Turkish baths in the Rue Poncelet is not *la douceur de vivre*: it is to catch a dose of syphilis and infect the world, infect it even in foetuses which are budding at this moment. To inject the tertiary stage right away. But now, lying in the big bed, it is not so easy to shut one's eyes, nor is it to be hoped for. The hum of the refrigerator in my ear is as great a plague as a bulldozer. I am exhausted and there is no dark that lasts. I see all the room as if it were lit by powerful lamps. I feel like shouting. When I used to wake up between Carolina and Primo, my godparents, Carolina used to say to me: 'If you feel like shouting when you wake up, do!' And we began to shout together.

And in front of me there is that little neon light that ripples through the metal slats without pause, persistently. I can't sleep, I can't sleep, I shall never sleep.

It's the last vestige of Geneviève's sacrificial passage through this room. To buy a little cage, kill oneself, embalm oneself, get into it and shut it, arrange oneself on the perch with one's neck stretched out, in the act of singing, to make a present of oneself and be hung in the air in an imitation of life.

The time has already come to go and meet Jesuisraide at the Gare Saint-Lazare. She will have the usual basket full of home-made jams, a sausage, maybe even a stuffed guinea-fowl. I always ask her to be sure to bring one.

'My mother was a little worried even if she is pleased to see that I have put on a little weight. She didn't say anything, watched me fill the basket and these two plastic bags and had her eyes full of tears. I have never taken as much stuff as this. Then, summoning all her strength, she said in a broken voice: "Arlette, tell me the truth." "But, mamma," I said, "there is no truth," she gave a sigh of relief and said "You haven't gone to live in a commune too, have you?" I calmed her. I made a long speech about one's appetite in the springtime etc. She told me to let her know "if there is anything new".'

'The only thing mothers want from their daughters is to become nuns,' I say, taking the basket, the two bags, the little suitcase.

'Yes, but with a son-in-law in the background. No flowers today?' she asks, looking straight ahead, walking a step in front of me. She makes an effort – a successful one – at waggling her hips.

'No, I'm sorry, I hope you brought a change of sheets, I spent the night in a sweat... You know, on the whole, I sleep better on the carpet. I feel I'm not taking over anything.'

'It's spring. A touch of depression.'

'You know, I'm not going to the pizzeria any more. You convinced me.'

'It didn't take much...'

'You know – about the flower... the manager wasn't there. They told me to come by tomorrow for my pay.'

'Oh, it doesn't matter – if that's how it is.'

Today Arlette evades me. She chatters away, with a hint of something femininely domineering, even of something insistent. You would think she needs confirmation. But I think that it is this little yellow dress of broderie anglaise that gives her these crested tremors. Will-of-the-wisps. She is incapable of subtleties, hers is a forced gaiety; behind it there is the tension of the suspicious ex-peasant who has hidden his money all his life under the brick in the floor and will never get used to the ease of cheques. The nuns have never been experts in banking techniques, they made their money by exchange in kind. But her dress suits her, some men look at her, she is curt with me as if I were a porter. She gives orders; put this here so that it isn't squashed; that one there so that it isn't spoiled; take this yourself. The taxi-driver gives a hand with the baggage and off we go. At home I know how to cut her down to size. I say nothing. I say nothing until she droops over me who am busy peeling potatoes in silence, grating carrots, who am following my own thoughts, hearing my own confession. And giving myself full absolution. I must get on. My ineffable smile is the final crack in her self-confidence. Let her at least take the trouble to give orders. I shall carry them out.

I arrive home in high spirits. It was my most secret aspiration! How did I not think of it earlier?

'Arlette, could you be very kind and buy me a pair of gym shoes? I have the chance of a job.'

'In a circus?'

'No, a dancer. I read it in the papers, my friend from Tahiti at the Alliance showed it to me this morning. He's the one that works at the Folies-Bergère. I wouldn't have asked if the pizzeria had given me the money that's due to me. They told me to call again, that the manager wasn't there.'

'But what about Suzanne and Geneviève? if the job at the bank turns up.'

'But Arlette, I can't wait for ever. Thanks all the same. If they can only get somewhere with diplomas and degrees what can I do about it? Someone with degrees gets there by himself, doesn't he?'

'Ah bon.'

Damn that *mafioso* of a manager. To have to stay here and throw pearls before hypocritical vipers. She pretends to be sleeping. As if it had not become a duty to be always there waiting for her below the office and to go for dinner together. I could get myself taken on by Monsieur Dreyfus, be his ponce, and spare him the labour of negotiations. Just to come home when I like. I would have put it to him this evening if he hadn't put away half a bottle of Beaujolais for each frog's leg.

'Goodnight, Arlette.'

No reply as usual. And Gina in Cortina, what will have become of her? where will they have sent her? to Trieste? Will they at least have given her a pack of Tarot cards? If at least this insomnia and suffering could be dedicated to her.

'Are you sleeping? No Tuesday at Suzanne's – an unexpected engagement.'

'No, Arlette. I can't manage... I keep shooting the same films for myself. What pizzas!'

'I was – caressing myself and saying to myself –'

'Go on caressing yourself, Arlette. That's good. It makes one feel one has company. The serpent never bites its own tail, it kisses it. I know something about that myself. One can't have everything.'

'I feel very bad.'

'Be patient. I feel I'm dying.'

'No, you only want to have the last word. It doesn't matter what it is. And to throw discredit on my dearest friends.'

'Goodnight for the last time, Arlette.'

'You see?'

I shall never sleep.

'And to think that I had a surprise for you. Suzanne and Geneviève had made the appointment with – But now, with this business about the acrobat...'

'Talk more clearly, Arlette, please.'

'But have you already been at these Folies? did you phone?'

'Of course I've been there. First they want the physical check-up. The audition I have on Thursday afternoon.... It isn't something you can improvise. Maybe it won't even be necessary for you to buy the gym shoes for me if this manager decides to turn up. So?'

'You know, even Suzanne and Geneviève are human. I asked them about the Eiffel Tower and even they have never once gone up it. And so...'

The technique of the Passionaires du Sacré-Cœur is the oldest of all: the carrot and the stick, the stick and the carrot. Then a diploma.

We get into the lift and see Paris rise up under 8,000 tons of iron. Suzanne, garrulous, keeps on talking to Arlette about myrmecology, a discussion probably begun ten years ago, a discussion that is a passion of the deputy director's, and Geneviève listens, absent-minded and beautiful, as her eyes strain in the attempt to follow the gradual change of perspective. But the horizon has always been the focus of her immaterial gaze. Suzanne has a dress with a high waist but not very tight, mauve-coloured, with pleats, which falls abundantly below the knee. Geneviève is more tall and slender than ever in a long dress to her ankles, black shot with some threads of lamé, a tiny purse with, I could swear, gold trimmings, like the chain which if loosened on her shoulder would reach almost to her hips. Arlette has no evening dresses but a black dress, which depending on the jewellery, the gloves and the shoes, can be whatever you like – for evening or a funeral. I have done my best. We get out of the lift, each one goes separately to the parapet and after a little, in silence, we enter the restaurant. The *maître* accompanies us to the table – it is covered with candles – reserved by Geneviève to celebrate 'our humanity', the watchword for this invitation, which made us smile at first. The menu, based on oysters and lobster and fish in general, has already been arranged by Geneviève – and the wines too – by telephone. The sea urchins are opened in front of our eyes by two waiters and I am a little absent-minded because embarrassed: Geneviève inspires in me fear and reverence, I cannot open my mouth. Her laconic manner, which is so eloquent, freezes me, her elegance which seems to be offered only to herself, her dazzling hair, flowing but not too thick, sends out electricity and so do her eyelashes, her eyebrows, the down on her nose and arms. Arlette gives me a secret signal with her shoe under the table, going on speaking about the kingdom and social organization of ants; Suzanne does not touch at all on the sexuality of ants; how they reproduce themselves simply does not interest her. She takes it for granted that we all know. She likes their hardworking nature. And going on from ants, she mentions the names of shrubs, of wild flowers, and gets on to English gardens, to hothouses – orchids, on which she is an expert – and finally ends up on her favourite subject: roses. Say it with flowers.

'Ah! bon!'

'If only I could have a rose-garden one day! I'd want it to be all *Blue Moons* and *Stanwell Perpetuals*. My mother can't stand roses and hates animals, she doesn't want to leave that flat in the second month – I beg your pardon – on the second floor, in case she ends up in some detached house or other with maybe a garden, a gazebo and toolshed and a kennel! I'd love to do a little hoeing! And you, mon petit, do you like roses? Do you know *Dearest*? It looks like porcelain with the faded pinks of old Japan and always reminds me of silent films. Now don't laugh! I was hardly born. Even if the palm of youth would go to Arlette, who is such a little girl, so young in spite of her birthdays.'

'I hope you like this menu, mon cher,' Geneviève breathes: it is incredible, she is speaking: 'You can order a steak, *of course* – she says it in English – And the wine? Blanc de Blanc was my mother's favourite wine. Between one animal being served and the next, she had nothing bu Blanc de Blanc given to her in the stable and amid the absolute silence of her managers and assistants and veterinary surgeons sipped this nectar, rolling her eyes slowly from left to right. The rule was that all the men had to drop theirs for a second. As for the women she passed over them. Anyone who didn't do it was thrown out at the first opportunity. She never offered a drop to anyone. Except to me, naturally. À la santé.'

'I am so confused – you are all so nice to me, give me ten minutes to take in this place, I feel as if I were on the moon.'

'Do you have flat feet?' Geneviève asks suddenly, smiling amiably.

'No, I don't think so, at least no one has ever said so to me. I have – a hole in my right sole. Right at the tip. I walk like that so that no one will see.'

'Ah, you're so funny, ah, so nice!' exclaims Suzanne. 'Oh, Arlette, what an ideal friend! so full of fun, always ready to have a joke! À la santé.'

'And what stories he can tell! and – well, maybe it's a bit soon but one could have a word with Monsieur Hippolyte...'

'Oh, he's so sorry he couldn't come. Buried under letters from women readers. You know, with the spring –' Geneviève interrupts her.

'But he has this idea in his head – I can tell them, can't I?' Arlette goes on, trying to assume a woman-of-the-world tone that she finds impossible, and looking at me. 'Well, maybe one day something can be found for him in some newspaper office. His French is magnificent, isn't it, don't you think? And he writes as well as he speaks.'

'Oh, everything is possible. One just has to have a little patience and never give up hope,' says Suzanne with a consoling look. 'We don't want to make you go back to that restaurant. The men who escort us are so boring. Even about the bank, don't worry, it's probably only a matter of a week but we'll manage, you'll manage! À la santé.'

'À la santé!'

'À la santé!'

'If you come to my place next Tuesday,' said Suzanne delicately sucking a silvery oyster into her mouth which is a little more red than usual this evening, 'you will have to be careful with my mother. One can't talk freely like here; she is a very religious woman and for her roses – But I'll arrange it so that she goes to her own room. She is a very nice woman and I hope she lives to be a hundred but don't dare to remind her that even Santa Teresa of Avila and Santa Rita of Cascia did not spurn the symbol of sin, and are always painted with their garland of *Lilì Marlenes* or with the more humble and intriguing *Masquerades*. À la santé!'

'Ah bon.'

Geneviève and Suzanne are drinking like mirages in a desert. In Montichiari they would say: drinking and smoking like a couple of Turks. Even if Suzanne doesn't smoke at all and Geneviève very little.

'I think I'll come back here again,' says Geneviève with that Pyrenean cadence of hers. 'I remember Perpignan, especially the drives in the gig with my mother who took me to Andorra with her on business.

We had bulls there too.'

Suzanne throws a panic glance at the liquid of her umpteenth oyster which is quivering on the plate.

'Oh, mon Dieu, we forgot the mineral water! Garçon, s'il vous plaît!'

'Height brings back memories. It's a little like a dream,' says Geneviève, laying her hand on Suzanne's. 'The way the air gets thin. Ma chère Arlette, what a wonderful idea to remind us of our humanity. Ça vous plaît?'

'Marvellous,' I say. 'About dreams. I have had one universal and current one: I have dreamt about snakes. They slithered over my body peacefully, they adapted to my extremely slow gestures – slow so as not to disturb their calm, so that they would not bite me. I was exhausted with the time it took to do anything and even not to do it. They were the measure of the meditation which is inherent in any hint of action, the moderators of any impulse. If I was in the open air and ran no risk of catching one of them by brushing against some projecting surface or object the dream took its own way and seemed destined, as it went along, to lose snakes in clusters, without fuss, without pain, like falling hair. But then I arrived at a gap, I'd have found it difficult to pass through it, the snakes began to slide along nervously and to hiss. If I took a step back to the side I would fall straight into an orifice; then I dreamt that I was awake and thinking of a better solution. The better solution was the only one – to take a step forward. Something I did, accepting the risk. And the barrier disappeared, and once more I found myself in the open, once more the snakes began to migrate from my body. When I woke I was on the point of freeing myself even of the last one. For years I have been dreaming this dream, and I have never had the experience of knowing how the dream would turn out once that last one was gone.' Geneviève, Suzanne and Arlette, spellbound, began to dream their own dreams indulging themselves with the images of mine, continuing to suck mussels or out of good manners to watch the waiter dress the sole and pass it to the *commis*.

'Your dreams are free. Mine are tied to other animals – bulls mounting mechanical cows, test-tubes of sperm frozen at one hundred and ninety degrees, the irrefutable coercion into involvement in the selection of the race, *pardon*, breed,' says Geneviève, without any sadness, with the calculated indifference of the female

89

captains of industry, of successful women who have adopted the language of men, they are the only people capable of saying the most romantic things with all the freshness of a female calculating machine. 'Oh, I feel so safe. I don't know how to say it – I feel so well!'

Suzanne turns to me almost as if to interrupt Geneviève who, in any case, has already finished her very long speech.

'And so you want to try dancing? Certainly you have the *physique du rôle* and why not? Better to begin there then one appreciates all the more proper sedentary jobs. And what about me who love only yellow roses and constantly dream about *Sutter's Gold, All Golds*?'

Arlette, very proud of me, says nothing and follows me with her eyes on the corners of my mouth.

'À la santé!'

'À la santé!'

'À la santé!'

Once on the quadrangular terrace Geneviève abandons herself to the night breeze while Suzanne and Arlette take a stroll round.

'Geneviève, my dreams aren't any freer than yours –'

'Oh, but at my age! to wake up and find myself there face to face with Jean d'Arc, another of my mother's crazy ideas. An immense white bull, of the Val di Chiana breed, which my mother had imported from your Tuscany a week after I had my first – I mean, after my fourteenth birthday. Oh I feel how understanding you are. As for Suzanne, if she heard me talking like this... Oh look, here they are. Well, try it – if it amuses you – but pay attention to our dear Suzanne – the Folies-Bergère, yes, if you feel like jumping about a bit, but we shall have to think of something more sensible, more stable. Oh, of course we don't want to put your future in liquid nitrogen.'

'The lift, when it is going down, has a tremendous effect on me,' says Suzanne in a jocular voice, almost to herself. 'It's as if I became light, funny isn't it? And this perfume of *Message* everywhere even in the hinges.'

'Ah bon,'

'Here we are! Till tomorrow. Arlette, goodnight, mes chers. Oh mon Dieu, I'm a little tipsy.'

'Till tomorrow, Suzanne, and merci. Geneviève, merci.'

'Oh how wonderful!' exclaims Geneviève. 'Here at last, inhuman at last like everyone else. *Aurevoioioir, mes chères,*' and she looks at me. Our two friends climb into a taxi. Hands waving.

'I am nothing, I am no one, not even for her,' says Arlette, looking for her handkerchief in her little black bag, slightly annoyed at not having been able to get a word in.

'It's not true,' I say taking her by the arm and giving her a little kiss on the cheek, which is still perfumed by Suzanne's kisses (Geneviève does not wear perfume). 'I like you a lot.'

I feel her shake like a dry leaf; Arlette is really a little shapeless unfortunate thing, full of sighs past and present.

'Tomorrow I'll come with you to get the gym-shoes. I'll get myself a pair too.'

'I wonder if the manager will be in the office tomorrow.'

'Take a hundred francs. That doesn't include the shoes. You pay the taxi. What things they talked about! Cattle, ants, roses in the hinges. Never anything real,' she says to me, squeezing my arm with all her might. 'Never anything.'

Poor Arlette. She is really stupid. And it is only Tuesday.

At home, after midnight.

'And is this real, Arlette?'

'I didn't mean to be nasty about Suzanne and Geneviève, I wasn't fair. They're so nice to me and to you. But they always treat me like a little girl. They say something to you and make you feel it is one of a thousand others, chosen by chance, and that they have an inexhaustible store of them. Apart from ants and roses. I cannot compete, I shall never be able to. I have only one or two things to say then I am ...'

'– finished?'

'Yes, what can I say? they are things one has there, as heavy as boulders that are impossible to move, to break down, to chisel away. Oh, look how I am talking? You are taking me over.'

'Oh no, Arlette, don't let's start on that. I'm not interested. You are simply levering away under these boulders and haven't even noticed. You will see – they are no longer what they were. Think about it.'

'You've got something there. And I never dream, that's to say, I never remember anything.'

'Of course, you dream with your eyes open and hardly ever sleep.

91

You sleep less than I do.'

'But what are all these disclosures about? I sleep, of course I do.'

'Then shall we put out the light?'

'Not right away, please. That story about the snakes. They disgust me. And at table.'

'At table, at table! What idiotic reservations.'

'How dare you? Do you want to quarrel?'

'No, I want to sleep, to sleep, if you'll let me. I have an audition the day after tomorrow, I must be in good shape. Oh...!' It is only Tuesday, soon Wednesday's dawn with my eyes burning and sizzling; but she too, poor thing, is tired, is exhausted.

'Oh, Arlette, why do we kill each other like this?'

'That's what I ask myself too.'

'Poor Brother Fox, Tarzan of marketing! If he goes on like this he'll undoubtedly be shoved back into the publishing trade, which is the other side of the coin for ambitious and untalented ex-members of the Catholic Trade Union. You have no idea how many people put a book together by dint of going through manuscripts returned to the sender – like my *Diary of a Barman* – with a toothcomb. One should publish things only in the wind or on the sand. And kill more and in other directions. But the poor sods are so ignorant militarily, they kill in the only way they have been taught – one another. Forgive the diversion.'

'The important thing is that they shouldn't reject your footwork at the Folies as well.' Arlette laughs heartily, stripping a celery heart. Both of us have our feet in our gym shoes, identical ones.

'Tomorrow. I must try to sleep.'

'You're telling me: I imagine you'll have to turn a cartwheel. Can you do a cartwheel?'

'No, no.'

'I can,' she drops the carrot into the plate and pirouettes on the carpet. Her skirt falls over her head. She is wearing pants of straw-coloured yellow silk, very tight and transparent. Comment: tawny hair, longer than normal – a little sticks out in two strips – on milk-white thighs, very slim and well formed. A most beautiful human body.

'You see? It's easy. The nuns taught me.'

'I wouldn't dream of trying. I can't injure myself – not now.'

She sits down again and fans herself with her napkin, she smiles sinking her little head into her shoulders like a chicken astonished at having emerged from the egg, capable of incredible things: to turn cartwheels, to provoke one slily, to get her teeth into a cutlet *alla milanese*, to have memories of spiritual gymnastic exercises inside the cloister of the shell and to be called Arlette, an actress's name, the very last name for a nun.

'Oh, I would like to do it again!'

'But the food will go down the wrong way!' I must absolutely change the subject, run for cover. 'Today at the Alliance the professor said that Proust was sick. In spite of all the foreign *folles* there no one spoke up, I jumped to my feet and asked him in what way a little asthma could affect his work, would he kindly explain. He seemed relieved, he felt he had been perfectly clear, the illness was – And he did not mention the unmentionable. Was what? I insisted, tell us so that we can understand better and get on. He kept avoiding the question, tried to send me up without succeeding. Finally he said the sick word. Listen, I say, if you have come here to give us a sermon on his use of his arsehole you are making a big mistake. Look round you – you are squandering the contributions of your French fellow-citizens playing the nurse to a gathering that is half made up of sick people. But it's you that are sick. And I emptied the classroom, I began to shout like a madman. I could have killed him. Perhaps I won't be able to set foot there again; and no one came to express solidarity to me, all of them off with their tails between their legs. It is they that create in people the need for a Universal Repudiator of the Repudiated.

'Don't you think you are overdoing things? Calm down, please, you'll wake the whole block.'

'And then, to send me up, they began to wriggle their bottoms, including the Tahitian who has a job as a dancer – a man who comes from a place where they throw people like him to the sharks when they are no use any longer – like in Argentina in Cuba in Russia.'

And suddenly I think: I have a wonderful woman here who even turns cartwheels for me and wears straw-yellow transparent pants and is squandering her savings for me and only wants a little love, a little sex, and is healthy, clean and trembling, and she doesn't interest me at all. Then I get up, full of a sense of guilt, take her under the chin with my hand and raise her head; she lets me without expression, not even amazed.

'I'm so fond of you, Arlette,' and I give her a kiss on the forehead.

'Oh, assez avec votre charme,' she says, a little disappointed, but coming to life again, laughing at herself. 'Do you know why I asked about the flowers on Sunday?' A thing like that, said with such melancholy, toying with her dessert fork among the crumbs of the walnut cake, touches me to the quick, at unfathomable depths which I do not even know I have. Oh if I could love her! make her a little happy, give her a little relief! the nuns will have even stopped her from peeing except at the prescribed times.

'Well, you came twice to meet me at the Gare and both times with a flower. Then I thought you would come the third time and I would say: it is the nicest present anyone could give me on the day of my thirtieth birthday, merci. Instead of which.'

I turn my head away and – fatigue, humiliation, sleep, Gina – begin to sob. Upset, stroking my hair, she managed to calm me after three hours of violent weeping. When I woke up she was no longer in the room. I called her in the dark and I felt well, rested, in great form, ready for the audition. I have slept in the big bed! I drew the curtains the pillow next to me was untouched, and I stood looking at the blanket heaped on the floor.

And here I am behind the scenes at the Folies-Bergère, the only Italian in the world incapable of getting himself a false diploma, with one black eye and a thigh that hurts and nice gym shoes on my feet. The Tahitian dancer looks at me from the other side of the stage and crosses his fingers. My knees are shaking. Did I think then that I was going to dance in a booth at a fair? Who will ever manage to twirl a top hat like that on the tips of his fingers and pass that walking stick from one hand to another? and yet I am here to try to do it. And there are such things as fourth-row dancers, if I'm not mistaken, maybe fifth-row ones, on this stage there could be a military parade of dancers of up to a hundred rows, I mustn't despair. I could be in a worse state, could be in hospital with a few broken ribs or a broken femur, like Carolina. For two hundred and fifty francs! They made difficulties, they accused me of having left them in the lurch on Sunday, I said no one likes being exploited all the time, they told me to clear out, I said they were members of the *camorra*, they jumped on me two and then three at a time, bloody Italians, who then go back to their little village with their smart cars and 'have made it'.

Now they are rehearsing a routine where you have to pass a cage with stuffed parakeets under your arm, then behind your back, then in front of you on to the right shoulder, and then the same thing to end up on the left shoulder. To watch it it might seem child's play. There are only five of us and they are looking for twice as many. I have heard that it is because all the boys are waiting to be cast in *Hair* at the Porte Saint-Martin and because no one wanted to have his hair cut, they set their hair to make it curly like mine; here instead one needs a *Longest Day* type American haircut with brilliantine, or at any rate to be well and truly shorn. I don't mind if they cut mine and if possible put me as far back as possible where no one can see me. And don't let them give me any ballerinas to lift because it would be a disaster for both of us.

Taken on. Bring passport, fill up the form, go to the aliens office with the book they issued you with in Lille. With the canteen coupons in my hand. An industry. They do things seriously. The ballet master, Slav or Hungarian, I don't know which, said to me: 'You have the instinct: a few lessons in jazz steps so that you don't hurt your neighbours with the walking-stick and please try to lose that mad look you have,' and he handed me over to the trainer in the house school – school, gym. I know already what I get: one thousand five hundred francs a month net and they have given me a ticket so that I can come and see the show tomorrow, so that I'll get an idea. I begin in about a week from tomorrow, rehearsals, three hours every afternoon. There is only one thing that bothers me: that I can certainly *act* the dancer but I don't want to *be* a dancer, I don't want to run the risk of becoming like that Tahitian and so many other actors: he has exchanged the Alliance for a number at the Folies-Bergère and he believes he must dance for ever. They should have given him the letter saying 'not wanted' but still it's better as it is, without the Alliance, that way I can begin on English. It is terrible to have to do something and then to think you have become that thing, that role. For this reason it is better for us to use things up, to be a rolling stone, to change professions, *changer la dame*, life.

'Well, tomorrow is Saturday again. But I have good news for you. On Monday you must go to the Banque de Paris et des Pays Bas,

95

third floor, personnel office, there is no need to trouble Madame Bonsants. Ask for a certain M. Lefie, he knows all about it; on the form put the name of any Italian institute of further education. Then leave the telephone number of my office. But now shut your eyes, I have to give you salt water compresses. It isn't any better than yesterday, it really is nasty.' And with the cloth she can caress me at last – I wouldn't let her yesterday – as much as she likes. She mutters and says one should report them, I reply with indifference that there is always the consolation that these people all end up by throwing cans of petrol at each other – like in Marseilles – and that no intelligent insurance company insures an Italian pizzeria. I am very undecided between the bank and the Folies: there I would be independent, at the bank, no, because I would earn less, I have already asked around. But here I would be protected by three maidens, even if I was a bit of a slave. Suzanne and Geneviève would take it badly. Who knows. But I can't stand the idea either of being made up and oiled from head to foot – and besides, total depilation is obligatory, over and above a haircut à la Fred Astaire. In the ballet all the women have to be feminine, the men effeminate angels. It's too much – I feel that it's precisely by beginning with little things like this that one ends up becoming an Italo-Tahitian.

'I'm not putting compresses on your mouth. Why this silence? Your francs for the weekend are in the glass already.'

'That's not it. A little homesickness. It happens.'

To be able to see Giacomino again, now that he is going to university, how elegant and goodlooking and triumphant he will be, if only I could do something to have my revenge for my reviled adolescent love. And to think that in my poems I used to call him Homerically 'No One'! How would it ever have been possible to sail beyond the Pillars of Hercules with someone so truly *nobody* by name and in fact. When I said I loved him with all of me he said to me: 'Go and get fucked somewhere else, you disgusting queer.' He was glad to get rid of me after the business with the chains that went wrong. That was all he was waiting for to avenge his shame. He insisted on seeing me only at night, when there were no witnesses. Mine is a longing for an impossible vendetta. Another one...

It is incredible how these women have busied themselves over me; incredible the timing of their liaison with Madame Bonsants and M. Lefie during the last eight hours. When the cats are away does the mouse dare to play? Never. And to think that only a month ago Arlette was so much on the defensive if I said anything to her she seemed to reject me utterly. Now she is afraid of losing me. And I, like a fool, felt I had a duty to tell her right away where I stood! She had given me a pleased look as if to say: 'That's exactly why I am interested in you.' And my feeling of relief, there would be no misunderstandings, was no longer possible. And now here she is bathing me with one hand and with the other drying the drop that runs down the collar of my shirt. Is she really afraid to lose me? Is she making concessions to me provided I take the bank and turn down the Folies? I need her and her floor and the thick atmosphere in which we live and her refrigerator. But by going to the Folies-Bergère I could also try to do without her, stand on my points, or buy myself a tape-recorder and say goodbye. Her upper lip no longer detaches itself to order me to speak, if possible never to stop. It is as if she wanted to delude herself that she has been at the pillow of an invalid who only now is slightly convalescent 'on the way to recovery.' Better not touch on that.

'That's enough compresses, Arlette. I'm sorry but you know I have to run along to see the show. I'm sorry, I told you, it's a single ticket. Even if I'm late, tomorrow morning I shall be in time to take you to the station.'

She shrugs, goes to the bathroom with the basin and forces herself to whistle 'Ay, trece de mayo', she takes her time. When she comes out she looks about her as if I weren't there at all, I try to look into her eyes to say goodbye, she doesn't stop gazing into empty space, I slip out of the door and, involuntarily, when closing it, make it bang. It is the annoying sound of an unclear goodbye, of an affection that has lost patience by mistake, of a love with a good deal of involuntary anger and no sense of passion. I certainly did not forget to slip the bank notes out of the glass first.

A troop of tired and bored people is climbing on to the stage again to simulate the evening's merriment with which they earn their living. After going to the canteen – delicious choices – I stand here a little apart from them all, in any case no one deigns to glance at me, the beauties are quite different from me and they all are in a hurry to get it over and go away – to play in life the part they play so unwillingly on the stage. There are some relics of the post-war years, certain balding gentlemen with bellies who play the jungle savages when the moment comes for the tribal dance and certain old ladies, a bit wrinkled, who still play the saloon singers! And one sits in a stall, down there, and everything is so beautiful and credible, four-dimensional; there is even a carriage with horses that run while standing still, real horses, a piece of magic. And now they are calling me to go up into the gym. Then I shall go in search of Colonel Jacques Dreyfus. His gloved hand isn't of wood at all as it seemed to me at first, it moves under thin and very old leather, and as far as size goes will be half as big as the other.

'I hope you've been to the bank,' says Arlette on the Monday evening as we come out of the Gare and walk down the steps. The Mother Abbess's funeral has kept her unexpectedly. She smells her flower.

'Yes, of course, no bother. I asked for this M. Lafie etc. Filled up the form. Everything in order. They will call me.'

'You don't seem very enthusiastic.'

'Well, in the bank I'll get five hundred francs less, you know, don't you?'

'So what? you have no rent, light, gas or water – look at this – eggs and sausages and cheese. And we can buy a mattress, can't we?'

'I'd like to enrol for an English course.'

'English? Why?'

'Because, because – because I know French already. I know the place too, it's called Red College, not far from the Boulevard Raspail. The courses begin on Wednesday. Two hundred and fifty francs a month.'

'But that's an enormous sum! and for how long and how many times a week?'

'Three times a week, two hours each lesson.' It is twice a week for a month.

An hour and a quarter each lesson.

'All right then. You might as well start right away. Let's take the metro for once, what do you say?'

At home I am seized by a furious urge to get things over quickly, to go away, to run off, to throw out the ends of stories which I feel are old and tattered and no longer mine, to go on to something else; to set fire to the *Bella Napoli*, to set fire to the bank, to set fire to the Alliance, to set fire to the Folies-Bergère and take the first train to England with these three hundred francs for enrolling on the course, to get even more disorganized, to descend on the English without knowing a word, to go to Brother Fox and stuff down his throat all the letters I have written him and not posted. I've had enough. And Jesuisraide, what does she want of me? What does she know about me after all that *straight* talking? Who do I recall this time? Why doesn't she get it out of her system, make her boulder roll down on me, seeing that she too has bought me with her money hidden under the brick in the floor.

I have re-read the last letters to Brother Fox and they don't seem to be mine any more, I mean they don't tire me like others I have sent and then found scattered all over the place, like those sent to my mother and to my sister, letters so incurably despatched and said and definitive. I was never surprised to find a few of them even under the uneven legs of the kitchen table or the dresser: there was not a single thought disconnected or left in suspense, not a single brusque and fugitive feeling, they were the letters of a broker of lamentations, prepared to do anything provided he fanatically altered the substance of the facts. I never wrote to them saying how I was really getting on – it was always either very badly or very well, the only states of existence they could ever have understood, and I was forced to adapt to the state they expected of me at that moment, irrespective of the truth. From Cortina letters of a deportee in Siberia close to suicide, from Milan of the proprietor of a chain of hotels – I cleared the tables at the Hotel Terminus in the Piazza della Repubblica – from Lipari (where an unfrocked priest had been exploiting my priapism for four months spending hour after hour sitting on my prick and reading Ecclesiastes) of a celluloid star, celluloid because I felt nothing, my prick was erect from morning to night and completely deprived of the very slightest voluptuous feeling, it had nothing to do with me, as if it was full of artificial blood and the veins were of rubber and he, little Don Lucifer, who sat down so politely and stayed there, without ever turning round, without ever saying anything, turning the pages on his curule chair of flesh and stayed there, with a few little beads of sweat forming on his temples; but how ridiculous! His father, an ex-sergeant in the carabinieri famous for having hunted the bandit Giuliano, knew the score and, since he was employed in the kitchen along with a couple of maids when it was dinner-time, shouted: 'Lucio, are you finished having it stuck up you? it's ready.' He was so happy that his son had got back his mental equilibrium. Yes, like a Hollywood star, that was it, a bit of a snob, busy sending a description home, to a place where they kept looking at each other's plates, of the blow-outs of fish on the beach in the evening by torchlight.

To me priapism seemed a state of grace: it wasn't important to me that I felt nothing, the important thing was that, apparently, it cost me no exertion and that little Don Lucifer was very pleased with his sessions. I certainly did not foresee the umpteenth collapse that would follow it. Who gave it a thought? If nothing else, thanks to that boney piston, I now contrived to be taken seriously and to look forward with some hope to next day. Prostitution has always fascinated me; now it no longer seemed a chimera. It seemed to me to be the prelude to divinity to be able to have at one's disposal a body that performed a public service. But priapism followed by impotence, impotence by atrocious attempts to overcome it, then a state of physical impoverishment and, finally, this subscription to a dose.

In short, soon after, all my dreams of becoming an erethistic robot were wrecked. No immortality of the prick. And there was the bone turning to limestone, and my attempts at being a rent-boy failed miserably. I wasn't as good psychically as I had thought. I did some laborious 'jobs' like chemical experiments for which the basic elements are lacking. I might as well go back to being a bartender or something of that kind. With the egoism I had firmly implanted in my brain, that was all I deserved. But I did everything rather than put on the white jacket again. Since no one had yet shafted me perhaps the moment had come to give my backside a chance. At Milan, in the Piazza Duomo, down in Wanda's toilets, I met a kid who had run away from home; he had the smallest penis in circulation. I gave him five hundred lire. For good or ill I was on my way. It would never again be possible to attempt to elevate my arsehole to the status of *gift* as they all had done with me, these miserable failed heterosexuals. It was the best way to write off *the first time*, to kill the sentimental symbolism of the concession of genital and excremental organs, that is, 'the heart'. Impotence was a great teacher of peremptoriness: it gave me the taste for things that do not hide others – at least not intentionally.

I continue to converse mentally with Brother Fox because I want to eliminate him right away and in a natural manner, by saturation, by maturation to the point of putrefaction, of dryness, of dust. I want him to complete his course at once, not to leave traces; I must learn the total expulsion of foreign bodies. If I succeed – beginning with him – I shall succeed also with Giacomino, with my father, with my mother, my sister, all these sterile and repetitive loves and hates which cannot be easily uprooted because the sedimentation of infancy and childhood and adolescence come into it with their frustrated needs and sensuality, a sewer of repeated offers of love rejected, ridiculed and humiliated; and others too. I have to do this in order to set out again, to start living again, to evaporate from this stagnant water that rusts my head day and night. I think back to the belated caresses which have come my way recently from Brother Fox – too belatedly, induced by a beauty cure I gave my natural sex appeal, they almost disgusted me. His dependence on me does not interest me any more, it will not be difficult for me to eliminate him, a bubble that bursts and along with it goes any desire for revenge. My revenge is that it is now he who waits in vain for me to call him. When he invited me to the estate of this man Giscard d'Estaing and wanted to buy me riding-boots etc, I said yes – and disappeared from circulation. Now he is looking for me, my Tahitian friend tells me that someone was looking for me at the Alliance and described him – oh, all I need to know is that he cannot get to sleep and that his one ball is reduced to aspermic hardness of a horoscope without either aura or scope, so that I can sleep well for a week. I left him there in the worst possible condition, with a situation which is in suspense and which he will never be able to resolve without me. And I will not give him the chance. My situation is over and done with; I can even go on to other things.

The one with the old man never even existed; but for the *Diary of a Bar-Boy*, which I had in that suitcase, I would have left it with him. When Arlette told me I could come to her place I already felt as if I had been there for ever. Nothing upset me, neither the Arab voices at the door, nor the cut ribbon on the venetian blind, nor the dark; I opened the door before they did. In fact I was waiting for them. I politely asked the old man for my other suitcase and said I would go along with anything. I did not want there to be the slightest violence, I wanted the old man to be left feeling bad. While he went

off to get it I began to talk to the two Arabs and told them the old
man wanted them to do this and that and that it was all an act,
whims of old age, but that he mustn't suspect anything otherwise
he would have us start all over again and that I was tired and so
were they, I imagined. They were overcome by these occidental
refinements and were at my orders. When the old man appeared
with the suitcase, it seemed to me that his eye with the cast was
shining more than ever in the light of the candles and that he was
displaying a false-toothed smile suitable for a grand *soirée*; at last he
saw me totally bent to his will and then, who knows! who knows
whether I would not decide to explode with all the violence of my
anger! That is the kind of lust he has; it had taken a while to understand it; what excites him is non-co-operation, enforced gestures. I
had only to behave in the way that had always seemed natural to
me to make sure that afterwards he would make my suitcase disappear again and for me to be back where I was. He began to give me
caresses to which I replied with equal promptness. He offered to
kiss me, I had already kissed him. The Arabs pretended to be having
a job to get my trousers off, I told them not to bother, I took them
off and made a very serious invitation. Suddenly I felt hungry, hungry
for beans. I said we had all the time we wanted, why not use it?
There was a tin of beans on the top of the cupboard, would they
perhaps like a little? Maybe I would let off a fart or two, it would
be more amusing. The old man in his dressing-gown of red velvet
stood looking at me, on tenterhooks while I ate beans, and the pupil
of his right eye had almost fallen into his left socket. I ate them
calmly, the beans were the guarantee that no other greater violence
than the act of eating them would be done to me. I began to simper
to the old man who was beside himself and puffed away and could
not make head or tail of my volte-face. From my impulse to vomit
there came only a great feeling of philanthropy, the military tactic
of niceness right up to the last ditch. The old man was finished. I
went along with him in every possible way, that is, in no way at
all, because by so doing I had made him lose the urge. He sent the
Arabs away, after I had sworn eternal love. He said 'pfui' and told
me that I really couldn't stay there and I pretended to protest, swear-
ing affection, my filial dedication, the rosiness of our future perhaps
in some medieval castle. I heard him muttering to himself (but I
heard him perfectly well) *'Ah, what a queen, what a queen'*, he who

had laid the whole thing on so that it would end in a thrust of a knife, a massacre – I would have liked to strike him a mortal blow in that eye that wanders about on its own. So he put me down with his ricketty 4 hp car in front of a pension in the Place de la République, gave me three hundred francs, helped me to unload my baggage and I wished him 'all the best'. No revenge could have been as bloody as my hate, and if one considers that what he expected above all was blood, then one can understand better the effect of my total indifference. And the scene continues to improve in my memory: my tripping him up, him falling on to the gravel from the two steps of the pension, his cries for help and a little white ball that rolls down from his face and darts away into the gutter, me walking over his back with all the weight of the suitcases, of the bag with the books and of myself, I reach the glass eye, we look at each other for a moment, then I cover it with my heel and spin round until I feel myself glide down to earth again and I go down the metro leaving the old man raving and blind on the pavement. The truth is much more disturbing: he stumbled on the doormat, his glass eye – if you can call it glass – did fall out, I picked it up, pulled him to his feet, took him into the bathroom in the pension on the ground floor, washed it for him and he put it back saying to himself again: *'Quelle folle, quelle folle'*. I can't have had the least trace of blood in my face such was the effort not to spoil my painful story. I waited till he left, I gave the little Arab night-porter a small tip and went back to Arlette's to leave again immediately – I came back at six drunk with happiness and sleep. I had had my last meal at Les Halles and I gave the last five francs to a woman tramp.

But these are things I no longer tell Arlette in detail; it is all so far away and prosaic, all so much a story-line and she would in any case be disappointed with it because none of my stories *ever end*. So I prefer to disappoint her right away, going on immediately to theorize and summarize.

'You overestimate people's sensibility, my dear. I'm afraid no one ever knows about your vendettas,' says Arlette, sipping her tomato juice.

'Perhaps that is the greatest act of vengeance.'

'You see? You're not interested in discussing things, you're interested in having the last word.'

'Just imagine: someone knows he has enemies and has done things in the past to deserve them. All his life or for a great many years he waits for the settling of accounts at which he will have to give in, bow his head, be repaid in the same coin, and no one steps forward. He goes to the registry offices: No, he is told, this person and that are still alive and thriving, no one is dead. And everyone has forgotten him. Even his enemies. He goes home and kills himself.'

'And how did it end with the old man?'

'Nothing – he gave me back the suitcase and I came straight back to you by tube.'

'And your diary is in our flat now?'

'No, Arlette, I sent it home,' I say, lying; I would like to add: one must make new mistakes, allow the people of the moment to blackmail you over other things in life, those of the present moment. 'As far as postponing her Tuesdays goes, Suzanne is really a specialist. Perhaps her Tuesdays are the eighth day of the week.'

'No, it's that she is a bit tense. She was last week too. And on Friday Geneviève wasn't waiting for her. I think it has happened two or three times in ten years. But I beg you, not a word about it.'

Now I won't start asking questions, she would clam up at once. She measures out every piece of information about her two friends with a little jeweller's scale. I can make some hypotheses, obviously, but I keep them to myself. Hoping that she will continue of her own accord.

'The yellow of the bruise is beginning to get darker, a good sign. Does it hurt still?' and she is already thinking about an evening of compresses.

'No, not at all.' There, the trickle of information has already dried up. The caresses in prospect divert the course of her thoughts. And I give her so little, am hardly even a plank without nails for apprentice female fakirs.

I am all stiff: my arms, my legs; they have told me that after a couple of weeks of these exercises one gets used to it and the muscles tone up well and it is no longer a torture, becomes a habit like any other. Watch your diet. I'm supposed to make my first appearance next week – and there are no bad nights – the theatre is booked out for two months by the American tourist agencies.

Everyone seems better at it than me – if they keep me on it is only because they see that I put everything into it and that I have to show

I have learned something. The secretary – one of a whole lot of them – keeps on asking me for my work permit, if I have been to the Prefecture to renew it: each time I invent an excuse. What terrifies me is the depilation, postponed for the moment – it can be done at the last minute, in fact it's better that way, then you don't have to do it again and waste time. The important thing is to do it before going on stage. Depilation and economic independence, which from being progressive threatens to become total, seems to me an outcome that surpasses everything and is not negotiable.

Over all of us watches the secret and perfect organization of this theatrical machine, which feeds into its system a certain semblance of comradeship; but in fact, everyone thinks of himself, as in the bank, I imagine, and these people do not share a social life in private; they dance and sing together, simulate ardent passions, possible and impossible loves, Russian fairy tales about abandoned infancies in the midst of a Cossack ballet, blood bargains between whites and Red Indians, and then everyone goes home, to change clothes at last, to go out into the street. Here there are a lot of queers of all ages, all have women's names, it is horrible, it feels like being back in Milan, in the circle of Rick's Bar or the Storkino. They haven't given me a nickname yet. However I ring Arlette twice a day to hear if there is news from the bank. Nothing yet. The high rate of unemployment – you can just see them taking on a foreign bank-messenger.

Independence first and foremost presents itself to me like this: to shave my chest and legs, to become a male dancer and then, gradually, a schizophrenic doll with a prick.

'Good evening, Arlette, I'm dead tired. Couldn't possibly meet you at the office.'

I flop on a chair and shut my eyes.

'Take a shower while I finish cooking. Roast beef and roast potatoes and salad. I have that English sauce too that you like.'

'Oh no, the shower would wake me up. I so much want to lie down. I have to begin on Monday evening, it's been decided, I have already tried out all my routines, tomorrow I have to try on the various costumes. On Monday they depilate me completely, I have to look as if I was made of china. A *Dearest* rose. But the canteen is excellent.'

'You've told me twenty times already that the canteen is excellent. Get up, come on, you're all sweaty and sticky. A nice shower, a nice meal, a nice sleep.'

She takes a long time in the bathroom, looks for soap, salts, sponge, things which are all to hand. I have stopped at my T-shirt. She doesn't go away. I take off my trousers, my socks. My pants. And she is still there.

'The roast will burn. And not too cooked. Please Arlette. Turn the oven right up so that it gets crisp on the outside.'

She must have thought, looking at me: where have the basketfuls of food gone that I brought on my arm from the village?

Wrapped in her bathrobe – I don't have one, I use hers and tie it at the waist – I finish drying myself in the corridor which is sprayed with sound, with of all things *La Gazza Ladra* – at such a volume as to terrify any concierge. And Arlette accompanies the aria whistling. Cheerful? Something from the bank? Tuesdays have become Wednesdays, Thursdays, Fridays? She doesn't say anything. I get dressed again and sit down at table.

'I'd like so much to take you into the country to my parents. My mother when you called to know why I didn't arrive on Sunday asked me if you had serious intentions! But it is not possible, your intentions are not serious.'

'No, Arlette, it's not like that – I have no intentions. And then I still have rehearsals on Saturday and couldn't in any case.'

Then I begin to speak, she puts on the usual record of Conchita and I try to abstract myself from a metamorphosis which Arlette is going through before my eyes. An orgasmic wrinkle disfigures her face, which is suddenly stupid, avid. Nothing I say upsets her at all, or distracts her from her brazen aim of humiliating me with the shamelessness of her sexuality, now she exhibits it without taking her eyes off me for a moment. She has her little hands thrust into her nightdress against the groin, her thighs closed tight and suddenly opened wide, a little statue of debauchery I don't know how unconscious and bestial, but of explosive violence. She almost disgusts me. Her half-shut eyes are romantic in their depravity – aesthetically very beautiful. Then she abandons herself on the chair and murmurs:

'Oh Pablo, Pablito, me voy . . . . me voyyy!'

At last the glass of her obscure and elementary past cracks, it melts under the narrative lash of her private bard. I, as always, have nothing

106

to do with it. I would simply like as always to leave.

'.... but no one must know that I only apparently betray or betray to make amends and make amends in silence to get used to a public betrayal without having to give explanations.' Perhaps Arlette, there on the platform (the train is late), has understood that my story was not gratis like the others; knows I presume that when she comes back I won't be there. She can come and look for me at the Folies-Bergère and then I will be really nasty, I will remind her that the worst people are those who give themselves a power they do not possess, those who pretend to get jobs and work and then in the end have only raised a lot of dust like her two nice, ineffectual, stupid, racist and reactionary friends. I shall have to depilate myself and try to get myself fixed up, but she is finished with me. And the moment I leave her I shall phone the colonel. All or nothing. As soon as possible I shall let her have the money back for the Red College, by letter. Anyway she has conjured up her Pablo, the train has arrived in the station; she has taken my arm lovingly, like an old unhappy friend, or a brother who has just left a clinic and who doesn't mean very much to her. She climbs into the train.

'Goodbye then.' She doesn't say, for example, as she always did: 'till Sunday evening then.' 'I'm very confused about the bank. Suzanne and Geneviève have forgotten about us. They've been so odd lately. I'm sorry, oh, I'm sorry.'

'It doesn't matter, I have a job and earn a lot more and don't need to thank anyone. Never mind. Have a good journey.'

'I'll miss you, you know,' she says leaning out of the window.

I don't reply. I merely look at her. She is beautiful, Arlette. I could make some kind of reply but I cannot use the old 'vous' nor her sudden 'tu'. Either would sound false now.

The train leaves. I'd like to say to her: 'Goodbye, you obsessed creature.'

And she shouts: 'I'll bring you a guinea fowl. Stuffed – the way you like iiiiiit!'

No trace of the Colonel, at any time of the day or night. I'm fed up with going down into the street to telephone him. He goes to rock concerts, at his age, to pick up little boys. Who knows what hell he is in at this moment and who knows how often he has twisted and turned that little cube of hash in his little gloved hand. Poor thing, his enthusiasm as a corrupter of minors must be equalled only by his patience and trust. I begin to empty the bathroom of all my things, I open both suitcases and set about stuffing them. If anything I'll go to my Tahitian at the Folies and ask if I can possibly stay at his place till I have got an advance. Here is my diary, of course I didn't send it to Italy, I always keep it close to me wherever I go. It is a rectangle twenty-five centimetres long, brick-red, and it begins like this:

"THE DIARY OF A BAR-BOY"

I have bought a new exercise-book, I had a great desire to set about writing something, I don't know what. I have so much time at my disposal that I don't know what to do with it. In the family, now that I am seriously ill because of the trigeminal neuralgia, a certain calm has been established, a somewhat tense truce which I shall nevertheless be able to upset, thus getting something to write about. I went to the military headquarters at Ghedi, to the one at Brescia, and then to the Registry: they read this number on my discharge – 28 – and then looked at me and at the number again incredulously.

Why have I decided to acquire these blank pages to fill? Yesterday, as if by magic after so much waiting, I felt that my thoughts were spontaneously composing themselves into images of written language, without any intentionality on my part, as has happened before, and that, at the same time, this wire which burns all round my face cooled and I felt better and my headache went away. The thoughts weren't important to me and I don't remember one of them; they were the annunciation of a poetic idea which is ripening in secret and which I must keep myself ready to realize when the moment comes. I wait without forcing the moment of waiting. I go for long bicycle rides to the river to distract myself from the psychological oppression of this gratuitous event, so as not to disturb it with the impatience of an invalid who cannot wait to break free. The important thing is not to reduce everything to a story-line.

I pay visits here and there, now and again, if the pain dies down a little; I tell them about my *military* experience.

The other day I worked for my brother Dolfo. There is nothing more pleasurable than to feel the blisters on the palms of the hands swell and burst and grow again and burst again, until *the callous has formed*. It is a bearable pain, if only because a labourer or a mason or a plasterer cannot admit to it: if they want at all costs to give vent to their feelings they begin to make fun of themselves after each grimace of pain, otherwise they would end up losing their job if they are dependent workers and have the silly idea of making heavy weather of it, maybe to get more money. Pain exists and to all intents and purposes is useless.

Luckily then with the passing of time the palms of the hands harden like the mortar they have turned over and over and carried in buckets, lucky that the pain stratifies and is no longer the same, becomes a habit no more wearing than many others and those who are forced to make suffering a life-long profession no longer laugh about it even in jest, no longer make the faces which are typical of the apprentices, and end up forgetting about this pain, this violence, because it is too deep within them, almost born inside them like the spleen and liver. *Natural* that is.

One must rebel while there is still time, before what we suffer is not so internalized and made our own as to seem *that's the way it is*; we must expel it, create a gap between ourselves and our own suffering, not allow it to eat us up like phagocytes, to use our pronouns in our place, not to let it say 'I'; one must always rebel, reject it, throw it in the face of whoever makes us undergo it, or make of it a sharp weapon always suspended, which acts as a counterweight in contracts, which becomes hard scabs; that is capital, that is contractual power. It is very difficult, however, for someone who makes walls – for someone who *is* the work he *does* – not to become a wall himself. Like Dolfo: he works as a tile-layer and a couple of years ago set up on his own and actually makes quite a good living. But I believe that of all those who trample about around him I am the only one who takes care where I put my feet. Because it is too late – because he has become in his turn a floor for everyone else seeing that he first and foremost did nothing not to become one. By now there is no difference between him and a floor: you can walk on him and he will make no more complaint than a tiled mosaic, of little tiles, even if they were laid live, and he knows it and it irritates me that he doesn't give a squeak of rebellion. Nothing. You could measure him, take his dimensions, he is so flat and amorphous, cover him in special paper to deaden the noise when you walk on him (like my

110

father or his wife who actually walks somewhere else) and he will not complain, will not react, he will feel that if this is how it is it cannot be otherwise.

And the certainty that he *knows* (did he not stay awake at night for pleasure translating from the Latin until a little while ago?) disturbs me, because it prevents me from despising him totally, because it makes my contempt problematic in the face of his resignation, his consciousness of this state of his which accepts social and intellectual and familial slavery and throws into crisis my continual and total state of rebellion: I cannot bring myself to condemn his moral passivity and, seeing that he has not sufficient power to make himself respected, he has decided once and for all that to *bear the cross* is more rewarding. His indifference, his total acceptance of his human condition as someone who is on his knees fifteen hours a day making floors without any other thought than that of continuing to increase his rate of work even more, while his wife indulges in all manner of restlessness, sets up a friction between me and my way of thinking and living which demands immediate rebellion (and social rather than 'human') against any state of affairs the moment one becomes conscious of it.

Who knows what I am about to write in this emotional state of waiting? Predict? no, I will know nothing of it until the last moment, it is better not to think about it, to redeem the stylistic mortgages, and 'the stories' and the plots, to isolate oneself for the time being in some spring landscape and breathe to the bottom of one's lungs.

Do eye-exercises, let them rest on the peach-tree branches, the erupting hawthorn hedges, the country paths, the streams, the undergrowth by the river, to be fit for that intuition of renewal which I had from contact with a swallow. Is the vernal presumption to relive in one's self the sensations of a swallow, which having passed over land and sea, returns to its territory under the eaves and finds its nest again, not a fantastic one? And I, with a new concentrate of human essences, will travel across the world of men and will return to myself, with wings spread wide, muscles tense and eyes incandescent.

During my first long absence from home Lucia painted on the wall opposite the little desk at which I write, a big blue flower, with excessively orange pistils. Round it she sketched in with her brush dipped in turpentine a shimmering halo of wayward green – the childish desire to enclose things *in something pretty*. She painted it for me and from the cracks in the petals there comes an affectionate perfume, the desire made manifest that my being far away might not last too long.

Certainly in the morning, without my noticing, butterflies flutter out from under the plaster and palpitate with joy when I throw the window wide open. But they do not go away. It is in the room that they use up their flight and if they die in secret they certainly first restore the nectar to Lucia's flower.

On the little terrace, which is the naked cement roof of the small kitchen, handkerchiefs, shirts, pants, a sheet, a cover, T-shirts, stockings: which I see as so many imprints left by my mother's good hands. And then there is the cage of dozing chickens heaped one on the other, a whole yellow mass of ignorant lives.

Whisky, the red female cat which I took in a year ago when it was still a bundle of rags, goes up and down on the pergola in the little courtyard, permits herself a pleasure trip among the vine shoots, pokes her way into the letter A of the luminous sign which in the evening goes CAFÉ...CAFÉ, takes a jump on to the sloping tin roof and stares at the wind she has raised. She thinks it is a ghostly mouse, the most invincible prey of her feline career.

I have gone back to loving guffaws of laughter, the relationship with nature – it is not superficial – which during this spring represents my subterranean rebirth to simpler, more complete, more reserved forms of life. The doubt does not even skim past me that what is happening is due to the physical weakness that comes over me with the crisis in the trigeminal nerves. I profit from these moments of serenity and don't look them in the mouth, so rare are they and so memorable. Then I will leave again. I shall go to Paris.

Certainly the words are not bursting out as they once did, beautiful and daring as they were then. I and my pain have crystallized a little, but we knew this before we became one, and there is no ill-feeling between us. So long as there are feelings and ink we shall progress, then when the bad time for *ideas* comes, we will dismiss each other, say goodbye without regrets.

Mid-April, and already the flies are coming out. For me they are not a nuisance. I look on them as the private swallows of my room. Today I could no longer kill one: did I ever kill one of the many people who sucked my blood? And yet they were all much more conscious than these mosquitoes of thinning my blood and lowering my blood-pressure. And it is when I think of these mosquito-people, of those insects that wear out your cock, whom I have hated without reacting to, that I find sufficient patience to put up with these mosquito-mosquitoes.

Nanda dear, this morning I pretended to myself that you were turning the corner by the town hall and coming towards my house. My eyes lit up, I began to run, I joyfully shouted the blind alley of your name several times, threw myself into it and hugged you tight to me. From behind me you had come down the bus and sat beside me and said:

'Ciao, Barbino, do you remember when you used to come to borrow my earrings and began to dance on the chair?'

After so many years you were there behind me and I wanted to say: 'You haven't changed at all' and it wouldn't have been something said casually. I always have the feeling of remorse in me: that I disappeared, that I didn't show up again after that time in a bus in Milan. But a certain desire to be in your company has always stayed with me, to learn what other things you remember about our childhood in Vighizzolo. But there was your present that stifled everything – on the one hand, the repetition of similar situations (your three-year-old child being looked after in Bergamo; your obviously carrying on the same trade as your mother – 'manicurist' – or something of that sort) and on the other, that detailed history of the cancer you carried about on you with too much desperate coolness. Your self-mortifying language wounded me, gave birth within me to an inexpressible emotion. In this world of puffed up balloons nothing pleases me more than self-contempt, when it is genuine like this. You used to put on your long, long earrings. With a single glance you dominated the looks of all the other children. A goddess of stone, an immortal woman, determined to dominate by distance, never to be brushed by an unknown hand come from who knows where to force you to bend, to constrain you to accept the filthy caress of the most icy and witty excuses so as to give vent to fear of a death, that is always imminent. You have remained here in me, like a fishbone in my throat; after we greeted each other and I took your telephone number, I knew immediately that I would not phone you – all that afternoon and that evening and all the next day I went about and felt myself to be *you*, I tried to localize your carefree tumour and under my hands I even felt that it was your clothes that rustled not mine. And in my head I felt like a body that didn't belong in its skin, which did not fit well, which slipped about, like a wig put on in haste or with complete lack of care. Because I didn't say a word, but it was clear that these hairs were not yours, that these hairs were opaque, like black spaghetti, although the frantic cut had remained the same as when you were a little girl.

But it was not possible for it to be you, it was a mirage; and my fishbone was back in its old place. Will you ever be able to pardon me? Then, searching in the little flowerbed under the vine, I noticed that the lilies of the valley are still green, that the pansies are finished, that the salad for the doves is still a remote intention, that the geranium has brass arms, that the dahlia will flower only in a few weeks' time.

Then I began to rub my brow and cheeks, while the new brood of doves started to cheep in the black-painted cage.

I look around me not looking for anything in particular: my bedroom is very ordinary, it does not lend itself to dazzling descriptions.

There are brown spiders' webs on the beams, nails and tacks in the walls, a big stable-door key hanging on a nail, the peeling patches of decades. To stay here alone when my folk forget for a little to inveigh against my lazy ways and my facial suffering ('all an excuse not to do anything!' bawled my mother) means to be ready to open the door to someone provided they are able to get up the first little flight of stairs before being thrown out on to the courtyard by *my folk*.

At least in the evening – above all in the evening – I should like to meet someone to talk to, to let my emotions circulate, to get some air, to discover through that person myself, my sensibility which has never been formulated except palely on paper. In the evening the feeling of emptiness, although it is not distressing, gives rise to an unnecessary and annoying feeling of melancholy in my thoughts, because melancholy models them on itself, and spoils them and on my own I am unable to detach myself from it and overcome my unease.

And when, walking through the village streets, I no longer manage to brighten my glance by imagining this person walking towards me, I climb up here, light a cigarette, look round the walls and the trunk and over the beds, until I fall asleep – and if I do not succeed – either go down again, recharged with hope, ready once more to search those faces which I know by heart for an understanding which has never been there and never will be, in these homogeneous and inexpressive faces, which do not accept my obvious desire for them. There is no desire about – or if there is, there is also the funereal refusal to bring it into play; fear that the deformed creature which we have shut up inside us will poke out its head. Nanda and I are the only persons whom I have known until now capable of talking of our own cancer and of living out the vital part of what is superficially considered death or dishonour: we talk about it and then go on to other things. The others do not talk about it and are stuck there, for ever, and all their lives long what they chase out at the door comes in again at the window – and in horrible forms and all the more monstrous. There is no commonsense about, no one who sniffs at his own brain with the least discernment. Every single one is so disgustingly sentimental – and putrid from the habit of using clichés which are the other face of being mute, of mental pornography.

And having nothing better to do, I observe how I hold the cigarette in my fingers, how I place it between my lips, which are full of blood that has coagulated with abstinence, how I expel the smoke, calculating its intensity. I look at myself in the mirror with acute pleasure and think of nothing else but how to increase that self-satisfaction. And then if I describe a little circle in the smoke, I feel myself, and can also feel myself to be happy. In this way I like to go fishing in my minutes between one solitude and another. I like my neck, so high and strong, when my eyes dig into my reflected image. I like the imperceptible play of my limbs which penetrate the mirror and leave their own outlines even when they move away to come back quickly to see if they are still there. I appraise my delinquent face.

And at the peak of erotic pleasure (which there has never been – sex is a damnably painful business, psychologically, physically and *socially*; and then there is a whole little-explored business of coming to terms at last; in short, a hell made up of little worries, of childish

115

anxieties, of cretinous good resolutions etc), uttering little cries, I masturbate words like *femurs, crustacean, ecpirosi, mechocan*.

An expanse of roasted almonds in sugar and vanilla, little villas of white *torrone*, a friend of whipped albumen, a little bench of candied sugar and to stretch out on it, my belly on yours, *and to experience the sweetness of living*.

And let us by all means talk less about it: let the tongue be silent and the lips become apple-flavoured ice-cream.

I should like to write all day today, I feel I shall never stop. I have got cigarettes in exchange for a book – one less that will finish up on the stove, the moment my mother 'isn't thinking' as she says – and I have come up here with the task of having many things to say. I could begin by saying that today is Easter Monday and that it is drizzling and that the birds are making a great din in the tiles. And I remember that Easter Monday in Milan two years ago, in the afternoon, the sun, in a public garden, seated on a bench near the refreshment kiosk and in front of me was a boy of my age, of a delicate and virile beauty, with something very ironical in the turn of his lips; beside him, on the bench, he had schoolbooks held together by a belt, and I was already thinking that I had only two hours free and then had to go back to the Hotel Terminus to prepare the tables for dinner.

From behind his dark glasses he could look at me as much as he liked without my noticing and this embarrassed me – too much in common with Giacomino – and in defence I adopted the oddest poses so as not to be studied with impunity, defined. Probably only a contortionist could have knotted arms and legs as I did in this ticklish position. Perhaps he simply thought I was mad. He turned the pages of a motoring magazine, I had a paper which I was unable to concentrate on reading so great was the strength of feeling I experienced at that moment; if only I could go up to him and talk to him! He was so beautiful. You could see he did not have to eat pork morning and night. I felt I was burning. But I did not feel any envy, I have never for an instant wished to be anyone other than myself.

I began to scribble words somewhere but I had not time for words, they could never have equalled in intensity those emotions which darted to and fro between us, absolute and mute. Every so often we caught each other's eye, very briefly; I mean that I pretended that he was staring at me and every so often I improvised a stare in reply. He must have thought I was a case. Perhaps he was already so privileged, perhaps he was already so concentrated on the driving-school, and he would feel it a duty to find me touching.

And this state of having him a few metres away and not knowing each other and being attracted to each other in this virulent manner lasted two and a half hours, more than enough time to deduce that not only I but he too had picked up those telepathic signals.

For some time he had stopped turning the pages of his magazine. My paper had finished up in a ball in the rubbish basket. I waited. He waited. We waited for sufficient spontaneity to ripen to ask for a match, a banal pretext or – what else could we have asked for? I tried not to think about it, to have a snooze, to simulate sleepiness, to distract myself by turning my back to him, staring into the beak of a black swan which seemed to me to be yawning, tired of staying anchored there to be the witness of something which never happened, which had already happened ineffably and which in the animal world makes no sense. I ate a mass of ices – and I hate ices. That was it – offer him an ice. But no, how on earth, someone you've never seen before and you go there with an ice-cream cone and say, excuse me, would you like a lick? And the thought never even so much as touched me to start to walk, to change path, seat, swan, to follow each other in order to get talking... He takes off his glasses, his eyes are black, almost angry, and they looked at me haughtily, with ill-concealed annoyance towards me for not launching an attack, that I had beaten him in bouts which were too long, bouts typical of an intellectual or of impotence. And he is taking the first step towards me. And in the fraction of a second I have time to see his lips which open in a smile, his eyes which, like coiled snakes at sloughing-time, disentangle themselves in a new sweet skin, while I was running away with tears of fear held back only by the need to rush straight to the hotel. He looked like Giacomino, he was another No One.

I got told off thoroughly by the chef and next day had to give up my time off because of being late. So I never saw him again.

I look at the X-ray of my skull: I sincerely feared to find it in the same state as I feel myself to be in – in pieces: little bony islands each going its own way, a cerebral ferment of wandering stars, spherical, triangular, rhomboid, splinters of every shape, perfect and imperfect, with and without volume.

Against the light: that whitish arch recalls death, death photographed at last. I am contained in there.

It has been established that I have tissues more developed than normal, hyperplasia of the forehead, I think they say. I do not know what it means clinically. Nothing, I imagine. They simply wanted to find out if I had sinusitis – that was all.

I like to think that it means that I am inclined more than others to extremes and to balance, that is to say that I possess a proper equilibrium of stupidity and intelligence and balance, to a superlative degree, because to be only either the most stupid or the most intelligent or the most balanced would be a misfortune which in the end would be equivalent to the other two which are left open by the genetic and existential alternative. But in three misfortunes, opposed and consubstantial to a superlative degree, which co-exist and compensate each other, *I*. . . . That is the point: to begin by knocking a hole in this pronoun.

Here I am in Milan again, looking for a little luck, like so many others as thwarted as myself. As if the previous lesson hadn't been enough for me. But it will not be for long; if I have to pick up lice they might as well be Parisian lice.

I am working at the very exclusive Bar Pinguino in Via Verri, I am a waiter, or rather I go round the shops and beauty-parlours carrying through the traffic trays piled with ices with their little paper umbrellas and martinis with glacé cherries in them. I have found lodgings just a step away, in Via Bigli, in a ramshackle attic belonging to a tailor: a camp-bed there was already, and with a bit here and bit there I have managed to put together a bed. Hundreds of beetles about – they don't even wait for the dark; I don't even squash them. There are so many of them that they squash each other I imagine. Now there is one peeping out from this page, who knows what it is trying to say to me.

My legs are giving way from walking upstairs and kilometres up and down the Via Montenapoleone. Use of lifts forbidden. These shitty jewellers and bankers and hairdressers. 'Put it there,' they say always impatiently pointing to some level space – who knows why; I am a real marathon runner for speed. And addressing me with 'tu', and making me feel like a cigarette-butt that they don't crush with their heels because it is too high for their legs. And then the affected and grammatically deformed language of these new rich! 'This way, that way if you please, modom countess!' Like that shit Bergottini, who every time I put a glass on the little table shoos me away not only with his hand but out loud. In fact I think I get on the tits of everyone with my manners, which are free-and-easy and very polite. I never say anything, but when they nettle me I always find a pretext to leave behind me a sentence the construction and shades of meaning of which are of such vast scope that they must feel that they are being sent up by the correctness of my sober language. And they reply with violence and contempt but you can feel that from the beginning they have in some way thrown in the sponge and, if they could, would start kicking me. I haven't time to close the door behind me before I always hear '. . . . rtinent' trailing behind me. Fortunately they are not all like that, otherwise I would already have lost the job because of complaints – but there have not been any really bad ones. Not even the two brothers here who run the bar with their father know which way to take the situation: there is a vague dissatisfaction with me which comes from outside and yet I know from Rino, my colleague-boss, that since 'I've been working in the street', as he puts it, I have doubled the orders and therefore the takings and the two brothers keep saying 'But what do you do to the customers?' and you can tell right away what they mean. Since I do nothing special apart from getting secretly into these shit-heads the notion that even a waiter, all beliefs to the contrary, is a thinking human being, I shrug and say 'I don't understand' and they don't dare to go any further, apart from anything else because I have already dashed out with another tray – and then the ones who are my salvation are the women, I mean the shop-girls. All the seamstresses give me the glad eye – and keep ordering by telephone. Since there is a young boy full of pimples who takes my place sometimes, just to be sure they say: 'Please, will you send the one with curly hair, eh?' which is me, seeing that the other has hair as straight as wire. When there are no orders from outside I stay behind the counter or serve in the saloon. Sometimes I have to contend with pairs of wrinkled eyes which stare at me shamelessly and do not allow me to work in peace. You feel them on you like slimy eels on your skin. There is not the least discretion in people who are used only to give orders – they look at you as if they wished to take possession of the sight of you. They suck you; suck in the abundant curls, the little deep eyes, the fleshy mouth, the colour of the skin. Especially if they are old. There is a grand lady who comes accompanied by an adolescent in livery – purple with gilt buttons like door-knobs – and she looks at me and sips her grapefruit juice and gin contriving to turn the usual five minutes into five days. She's as thin as a beanpole, bent slightly forward, her hair drawn very tight at the back of the neck, an enormous bosom, who always wears showy dresses – flowers, ducks, aeroplanes. And other eyes, like pinheads, which seem to give off humidity, which must inevitably blur my image after they have brooded on me insistently for a little. And they all leave ridiculous tips – practically another wage. Better still if you have the wit to address them with a title, whether real or false, as Rino does – it is a never-ending whirl of 'doctors' and 'professors' and 'advocates' from morning to evening. No doubt they have money but what a depressing life they must lead if, in the end, all they need is a bit of pimping by a waiter to make them feel important. Eugenio Montale, whom I met at the baker's, amused me a couple of evenings ago: I mean that without him I would never have put my finger on the difference, which is for a waiter always essentially literary, between being one and not being one. Well, since Montale is someone who would never stop walking about simply because he keeps on stumbling and stopping, just outside the baker's strikes up a conversation with me pointblank and tells me he would like very much to go for walks with me if I am free. I must say that I took a liking to this old man at first sight. He looks like a pachyderm pickled in spirits, totally unable to do either good or ill – a physiological shape redeemed by the fact of having produced the right poetry at the right moment and then of having contrived to administer it for all the decades to come. Well, so we arrange for the next day at three, seeing that I can go out from three to six. And so we go on for a week with him hanging on to my arm; I like very much the honesty with which he openly shows his physical dependence; when he has managed to put out his third match as well, I light his cigarette for him with him smiling away like a new-born babe in ecstasy – a bit idiotic to tell the truth. But certainly he is not like all the people who operate round here – it doesn't matter to him if a waiter is a human being – in fact he recommended to me a book

120

by Thomas Mann, *Felix Krull*, which I enjoyed very much. A week ago that was. But I ring him every day and his housekeeper answers the telephone and he seems to have sprinted up and says all in one breath but almost singing 'How are you?' as if it was a piece from an opera, shouting it. Two days ago he says to me could I go with him somewhere later on, at about nine o'clock, nearby at the Mondadori bookshop; he says 'Seeing you like reading, I'll introduce you to a few writers', and off he goes. I put on my nice blue trousers, a blue shirt, a loose neck-tie and am down there waiting for him. As usual he is very nice and says on the entry-phone: 'Why don't you come up?' but there are at least three thousand reasons why I don't want to go up to his place and I pretend to feel a little shy. In fact, so long as we go for walks and bumble about I like it but I wouldn't like to find myself in some painful situation, I have absolutely no wish to wound him or to be wounded: we are both very fragile – that I feel deeply and a certain distance does not harm this peripatetic friendship.

So once we are down in the basement of the bookshop – it was the launch of a book by Bassani, *The Heron* – he completely forgets about me: by this time I had got him down the stairs. But everyone had had time to see that I supported him right down to the last step and that he smiled to me saying to wait for him, not to go away. Immediately the grand lady of the gin and grapefruit comes forward: charming, an ocean of scents each one different from the other, offers her sleeping hand and starts off: But where have we seen each other? wasn't it in Rio in that lovely little place behind the Sheraton? and I shake my head in terror: but I realize at once that she is not sending me up because she goes on: Then perhaps at the Biennale? No, not this year's, the one two years ago. I shake my head, but very decidedly, but I still say nothing: all I should like to say to her is, shithead, but what if this morning you drank two fruit juices made by me! but you never even buy a lemonade for your little slave! Then it must have been at Spoleto, at dinner with Carlo. And I say, yes, it must have been a dinner with Carlo, and not to go and put my foot in it, smile politely: at dinner with Carlo to me means a restaurant as big as a parade ground with three hundred places and three hundred and one with me. But it could also be a private occasion and then I would easily be unmasked. So I begin to look round, catch glasses of champagne on the wing, empty a couple, she too, and gazes at me and bends forward still more and makes odd grimaces with her mouth, which looks like a drunken boat on a swamp of perfectly motionless make-up. I give a slight bow, I am embarrassed to death, and lo and behold I catch the eye of a director of a bank or something of the kind, the one with pinhead eyes. He makes a gesture with his chin by way of greeting, comes up to me, while that lifelong festival-going lady is caught up in the vortex of some other fashionable and geographical whim with a lady close by, and says to me: 'How is the Maestro? tell me, tell me how is he *really*.' Since the 'maestro' does nothing but tell me his ailments for two hours a day, like any other wise old man in this world, I know all about it, reassure the banker about his health. After chatting for a good while, lo and behold this one too gets going but without asking questions, simply making assertions. He asks if it is worth while renewing one's subscription at the Scala because 'there are very few real premières', if I shall be spending the summer at Versilia this year too, and don't I find that they are overdoing it a bit with the prices at *La Bussola* seeing that 'the Agnelli's have moved away'. I am dumbfounded by the whole of this snobbish and slightly mad soliloquy and keep on saying to myself 'my God, it isn't possible'. Even this guy hadn't recognized me. And down goes another glass of champagne to the health of the world of culture; wondering who is the fortunate person for whom he has mistaken me, certainly the scion of some distinguished family or some high class rent-boy, I don't know and will never know.

The real amusement came this morning, whereas all that evening I felt like a fish out of water and seemed to have been there since time immemorial – instead of which we were back at half-past ten. Well, the lady with the camellias arrives: the usual grapefruit juice, gin, the usual silent cud-chewing with the lips, the usual sucking glance. Now I know the score, I think: maybe I can teach her a lesson or at least, make her wonder whether there was a waiter at dinner with Carlo, maybe seated next to *her*! absolutely officially! But not at all – she opens that huge mouth somewhere and says: 'I think I have seen you before' and looks at me with ash-coloured eyes, to which, holding back a laugh and biting the inside of my cheeks to restrain an incipient giggle, I say 'Oh, signora, very likely. I have been working here for three months.'

The same thing happened with the banker: I'd really like to know what it is they look at when they look at someone as they do at me. They are certainly pursuing some phantom or a myth of a big dirty boy who is scratching about for food, I don't know. The fact is that these people don't use their eyes to see something, but to continue to pursue a reflection of themselves, in perpetuation of a visual egotism in which there is no room for the world. And so I can console myself for my camp-bed and this slum and these immensely respectful and polite beetles, seeing that I enjoy excellent sight which is less uselessly abrasive than theirs.

Then Bergottini says to me: 'Listen you, how dare you serve my clients with these dirty nails? aren't you ashamed?'

In fact my nails are not dirty: they are pink to the cuticle and the hundreds of cups and glass washed do the rest. It is not so much the nails as my hands which are in some way filthy and obscene. But even for him, to say such a thing to me in front of all these people! I cleared my throat, I didn't feel like trying on anything classical and I said to him: first of all 'tu' is what you say to your brother, then secondly, you can ring some other bar and thirdly, you know what to do with it!

I was shaking with anger, I could have killed him: he does this with all the waiters Rino told me, he wants to make them feel like shit, it amuses him 'and just thank heaven you're not working for him!' I turned on my heel and ran down the stairs, while all hell broke loose upstairs, a couple of cups of coffee fell, someone stumbled. When I arrived in the bar I was already prepared for my fate – in fact I came in with my jacket folded on the tray and went straight into the basement to get my things. And then one telephone call after another and the father of the two brothers who goes personally to Bergottini to offer his apologies and that I am a criminal, a good-for-nothing, that I am ruining the good name of the firm, and that they hadn't expected this of me etc. And here I am without a job, and almost back where I was economically because I got the idea into my head of buying the washing-machine for my mother, so there was no longer any question about who to give the money to (as much as I liked, however, not like when I was on the lake and he still came at the end of each month to draw my pay although I had left home a while ago; and I, like a fool, who let him, in any case, I said to myself, it's not the end of the world, I still have the tips). And my mother who looked at this square piece of bodywork a little disappointed and didn't see any sacrifice behind it, as if I had stolen it or that it was the result of some whim on my part which she didn't understand. But, I said to her, you'll soon see this winter the difference not to have to go down to the stream with the washing and her twisting her mouth in a resigned way as if she were still always thinking the usual refrain of 'it would be better if you gave me the money'. The money in lieu isn't very much and I had bought myself a semi-linen suit. When I told Montale that I had been dismissed and that that Felix of his had gone to my head a bit with his picaresque aristocracy and that, for all the waiters I have known, I never came across one who... In short, in a certain sense, by making a big thing of it I wanted to make him share the responsibility for my misfortune, that was it (my god, with all the money his melancholy must bring in). He said to me: 'Ah, but you know I am leaving for Versilia and afterwards who knows,' singing as if it was a verse from *Nabucco* and then in my mind I told him to fuck off there and didn't phone again. What can a person understand of life distilled into literature who has never lived where literature is not made for nothing, but at most is endured from on high and that's all. Well, I went to the Piazza Duomo, the usual little visit to Wanda, down in the loos; we talked about this and that, of the raids by the vice squad, of the fear that in the baggage she keeps in the left-luggage they may have put a bomb and about her face which after ten years as an attendant in underground lavatories, is grey and full of little broken veins and 'she too has become a shithouse' – she says it not me. Then I go up top again and get talking to an extraordinary type, a nice piece with cowlike eyes and a tall slender figure, and the talk gets round to his job: private waiter, he works for Buzzati the writer 'even he doesn't know how many thousands he has! and he seems always as if he had dropped from the sky, so uncontaminated by money, him, the fox!' and we begin to scatter poison on the grand families that determine the fate of culture in Italy, people who so as not to lose their grip on things are all dressing up in red (Rooshia, Rooshia!).

And then by dint of finding things to do, of going round cafés and bars, about the streets, to the station (the ticket to Paris wouldn't even be dear but I have no idea how expensive life is there and I have to pay the tailor, the owner of this hole here) I make the acquaintance of a type of about fifty, plump, a sad look, well-dressed but with a grease-spot here and a coffee-stain there, who when he speaks interrogates and snorts and then rolls his eyes to heaven, then takes nervous little steps backwards, always struck by a non-existent spotlight, hair thin – dyed red. Theatre impresario he said he was. Would I like to go to Venice with him? for two days? He has to put on an operetta.

He makes an appointment with me for the next day early, he dries the sweat with a red handkerchief; right, I say, come home with me seeing you've got a car and we'll talk about it. We talked about it. Naturally although I call upon all the patron saints of useless tarts I can't make it and I am disgusted by the way he moans down my neck, these streaks of saliva he sticks to my ear while I move about and wriggle like a little virgin and meantime talk to him about the rent. The gist of it is that for the trifling job I have done I earn ten thousand lire and at once make a date with him for Venice. It will be up to him to know whether he still wants to or not; the most I can manage is not to participate.

Venice is full of memories for me – the games of rummy with Guidi and the Padovan woman, I was not much more than sixteen or seventeen, it all seems very far off, I wonder whether Guidi still remembers me, or Anna Paganella, about me who was dying to know all about Tancredi. It is odd but I remember nothing about Guidi or what he said to me during those three months when we saw each other at least once a day after I gave up my job on the Lido in a restaurant on the beach where I worked by the hour (and which was shut when the weather was bad). In fact it is because I did not *understand* anything, in the sense that he muttered everything to himself, for hours, in an incomprehensible language which was mumbled, clipped, made up of unexpected jumps, flat calms of vowels, the hissing of consonants which could last the time it took to cross the bridge at the Accademia. He and I in front, the retinue of journalists, dealers, relatives and inquisitive people behind. Every so often he turned and made a gesture at them as if to say – go to hell all of you. And all that time when I wasn't working at all because a series of storms broke out he took me one evening into a dark *calle* and said to the others that he wanted to be alone with me and took out a roll of ten thousand lira notes and put them in my hand and said to me – 'Take this, it's better for me not to give you drawings otherwise you know – the gossip.' In fact he must have known that I, like everyone else, had on various occasions been approached by hotel-keepers and art-lovers who asked me for drawings of his, seeing that they always saw me with him. Dear Guidi, who enabled me to pay for my room and to have food assured for two months (admittedly I ate only bread and mortadella and slept in a basement in the house of a widow from Calabria who couldn't stand me because, she said, I kept the light on all night and she should at least raise the rent and, in short, it would be better if I went etc). Until a relative of the painter threatened me and talked about 'taking advantage of an old man' – Guidi for those three months was crazy for my company and never once took a brush in his hand, and never did any more than stuff me with lemon ices in Campo Santo Stefano and my presence was as vital for him as it was harmful and unproductive *tout court* for the heirs. I don't believe that I ever touched on the topic of sex with Guidi – to tell the truth I do not remember touching on any topic. He had fallen in love with my youth, probably with the impudence with which I had done everything possible to get to know him, because I very much liked his blue faces – that was all – and perhaps because I said so many unimportant things which were nice and thoughtless and clumsy. And so the moment I got the feeling that by now I had stood on enough corns right and left in Venice I got away in time before being run out of town. And I explained it all to Guidi in a letter and he said he knew all about it and that it was normal that like all the others I too should have only one aspiration: to manage to get a present not of a drawing but of an oil and then disappear. That is, he totally supported the theory of my opponents and the matter didn't seem in the least blameworthy to him. The fun my company had given him was well worth a picture, I should look in at Harry's Bar, where he had a studio and come and choose it. The whole thing moved me very much and I disappeared from circulation for a couple of days, tortured by this temptation, by this picture with the proceeds from which I could certainly start studying again. Then on the second day I rang him, he said he wanted to see me before I left, that the picture was ready there, that his pictures were still his own and he did with them what he wanted and was not 'forbidden' to do so as some people wanted him to believe. But I didn't go, something held me back. And when we saw each other for the last time it was raining and he held the

126

umbrella and walked with me to the *vaporetto* and I didn't understand
a thing of what he was saying and then, suddenly, he began to cry
and I jumped on to the boat and never saw him again. And it seemed
to me that this gesture of wishing at all costs to preserve a dignity
which I did not even possess, had made me more nasty and I left,
cursing him, him and his pictures and Venice and this wretched
wandering life of mine which allowed itself the luxury of certain
heroic gestures on the grand scale, and then, perhaps, was there on
the Riva degli Schiavoni on the job in return for a *pastasciutta*.

In short, I had reasons for wanting to go back to Venice: to visit
Virgilio Guidi, and, who knows, take back my picture.

Well, the impresario was on time and in his car full of waste paper
and matches and dirty linen and little plastic bags of ostrich feathers
and spangles, we arrived at Mestre and then put up at the Hotel
della Fenice. He drove in an amazing way whistling tunes and clearing his throat: I was already wondering about the evening which I
might possibly have to spend in a double bed. And in fact, he had
booked one and in the morning I already began to complain of the
heat, a headache. At the sight of that whitish blemished skin, which
had run everywhere, from which there came an adoring and vaguely
charming glance, I pretended to faint, I ran into the bathroom with
him naked, following me, covering his privates with his hand like
a Botticelli Venus from an old people's home, and me running the
water as hard as I could so as not to pay any attention to his entreaties.
But then I had to come out after all and said to him with a touch of
flirtatiousness that, by the way, little incontinent satyr that he was,
it was dinnertime. What impatience! Seeing me so whoreish, doing
the whole bit, it began to go to his head and he came *by himself* at
his age. I gave a great sigh of relief and ran out, telling him to go
ahead and order something, that I would be back in ten minutes.
Guidi was painting frescoes in the Fenice theatre and I didn't take
long to find the right door to get up into the gods. But there the
doors were shut and from inside I heard his cavernous voice giving
orders. I knocked hard enough to break down the door until some
on the inside undid the bolt.

'What do you want?' asked a boy of my own age in a white shirt
dirty with patches and streaks of colour.

'I want to see Virgilio Guidi.'

127

'It's impossible, he's working.'

I tell him to say who I am. He pulls his head back behind the door, puts the bolt in again, comes back and, without opening says:

'It's like I said. The Maestro doesn't wish to be disturbed by any one.'

'When does he finish?'

'Ah, that we don't know.'

'But did you tell him my name properly?'

'Yes.'

'What about him?'

'It didn't seem to mean anything to him. Good evening.' I hear footsteps going away and then they stop and come close again. 'But if you like when he finishes he always goes to the bar of the Fenice for an aperitif.'

'Thank you.'

Poor old thing, I'd like to tell him to report back, tell him he is a poor old thing.

I take my courage in both hands, go to my nice bankrupt impresario, who is now talking with other theatre people, all bald dolls – the kind you can unscrew bits of – I make a sign to him and he gets up and introduces me, and they all bow and praise my hair – and what else could they praise with those toupees and bald heads? My impresario is very proud of me as a social object for display: I say something very elegant and polished but not too much so, I leave my mite for the benefit of my protector; he chooses the most prominent table in the whole restaurant, we eat, I leave a note on the double bed and go back to Milan by train. Thirty thousand lire he had already given me for pocket-money the moment we set foot on the laguna.

It was at the Cortina Gallery that I met Enzo Macigna; I never miss a *vernissage*: there is always a fantastic cold buffet, the Yugoslav naïve painters are allowed to bring out Prague ham, while the smoked salmon goes well with Buzzati's little deformed figures. He was standing in the centre once, down below, in a glass cage, alone, with the naturalness of someone reading the news of the day in the bar at the corner of the street who discovers, discreetly stroking his nose with two fingers, that – imagine! – war has broken out in the neighbouring district.

That evening there was an exhibition by an ex-singer: masses of big bowls piled high, and any amount of pizzas and wine. There are always *grissini* with raw ham, along with a big Parma cheese and lots of spring-onions and celery and young carrots. Well, I am there at the buffet, I fill up and go to a wall, go back to fill up again and walk towards another bowl. Always like that. Until I see there is another person, at least one, who is doing the same as me and is watching me. A glance and we are outside already, in his little Fiat. I go to his place. He is a painter (pictures a couple of metres square full of details of glands and nerves and capillary bulbs seen through a magnifying glass – a disturbing way of painting, physiological, stomach-turning: beautiful colours). We fuck and next day I cancel my little pokey room and I am in his little Fiat with my household goods which are not very bulky and we are off to his place, happy and content. Two days later it feels as if all hell has broken loose. Reason: his jealousy. Now I understand that one can be jealous and some people may like to be the object of it but frankly a *maudit* painter who gives himself such airs – above all that of being misunderstood and then has a complex about his fat belly and wraps himself in an elastic girdle and buys jeans two sizes too small and tightens his belt like a hairshirt into the bargain – should think first and foremost of dieting, of getting rid of some of his real aesthetic worries situated outside his art (in his belly) and then, maybe after gymnastics and physical training, could allow himself to be jealous. Jealousy has a quality in thin people which is entirely missing in fat people: credibility. Fat, especially when it is concealed, covers the nerves too much, perhaps the brain-cells too, and allows only distorted and literary passions, which lack impatient and necessary immanence. I mean that his jealousy was out of proportion to the events which involved me and was not directed at me: he was jealous of the whole world, of those who had achieved 'success' or those who didn't give a damn about it especially if they were young – like me (he is fifteen years older than me). In short: it was a metaphysical jealousy, one of the most dangerous kinds because of a hysterical and not a loving nature. That haughty and lugubrious face of his, hidden behind the amiable and carefree mask he had presented the first evening, this continual chewing over 'me and the others', this denigration of other people's success, while pursuing it in vain with acts of self-abasement and politeness which had not produced and were not producing any positive result, made him antipathetic and unbearable to me.

And I go to bed with him much against my will, but we're stuck there: by now autumn is far on, it is beginning to be cold, where shall I go? not home certainly and without a lira. He is easily made angry, all he wanted was to find someone on whom to vent himself. And he shouts from morning to evening and often doesn't have a coin in his pocket either and then we open a tin of beans – I don't know how he manages to get them but he must have at least two hundred tins on the shelf in the cupboard. But then he comes home maybe with an alpaca scarf, a double-breasted jacket, patent leather shoes and smiles at me, goodnaturedly, his eyes begin to shine: it means that he's getting a hard-on and I do everything I can not to make him fly into a temper, but refuse to have sex. Then he begins to say that sex isn't important, and so on and so forth, that the important thing is intellectual understanding, that is, tries to convince me to fuck with nice talk, with nice feelings. Well, one evening I say to him: 'Why don't we go and look for some one and have a threesome?'

If nothing else the third party will have to put up with half the boring job and my part will be made lighter by the fact that, even sharing half-and-half, I can still have some fun. He doesn't dislike the idea. And so we begin our erotic excursions in the obvious places. Our very first evening was a great success: we pick up a couple of them in a public urinal and it ends up with me managing to keep out of things or to participate as little as possible. Meantime, when the two of them go to the bathroom, I say to both of them, under my breath, one after the other: 'Listen, couldn't you put me up? but don't tell him, he'd beat me.' But no one seems to welcome my request. If there is a third he doesn't mind what I do with the other: the important thing is that I don't fuck with the other one but with him, something which is more and more difficult for me because by now Macigna simply disgusts me and nothing else and I'd like to leave – also because my head has begun to ache again seriously and I fear a relapse.

Until a guy from Genoa, who had taken me home and made love to me as if it was a case of the last time because his days were numbered, rings him up and asks him if we can do it again. Seeing I like him quite a lot and Macigna noticed and it was me who gave him the telephone number, Macigna was very careful not to say yes, wanting to give the impression that it all depended on external circumstances (the things one invents on the phone! an exhibition in Caracas, a meeting on the Martini terrace, a new secret studio with an ex-directory number, business trips to Basel), began to act grand, to use a high-class vocabulary, and it is obvious that the other guy returned to the attack and asked for me to come to the telephone until Macigna got annoyed and said, passing from 'tu' to 'lei': 'But who are you? how can you permit yourself to pester my friend? He's not in, he's not in!'

The guy from Genoa must have said something like this to him: first of all go and get stuffed and then told him about how I wanted to leave and that I had asked if I could move in with him because *he* was a *madman* and a *mythomaniac*. Macigna banged down the phone and came towards me with his eyes blood-shot, he took me by the arm (I didn't even defend myself) gave me a shove and shut me in the cupboard with the beans. Locked on the outside, total darkness, apart from that crack under the door which very quickly got dark when he quietly shut the outside door and went off. And very shortly afterwards the crack of light reappeared and I gave a sigh of relief – I hadn't said anything: neither shouted, nor banged on the door with my fists, and was not even resigned: I was certainly prey to a shock as snobbish as it was terrible: that the whole thing was staged. In fact, all the tension went away on seeing the crack of light under the door. Then I heard him open a drawer, a noise of metal, and the scraping sound of something being put under the door: a tin-opener. And again the dark. And him going away. As soon as my eyes are used to it, they also notice a glimmer of light which is like a layer of cotton wool on top of the suffocating atmosphere and lift themselves up: up there is a kind of little porthole without glass which gives on to the kitchen, which in its turn gives on to the street and this wall isn't a common wall with the adjacent houses at all but is on the side of the building.

What does one feel in the dark for so long? nothing that can be really described. To be walled in alive – after the first twenty-four hours, when the light from the porthole has lit up the cupboard almost as if it were day and has gradually transformed itself once more into the initial darkness – becomes a habit encapsulated in an incredibly unreal event; and yet it is you that is there, with your bodily needs, your hands which have lost their skin on the door,

131

your throat which let out a few cries and then gave up, the first tin opened, trembling, and the first cut on the thumb, and the desperate need to eat, to empty the tin and go on to another. And then obviously, along with the flatulence the mucus appears. The mucus that runs in buckets from the nose and I think also from the mouth and the eyes too: everything is thick, sticky: on the second day, you have become a kind of slime teeming with itches and new smells. I defecate in the tins and then try to take good aim at the porthole and throw them through it but I don't always succeed first time. And it's a case of knocks on the shoulders, on the head, a graze in the cheek – apart from hair standing on end, from which a nasty sort of liquid stuff full of crusts runs down. Will he come back? will I survive? but these are questions which very soon it is no longer possible to formulate mentally, the very notion of language crumbles away. The pupils dilate, they see everything except what is in front of you, tins without labels, and scores of pieces of silverware hidden in bits of velvet. They see, still dare to see imaginary love and language (incapable of facing up to the nervous shock second after second) reshapes itself, because the phrases are old, like commonplaces, learned by heart once and for all. And I talk to myself aloud: I have decided that I must create you in my thoughts and give you all my darkness, and the past too, and a story for us who have never existed, have been made of darkness in the dark. I have never accused you of not existing, of being my pure mental invention, I took you for what you weren't, sensation of love, thoughtless boy, metaphysical purity, scapegoat. No One. – And before uttering the last sentence a need to laugh – but theatrically, a studied laugh, and a need to make certain gestures with my hand and to move the muscles of my face in a certain way, to try over again the behavioural imprints left on me by certain persons: Helmer's way of popping his eyes when he wanted to say something incredible with the most natural air in the world: the hand of the unfrocked Sicilian priest raised delicately by an imaginary forearm and then, once in mid-air, closed into a fist that was opened with a simultaneous beat of the eye-lashes as a sign of gentlemanly dismay: Giacomino's first finger when it rose to the height of his right cheek and stayed suspended for an instant before going to nestle in the dimple of his chin, on which he imprinted half-turns, slightly bashful, as if he did it because he couldn't help it and because he was with a friend, but that he still would rather have done it in private: because it had to be the sign of an important reflection on something trifling, and of a decision to be taken, whereas it was quite the contrary of what he wanted to make out, which was that the decision had already been taken. I made all these gestures which have adhered to me and which were not mine once, but are mine now, as much mine as their legitimate owners', the mark of which I shall always carry on me: and while I produce myself through the mimesis of what with time has become me so that I can no longer separate it in normal circumstances from what could have been an individual gesture of mine, of hands fingers eyes, I feel a tug in me somewhere, very remote and a noise rises in my throat, *I*, and I begin to laugh like a madman: *I, I, I!* I go on repeating to myself and can't believe how many 'I's' I have been made up of till now, how many 'I's' there are now, in the dark, along with me, and then his terrible voice booms in my ears, when he wedged me as a child in the angle of the door and made a barrier with his knee in the corner of the wall and began to bring his fists down on me and with the same terrible voice I cry something nice: 'Your tongue was liquid cork and your kisses rusted gooold...liiiife.'

Is this what they call the mouse's end? to die little by little consciously? squeaking out dreams of life not as it *is* but as I should have liked it to be? rummaging in myself for a crumb of astonishment like what is called happiness? clutching at painless sentimental concepts which are not verified but presented on a tray of mock gold dressed up in sequins?

'Besides, although distant and unknown, we will never become bored with ourselves: there will always be something of you and me which will arouse our curiosity for another few seconds.' Or else: 'I feel you even more near and understanding and the illness which I create to give myself time to cure myself completely of myself does not frighten me. I am suffering in my own filth, oh youth that never ends!' Or else I utter a question and an answer: 'They are carrying her away.' 'Where to?' 'Poor thing. Poor woman.' Or I declaim: 'I have at last found in myself something that resembles me and is in one piece. The mouse looks at the porthole which is submerged little by little in the darkness and is happy even like this – just as it is not. I am happy to make amends.'

Like this for three days. Making a great mystery to myself with two unnamed names: Giacomino and Gina.

When he unlocked the door I fell into his arms and he began to kiss me all over, filthy as I was, and whimpered, he did, and asked me to forgive him and laid me on the bed and went to get a basin of water and a sponge and began to wash me down. I smiled while he disinfected the cuts on my thumb and cheek, I begged him solemnly not to blame himself, that it had been a well-deserved lesson and I thought: the moment I recover I shall kill you in your sleep without letting you know. You will suffer much more.

The first time I met Adel was at a party at his house: Macigna had sent me on ahead, to spy out the land, because he wanted to have some pictures bought and I served as a bait. Perhaps Adel had seen me somewhere in his company and had been interested in me and Macigna had jumped at the chance. (I didn't kill him for a very simple reason: which is that if you kill a man then you kill another and yet another and it is very probable that sooner or later you will be caught and put in prison. And I do not wish to have anything at all to do, even indirectly, with *justice* after the affair with the jewels.)

We had arrived when the party was well under way – Macigna was very keen to arrive late everywhere – and I found myself catapulted into the high society of Jewish jewellers, male photographic models from *Vogue* and antique dealers. Adel had an antique-dealer's business in partnership with an old friend of his. Both had escaped from Egypt after the fall of Farouk and had built up another fortune in Milan. There was a very famous surgeon, a professor of German at the Catholic University and a very distinguished gentleman who had a lock of white hair in the middle of his forehead.

Although I was not unaware of Macigna's intentions, I had an aim of my own: either to find myself a lover – a rich one at last – who would at least please me enough to give me an erection without trouble or, if things turned out badly, to get some sort of introduction to the editor of some paper. Or, if the worse came to the worst, to work in a book shop and thus, now that I had learned the tremendous possibilities inherent in Felix K, to stop being a waiter.

Macigna, who by now considered me a dead weight chiefly because of the after-effects of the trauma, had told me that Adel, with his circle of friends, would be able to help me if I 'was nice to him'. When Adel came and opened the door my heart thumped,

I don't know how long it stopped beating. Then I said to myself that I mustn't give up, that I had to risk everything, that with Macigna I had in any case reached the peak of aberrations and fear and disgust and that anything was preferable to him, to staying with him. Adel was over sixty-five and was a disintegrated Egyptian mask: his jowls, his eyes with their cataracts, a long curved neck like a length of a gutter covered with fat and warts. And Adel devoted himself entirely to me: cognac, champagne, pilaff, do I know Bécaud? do I know Jacques Brel? The drawing-room is the biggest I have ever seen in my life: full of brocades on the windows and works of art and carpets and photos of distinguished persons with dedications – him and Maria José, him and Farouk, him and Umberto di Savoia, he names them to me one by one, lightly embracing my waist. Macigna is ignored, I think, although he makes an effort to cut a social figure and to be very much at home. Clearly he is not very well known. And he gives me encouraging smiles. Then he and Adel go to one side, Adel winks, Macigna winks too and both look at me. Then I see from Macigna's gestures that he is speaking about his pictures, this high, this wide, and Adel who shakes his head several times and seems to mutter 'you can count on it, you can count on it' and can't wait to change the subject. And Macigna goes away after Adel has held him back when he wanted to go round saying goodbye to those present as if to say, don't worry, I won't fail, I'll see to it.

Adel comes straight up to me: another cognac, another glass of champagne, wouldn't I like to learn French? But I am distracted by the penetrating eyes of the distinguished gentleman with the white lock. He is the one that interests me. Whom I like. Then the lackeys begin to go off discreetly, I and the Pharaoh are left more and more alone and embalmed, he by nature and I from fear; the one I liked best, with whom I have not exchanged a word all afternoon, slips a note into my jacket pocket, until even the waiter who was tidying things up a little is gone. Adel disappears: in the course of five minutes I have the impression that the temperature has gone up – indeed the radiators have gone from hot to boiling. Adel comes back, wrapped in a purple damask dressing-gown waving the sign of power: a cheque book.

'I know what you are after. Here, don't let's mention it again.'

And he tears off a cheque for two hundred thousand lire. Then he fills my glass again. He asks 'if am I not hot.'

'Make yourself comfortable.'

To make myself comfortable I have to restrain the mad desire to distract him by telling him about the dark, about Macigna, about the violence he made me suffer. Generally if you can awaken sympathy then automatically you get a dispensation from the rest. But Adel makes a sign for me to be quiet.

'My dear, I don't have much time.'

He notices the annoyed look I give and softens the message by making it more astounding than before.

'I mean I don't have much time in any sense of the word.'

I understand and I don't understand: you mustn't take everyone at the letter of the word, I tell myself.

'Are you not... well?'

'There, you've said it.' When he speaks at the end of every sentence he loses a thin trickle of spittle.

'My head is spinning,' I say to him, 'I'm not used to drinking.'

'Take this,' he says and gives me a little transparent ball. After a couple of minutes I feel in some ways worse but well. And he fills the glass up again. And he gives me another little ball. And I drink. I lose something in my joints, I give sudden jerks which I have never had before. And I have a desire to laugh. And I count: one little ball, two little balls, three little balls, four little balls. Nine little balls.

Between the third and the ninth I have been unbuttoned and put on the divan, my shoes have been taken off, they have stripped me naked.

'I'll rub you down with pure alcohol. You'll feel better in a minute.'

Naked and paralysed, I grit my teeth with anger and feel the taste of blood on my palate. He begins to rub me with cottonwool and slaver. I feel like lead, I cannot move a finger, the alcohol on my genitals makes me shrink even more, I seem to be contracting, going into a ball.

'It's the first time it has had this effect,' he says. I understand that he is talking about the little balls. 'Usually it liberates one.' And he takes me under the arms and drags me to his bed puffing.

'I want to leave. Please.'

'Don't worry. Everything will be fine.'

'Call a doctor,' I manage to murmur. 'I feel I am dying.'

136

He has begun to drag his breath up from the bottom of his lungs and he does not listen to a single word of my entreaty. He strips with brusque and clumsy haste and no longer sees me but a mirage which might vanish from one moment to the next.

'You are letting yourself go, you'll have a marvellous time.'

'What was it?' I ask, curious even although close to collapse.

'Coke in gelatine.'

Coke in gelatine. I am no wiser. Coca cola in gelatine. I feel a great desire to shout but I think of the cheque, I think that tomorrow I shall have left for Paris, and it doesn't matter any more that my limbs no longer react nor that, if they were capable of any sort of autonomy, they would make for the window and throw themselves down among the snow. I would feel the irrepressible desire to kill myself. Finish with things. I see my face in the mirror in front of me: I reply to its cadaverous pallor with an idiotic smile. I review many circumstances which have brought me here. I feel that there is an unknown thread which leads back to my childhood, to a period when the boys of the district lay in wait for me when I came home late on my bicycle and, jumping out from every hole and corner four or five at a time, began to drag me to the ground and to shout after me 'ugly little arse', angry because one by one they had made love to me and had enjoyed it. And that for one reason or another, I can't help landing myself in suffering which affects me more and more. And there is Adel puffing away and pressing against me from behind and then he lets out a sigh and something in Arabic with 'Allah' in it and says a second later.

'I must ask you to dress as quickly as possible, I have guests coming shortly.'

Get dressed: it is easily said. But I don't answer back: he helps me to put on my shoes and socks and I don't even dare to take the time to go into the bathroom to wash myself, I feel my thighs all sticky and it seems as if everything I do with my right hand is done with the left instead, I feel something coiled round me and I can't get out of it.

Staggering, a rickety load of traumas, of glassy pains, of walks through the meanders of madness, taken and thrown away, a well-trained guinea-pig which can anaesthetize itself and doesn't create problems, in the entrance-hall, while Adel gives me cast-off ties which I am unable to refuse, I look at him with gratitude. I think I shall leave and go and throw myself from the Duomo.

137

'You mustn't think about it any more,' says Sebastian, the handsome thirty-five year old man with the white lock, a week later as we leave for Perugia, Urbino, Assisi, in his Rolls-Royce. 'Adel does that with all the boys like you; he makes them drink and drugs them a little. Evidently he has increased the dose lately. Everybody in his entourage knows about it: I know that it is a matter for the courts. I have known Adel for ten years: apart from that he is a very generous person. He does it for one simple reason: he knows he is repellent and with the drug he believes he can get close to his victims, very expensive ones too, aren't they?'

In the course of this week I have done a lot of things: I have gone to live in a pensione not far from Adel's flat, I telephoned Sebastian the next day already, and up to a couple of hours ago – we had arrived in Alessandria in an old Renault and he had made me wait in a bar because 'he couldn't take me home with him' – he had passed himself off as someone who puts up television aerials and then he appeared in this liner out of the Arabian Nights which lacks only a telephone and a swimming-pool. I pretended not to notice, deeply offended at having been made a fool of by someone who, as far as I am concerned, could have been a street-sweeper he pleases me so much in bed. And now, having appeased the complex of someone who 'is loved only for his money', he has decided to spend a week's holiday with me. And I kept saying to him: 'But, I'm sorry, what need is there to go away? to spend money?' and he kept saying that he will see to things and there was me full of scruples because I always imagined him on top of the roofs in this snow and frost getting chilblains from sticking aerials between the tiles. And I never even thought of looking at the state of his hands. In fact, if I know nothing about him, he didn't know that I continued to meet Adel and that I had absolutely no wish to let him know that I would even have been in a position to pay for this week's holiday myself. Or has Adel perhaps told him? and he, while still thinking I am a hardened whore, derives satisfaction from the fact that a rent-boy goes with him 'gratis'?

Macigna was very happy because Adel, even if he has not bought even a single picture directly has taken four on approval and has put them among his antiques. Certainly with those baroque frames, in such contrast with the subject matter of highly-coloured glands, they look quite different. For the rest, when I met him by chance two days ago in the Galleria – I was with Sebastian but truth to tell, seeing that we were taking the same route to go together to a place he knew of, Sebastian had asked me to follow him at a distance on the other side, and Macigna didn't notice anything – it was as if he bumped into an acquaintance whom he hadn't seen for a while and with whom the usual topic of conversation was the weather and the ballet at the Scala. But the conversation – a very formal one – lasted a very short time and I caught up with Sebastian who had already crossed the Piazza Duomo.

In fact I am so dejected by these unexpected social volte-faces of Sebastian's that this Rolls-Royce is a disappointment. I preferred the Renault, I felt more at my ease. I feel myself bought this time too, little by little fitted into a role – that of his past fantasies, from which he has not freed himself even with me.

'So you knew about the drug and didn't do anything about it. That's great,' I say, looking out of the window; even if he leaves me here on the autostrada it doesn't matter, I shall manage.

'Adel, when it's a question of sex, doesn't connect any more. I couldn't do a thing. Do you think that everything is as easy as that? I have a promissory note for tens of millions with him. Now don't think about it any more, you are with me. And don't worry: Adel hasn't got venereal disease, I would know. I know his medical record by heart. Otherwise you wouldn't be with me. You have a bit of a bee in your bonnet, with these stories. You'll like Perugia.'

'What does it mean you know his medical record by heart?'

'Well, I and his friend check up on him a lot, because of his diabetes. He was in a coma for four days three months ago. You know how it is.'

No, I don't know how it is and I don't care either.

'Adel was generous with me because he can't help it,' I say, trying to lower the opinion he has of generous Adel and at the same time to put him on a bit of a spot.

'What do you mean?'

'That Adel pays because he wants to take us with him. Into the tomb, alive, with him. Like the Pharaohs.'

Sebastian remains silent and then says:

'You are too much of a moralist,' but it doesn't sound at all like a compliment, he seems disappointed in some way.

'I know.'

After a long pause in which I feel that something is giving way between us he says:

'With the years you will understand Adel's reasons too' – but his is an indirect speech in defence of the logic of capital and of the egoisms which it begets: a speech therefore to justify himself, his billions (because it is a question of billions: a jeweller's workshop at Valenza Po with a hundred and fifty workers, one of the biggest in the world), his veiled neuroses. Because the rich are neurotic too, inexplicably, not only starving people like me. An authentic discovery while the car slips along the autostrada towards this kind of pilgrimage to the snowy plains of disinterested love. Then he stops at a pull-in, lets the windows mist over well and we make love. But it doesn't work any more for me. I think how much I shall be able to get out of this guy and I need a little time to reflect. I convince him to wait a bit, that I don't feel well. He starts up again. He turns off at the first exit. Bologna.

'You don't mind, do you, going back by train? Now that I'm here I'd like to look up some people,' and he takes out an envelope.

'Half this money is from Adel. He asked me to tell you not to bother him any more, you understand. A pity.'

'A real pity.'

'Good luck.'

'The same to you.'

And I am rather happy: a real, dirty, distinguished fascist gentleman. And with this money, fruit of my participation in more comas, I go back to Milan with a desperate thirst for life: I put on one side the necessary for the ticket and in ten days, taken by an insane desire for revenge, to do something without knowing quite what, I fall into the usual trap: in ten days I squander what normally would be sufficient for me to live in comfort for three months. I eat, that is to say, four or five times a day.

And am back where I started from, without a lira: and that woman at the pensione who has been asking for my arrears for a week already.

I only once telephoned Adel, but he hung up. Had he understood that I would never really have *followed* him?

If things go badly in Paris, I already know someone who will put me up in Lille. Tonight I shall really leave.

Mine is not a heart but a platoon, disconcerted by the impossibility of recognizing an enemy, any enemy. A heart which explodes in all directions like a shell, which in its fear of missing one, loses time marking all the existing targets until it explodes in one's hands.

Gare de Lyon, just arrived. I do not know in what direction to direct my steps. And what will have become of that latest serpent from whom I have not been able to free myself? It will be wonderful one day to have everything behind me.

THE PORTRAIT OF MADAME D'ORIAN

'This evening we are all going to celebrate – what do you say to going to the Opéra-Comique? There's Mozart – *Così fan tutte*. It's such a nice place and such odd days – Monday and Wednesday when there's no one about and the other theatres are shut.'

'You know, really, I'm not one for opera – and besides –'

'Oh, come on, a little bit of effort –'

'No – I was saying that I'm still at sixes and sevens – the job today, a new set-up and I ate too much in the canteen and now three-quarters of a guinea-fowl.'

'Suzanne and Geneviève are so anxious to hear how it went. And in any case one can't – they've already got tickets for all four of us.'

'*Così fan tutte* – but what do they do?'

And Arlette saying to me before we go into the foyer:

'They'll be there waiting for us – we're late. Give me your arm.'

And during the performance she follows me out of the corner of her eye and her friends also look at me with their usual benevolence and smile at me and smile to each other, if there was any sort of friction between them it has been completely overcome and not one of the four of us, in my view, has any real idea of what is happening on the stage. This morning, five minutes after Arlette left the house, the concierge came to call me, told me to come down to her place, that there was an urgent telephone call, very urgent. It was Suzanne, who told me to go along to the bank at once, that I was starting there right away, in the print-shop, Monsieur Rigot, to report to Monsieur Rigot.

I feel as if I were the hostage of a Marseilles gang and I don't mind although I don't so much feel protected as under surveillance. With three guardians of this kind nothing can happen to me. It is odd how for me our acquaintanceship has suddenly been completely altered: I seem to be seeing Arlette, Suzanne, Geneviève, for the first time. Now they are part of me – in that little knowledge we have of each other there is a subtle and exclusive sense of belonging which was not there before. I feel as if I am having to watch the first reel of the same film over again because I have come to suspect that my cold curiosity may conceal a considerable degree of distraction.

Geneviève puts up with some *tranches* of my repertory (in this case the concept of *Grandeur* linked exclusively to the glances of the tramps under the bridges) and says to me in her usual calm way:

'Ah, mon cher, you'll not only make it to the Presidency – you'll make it to the Throne.'

Suzanne, who should fill the role of the protective and supportive mother is always very moderately amused and so optimistic about everything: she dispenses smiles of hope to the whole theatre, and confidence to the bit-actors, and asks nothing for herself, only to have someone constantly to busy herself over or to worry over; this evening none of the three wears a trace of make-up, they are dressed very simply, and the seats too were in the circle and not in the stalls. No ostentation of any kind: Geneviève will say two or three more things which it is impossible to remember with her sing-song inflection that recalls the Pyrenees, flat statements – without an edge to them – yet which, if one thinks about them, end up by being somehow striking and even enchanting in a woman who has spent her life over books and in laboratories, and who this evening, for instance, is not worried in the least about being taken for a low-grade secretary. And she seems a woman without a past, without lovers, without a private life, an albino ghost, and I am not even sure what kind of friendship hers for Suzanne is. I feel that up to a week ago my perception was more neutral and penetrating perhaps because, after all, none of the three of them was of any importance to me, it was easier for me to see them from the outside, to analyse them and put some sort of pin through them and stick them in the little velvet box along with the other animals in my *human* collection. And after all what do I know about Suzanne? That she loves flowers, ants, nature in general, that her mother still stands guard over her and that theoretically she invites people to her place on Tuesdays. It isn't much. Perhaps one could assume from the second or third phantasmal Tuesday that this insistence on nature, roses, orchids, is an Orphic code. And that, in reality, terrible things are being communicated, of terrible resolution in the solitude they harbour, of which one knows only that they exist and that is all. And around this banal and (almost) resigned way of life of Suzanne and Geneviève a halo of mystery begins to become visible, of secrecy armoured against any eyes other than theirs; it is even probable that these three women only pretend to know each other, without in fact knowing anything of each other, merely assuming that they know, and in the end not attaching any importance either to the knowledge or the ignorance they hide from each other. Perhaps they simply like to meet after the office, to know that someone is waiting for them, or perhaps one of the two is in love with the other and the other knows nothing of it or pretends or rejects – and this Monsieur Hippolyte who every time (like this evening) apologizes for not being able to come because of his articles on gardening in half-a-dozen French weeklies? Together they are a primal force; destructive as well, if they feel like it. Desexed praying mantises, who have transferred elsewhere the lethal bite of their embrace. To social success, for instance. One can feel that they have an ambition, which one might call genetic and unlimited. Arlette, perhaps because she is the youngest, seems to me the most alive of the three, alive in a less reflecting sense. Moreover it cannot have been easy for her either to take a stranger in and it is not certain that she consulted the others. I mean that if Arlette decided to make someone her prisoner she would never be able to hide it from him and he would be able to notice in time; with the other two it would be different: one would become aware of the cage only when in it – for ever. And this closeness between the three women, all in some way intent on me and on my well-being – *but* being close to them – gives me food for thought. Mine must be some sort of persecution mania and I must be very careful not to create problems, and not to mess things up just because I can't get used to the idea that someone got me a job and offered me a roof 'without strings'.

So the days passed, quite quietly, but charged for me with an internal tension which I cannot grasp and tame: the fact that I have poured out all my stories to Arlette has let loose in me a new relationship with time as well, now I live in waves as it were, the minutes and seconds have dissolved into the trembling surge of a new sensibility; it is as if I rejected the draft version of description, of detachment, to make another nth attempt with the senses, with feelings. I am not really happy nor independent but I have chosen my chains and, all in all, I like them. I like to belong to Arlette, to Suzanne and to Geneviève, even with all the inconveniences that go along with it. For example, Arlette has become in some way more demanding towards me, seeing that I fall in with her over everything: since I leave work first, the ritual demands that I must go and pick her up regularly at the entrance to the office – where we always end up drinking an apéritif with Suzanne. But it is a wasted hour, that's for sure, and now that I have fallen in again with this habit which previously I had managed to break a little, it will be a problem to get out of it a second time. But the annoyance I feel at my weakness is largely compensated by the thought that somewhere in Paris there is a little person who is covering her typewriter and who possesses almost in its entirety the history and the histories of my existence.

Then in the evening, when I go out alone, Arlette gives me a smile which tries to be happy and says to me 'Have a gay time' and I am not even in the street when a sense of guilt has already ruined my evening and my search for some adventure. I am tortured by the thought that she is waiting for me all the time, manicuring little hands which are already so irremediably cared for and perfect.

When I came back she was pretending to be sleeping, her sighs were too intense, they were like waves of flame out of patience because the firemen haven't arrived yet: I knew the score and said to her:
    'Do you want me to tell you a story?'
    'Oh, yes. I can't get to sleep. Where have you been?'
    'Silly: silly boy, I made myself a swing from the wool and the little dangling balls of the poplars and I myself am a piece of poplar wool, something nature has expelled. Running along the pavements I buffet the wind with my bare chest and make leaps like a flying dinosaur. All my life for six fabulous days of love and the fullness of life! all my golden body for long silver kisses, bird-like kisses under the hips!'
    I feel that I have been clear enough – by now the *facts* bore me to death, suddenly they seem like the chronicles of an unreal city. And as for where I have been, I must teach her that how I got there

embraces every meridian of the shifts in my internal geography. She looks at me incredulously, sideways.

'And then?'

'And then goodnight, Arlette. Put away your wax tablets, the session is closed.'

Or else:

'The red violet of autumn grows only in our thoughts, which are mutilated by the cruellest month without particular aspirations. To live is sufficient. Have a new April fool each day and photocopy the palms of your hands. How funny to call a bull Joan of Arc. As soon as I get another cat I'll call her William Tell. Night.'

Arlette becomes more pressing: she demands a lullaby from me each evening with this difference that my lullaby has the result that in the morning she has rings round her eyes that point to a sleepless night, exactly like when I told her in detail about rapes, vampires, dead brought back to life. Sometimes she even makes me repeat the same lullaby at dead of night. For this reason, not because I am annoyed with her, I keep dreaming how wonderful it will be to sink into her big bed when she goes off to the country. I continue to sleep – badly – on the floor. And to be nice and obliging to the point of exasperation – I feel I shall be completely myself again when I manage to put her down or tell her without beating about the bush to let me sleep, I am exhausted. On the contrary, every time I feel like doing it, it is I who overcome my tiredness and laziness and suggest a walk to her – perhaps when dawn is just breaking. We walk close together, shoring each other up, making little jumps only when the lorry that waters the streets turns up. She always says Yes enthusiastically whatever the time and both of us pretend to be fit whereas we are more exhausted than ever by the fatigue which, for different reasons, living together causes us. You can make the usual traditional three o'clock in the morning proposal to Arlette: 'Let's go to Les Halles and have an onion soup' and she will discover that that was just what she was waiting for and that she is ravenous; and once there, with the bowl in front of her, she can scarcely lift the spoon because after all the preparations, the excitement, the ride in the taxi which had to be waited for in a downpour of rain, there is nothing there after all except a bowl with the usual dark onions in it. And it is clear that this is not what she wanted. And then it will be torture to fall asleep for fear of not hearing the alarm in a couple of hours and then, she will decide into the bargain that one must crown with a parable this dawn which has already been shattered by epic yawns.

I feel I know nothing about Arlette and she has not said another word about Pablo–Pablito. To sum it up: a normal childhood, only daughter, then school with the nuns, then London *au pair*, then this job she has had for ten years, the maternal protection of Suzanne. She only cut off her pigtails a few years ago – her parents went on as if she had something wrong with her, 'they still treat me like a child.'

'But they know nothing about my life; my mother, imagine, still can't get used to the idea that I left home to live in Paris. Ah, if I could just give them a surprise. Come on, why don't you come too?'

'Look, let's be serious. You're talking about a proper, formal introduction. Be sensible.'

On the platform Arlette has wet eyes; I understand it all, it hurts me; I like her but I am glad she is going away for two days; if she were always here I would go mad, but I would be driving myself mad because of her – not she, poor thing. I do nothing either to comfort her or to encourage her to say what she is feeling. I pretend I haven't noticed, I don't want to touch on delicate and painful matters at this moment, perhaps she will change her mind – stay, or really insist that I go with her... and I am so undecided where she is concerned that I always end up being dragged along.

And the train that is late is always the one she has to take. Her look becomes more and more imploring, and mine more and more nonchalant, so much so that I decide to tell her another fairy-tale.

'Falling stars, falling one on top of the other, rescue each other – except for the first one, the star which led the way. It dies when it enters the trajectory of the planet Earth. In fact there is no gravitation for spirits here – the earth is earth and that's all. The falling star that fell into my garden cut with its biggest point my only strawberry tree, on which as an adolescent – just as in the fairy-tale – I used to hang myself once a day. The crowd of neighbours are fascinated and hail a miracle... Meantime my strawberry tree bleeds, and the ground round it has become muddy and reddish. I have left the gate open and the children – their children – come in and make castles with a star that has really fallen. My existence has become a paradise, my garden an animals' Eden – astral presences, milky vapours which only I see and whip up. I feel as if I had in my pupil a satellite in orbit transmitting for my use images dear to Disney. Involuntary but happy guardian of a falling star landed right by me. Me, in short, the chosen one – at last a stroke of Fortune, a terrestrial sign.' And she wants to know what the fairy-tale is.

Her eyes have dried, she smiles again and puts her right hand on mine and squeezes it, then suddenly rises, runs to the step of the carriage, climbs up, disappears, appears again at the window, says again: 'Till Sunday evening!' 'Till Monday if another nun dies,' say I and the train can't make up its mind to leave.

'Right, I'm off – it's never going to start.'

'Ah, bon.'

Then here comes the scene I hate most of all: her little face thrusts itself up from her bust as far as it can, a joint that waves until she can no longer see me. And there I am falling in with it all, feeling a sense of shame, terrible disgust. As if she were going off to the wars, as if she were leaving behind her Dr Zhivago. Let's hope there are lots of convents there.

First thing: a quick visit to the public lavatories, just to put my hand on the fact that I am free and that I can dispose of my time as I like, that is to say, meditating. As usual, after three minutes I am no longer looking at the pricks but automatically follow the flight of the mosquitoes and when they come within range, smack, I squash them. On the tiles there are still signs of my previous visits. I can even spend two or three hours like this – and the remaining white tiles above the stalls fill with black graffiti and streaks of blood.

Every so often the vice-squad boys arrive and want to see your documents: four of them surround you, one of them no other than that fine figure of a man who stuck thirty centimetres of cock under my nose for ten minutes. Never mind – clearly they have nothing better to do and the barricades are over and done with. You are left so bemused by the stupid questions they ask: What were you doing there? why do you keep walking to and fro? they seem to me such unhealthy kinds of curiosity, so humiliating for them – seeing that legally there's nothing they can do. I'd love to say: I am behaving in an obscene manner in a public place. Then I have an idea: I tell them the truth.

'I was squashing mosquitoes.'

One of them takes me by the arm and twists it and I begin to yelp.

'What?'

'Mosquitoes. Take a look if you don't believe me. You're pulling it off.'

Then we all leave the lavatory and they tell me to clear off and make signs to each other as if to say: he's a bit touched. Let them count them, if they feel like it; there will be more than a hundred and there has never been such a perfect example of pest control in any public place in Paris. Besides the real cases of obscene behaviour are never public – they are part of a puritanical and pharisaical mentality which reveals itself only in private. When an obscene act is public it loses all its obscenity to become solely and exquisitely public – the fact that it is still obscene is a distortion of the morality of respectable people, which thus sees itself deprived of part of the obscenity it claims entirely as its own and does not wish to see scattered about in any old place and within anyone's grasp. The great thing about public lavatories is that the sexual organs are made less sensational: they became democratic toys which everyone – almost everyone – can have a quick look at or give a little touch to. A kind of universal greeting. Obscenity reduced to a way of passing the time, that is what annoys political power and its guardians: the dangerous and gratuitous gesture of standing for two hours squashing mosquitoes without feeling any nostalgia for the great social-erotic apparatus which the State controls for the satisfaction of the 'instincts' of the taxpayers. Paradoxically, if everyone begins to enjoy staying there jumping about and chasing mosquitoes, everything will collapse: from legalized brothels to the various *pro loco* Arcadias, to the matrimonial and inquiry agencies to the Mafia of the night-spots dedicated to sex. And they would have to get rid of a whole lot of idlers like the members of the vice-squad and a lot of other useless guardians of law and order. My God, what a crash you would begin to hear, what a creaking. And I would have invented May '69 just as Arlette has May '58.

Then I take the metro which brings me to the Étoile and in a flash I am in the cellars of the Rue Poncelet and among its five hundred strangers who are making love on that three-storeyed, foam-rubber circle. To come here is, in a sense, not so nice as standing in a public lavatory for two hours because here, alas, one comes with a specific aim – to have sexual pleasure until the last spermatozoon is exhausted; there, on the other hand, one contemplates one's own psychic energy, which is held in suspension by the tickling sensation in the soles of one's feet – not employed for no real purpose. And to go back there is in a kind of a way to have a guarantee that I am learning the art and I always get rid of it. Here at Poncelet one feels around one the anxious need most people have to live something which can fill the gap of the return home; there, in the lavatory, on the other hand, after the first half-hour, only one's own aesthetic theories are put up for auction. Given that all my life has been marked by the need to combine the useful with the enjoyable – provided the useful is very evident, seeing that the enjoyable has usually been outside the law – or at least to trade the very last of my energies, to be able to stand there squashing mosquitoes seems to me an unheard of luxury, an unheard of display of power. At last something that doesn't have a price-tag: nothing to sell, nothing to buy, nothing to barter. Just standing there, shifting one's feet, watching the hunks of flesh that come down and go up again, seeing who arrives and who leaves, until one forgets even all that and lays oneself open to all the most unthinkable intuitions, and the brain, emptied of any other contingent sexual concern, is purified – perhaps also because of the circulation of the blood – and breaks through the wall of the known to give you a glimpse of new forms, new possible ways of putting words together, and other mosquitoes. At Poncelet, on the other hand, there are men of every nationality, Arabs above all, and they make demands: all you hear is the door slamming, the sound of feet, the coughs, noses being blown. Groups of bodies which arrange themselves and undo themselves to take up new positions in some other extremity of the half-dark cellar; laughter and an occasional entreaty. The eyes are more dilated than normal, with the intoxication of taking in as many sizes and colours as is possible: toothless mouths, triple paunches and, every now and then, a beautiful, athletic and polite man who talks to you about Maldoror; in the corners of the corridors outside, dandies, the ephebes of the Lido and the Folies pose, contenting themselves with the admiring glances of men to whom they do not pay the slightest attention: they want to fix things up for outside and to be given a little present. I wander frenetically up and down because here, naked in front of other naked men, my sexuality is unleashed and the mind rids itself of all thought

150

and, above all, one can forget about all the *mise-en-scène* of seduction, the burden of amorous tactics which, in the end, make one so tired and exhausted that the man who to begin with interested you and who wanted to be conquered makes you feel a little sick and looks like nothing more nor less than a coquettish, shy little piece of pussy. Here everything is immediate or isn't – and one can go on to others without feeling in the least the blight of rejection. And today it seems better than ever because I feel I have snatched this day from Arlette's grip, which is definitely jealous, because I have been capable of not letting myself be persuaded to get on to the train. All week I have thought of nothing but this day of oblivion, of these hours enjoyed minute by minute, stretched out, liberating one in a dimension out of time, for she is not there waiting for me with her scissors and tweezers in her hand, and the space around me is that of pure pleasure, self-contained, which I can fill and empty as I please. She is not there looking at the clock every five minutes and staring at the little cage.

I have a free snack, I fall asleep and then, because I am exhausted, I feel as if I were happy; but towards evening sadness intervenes at not having been able to cuddle up to Giacomino and to have begun living only when I had begun to lose myself further and further away from him without leaving any trace: when I transformed myself from the imaginary and painful dam that I was into a real puddle – but one that allows me to splash about and which, secretly, I sometimes experience not as a triumph over an adolescent's weaving of myths around his passions but as a complete existential mud-bath. But it is inevitable – it always happens to me when I have plucked at all my nerves and it is no longer possible, for a short time, to impose on one's spinal column.

It is at that moment that from the bladder there rises something hyper-lyrical, full of ideal shapes that have gone wrong, the worn-out present weeping over the milk that has been urinated. Hence the distressing nature of that insolent phrase that is born within me: 'Why did it have to finish like this?' even if it is precisely this 'like this' which let loose that youth of mine, feverish with desires that now wish to be satisfied, not to be repressed or deferred, at the risk of assuming forms that are pathological or unnatural – ecclesiastical, I almost feel like saying. And on this waterproof couch, sated and exhausted by acts of generosity given and taken, I think I should have died that day by the river when I loved him silently, forcing myself to hold back my desire this side of the retina, so that my glance would disintegrate before it was dispatched and could not betray me. In truth my heart could have burst at any moment of that day so greatly did he and his olive and inaccessible body press on my aortas, which were choked with desire. Badly dressed, always wavering on the edge of the banks, he clutched at clumps of wild mint so as not to roll down. And there was I always quick to put out a hand to restore his balance, to touch his fingers lightly.

There were incandescent suns above our heads, now strangely drained of blood but burning, impalpable like hallucinations, as dense as the madness of my reined-in passion, the accumulation of the nights in which, silent at his side, I had to bite at the inside of my cheeks so as not to cry out and jump on him, while I came in my trousers: I who knew that he knew and remained indifferent and enjoyed my suffering and could not get over the fact that a poor ordinary boy could have so much power.

'Are you afraid of snakes?' I asked him.

'You bet,' he said.

'Watch where you put your feet then.' He stayed there looking at me, nailed to the spot as if he was hoping to catch in my face a jesting expression; but I pretended not to notice and went on with my eyes glued to the ground, searching among the bushes before going through them, considering a step, measuring a leap.

'Come on, get a move on! In any case if it's fate –' I said.

'But take care, please. And if a snake bites me who will suck my blood?' and he became sulky, pretended to be a child so as not to lose his balance, not to let it be seen that just for once he was worried.

'But *I* will, *I* will,' I reassured him, only too sincerely, even though I knew he would have taken to his heels if it had happened to me.

'Have you got matches too to burn away the germs?'

'Of course, matches too, and then we tie it a bit further up with *my* vest so that *yours* doesn't get dirty..,' I wanted to be ironical but it must all have sounded terribly serious.

'Then if you have matches it means you have cigarettes too, give me one,' and I handed him a cigarette; I handed him cigarettes for years on the pretext that the sons of the rich never have a penny, because tennis costs a lot, the piano lessons cost a lot, skiing costs a lot etc and I who went to work by the hour at the Swan Hotel and

152

on Fridays to the market to fry fish at Fanel's, kept him in things which don't cost much: ices, cigarettes, the cinema – in town, because he was ashamed to be seen with me in the village, that I had understood. And there was no way of just standing there for five minutes without having to do anything, letting one's gaze wander over the stones, the carcasses of cats, the wine-bottle stripped of its straw, a broom stuck in a metal drum, the cemetery that was the river.

'What shall we do?' he began.

'Shall we go and have an ice?' I proposed.

He had still three spoonfuls left and already he was starting up again:

'What shall we do?'

I could have taken him by the neck – but also to be able to kiss him till I suffocated.

And now, on this slippery bed, half-awake, like a coward, dominated by a hypocrisy of the feelings that is stronger than me, which bewitches me with the power of its clichés, I think that what happened in the years that followed was not worthy of me and that today it is counterproductive that I didn't die for that sublime reason, for 'love'. With my body drained of any impetus and passion, I realize that I too am a rotter wherever in the world there is a plate of spaghetti and *stracchino* (the standard fare of washer-uppers) and that, even if I changed job and menu (for example, *minestrone* and pork morning and evening for eight months on end), the men-jobs-menus were equally indigestible to me and all gulped down in the same way. Because ideally I remain rooted in Giacomino. I exhausted millennia of love on him, arid in the way pleasures are arid that are not pleasures and which I cultivate without conviction, carry on with my little messy bits of sex and get no further, do not ask, do not speak and see in my human encounters only a momentary orificial hiding-place. I know that my breath has reached the limits of noise; I know that any possible outburst of joy would be the hired death-rattle of an animal which has lost teeth, claws and placenta, that I am a dead cat prey to the ants and the singing cicadas. Motionless in my nitrogen ghost I toss and turn like someone in his sleep and defend myself against my past nightmares by creating new ones in which to forget my troubles. Etcetera. Before that etcetera there is more as follows: why did I not slip into the water like a frog that day by the river? why did I die differently, somewhere else, hour by hour, like everyone else? and continue to live and to die and one life is much the same as another – ah bon. You are putting up a tremendous bluff, Barbino, here you are telling yourself a story, understand that; now, because you work and sleep, are you falling back on to the fine phrases of your repertory? now that you have a full belly do you feel it your duty to feel nostalgia for when it was empty? and are you crying over the twilight quality of 'life at five percent'? do you feel guilty because you are diminished and content? because are you ashamed that the absolute can fall away after five fucks? Then I get up, smiling at myself, happy to be here and not at Leopardi's Recanati, to be standing upright and not with bowed shoulders, to have had the good fortune to be repudiated and mocked by his friend Ranieri and to be able to whisper to a stunning Argentinian boy with a silvery lock on his forehead: 'There's always a sixth after the fifth.' Because if the infinite is real, it must perforce pass that way, numerically speaking.

After supper it must be indigestion that wraps me in melancholy as I leave the Banque de Paris et des Pays-Bas. Jacques Dreyfus, on the telephone, has again discussed with me the difference in size between the cocks of Southern Italians and Moroccans – he wanted to reach some conclusions and I gave him a hand. But for him the needle of the balance always tilts towards the greater quantity of seminal fluid. I feel like crossing myself because, being no longer fourteen or fifteen, I don't run the risk of bumping into him. Besides he always talks undaunted about 'Greek love'.

Night is much kinder to me than the day and my throat, wrapped in a bath-towel, warms up and loosens its catarrhal filth which collects in the first morning spit. The presence of Arlette in her big bed is becoming more and more disturbing and I shall not be able to sleep on the floor for ever – but I stopped her from buying an extra mattress – because now, after so many weeks on this indoor bench my back is beginning to give a shooting pain in the middle of the morning when I have to stand at the photocopying machine.

I work in the printing-shop at the bank, I print forms, cheques, I cut balance-sheets twenty centimetres high, I go into the offices on the seventh floor to hand over the work they are waiting for. Ah,

154

to be able to sleep alone in a big bed, without that fluid she emits even when she isn't there and which is suffocating me slowly and all the more intensely the more I pretend not to notice it. I have had to put up with enough disgusting bodies which cling to mine, and I have sacrificed so many nights of sleep and so many possibilities of new images to acres of human organs which wanted to impose themselves on me, to fit into me, to entwine themselves round me. I have been very nice and patient. Oh I don't mean to say by that that Arlette is repellent, on the contrary – a pity about her mouth which is a bit sulky, but she has a nice, well-proportioned little body, she is agile, a milky little thing and much less thin than she appears – even if she has never dared to try seductive routines such as letting a shoulder-strap fall, coming out of the bathroom with half a breast showing, crossing her legs when she is wearing a dressing-gown (like the woman at The Swan). Arlette is in no way a vulgar woman: she tries to seduce me physically, with that fluid which has also something to do with the sense of smell. And probably I was confused when I could have sworn she was masturbating in front of me that time. Even if she doesn't succeed in seducing me, this fluid is so intense that I feel it on me even when I am out, at the bank or on the prowl. I mean that her femininity is always encircling even when she pretends to be reading the paper or when she says: 'Sorry, what were you saying?' But when her desire for me, which I keep at a distance, reaches its peak, she makes me feel all her contempt if I have dared to go for a mere ten minutes without speaking, without somehow justifying – metaphorically speaking – the fact that I cannot make up my mind to penetrate her. Then I have to do it with words, entertain her, amuse her, transform myself into her 'Rigoletto' (Friday at the Opéra – remember the tickets – go to the box office this evening in the name of Geneviève d'Orian), mask what she believes to be my insolence or my supposed secret plans, which is nothing other than simple indifference.

But I have to recognize that Arlette wakens great tenderness in me, that I bear her no ill-will and that I am more than careful not to wound her, and not only because without her, with what I earn at the bank, I couldn't keep myself and even save a franc to be able to leave when the moment comes – it is she who pays the light, the gas, she who will pay the rent and she who continually *lends* me the ten, twenty francs until I draw my first month's wages (one can't call it a salary) – but because she has begun in broad outline to dig a little deeper into her past, admits for the first time to certain things. What is certain, according to me, although I know nothing concrete as yet, is that Arlette, if she had ever had a man, let's say the last one she had, this Pablo-Pablito, who maybe was also the first (May '58?) it must really have been a good many years ago – then she drew back into her shell. I have the sensation that I am dealing with a convalescent who knows no other state, and clings to it fiercely: I am terrified to scratch old wounds or weeping scars of which I am unaware. Certainly I have my ideas – even because, usually, a minimum aesthetic sense says that it's the same old story. As a precaution I never utter certain words like 'abortion', which is a classic thing for a little girl from the provinces who leaves a church school; from first communion straight to the lady-quack without half-way houses, knowing nothing about anything, only a great confusion in her head – about love, God, sex, sin and *dulcis in fundo* the bitterness of a scrape carried out who knows how, who knows by whom.

And so, even if after work my only wish would be to go home and sleep until tomorrow in her bed, which grows bigger and bigger and more chimerical, I see to the shopping, I arrive outside her office with the plastic bags, I too give her a little kiss on the cheek, let myself be taken by tram or the metro to a somewhat out of the way place to eat something horrible made of fruit and whipped cream and at the till there is an albino lady who vaguely resembles Geneviève (so as not to annoy her I don't even tell her that whipped cream turns my stomach); and she is always so pleased and puts at the end of her sentences *pendants* of exclamation marks and constantly needs to touch me, to put one little arm here and the other there, a little hand on my knee, to take a hair off me somewhere, and when I feel like telling her to give over, that she will fall ill, because I don't know how long I shall be able to put up with this long hand of hers on my future, I come up with a thousand nice gestures and attentions, open the door for her, open the door of the taxi, help her to take off her coat and put it on again, and the more tired I am, and the more I feel like pretending to faint, the more I brush up games with words and stories, recite things, whistle, clap my hands ('clap harder, harder!' she says). We are pushing each other to the edge of the abyss – and I shall be the first to fall in, because I shall be the first to give

156

in to reality, whether nice or nasty, and shall start over again with only a single hope: not to commit the same error all the time but to commit new and vital ones.

I feel more and more need for freedom, to walk for miles and miles where my whim takes me, to stop and talk to people on bridges and in gardens, without stopping, if possible, in anyone's house, but eating on the spot wherever that may be. The interiors where people live fill me with dismay: they are always so indiscreet in the way they reveal too much about whoever lives there – the photos in particular, those faces of young and old: I don't want to know about them, I don't even want to see them; they end up by making me feel sorry for them, these testimonies to the impossibility of doing without, of getting rid of certain memories, of certain knick-knacks from the past. And the opulence of stylish furniture or the ostentation of certain fashions on the other hand annoy me; the end of it always is that my adventure assumes a certain homely quality because it is too well known, too like myself, or too responsive to the dictates of the world, and the individual that stands in front of me loses his outlines, becomes from being the unique person he was a housewife like any other who has the things that more or less everybody has or wants to have. And I, I always say it about cars, don't fuck a chassis, I fuck a man. I'm not in the least fetishistic: for me the best sex is the *naked* kind, the kind without metaphors – the metaphor is already in us, and it is *that* that excites if at all and you can feel it pulsate, as it looks for a way out, more in one of those circular *vespasiens* in Montmartre or up against a lime tree at the Orangerie than in the *comfort* of a drawing-room or in the squalor of a hovel. And the person who sets store by his neo-classical bits and pieces or his Gobelins ends up wanting to 'count for something' along with them and the person who lives with dirty dishes and dirty sheets is lazy and filthy, not a person detached from things and bent on nirvana and I cannot but take account of that – and in either case the end of it all is that I don't feel like fucking a whole way of life, to become infected by the secret ambitions and frustrations and spiritual squalors that it gives off.

I prefer, besides the plank beds of the Rue Poncelet, the impersonality of open spaces – or of a lift in a building where the man of the moment doesn't live however. But Arlette's diffused presence at all my little adventures transforms itself into an all–embracing complex of guilt; and so, knowing I shall at all events get back late and that the shops shut at six, if I don't come to the office, I am already thinking about the little present which I shall bring her at eleven o'clock – a plastic brooch, a tiny bottle of toilet-water, and this little weight in my pocket is like a thorn in the flesh of all my hours of freedom, the palpable limit to my evening escapade.

Then, like yesterday evening, with the door scarcely opened, she transfixes me with a defiant look and presents herself in all the ostentation of her frustrated expectations: got up from head to foot, a pretty silk dress with red and blue and white flowers, red patent leather shoes, the traces – already slipping somewhat – of a permanent wave done at the midday break.

And now she has started to smoke – how funny she is when she smokes: she holds the cigarette right in the centre of her mouth, stretches her neck and breathes in, and every time with a grimace, like a schoolgirl – and now the grimaces follow each other frantically, because she takes mouthful after mouthful and I offer her the little bottle of perfume.

She gets up, undoes the stopper and goes to the sink, empties the bottle and says:

'Are you ready?'

'Ready for what? I feel ready to sleep, if you don't mind.'

'Sleep? but weren't we going dancing?'

It never entered my head to take her dancing – oh, that's why! it's because it was her idea and not mine – and then no perfume is any good, seeing that Arlette, like a good instinctive woman, has identified it as instrument of blackmail: I give you the perfume and you let me sleep in peace.

And so we went dancing at a place where Geneviève and M. Hippolyte – so she has a boy friend who takes her dancing and who knows what else – usually go to have a drink, without Suzanne. An *ancien régime* setting, low lights, lots of blues, a purgatory. And, when madness is at its pitch, a beguine: we were five couples in all – not even the champagne had bubbles. We acted *the couple*, seating in the alcove, without anything to say to each other, with me who couldn't hold up my head for sleep – and she was trying to find out how much I had paid for the perfume, because she would let me have the money back (but it was she who paid for it!) and said she was sorry and kept on saying 'this is the last dance then we'll go', and we hadn't even got on to the dance-floor. Dancing! standing practically still trying to look good and to say witty things because everyone – they were doing exactly the same as us – would think we were having a whale of a time. Then it got on my tits and I said to myself: 'You are dancing, then dance!' But Arlette is no use at dancing, so that at a certain point I said as a joke:

'You'd better put your shoes on mine, that way we'll take a couple of whirls and I won't have pins and needles in my feet any more.'

And she took me at my word. I felt I couldn't resist and I held her close to me, this obstinate chaffinch with its beak adorned with fiery red. And then I asked for a tango. A tango? and who dances a tango? We do. So on with the tango: I and Arlette like a feather in my arms and I drag her along, like a pillow from the big bed, not so much following the music that is really there as imagining it, alone on the floor, and she laughs and clings to me with all her might, I make her spin round, kneel before her, improvise a flamenco step and lo and behold the second couple arrives and 'olé muchachita, let yourself go on my arm' and she obeys at once – she abandons herself completely, with blind trust, and I make her do a *casqué* which is perfect. Applause all round. Arlette's face is pearled with sweat. She looks at me and says:

'My God, how happy I am. My God, a tango. My God, tomorrow –'

'– this morning'

'. . . when Suzanne and Geneviève learn what you made me do!'

Then in the taxi I am a wreck, she sleeps exhausted on my shoulder, tomorrow – this morning – yet another day when I shall be dropping with sleep, and I begin to hate her, but it's better not to start arguments now, better not to spoil for her this illusion of fulfillment which will last her for another working day; and I have to take her under the arms and drag her up the two flights to the bed, where she begins to snore slightly – I undress her, taking care not to wake her, all her little face is relaxed in an expression of beatitude. Her skin is white, an invisible down makes it softer still; with a paper handkerchief I take off her make-up, she lets me and says 'Mmmmm', I feel like laughing. What a character! And then for the first time, to hell with good behaviour and pacts, I lie down at her side, my God, the alarm! I wind it and fall asleep.

159

A few days ago Arlette reacted in a somewhat worrying way. I have never rummaged in the wardrobe, I have never allowed myself to poke about among her personal things, but taking my tin suitcase down from the cupboard I must have torn the wallpaper that covers the shelves and two photos fell on top of me, one black-and-white. She was at the cooker and I picked them up and looked at them. In one, presumably shot from below, one sees a figure in a dressing-gown on the sill of a window – the height of the storey is difficult to define – and I at once thought of Geneviève because of the white hair; the other showed a little girl with plaits smiling with her mouth wide open, in a little sleeveless summer dress and Suzanne, much younger than now, beside an imposing old lady of about a hundred, dressed in black, the flounces and puffs of a costume which if not folk is far from traditional either, serious, with burning eyes, and behind them a huge white out-of-focus blob – it must have been taken badly against the light or else it is an animal – with a few twigs which stick up from somewhere or other beyond a fence, and then I asked Arlette:

'And what was Geneviève doing perched on the skyscraper?'

'Put down those photos!' Arlette began to shout, suddenly in a temper. 'Give me them, give me them!'

I gave her them saying:

'Calm down, I didn't think it would affect you like that. It's not because of the plaits, eh!'

She gave a sigh and said she was sorry.

'Yes, it is Geneviève, I snapped her without her knowing. It seemed odd to me to see her up there, busy washing the windows on the seventh floor. She hates to be photographed – there would be trouble if she knew. Promise never to tell her? never?'

'Promise. And the other one?' If I had them in my hands I could ask her to explain details to me – the hair-grip on the lock of hair that holds the right-hand plait, I remember, a sort of ski-stick the formidable old lady held in her hand, and a kind of red cloth in the other picture, but she had put them away in a box and locked it.

'You've guessed – I am so ashamed of these plaits.'

'But you were a little girl! All little girls have plaits.'

'Yes, a little girl! I was nineteen, almost twenty. I was already in Paris. Got up like that. And got up like that when I went to London. When I think of it.'

'And that lady in black?' Arlette turns her head to one side a little, says with an indifferent voice:

'You are nosy! have I ever asked you questions?' Not much, I feel like saying. 'A lady... a relative of mine who had a farm. Happy?'

'But why do you take it like that? over a pair of plaits. Come on, let's put on Conchita.'

'No,' she shouts, 'not Conchita.'

'Everything's burning,' I venture to say.

'So much the better. Better that everything should burn. You eat, I'm not hungry.' She put the box under her arm and went out. She must have been away half-an-hour.

On the sole of my right foot three dark red patches. They ought to be the symptoms of secondary syphilis. Which means first and foremost that I shall have to start sleeping on the floor again – it's better not to take risks in case the germs are transmitted through the air, under the blankets. But I won't make a mystery of it to Arlette, so she will be forced to make a little adjustment to that strong smell she gives off at certain times – it will inhibit the relevant glands. My gums continue to bleed and my mouth has a nauseating taste. At last the bogeyman has arrived: I have been expecting him for years and my terror has been inflated through seeing him everywhere for years.

I go down at once to telephone the Colonel. Existences like mine cannot hold out long where time is concerned, and never sufficiently where it's a question of needing to make up sleep. Now that I could sleep I have to go back on to the floor, get used to it slowly; she will be back in an hour with that very elegant bag of hers full of vegetables, a rabbit at the very least, two chickens already plucked, and gherkins and little onions, aubergines in oil – and I must naturally go and fetch her from the station.

'Noblesse oblige,' is all the Colonel says and adds: 'Come with me to Chamonix next month, I'll treat you.'

'To Chamonix? I'm not even sure yet that I've got it. I've got to take tests. And then – to Chamonix?'

'Yes, right next door to Italy. I've been going there in mid-June for years, but I can put it off for a little. I have an old lady friend there – in the sanatorium – an old companion from Africa.'

A female companion from Africa in a sanatorium: the Congo and the snows, terrible viruses and avalanches, and you're back with the usual old-fashioned consumption.

'But I tell you I have to take the tests first. And in any case don't talk to me about Chamonix, I've no money.'

'I have. Come on, keep me company. If you like you can take a quick trip home. All you can do there is rest and eat well. A week. Admittedly there are only women in the sanatorium. Ravenous they are.'

'I'm not coming.'

'But they are locked up again in the evening,' he says laughing softly.

'I'll see. Have you ever had it?'

'Who knows? I've never had a blood test in my life. And then at my age –'

'All right, but the others?'

'What about it? I'm one of them too.'

The cynicism of this old soldier who, into the bargain, pretends to have dropped from the clouds when you mention the word 'corruptor' to him, is absolutely out of this world. It is never possible to pin him down: not that he is always right – it's worse than that, he isn't the least interested in being right. Once I asked him about his gloved hand, if it was a skin disease or what, because it seemed to dwindle visibly inside the worn leather and he said: 'Ballocks' then, after a few glasses he begins to mutter and no longer makes sense, fragments of words which explode here and there in the middle of the black hole of his fuddled mouth. A very laid-back man – who invites me to Chamonix at his expense or to the restaurant beneath his *hôtel particulier* and yet who would leave you to die of thirst if you asked him for a sip of water. Chamonix-Montichiari, by way of Genoa or Turin, I imagine: only a step. And after I've had my month's wages. It might be an idea.

'But can you give injections?'

'Injections! but suppose we have a nurse all to ourselves! Nougatine was the company nurse.'

'Nougatine? That's a nice name! But syphilis – a woman –'

'She's seen a few things, dear boy, you've no idea how many – scabs that fell to the ground when you did this to them with your finger.'

'Oh give over, ciao. We'll see.'

I am listening to the little transistor, a present from Suzanne, on the periwinkle-coloured bed-spread; cutting my toe-nails I wait for death, that is a little eternal and restful sleep, and I feel it's going to take some time. Oh, having to get up and go once again to Saint-Lazare! Oh no! Worn out by this physical need which I cannot satisfy, I would begin to cry if a voice did not distract me. It is the voice of the sprigs of lavender which I picked in the heath with Maurice, a crazy and infantile painter, thirty-nine years old and nine – nine! – children to support, with which I have filled all the vases and containers in the flat. I prowl about like a wounded beast, a prey to nervous impulses, the results of a clinging worry which recalls something in vain, like a robot of gelatine walking about in my head, which I am unable to define. If only I could free myself of that itch.

On the radio all one hears is one word: *Vietnam* then a little bit of music and then: 'Washington. In Vietnam –'

I shave (if I went to fetch her with a beard she would have a fit, I would be accused of doing it on purpose, I ought to know that 'I cannot put up with scruffiness when you have to give me your arm'), go down to the bar below the flat; so as not risk falling asleep, I have a cognac. Images on the television: children with their heads cut off like buds from their stem, one beside the other in a field where death has reaped its weekly harvest of Asiatic victims – question: the victims of war, I mean, those who know nothing, the women, the children, the old people, are they always entirely *innocent*? – And mothers with withered breasts, spattered with blood, happy to no longer exist, to have left to others the duty of offering atrophied glands. And I ask myself: these mute and shattered mothers, isn't it the case that they secretly wished for it too, (for example, by teaching their sons to look on them as servants, making real little men of them, all of one piece)? Plains where the bombs explode silently – no sound-track – blowing up, without a sound, the fate of someone who has spent a whole life getting an artesian well or an irrigation ditch to work again. Armoured cars which flatten the first gleams of civilization – hospitals, houses, trellises – like bitter walnuts, leaving behind them a wake of slurry and human sludge wrapped in white habits and sliding about in the village mud. And so, overcoming the cunning of this reactionary vision, I manage to restore order to things no one understands, and not to suffer and to say 'other people'. Old men with an empty gaze, dispossessed, the look of being accustomed to resignation as the only reality in life, a habit like any other, like not eating, not sleeping, always escaping with their utensils on their shoulders, or staying totally dazed beside their animals which have died one after another, like this, passing in slow motion from an upright position to a supine one, falling down once and for all. Indifference is the most difficult feeling to develop and my eyes shut instinctively; it is almost seven o'clock, I had better get on my way, go to the station, carry her big bag once more, ask her again if the journey was comfortable, give her my arm as she steps down ('If a woman is out walking with a man and he doesn't give her his arm, what reason have they for being together?'), to reply to her questions once more, while I have this word on the tip of my tongue 'treponema' and I must find a gap to let it pass through; but not this evening, this evening I shall have to ask her a lot of questions to delude her into thinking that I want to know everything she did during these three days (did she have to celebrate the 25th of May? I'd like to ask her; Can it be that a nun really dies every so often and that in your office they go along with this?). I get up, pay for the cognac, attempt a smile in the mirror and go out.

The printing and binding department where I work is strewn with old-fashioned fans which turn slowly so as not to disturb the papers which come up to our knees and continue on the tables, the shelves and the conveyor belt. Almost every day I photocopy the palm of my hand a hundred copies at a time, then I throw the photocopies into the wastepaper basket and there, in the rubbish bins in the courtyard, the bolder mice read my future – my past is not there yet even if there is more of it than there was. There are too many things I do not understand: for example why at twelve I no longer felt any affection for Carolina who had taken me in to her house for years to the great relief of my family, who for my sake made journeys on her bicycle, climbed up cherry trees, who made me snug and 'spoiled' me as my mother still says, only because for all my birthdays – both name days and anniversaries, and the festivals of Santa Lucia – she let me find a tray of cakes. Then, for no reason, I no longer went to see her and she must have felt bad about it and never reproached me. And why did my father not want to see me for three weeks when I was born only because I wasn't a girl (certainly no

question of cuckoldry – my mother 'sinned' too perfectly with him).
I have never found an explanation for these two facts – and that is
why it is odd that they come back to me at the most extraordinary
times and it is funny that at this moment, twenty years after the one
and nine after the other, I am entering the office of Madame Bonsants, Suzanne's cousin, to pay my respects and to learn from her
what impression M. Rigot has of me down there in the binding
department. Madame Bonsants is about fifty and deals with complaints – through her hands pass the invisible hurricanes of shattered
dreams or of frauds that have come off, by the thousand; perhaps
that is why she seems to be carved out of ice and nothing has the
power to shake her, and she seemed to welcome me with the same
polite detached air with which she handles her rectangles of paper,
which are branded with fire.

'Oh,' she says with an effort at cordiality, 'you're managing very
well, you got the knack quickly.'

'A pity I can't go to the Alliance any longer,' I come out with it;
she obviously doesn't know the reason, but now, after this period
of quarantine, they would take me back.

'How often a week is it?' she pretends to take an interest and lights
a cigarette without offering me one.

'Twice, from ten to twelve. But you have done so much for me
already. And Mademoiselle Suzanne and Mademoiselle Geneviève
and Mademoiselle Arlette –'

'I shall talk to M. Rigot: there shouldn't be any problem about
taking a couple of hours off for the Alliance. How is Mademoiselle
Jarre?'

'Well,' the question throws me a little because it excludes the
health of the other two. 'We go a lot to the Opéra and to the cinema
and to dine and –' I feel that if I go on like this I shall reveal that
Arlette is not at all well, that she who has vampirized herself is
vampirizing me slowly and relentlessly, and end up with how when
I was nine my father shut me up in the hutch with the white rabbits
and, since I started to pee, the female rabbit came and bit my willy.

'How glad I am! she needs it so badly!' then she sees my astonished
expression (needs what so badly? I think) and is aware of having
said (intentionally?) more than she intended and dismisses me.

'Thank you for the visit and give my regards to our friends. We
see each other so seldom – you know – commitments –'

165

Indeed: in fact they never see each other at all and Madame Bonsants' name is never mentioned by them, neither when we are all together nor when they are alone with me. And how many godmothers does Arlette have? I ask no questions: besides there are so many things I don't know about these women and this is not the moment to start asking questions in all directions, upsetting the congealed balance of their relationships, which are apparently – and perhaps also in reality – so formal. Besides this hint – she needs it so much! – might be the riposte to my indiscreet remark about Geneviève the day before yesterday when I had the unfortunate idea of going and sitting beside Madame Bonsants in the canteen. Realizing that she did not at all appreciate my gesture (merely a question of internal hierarchies, nothing personal) deeply embarrassed, unable to remedy matters (I certainly couldn't get up, excuse myself and change my place) I began very blandly to talk about Geneviève. I saw that she raised her eyebrows and began to cut her meat into cubes that got smaller and smaller without being able to make up her mind to stick her fork into one. Yet I made it clear that she was very much the superior – one of these who have the power to put you in your place and leave you puzzled and almost grateful.

'And let me know how things are in the printing shop. If I can ever do anything –'

I thanked her a dozen times as I followed her, unable to take my eyes off her tray where the little cubes of meat floated wretchedly in the gravy.

Since the blood samples are taken right here in the bank – but what isn't done in this bank-city from kindergartens to cruising holidays? – I go up to the top floor, to the sick-bay. The two ladies at the *réception* are directing a dozen patients towards the dentist, the oculist and the gynaecologist – obviously it would never occur to anyone to ask for a dermatologist or a urologist inside the bank, and so these in-house services are lacking, like the blood tests, which are entrusted to a confidential institution; the answers, sealed, are delivered directly to the person interested together with a list of the external specialists for all branches of medicine not practised in the building. You can go to any of these specialists free in case of need, presenting your employee's *fiche*. These doctors, since they are paid by contract, once they have satisfied themselves that you belong to this banking élite, don't even ask your name and, since there is no bill to be presented each time to the administration, no one at the bank can know anything about abortions or cases of syphilis or cancer or psoriasis or tuberculosis or about organs removed, nothing, that is to say, about socially prejudicial illnesses.

So, with my heart beating like mad, I open the envelope and, since one name is as good as the next, I phone the one nearest the bank, and make an appointment with Dr Chan Li Pao. Then for the rest of the morning the ringing of the telephones and the crowd at the photocopying machine do not disturb my musings: to visit Brother Fox and infect him in a last fatal embrace; to keep it without having it treated; to kill myself (you must be joking!); to pack my suitcases this evening and leave Arlette, or if I do really decide on suicide, to kill another two with me, drag them away because they are mine: my father, pure hatred, and Giacomino, love covered with a fungus of hate.

Instead I am seized by furious gaiety and begin to joke with everyone and the photocopying machine becomes the centre of a salon and no one wants to go away any more. I have begun to sing *La vie en rose* for the ladies of the bank.

'Quel charmeur alors celui-là!' say three or four elderly ladies to M. Rigot, who is visibly pleased that I have the ability to calm the whole establishment with my chat and to silence the demands for work in arrears – his, not mine.

I follow the syringe in the vein of my arm – the liquid is called 'bismuth' – and I imagine I have yellow blood, perhaps because the person who is treating me is a Chinese dermatologist in a straw-coloured surgery. How odd, I feel as if I were under a transparent parachute, a spore of Arlette's odour, seeing the world upside down during a gymnastic exercise – but these are not the hairs that come out from under her pants, they are the drooping moustaches of the Chinese doctor.

'But where the devil did you catch it? Have you told your partner?'

'I go with men.'

'Ah, couldn't you have said that before?'

'You didn't ask me.'

'Let's take a look behind. That's why there was nothing to be seen on the penis – apart from the feet. But the tests are quite definite. You don't feel anything in the anus?'

'A hell of an itch.'

It's typical: first they treat you on the basis of the little ticks on the chemical report, then they examine you. Here he is putting on a transparent glove, he greases it with vaseline, but he doesn't need to stick his finger in: 'A fine anal syphiloma, look at it!' he says, exultantly, as if he had at last harpooned Moby Dick. 'Who knows how many people you have poxed up.'

'I am people too,' I say, mirroring myself in the Colonel's phrase. 'I hope you're not going to preach at me!'

This shut him up for good, his tone becomes detached, less triumphant. They are all the same, just like the people in the VD clinic: they live on it; they see tens of thousands and all give you the same lecture, especially if it is a case of homosexuals, at the slightest staphylococcus they rush on to the balcony to harangue the crowd. The only thing to do is to send them to the devil right away.

'Another six of these intravenous injections I shall do personally, the other intramuscular ones you can have done in the bank.'

'How many others will there be?'

'About eighty. One a day. Let's say ninety.'

I calculate in my head whether a mere two hips can have enough room for eighty holes and leave, feeling like a sieve, talking to my hips:

'Poor right hip, painted on a winter's night with the white rigours of solitude, and you, my inflamed left hip, lined with desperate poems in an afternoon of Argentinian *fuego*, my whole sacrum of no more use after being squeezed a good dozen times in one single day –'

When she comes home, she finds me on my lair on the floor, as at the beginning of our time together. She looks at me:

'Ah, bon.'

I make no reply, I first let her imagine all the wrong things which can act like yeast on her sense of guilt: for example, that I have noticed her furtive caresses on my hair and that I have gone back here because I can't stand them. Then in one breath I say:

'I have syphilis!'

'And I have had two abortions: one at nineteen and one at twenty-one.'

And we both add:

'Ah bon!'

And we burst out laughing and suddenly it is a party: we empty the refrigerator, uncork the bottle of champagne – which neither of us likes much – and we begin to get down to details.

Me: 'Let's talk about your abortions.'

She: 'Right. On the twenty-fifth of May in the year one thousand nine hundred and fifty eight I meet a Spaniard, as shy as myself; I meet him on the beach and that evening am already – All that memory is a great pain and then the fear, the fear my mother might get to know. So Suzanne takes me to a woman, very good at her job, a professional; but I wanted to keep the baby, I'd have liked to keep it. But he takes off, goes back to Spain – I had just started working in Paris: it meant going home, a girl-mother, in that set-up. No, no, it was better to have an abortion, Suzanne insisted. I have an abortion and Suzanne sends me to London for a year, to perfect my English, she even gets into touch with my parents, gets to know them, persuades them to let me go, guaranteeing that when I come back I'll find my job and will earn a lot more. And so I went to the Bradleys. But I suffered a year of remorse and breakdowns – if it hadn't been for Suzanne, I don't know, I don't know.'

Me: 'The first. And the second?'

'At this second question Arlette gets up from the edge of the bed and begins to make circles round my lair which is flooded by the light from the wide-open window, as if she were looking for something. But she doesn't find it: clearly she was looking for a new version, or perhaps trying to improve on the first statement. As if she were making an effort to hear her own words, the sound of them, but they have already flown out of the window. She taps the cage which begins to sway, I hear two sighs, see her shake her head and light a cigarette with trembling hands. I have to be a spectator of the usual pantomime when she draws on it like an idiot child from the backwoods before she begins again:

'I start working again. The Spaniard comes back to Paris. He turns up two days after I had started again because, he says, he wanted to know if it is a boy or a girl, and then he will disappear for ever. I don't tell Suzanne, who would never have allowed me to see him again; so he phones the office and, as usual, Suzanne is there at the desk opposite, going through a ledger and talking about bees and pollen; I behave as if nothing were wrong and I feel as if my heart were bursting, I don't know what to do, I simply say 'yes' to all the questions put to me. I wanted to see him again for all the hurt he had caused me, above all because he had gone off like that; instead I keep things to myself and when I make love to him – well. I despise him for his cowardice but –'

'You liked making love with him –'

'Exactly. He drove me mad. I shouted.'

'Don't look at me like that, Arlette. I don't have to emulate any one far less this Pablo.'

'What does that mean?'

'It means that I don't have to make love to you, simply because women leave me cold sexually. That's all – nothing personal. But you were looking at me as if you wanted me to consider the problem whether I'd ever be able to drive you mad like the Spaniard. I've just told you I have an anal syphiloma and you've already wiped it away like a sponge, and you invent for yourself an *escalation* between males.'

'But the one doesn't exclude the other.'

'Well, it does for me.'

'Pablo was a homosexual too. He was –'

'. . . . .'

'He breathed fire –'

'A minotaur. But it's ridiculous!'

'You're the ridiculous one,' says Arlette, looking at me furiously.

Now I begin to understand many things that went on in her head – things that never appealed to me: Arlette, on the basis of her experiences, has always followed the only logical thread she could and has never fallen into contradictions. If the Spaniard gives me so much, the Italian will give me just as much – abortions apart, or, maybe, including abortions, people are so odd. The Spaniard an erotic marvel, so be it with the Italian – both declare themselves homosexuals, so the ones who go with other men when they stop being cows and turn into bulls to go with a woman, the elect, the redeemer, the inspiring muse, the arena between whose high slopes the bull finds sublimity, and in death, finds *true love*.

'Well, you've got it wrong about me, Arlette.'

'Have I got it totally wrong? Why put the cart before the horse?'

Her glance has become sad; the little head that looks at me now from between the arms crossed on the edge of the bed is dejected.

'Arlette, please don't get upset for nothing. You know how much

I like you. And as for tauromachy, Montherlant is enough for me,'
I try to say, hoping to catch once more a little of the initial light-
heartedness with which the confessions of this little calf began – the
calf *matada* when she had barely emerged, covered with the pink
and white ribbons, from the throng of sacrificial virgins from a
convent school.

'Stop it!' she says raising her little head suddenly, looking at me
fixedly with a look which has lost its challenge and perhaps its hope.
I offer her another glass of champagne, light a cigarette for her.

'In short, after a month of this story – I miss you know what I
mean – after two months the same story. The woman had gone out
of circulation, dead or in prison, and I didn't have the courage to
ask Suzanne for help again and to ask Geneviève was practically the
same as asking Suzanne – I didn't know where to turn.'

'And the Spaniard, good God, he didn't run off this time too!'

'Yes, he did, and for ever. Vanished into thin air. Finally in the
third month I find a woman; she lived in the Camargue, I travel all
night in the train on a Friday evening. But it wasn't like the first
time. It was terrible. Terrible.'

Her voice has turned into a cry.

'I thought I was dying. And since then I haven't had any relationship with anyone.'

I get up, go to the side of the bed, put an arm round her shoulders
and hold her tightly to my breast and she begins to cry and then I
cry, but you can't hear it, this time, because when I cry a lot I often
don't shed more than a couple of tears – but they are so far apart
that my eyes turn red as if I had conjunctivitis.

'And you?' she asks, as if she was forgetting that I am not Suzanne
or Geneviève or someone else liable to have swallowed a concoction
of bleach and nettles or to have been done over in *petit point* at the
back of the womb with a knitting needle. Then she raises her head,
wipes her face with a fringe of the bed-cover which is spring-like,
blue, with little lavender flowers raining down all over it.

'Let's drink to us,' I propose. But she doesn't feel like it any more,
she looks at me full of suffering with that streak of eye-shadow on
her cheek and pushes the glass away. I take advantage of it to touch
on a subject she has forbidden.

'Can I ask you something?'

She hesitates, opens her eyes wide: she listens once more to the

171

words she has spoken, searches among the echo which has gone on beating in waves on the little cage, and then says with a broken voice:

'Yes –'

'But this Madame Bonsants and – Geneviève –'

'How do you know?' says she, betraying herself.

'I guessed. I imagined it.'

'Yes, but I know as much as you do. All I know is that Geneviève meets Madame Bonsants, a friend from her schooldays, after a number of years, fifteen years ago; Madame Bonsants had got married and had a little girl; she leaves her husband and goes to live with Geneviève for a time and both of them look after the little girl.'

'Intimate relations?'

'I've no idea. I can't even imagine it,' she says in a peremptory way, takes the glass and empties it. I go on:

'Then Geneviève gets to know the cousin, Suzanne, who is so much more beautiful, that Geneviève –'

'– leaves Madame Bonsants, who has a breakdown. Anything else?'

'But after all, you must have some idea about people you've known for ten years.'

'Suzanne is still so amazed at this constant attention after ten years that, although she has got rid of all her admirers, I don't think she has ever decided –'

'– to take the big step? Come down to earth, Arlette!'

'All I know is that Suzanne lives as a function of Geneviève, but the director has been in love with her for years –'

'Well, Geneviève has a boy friend too, doesn't she? This Hippolyte.'

'Oh, purely platonic relations –'

Her mouth closes again. I see that she has replaced the brick, having taken out just the number of coins that was necessary. But the brick doesn't fit perfectly into the floor, a tiny crack remains and a gleam of light continues to come from it. But she is not aware of it.

'I'd so much like to tell you something!' Here she is back playing the sentimental tune – was what I said not enough for her. No, she wants to increase the dose: repeat the same error, because she is somehow stuck with that error and all she can still ask of life is that it should permit her to repeat it in exactly the same terms, changing only the indispensable juvenile lead, who plays the abortionist, the innocent killer with the heart of gold.

'Keep it to yourself, Arlette, I don't want to hear it.'

'I love you.'

I take my glass and hurl it against the wall and she takes her head in her hands and begins to sob deeply and to hide her little head under the pillow. All I say is:

'And I don't!' and I go off banging the door.

Lately my sex has been clutching at a spider's web of mental exercises in order to be able to have an erection, I was always so tired; besides I always felt I was watching the same film: now comes this line of dialogue now that other one. What exhaustion. And I am so happy that syphilis, because of my great civic sense, obliges me to abstain from any sexual relation for at least a fortnight. What a relief not to have to ejaculate at all costs just to pass the time!

In the loo of the print-shop I continue to rub myself with cotton-wool after having been to the sick-bay where the nurses are always so nice and never ask questions. But the little boxes say inexorably: 500,000 units, a million units. They must certainly have guessed that it's not a question of doses of tonic. I breathe with enjoyment the air impregnated with alcohol, light a cigarette, then I perch with my shoes on the lavatory seat – I am always afraid of letting my colleagues catch crabs from me; not that I have any at the moment, but you never know – and little by little my sadness – the sadness of a human wreck – returns and the words in my head rise and fall and flow together into one question: How did I get here? in this closet rubbing my hip? Carolina used to take me over and over again to eat watermelon at the house of some people she knew at Piccinelle, where she lifted her elbow a little and they all began to laugh and said something to her which meant nothing at all to me: 'What about the Germans! and then you caught it after the Liberation, didn't you?' and she would say: 'But for the Germans I'd have died of hunger –'

'Monsieur!' says the cavernous voice of M. Rigot outside the door, 'Ce n'est concevable que vous gagniez votre argent en chiant tout le temps. Sortez vite, vite, s'il vous plaît.'

I have lost time too for another reason this morning: after being at the sick-bay I stopped the lift at the seventh floor which is also the most deserted floor in the Bank, the one where they hold the general meetings. I went straight to the end of the corridor that looks out on to the Avenue de l'Opéra, opened the window and leant out on to the sill and looked down. Then I took a look at the window panes – opaque ones – to see if they were clean. Suddenly I remembered that in the photo Arlette had snatched from my hand Geneviève's dressing-gown – blue – was unbuttoned in front – on the photo wasn't there a sort of spot, a sort of drop? But to know what it feels like at that height I'd have had to take my right hand as well from the window frame, the hand in which Geneviève held the bottle of cleaning fluid, instead I had to confine myself to balancing my left hand, the one that held the red rag, in the void. Geneviève was, what shall I say? leaning out towards the world in a gesture that was almost one of defiance, one unheard of in a houseowner who runs her finger over things when she has just finished dusting on Sunday. And I thought: if I was wearing a dressing-gown now and it came undone, the wind would create a sort of peal of bells to the joy of the curious and of some malicious photographer. From below some people were beginning to stop on the pavement and look up. God, how I felt like pissing on everybody. When I saw they were pointing at me I drew back in, shut the window and got down.

When I am in the metro, at each stop I look to see whether there is a new poster. Since underground men and women pay no attention to each other and I'd find it difficult to strike up a conversation with them – to justify my dirty face, the rings round my eyes, to take the first one that comes to hand and tie him to the seat and tell him *all my life* from the beginning because I feel I have left out too many important things or simply because that version I gave to Arlette no longer satisfies me (I could for example, start from the crumbling patriarchal rule of my paternal grandparents) – I read everything that comes to hand. Out loud. Billboards, plaques, titles of newspapers, numbers, labels on clothes, inscriptions in the cement and on the walls, everything, frenetically. Nothing, no reaction from anyone.

And so my story continues, calmly but tenaciously. I gnaw at my lips because I am always hungry even when I've just left the restaurant in the bank and I don't have a penny until the end of the month all because of Fleming, because the health insurance only pays 1p after three months because you are in a job and you have to buy the medicine yourself and I don't want to ask Arlette for more advances, for with her the situation has become tense to the point where simply to annoy me so as to find out what I made of her confession, she would force me to read the telephone directory to make me earn my place in bed. Reciprocal confidences have complicated the situation even more instead of clearing it up; when she saw that clarity would damage her, she retreated suddenly and began to say that she had never said this or that, that it was I who had misunderstood, and that she hadn't meant that at all, that is not really, and as for me, if you give me an inch I take a yard and she had seen through it all. A hell. So much so that I try to be at home as little as possible. And I should be careful not to repeat the confidences she told me in that off-balance moment, that moment of weakness, about Suzanne and Geneviève 'because I could get into big trouble' no less; that she had merely followed the thread of what I was saying, that she had never thought of certain things, Madame Bonsants, Geneviève, Suzanne, that she had been unpardonably thoughtless in letting me lead her on, and admit, no she didn't admit anything, it's me that gallops along in my fantasies. Etcetera. I have turned my last fifty cents into a telephone token (couldn't I buy the injections, maybe ten at a time with the advance? no, sir, all ninety of them at one go, as if the pharmaceutical industry ran the risk of losing the formula for mould!) to telephone Domenico, and ask him for a hundred francs. He is someone from Rome, a couple of years older than me, who has a job as a waiter in that pizzeria. He is studying the violin, a real passion – on his little camp-bed we always made love in a threesome – if it wasn't the violin-case it was the bow but some part of the violin was always there between us. One who pursues only his own thoughts; you talk to him, he looks at you pretending to pay attention and then you notice that he has not heard a word, that he was thinking about a chord, of producing a musical phrase. But I'm prepared to cut off my balls if he can play the violin; I have never heard anything more than exercises, never anything that had a beginning and an end. He plays jazz on the violin, he does – he plays whatever comes into his head and at the end says 'naturally you can't understand'. But with that dreamy look of his he is marvellous at fooling the customers by putting up the prices, and for him a hundred francs should be a trifle. But it seems not. I have leaden tears in the corner of each word, I have cries impeded by fungus and stinking firebrands when I think back to these days. And don't make me listen to chords on the phone, it simply isn't the right moment. He's sorry.

With the Colonel it's better not even to try – he lives in terror of being exploited, which is typical of corruptors and the greedy. In any case he too thinks that everyone fashions his own destiny and let them get on with it and I'd run the risk of throwing away the possibility of going to Chamonix and then home, with the trip almost all paid for. And Maurice! Oh he, loafer that he is, with that way he has of taking tellies, little tubes of oil-paint and *baguettes* on credit from the Porte de Clignancourt to the one at Clichy, will feed his nine brats for a month on a hundred francs – these sons of 'the young artist' were absolutely filthy, like so many beasts on the loose in a huge empty barracks where, out of pity, they had at least put in water and light for him: one day I had arrived with a packet of fruit to make friends with them and they kicked and punched me to go off with the biggest pieces. They were like monkeys, one more beautiful than the other, all half-naked, with the ravenous eyes of extraterrestrial beings in SF films. My God, nine children to feed and dying of hunger, while you go about having it off with young boys whom you bewitch with your beautiful flowing beard and your angelic face, your luminous eyes which are big and black and glowing, magnetic. One of his little hungry mouths – all in steps and stairs, one two three four five etc years old, with her in quarantine again as always with the latest one in her arms, that smiling asymmetrical face, of someone with a screw loose, low-set and a little squat into the bargain, Madame Trichomonasis, more of a child than the rest of them – had devoured two bananas and another who had been sleeping and had just come into the 'kitchen' (you had merely to push aside plywood panels and everywhere there were old cradles and metal nets and yellowish mattresses and darned blankets) well, this one, not having had a banana, after staring at me in a questioning way, had landed a gob between my mouth and nose. I smiled at him and to show that I wasn't to blame and that I was his friend promptly returned the spit, blinding him, to the mad hilarity of the others flourishing on the margins of the cowlike squinting mother, who is mad about you, and ready to turn herself into an egg-cup once again. You will understand that I couldn't go on with you, seeing you spend your family allowance on me ... And Montherlant, I wonder how he spends his royalties! and Sartre? That's it, I shall call them and say: Hello, couldn't you refund at least those royalties you have pocketed thanks to me?

That would leave me with Pierre, who is Pierre and that's that, someone to whom I had given an odd number of kisses one night, playing with the abacus of his teeth: a hundred and three or maybe a hundred and ninety one, but on waking another, very long and detailed, a Pythagorean table for himself. With gnawed lips, my tongue swollen and wounded, I lightly touched his big blue-streaked gusher and in Arlette's bed – she being in the country at her parents – said: Good morning, darling and ... see you soon. Pierre, gratefully made the coffee, cleaned up the room with its lavender twigs, remade the bed, and – on the doorstep by now – told me that I was the most absurd and stupid person he had ever met and politely told me to go to hell.

After that I don't know anyone else in Paris, that is, no one whose address I know. And there are certainly hundreds who have taken a piece of my time, maybe thousands. But Pierre has no telephone and if he had ... And the Hunchback at Poncelet might be upset and not let me in free anymore. In short, a desert. No one. I am abstracting myself from the meanings of the words I have used all these years to circumnavigate my depressing love for Giacomino and, never having completed the pentagram of my amorous sighs, I keep them pure and clean, only altering from time to time the space into which they end up falling to repeat themselves over and over again. Far from him I am also far from myself. I detest myself because I cannot manage to uproot this purulent root. Far from myself like the root farthest from the trunk, I hate myself, and wither to a skeleton and will never be able to reunite with the root which held me with my *fate* suspended. Everything is so colourless without his evil eyes, black when he would like to hug me and yellow when he does not do it, eyes which give rise in me to the sick desire which I cannot express: to love him without having to violate him, without tying him up in his sleep as he indicated I should do. But how could I put on stage something that, as far as I was concerned, was happening in the stalls? To watch me climb up the backcloth, aesthetically profane my desire only to satisfy pleasures which I did not know existed and which he must certainly have learned by going to the classical lycée. I didn't go to school and was a very simple kid who looked for work here and there and kept coming back because I could not do without seeing him beyond a certain time. To what psychological mechanism could I have traced those chains of petty bourgeois punitive desire which he made me discover on the bed that time when his parents had gone to the seaside? To none. At that time it seemed to me that the only thing worth doing was to liberate one's sex from any type of constraint and he, instead of enjoying freedom of will, already felt the need at eighteen to have chains if he was to experience pleasure. Like any old Lofty. And now I understand that perhaps the contempt he heaped on me when he dismissed me with those words was due not so much to my being 'queer' as to the fact that I had refused to tie him up, to rape him, become his accomplice, because I did not go along with dirtying my true feelings for him, perhaps because they were infinitely more important than him and he felt he did not have me in his grasp any more, because, oddly enough, it was I who dictated the rules with my incorruptibility – they were not yet *gaffes*. That is to say: was capable of renouncing anything that infringed my freedom even if it would have increased my pleasure.

But what is this dull bitterness before I go to bed, if not the certainty of taking there an empty body, full of a liberty which interests no one?

'Moral?' says Arlette with an effort, subdued. She is so tiny, so falsely fragile, with that little face scowling with myopia, but she has *most beautiful* breasts if one can ever speak of beauty in something of that kind, something that nourishes.

'There is a Lutheran proverb, maybe it's Sardinian, I think, which says: better an end with fear than a fear without end.'

She looks at me, not in the least afraid, as if to say: that is certainly not the end of the story – but I have turned on my other side which, by good luck, is not the hip that hurts – in the one that is uppermost the nurse has scored a direct hit on the sciatic nerve and has made me lame and it hurts a lot. Otherwise I would always be forced to have before me Arlette's set face, because I sleep in fits and starts and wake up every ten minutes and think that it is not very friendly to have gone back into the big bed almost at once and begin to wonder:

where am I? who am I? and who is this? and then, once I have found out, I begin to give vent to my anger. I shall not open my mouth for ten days. I am ruining my life and my vocal chords for her. I refuse to go on like this. All day long I think about nothing else but what I must invent to satisfy her, what new oral idiocies. Enough. Today I didn't feel well, they gave me a cognac, because I was thinking about her and me with a superhuman hatred – homicidal – and I turned pale. Besides she is too old for me. Two days, let her give me a little peace and I'll find myself a bed, I'll clear out as soon as possible if I get back some strength, if she lets me sleep for three days without dropping pans, moving furniture, dragging chairs about to wake me and then saying: 'Oh, I'm sorry, I didn't mean to, go on sleeping' and she turns on the radio, tactfully in the bathroom but at full blast. Oh, that's enough! And I've had enough of the story of her abortions, which she has confided to me alone, as if I could make money out of it! It's her business, I don't give a damn. When she had them I must have been about ten and was a thousand kilometres away from here. Sometimes she speaks to me as if I were Pablo-Pablito and I have no desire to stay there wondering by what logical concatenations she always confuses me with him – at least when she has to go into recriminations about her fate. She tries to involve me in a game of mirrors which I find as boring as a joke heard a dozen times over – she wants to get possession of me by using my feelings, which are those of a mesmeriser, who can take on out of pity, out of need, out of interest and then yes, I admit it, out of curiosity, the nasty secrets of other people's lives. I've had enough of the burden of other people, get on with it yourselves – her tearful stories of a petty bourgeois girl who couldn't confide in her bigot of a mum do not interest me. Mums get educated or else they take the consequences. And I don't want to be escort to her and Suzanne and Geneviève any more; she can go to the theatre with them by herself, they bore me to death with their mysteries: after so many veiled promises of exhilarating confidences and conversations about their own *sins* we have got to the point where we talk about what we ate today, what we will eat; and flowers and nature and animals have become, squalidly, merely flowers nature animals and Geneviève livens up only when she is given the chance to talk in unrecognizable oxymorons or about the absence of her boy friend. And this one here snores into the bargain, and nothing seems to

179

matter to her not even that I am having treatment; we say such nice things about friendship and mutual protection (against whom?) and this is the great result: inch by inch she rolls to my side and is not content till she has put a foot between my legs. And from this moment on I shall not shut my eyes even for an instant.

From the chink where the brick has been put back badly there suddenly emerges a different ray of light, an oblique one. I turn towards her and ask her straight out, withdrawing my leg.

'Arlette, but when you had your first abortion was Suzanne already Geneviève's girl–friend?'

'. . . mmm . . . why should I know . . . . why don't you ask her?'

'Don't you have a photo of Pablo to show me?'

'Go to sleep. I burnt them all. His too.'

Arlette is angry because I didn't go to meet her at the office. By now she has entirely abandoned the gloss of shyness and of hesitation and goes into the attack right away.

'Always that Montherlant! and what am I doing here? just keeping you?'

With an abrupt gesture she snatches the book from me and makes it finish up on the floor, goes into the bathroom, slamming the door as violently as she can, and locks herself in. Ten minutes pass, half-an-hour, an hour.

'Arlette, are you feeling ill?' No reply. 'What are you doing? answer me.'

I wish to God she had cut her veins in earnest.

'Come out, please, don't make me worry.'

I know! It's the concierge.

'But it's not true that I brought a man back to your place, who told you this story?'

And I was silly enough to tell Madame Bonsants my plans.

'And it's not true that I am leaving for London; how could I, I've just begun my treatment. Come out, for goodness sake. Come out, out you come.'

At the order 'come out' the door opens.

'Can't one have a bath now?'

'But I didn't hear the water running.'

'Or sit on the loo waiting until our little lord and master has finished acquiring a culture? You have all the time you want for reading.'

'When?' I dare to say.

'At the midday break. And leave Madame Bonsants alone, if you don't want to lose your job. Try to remember that I live here too, it's my house. And that it isn't a brothel. I'll have it disinfected.'

'But Arlette –'

'Well, not just because of you and the strangers you have brought here. Because of the beetles as well... Where shall we go? And no stupid questions.'

In the restaurant the usual scene: she begs pardon, I am touched (I am touched because it is the only way to cancel out, or to fuse to the point where they become unrecognizable, all my feelings of annoyance), then when her eyes are gleaming too, she cuts short the mutually painful situation by demanding that I tell a fairy-tale or say some nice suggestive things into which I have learned to insert an element which can implicitly disturb her: my stories are an antidote to the hatred I brood on night and day: that is why I say things-I-don't-mean as if I had learned them by heart for a charity performance.

'My happiness is to have many lives to donate to the earth which I tread daily without ever retracing my steps. And not to talk any more, not to look at you any more, not to know you, to want you to go away as quickly as possible. You have already definitely belonged, Arlette. And not to receive any more caresses, and to open the window and not breathe you any more; and not to remember my adolescence any more, to stop it from raging away with its constantly renewed palimpsests, to be a figure without a past; it is the game of lack of identity and of improvisation and of availability. My happiness has remained to walk alone and to go into the fields at sunset to listen to the crickets and throw myself into the sun. Let it carry me away. Then there are the fantasies and the chat outside the door at Panarea. I was shelling beans with a little servant-girl with unripe breasts, garlicky breath, a fleshy mouth, as beautiful as a wild kid; how I loved you! what love would have been like between us, the kiss, the caress with the tongue, the bites after having fought with our claws in bitter-sweet pursuit! an affair between northern satyrs and rustic nymphs; to drink the blood of your virginity so that nothing might be lost of your little salty body. And then to leave together, to carry you away from your masters, with guitars being plucked on the poop of the ferry to Corfù. You turned the skies orange playing with a ball against the sun and took me by the hand – I who was a confused gipsy who had left behind in a tattered memory his caravan, his tribe, the two of us, vagabond flowers, who have travelled far to live together.'

Arlette's cheeks are bright red and her forehead sweaty; there's no doubt, her armpits are like a natural spring. She stares at me disconcerted, amazed, bewitched. Exhausted by so much lyricism, I lean back in the chair and let my arms dangle, my hunger has left me entirely.

'And this servant-girl in Panarea, who was she? Where's Panarea?' she asks me, trying to concentrate on the menu.

'What servant-girl in Panarea?'

'The one you were in Corfù with. You've never talked about her before.'

'I've never been in Corfù with any servant-girl from the island of Panarea, Arlette.'

'How many things you must keep to yourself! And I've told you everything about myself!'

Naturally, there was nothing to tell, I'd like to point out to her, but I am enjoying too much this mystery I contrive to cloak myself in at the opportune moment,

'Listen who is talking.'

'Tell me about them.'

'Whether you want it or not, you know everything there was to know. In fact more – the atmosphere of the things that cannot be communicated. I really have told you all about myself.'

She lowers her eyes. Then when the waiter arrives for the order she chooses carefully: snails à la bourguignonne, leg of lamb with herbs in butter. All with garlic in it. As if the garlic at home wasn't enough. Get stuffed, little girl. For three months you have done nothing but drain me, I shall end up in the lunatic asylum. Why don't you look for a lady's man? Why are you chasing the impossible? With me you are only wasting your time, the little youth that is left to you. Don't you feel how I detest you, how much contempt there is behind my niceness, my patience, my accommodating spirit?

'For me braised bull's balls! Let's hope they're not Jean d'Arc's,' I say, staring at Arlette. She swallows, blinks and says: 'I'm keen to try them too.' I can't make out though whether she knows about Geneviève's dream or not. But when I hand her the fork-full it seems

182

to me that a drop of water dripping from somewhere or other falls on my buttock and I hear a sizzling of meat and am aware of the smell of unconditional belonging. And she meanwhile swallows it all exactly like the little face of the tobacconist's son lit by the match among the furrows and the bushes.

'Geneviève has invited us to dinner on Sunday.'

'Sunday?' I repeat as if I had been punched in the face. 'But Sunday is Sunday! Don't you have to go to the country? I beg you, Arlette, you know what Sunday means to me, if I don't sleep on Sunday either I –'

'She has asked other people besides Suzanne and us, her friend the gardening-journalist, Monsieur Hippolyte –'

'My God, what a catastrophe. But what about your parents, your mother?'

'I am of age as you keep pointing out to me. It's time they got used to not seeing me sometimes. They'd still like me to have white ribbons in my plaits. I'm not a little girl any more,' she says; but did she have to begin to emancipate herself now, at the weekend. 'I'll stay here on Sunday and we'll go to dinner at Geneviève's. For your good. And I have decided that next Sunday we'll go together to Versailles.'

'For my good?'

'Since there is this journalist, this chap here, after all you never know. Maybe he'll get you on to *France-Dimanche*.'

'Rather the print-shop at the bank for the term of my natural life than *France-Dimanche*.'

'Idiot, you have to begin somewhere; seeing you like to read and write so much, why not get a profession out of it? Oh, don't put on that face! You can leave your notebooks lying about as much as you like, first of all I don't know Italian and then I wouldn't even be able to make out your handwriting. I'm not inquisitive like you.'

I make no comment. But this trick to convince me to accept the invitation without making a fuss strikes me as brilliant.

'And please trot out what little you know or write something for the occasion.'

'To recite standing on a chair?'

'Why not? It wouldn't be the first time you've done it,' she says with a malignant air; she's undoubtedly harking back to the servant-girl from Panarea; and besides garlic doesn't agree with her.

183

'But this is absurd, I can't begin to recite to order, I'm not a puppet. And on Sundays I need to –'

'To do what? go to your filthy saunas? bring home venereal diseases? crabs? aren't you content with the ones you've got? do you want to infect the whole of France?'

'Damn the day that I laid my heart bare to you. Before you were all milk and honey, you played at seeing who could show most understanding and coolness, and now you amuse yourself by throwing everything back at me. What if I did the same with your two abortions –'

'Do it,' she exclaims in a peremptory voice.

'But it's only one day a week, even servants have a day off, I'd go mad if I didn't stay alone at least on Sundays.'

'Because you get bored with me, don't you? because I'm a drag, aren't I?'

'Besides the doctor told me that after the first ten injections I'm not infectious any more.'

'Sunday is the ninth. You couldn't in any case.'

So there: she counts them. Counts them for her own sake, not for the rest of France. Besides it isn't even true that she counts them properly because she hasn't stopped the furtive touching.

'This time you'll make an exception – like me,' she says, forgetful of the fact that she has already scheduled Versailles as well and then God knows what else, the chateaux of the Loire, etcetera, for all the Sundays to come. 'On Sunday we shall go to dinner at Geneviève's, you'll do your usual charming turn and you'll go to the sauna another time.'

I twist and turn my fork in the choucroute, hoping that my sullen expression will make her change her mind.

'Come on, my dear, try to understand, it's for your own good, for your future. I promise not to make a noise and tonight I shall let you sleep – As if it depended on me, *quel culot!*'

That's it – take a sausage with lots of cabbage and stick it up her everywhere, so that she can't breathe any more.

'Tell me about Venice, *ses musées, ses pigeons, ses* –' she says with a dreamy air, half-serious, half-joking. She is clearly making fun of me, enjoying twisting the knife in the Sunday wound. And I lay on thick.

'I love you, sweet little word, awkward kiss, cries of joy on seeing

184

you in the evening, your little hands laid on my cheeks, I love you, capricious little girl, sly swallow, malicious penguin. *Mais les petites pingouines, ça ne sert à rien.'*

While being introduced to Monsieur Hippolyte – tall, a horsey smile, blue jacket and grey trousers, an English school-tie and the exaggeratedly upright posture of natures aware of their tendency to servility – I immediately think of two things: how small the world is! and the second, which harks back to the line old Rampi came out with one day at the Centrale bar: 'If I find a woman who likes it limp I drive her mad.' Because this Hippolyte is that lamentable creature who roams in the bushes at Notre Dame with his trousers down and rushes about madly feeling people's pricks without ever finding one big enough for him. I have never let him and more than once I would willing have smashed his face in for the way he doesn't give a damn for any of the polite conventions between lovers eying each other. He is always kept at a distance; when people see him they move off with him after them. If then, when there is a group of four or five, he finally manages in the confusion to slip his hand on to the biggest prick, he has only one word to say: 'Mount me' and he turns his arse. Which is almost always rejected. Monsieur Hippolyte is impotent and some people say that once they forced him to unbutton his trousers and in them he had a head of maize wrapped in a handkerchief. It seems almost obvious to me now that he is interested in the coupling – of others.

'For designs, which can become delicious little works of art, one uses young, tiny seedlings, one arranges them in the container with a forceps or a little stick' – who knows whether he recognizes me, but such people never recognize anyone because they cannot recognize themselves. Besides it doesn't matter to me. Behind him and Geneviève and Suzanne, Arlette and I make our way from the big hall – Geneviève occupies the whole floor with terrace on her own – towards the dining-room. No sign of servants. The botanist walks with his legs slightly apart as if he constantly had a trowel up his arse. The kind of person who is capable of anything. What a disappointment that Geneviève uses a type like this for social cover!

It is Geneviève herself who serves at table, and like a grand lady, doesn't explain why. Hippolyte discusses flowers with Suzanne, he in a very scientific way, like an expert, she in her usual florid and romantic way; Arlette feels a bit left out as usual; Suzanne and Geneviève only where artificial manure for house plants is concerned; I by everything and everyone. It is incomprehensible to me how at that age they still have to go to such trouble – using gardening metaphors – to justify the failure of their own existence. 'The floriculturist, Madame de Gelpière, in that luminous, almost futuristic hothouse of hers near Tours, designs the elegant lines of her pots of Bohemian glass, shapes with the scalpel the beautiful palm trunks into which the tropical plants are inserted, oh, ma chère Suzanne, ma chère Geneviève, you see –' and the boor doesn't pay Arlette a single compliment as if she didn't even exist.

In Geneviève d'Orian's apartment everything is in violent or dark colours, from the table-cloth, purple with red embroidery, to the paint on the walls of emerald green. The glasses are of rock crystal, the seats have black backs and arms. A fair-ground with all the colours of *all* the rainbows – through which she must feel herself slide as if in a kaleidoscope bringing more and more dishes to the table, helped by Arlette. I do not believe, never mind the botanist, that there is a single flowering plant in the whole house – a living one, I mean; even some baroque pieces have been assaulted with yellow lacquer. *Consoles* and red furniture can be seen through the archway of the dining-room, edged with black; pictures on the walls with frames that try to look Spanish with their gold, their twirls – and in them American graphic art and oil paintings: gigantic tubes of toothpaste, lines and squares, flowers turned to plastic, an enormous foot – with six toes.

It is odd how this woman, seen here, today appears particularly exhausted, I'd say intentionally so, absent, that's it. Like someone who already has everything and has to beat her brains to find the slightest desire for something else. I want to leave. I don't feel safe. Arlette distributes smiles of agreement which Suzanne has not asked for; she has just finished saying; '. . . in Japan, for example, chrysanthemums are a symbol of happiness . . .' Arlette glances at me briefly as if asking me to come out of my cataleptic state and say something.

'Delicious, is it not, *mes chères*?' says Suzanne copying Geneviève's feminist use of the adjective, turning her eyes on to me and the other three. By now I have got thick-skinned and allow myself to be called *mademoiselle* when a plural is needed. But she turns them on to me in particular.

'Oh, I have never eaten so well in my life,' I say but feel the words die in my mouth, feel they sound forced, that I am starting up the mambo of politenesses in an ungrateful way.

'I found all the herbs it needed. They give the right aroma,' says Geneviève, wearily, immediately interrupted by her friend who begins a lecture on the qualities of tarragon, sage and a dozen other aromatic plants. And apart from everything else, apart from any extremely rosy theories about his potency and his most secret tastes, he seems to me a person who forces himself to court a woman like Geneviève precisely because with her he is on to something safe, in the sense that she will never *yield* – so that even if she didn't know about his anal itch and he that she is, let's say, lesbian, he can invent carnal desires and phoney anguishes in which to believe for the rest of his life, without ever having to come down to brass tacks and discover what really interests him apart from hothouse blooms.

Every so often he languidly lays his hand on Geneviève's who withdraws it delicately to do a hundred things – to raise her napkin to her mouth, to make a gesture in the air to ward off a compliment about the sauce. Arlette presses one of her little shoes on mine. But I shall not open my mouth.

'Oh excuse me, where is the bathroom?' I ask so as to get away.

'At the end on the right,' says Geneviève without batting an eyelid.

I get up and go through the whole hall, I pass a completely white sitting-room on the left with hundreds of white shells hanging on the wall, then another on the right, full of very old but not antique furniture jumbled together, as if it were a temporary store-room, then I turn to the left again and again to the right and no longer know where I am. I open a door: a bedroom. Another: a little room. A study where there is the unexpected ticking of a telex. Then, continuing to open doors, finally I see a washhand basin as big as the stone where I and Lenta went to do the washing, surmounted by a mirror decorated with gilt blossoms in Liberty style. And above the basin with its silver taps, a terrifying figure which seems to give off a smell of fumigation: the portrait of an old woman whom the steam from the hot water has totally discoloured. The original *pointillage* has come undone in little streaks and drops. The only thing remaining intact is the look with its exaggerated desire to transmit an authority worthy of Lucifer. The grey hair is a shapeless mass of brush-strokes by now, tangled by the damp. It vaguely resembles the late nineteenth century portraits of the benefactresses in the Municipal Hospital in Brescia: the bust, an imposing one, is covered up to the neck by a black dress, with round the neck a white ribbon with an enamel oval in which there is a little worn white figure. In her right hand she holds a rolled parchment and in her left hand a rather bizarre iron with painted on it in a semi-circle reddish-black letters, but the two in the middle are still a fiery red (the signature of the painter?): 8Ϩ6I Ǝ⅃ꟼAႱOꓷ, maybe a Greek – instinctively I turn my eyes to the mirror: DOJAPLE 1958. It is a branding-iron. And she is the old, white-and-black woman in the photo.

'I hope the portrait of the late Madame d'Orian didn't frighten you too much,' says the voice of Geneviève behind me. 'Oh, don't make excuses – I understand the curiosity of youth,' she goes on.

'I'm really sorry, Geneviève, I didn't mean to go all over the house, I couldn't find it,' I say profoundly embarrassed. I want to go. I shall never set foot here again. And then an exaggerated phrase comes to mind: if I get away with it.

'The bathroom was in fact at the end on the right but down there,' she says pointing to a door in the hall. 'Do you like the way it is furnished?'

She is still in the door. Her figure towers over me.

'Oh, it is marvellous, I adore pop art. And then the idea of putting your mother's portrait in the toilet, in the bathroom, I do beg your pardon – a delicious idea!'

She sighs and holds out her hand for me to kiss.

'Oh, ma chère, you are so intelligent. So quick. I can trust you, I feel it,' and she steps aside, giving me a caress on what remains of my curls. She can trust me, she feels it. But I don't.

The only thing it would interest me to know is how an albino functions physiologically and if this venerable gardener, who even uses the singular in a funny way, who at table gave me a look of total smugness, masturbates by sticking tubers up his behind. And what does Suzanne's pastoral act hide, in what kind of state of expectancy does she live – but these are not suitable topics for such a formal dinner.

'Oh but in this case one can also make a Macumba. One takes various tropical plants, such as pineapple, cryptanthus, orchids or others which live as parasites on a fragment of the trunk of a palm called Xaxine and –'

Then after the dessert and the coffee I get up and say:

'It has been a marvellous dinner: excuse me but I have to go. No, Arlette, do stay. I have an appointment. I'll see you this evening. Goodbye.'

Everyone gaped at my unexpected exit, I give Suzanne and Geneviève a little kiss and am already in the breakfast-room – ceiling with blue and white caissons.

'You've behaved like a brute,' says Arlette, she too barring my way, whispering. 'Half-an-hour in the bathroom and not a word. After all I have done for you. It's inadmissible.'

I don't want to give her new reasons, very recent ones: I have decided not to make blunders and I won't do so now.

'You know that on Sunday I want to be free to do as I like. So make your own arrangements for next Sunday. It's your fault – you shouldn't have brought me here. I don't have to amuse anyone. Ciao, let me go.'

'I'm coming too.'

'No, you stay or go home alone.'

'Right. You'll find your suitcase with the concierge, this time it's for real, don't think you'll get away with it. And don't even come up. Geneviève will be furious.'

'You're wrong, Geneviève has more sympathy for me than you think –'

'Maybe. Would you kindly give me my keys? The keys, please.'

'Oh no, not the keys, that's too easy, I'll give you them when I feel like it.'

'Oh yes? then I'll call the police. And then you'll lose your job at the bank.'

'Do as you like.'

'But,' says Suzanne, also coming towards us with her showy flowing dress of impalpable black satin covered with a gigantic poppy and tiny lilac lilies. 'We are going up into the garden, are you sure you don't want to come with us? Oh, I understand. Goodbye, *mon petit choux.*'

Suzanne opens the door and takes Arlette's arm, Geneviève appears in the background and waves her hand feebly. Geneviève's hand is bigger than mine, I think she is a little ashamed of it. For this reason she uses it always in a slightly remote and cautious way. In itself it could be a rapacious hand, even with all the delicacy it has when lifting things or laying them down. In my part of the world there are legends about men who with hands like that kill calves with a single blow. (Suddenly I notice that Geneviève's windows are like those in the bank, that is, it isn't at all necessary to risk your neck to clean the panes by clambering on to the ledge; all you would need do is pull back the shutters. Either Geneviève is mad or else she made a bet or is an exhibitionist. The fact remains that Geneviève up there was doing anything but cleaning the windows.) And I go out with the feeling that that faraway look of hers was like a shovel to gather something up and put it out of the house. Or maybe I am mistaken. Certainly I have disappointed her a little. But I didn't mean to offend her or be lacking in respect towards her. I call the lift, the door shuts behind me, once again Suzanne's flowered arm puts an obstacle between Arlette and my flight.

What happiness to be out of there! I feel like a hare that has escaped a lot of snares all at once. Who knows whether they are peering at me through the glass eye in the door – but I don't care, no lift, I see it as a cage which will deposit me in some unimagined and gloomy place. I begin to run down through the six floors. Free! With a thousand and more verses in my fingers to turn into poetry with my phantom, such a nice fellow, chains of tender hay which defy the impact of the one hundred and twenty-five stairs. It is a cloak of memories made from nothing, fiery brandmarks from which I shall free myself, which I shall peel off, I shall never belong once and for all. An afternoon of signals exchanged, my afternoon as a living being!

SHIFTING SANDS

I like the rhythm of sentimental enticement, to say certain words, to assume certain attitudes, to shape them like those of the other until they become in an illusory way an exact projection of his most unconfessable desires, so that in the end he entrusts me with his *soul*, throws it to me to feed on. And immediately afterwards I like to disappear like a mirage and to leave a desert when I am no longer there, a perfect specular fit with my partner – who is not a causal one. It is a kind of vendetta against Giacomino, which strikes everyone but him. I like to invade a person's life with my presence, making and unmaking its existence, almost always changing him into one which no longer knows who he is when I take my leave because I never reveal the code-word to break the spell. Like crumbling a loaf and leaving it there to decompose until time forces the crumbs to reach out to each other and come together again to find once more a kind of unity. In a sense because one has after all to live with a 'self', one cannot live with a 'self' that is in pieces. These immense forces set in motion to bring the scattered fragments back to a point of origin . . . . –

'If you could relax the leg a little –'

I shall have, infirm as I am in mind and limb, my lovely clutch of ghosts to keep me company and at the centenary of our death I shall have myself photographed and printed in the parish journal of the world. It will be a surprise for everyone, because by continuing to exist I shall have managed to render visible all the failed lives and . . . .

'Monsieur, we're not managing, if you do that you risk breaking my needle.' Then as for me and Giacomino, God – that is the only possible word for it – will have to summon me as absolute judge before giving him the position that he merits, let's say, in the beyond, and I shall be implacable: I shall destine him to be at my side until the end of time, both of us wandering through the universe and every second of that timeless time will inflict on my betrayed love, my humiliated pride, tortures neither more nor less terrestrial (tons of ice cream up to the chin, precipitous river-banks – not a single chain) until I manage to make him understand, through my sidereal hatred, the absolute nature of my love here, on this earth, now. And I shall begin again from the beginning.

'The liquid has all run out, we shall have to start again. Rub your thigh meantime – and relax, for heaven's sake. Let's see.' Maurice said to me: 'Think, if you too made some woman – a wreck like mine – have children, we could swap them, living companions for old age! And don't worry – the worst illness one can pick up in Paris isn't that, *mais de perdre sa vie par délicatesse.*'

And Lucia has written to me: 'Here the boat is leaking everywhere. There's always an IOU that holds everything up, I don't even have time to cash my salary. And you are away and don't send me a lira home. As for health, there's too much of it. Carolina is at her last gasp, she sends a greeting; they have put her other hip in plaster too, it's as if she were dissolving inside the plaster. Your little nieces are well, they keeping asking about you. And I beg you – do send me back this letter too with the mistakes underlined, I hope there are fewer of them this time.' Letters that get colder and colder, more laconic; perhaps she has begun to be ashamed of me: Catholic sister, active in the Christian Democrat Party, ashamed of a declared homosexual with Communist leanings and an adventurer who *knocks about the world.* The village doesn't forgive things: and who knows what sort of subtle annoyances they make my parents endure. As for my father – my mother doesn't bother too much about this business with men – he, the fine neo-realist Italian stud, who has brought into the world someone *abnormal.*

'You've never done this before, Monsieur, it's the first time. Don't you feel well?' How pleased he was – how pleased they all were – when the carabinieri turned up at home to tell him that his son had been accused of a theft at the Swan Hotel; and all these interrogations and that shadowing – as far as Milan even – everyone convinced that I was going to sell off the *jewels.* 'Put him inside,' said my father, 'at least there'll be an end to it for a while,' and that melancholy bitch of a proprietress and the carabiniere sergeant and a big industrialist, her boy-friend, consoling her at the trial, and me going mad because I knew they had had an eye on me to set me up because of my political talk in the bar and among the stupid blindfold youth of the village. But there were no proofs – and there they were already preparing the statement in which I confessed to something about which I was in the dark and the first pains in the cheek, in the temples, under the chin and up to the other temple, and my refusing to sign; I was so innocent that I could only have invented all my defence. In Milan they had discovered only one thing: that I went to the Storkino – a *chic* bar of *ill-repute* – and they had written 'he meets the exiled ballet-dancer Nureyev' only because he had courted me unrelentingly for three evenings in a row, 'he prostitutes himself to men' and it wasn't true yet. But their rage – the rage of my parents and of the others – was at my obstinacy, the fact that I wouldn't give in – 'confess, it's better, in any case you'll get away with a suspended sentence' – but I said no: I wasn't having it that someone should take the liberty of creating terrorism *in vitro* with me. If they so badly needed terrorist acts like those that are blossoming now, they could look elsewhere. I go down the stairs after the trial – not guilty because of insufficient evidence – and, splash, a fine gob in the face of the suffering cow from the Swan, supported in her agony, by that well-heeled boy-friend of hers who she was having it off with. I was rabid; and then right away I was called up and there my trigeminous nerve really exploded and they kept stuffing me full of cibalgine, those stupid employees of the state. And then my father sends me a photograph and a little news paragraph cut from the provincial paper: two faces, did I recognize them? Of course: they were those two, a couple of hotel sneak thieves, who had been at the Swan that time. In fact the stolen stuff was found – and no one came to apologize to me. Neither the cow nor the state. And she, the cow, whom they almost made shut the hotel because she hadn't filled up those clients' *fiches*, but everyone knows how often the carabinieri came there on a Sunday for a free meal, better to shut up about it all, everyone knew that they let out rooms and didn't fill up the documents. And I had escaped from the claws of *justice*. And from those of the army as well! And my psychological terrorism had been really strengthened: 'Your father didn't send you that cut-

193

ting for your sake, don't you believe it, he'd have preferred the suspicion to stick to you for the rest of your life; he did it because the Party asked him to, they were afraid the affair could affect the whole family, your sister in particular; seeing that those two had been arrested and had made a list of the hotels they visited, he might as well have got you out of the scrape in a gesture of paternal generosity' somebody from the police station told me later.

'That's that. Let's hope it goes better tomorrow, you put me into a cold sweat today, Monsieur,' says the nurse as she goes off.

At the photocopying machine there is a queue to the door and a colleague in my place, furious. No one knows that I go upstairs to get injections.

'Ah! et vous voilà, vous!'

'How many?'

'The whole lot.'

Giacomino – I don't think about you. Neither in my dreams nor in my thoughts, but only when I make an effort of memory: and during the business with the jewels, if you please, it was better if we didn't see each other, you know how it is, not even by night, and, please, don't greet me in the street, people talk so.

'I didn't have the heart to let you go in this rain. You always win. Lie down beside me, forgive me. But where were you last night? I've forgiven you already. Give me a glass of apple-juice. I have cooked some sausages, there's still a couple in the fridge if you are hungry. Where did you sleep, last night? Your voice, I want your voice. Speak, say something to me –' Arlette is a burst of machine-gun fire of worried phrases, which are a little incongruous because of the effort to get them all out without forgetting a single one.

'I'm hungry.'

'Please, you'll have plenty of time to eat later. Or else speak with your mouth full as usual. What did you do yesterday? Who put you up? you look terrible. When your face is tired there's no one to match you, the very words you say take on another shape.'

'Are you going to your parents this Saturday?'

'Yes, it's a promise. The one about the canary, for instance, I like it so much.'

I take off my shirt and my soaking black trousers and serve myself some sausages. I ask myself what I am doing here, in the midst of these apocryphal versions of existence.

'Have you ever heard Geneviève speak in – I don't know – a debate, a trial?'

'No. What is it now?'

'I can't even imagine her, the way she is – not a word to say – no, that's not it, it's that – how is it possible that someone with four degrees never says anything sensible or not sensible but always so full of hints, I mean, so difficult to grasp that it cast even doubts on the accuracy of any reaction on the part of her listener.'

'That's the effect she has on you. With her colleagues at the Ministry it certainly wouldn't be like that. Do you want to talk about Geneviève? I don't. I want to talk about the two of us.'

'What two of us? I want to take a little trip to Italy, I want to ask the bank to let me have my leave early.'

'But you have only been working for two and a half months!'

'What does that matter?'

'I'll come with you.'

I don't even answer her, I get up from the table without looking at her and make for the door.

'No, wait – I was joking.'

She drags me back from the corridor, she makes me sit down again. She goes into the bathroom to hide her tears. Lucky her, at least she can weep. But I don't fall for it. Besides I feel I am suffocating here, I see no bright porthole anywhere and there is a dull noise wherever I bang my head. Like yesterday. That décor and that portrait gave off a violent and sacrificial pain, the smell of burning flesh came from that decomposed portrait. But I don't want to find out any more, I only want to go away for a little.

'I want to go alone to Italy. It will be good for both of us. We need to rest, to think things over. I can't with you beside me, Arlette. You suck me up like a sponge,' I say out loud, without addressing her, imagining that that's exactly what she is expecting in there. She comes out saying:

'The canary. I'm done in too.'

'But you do nothing to improve the situation.'

'Nor do you, if it comes to that.'

'But what more am I supposed to do?' I cry desperately. She looks at her nails a little, presses the cuticle, thumb against thumb, and removes it:

195

'You know.'

'I am a canary and it is not true that I am stupid like one of my breed. First of all I am yellow, the colour of intelligence, then I sing and sing well because I have studied the musical knack of songs of praise –'

'Not so mechanically, put more inflections into it, make the right pauses.'

'Dressed in yellow and radiating notes from my throat beyond my cage, who remains insensible to my presence? The lettuce leaf hangs there fresh and the little containers of water and bird-seed are full and often refilled. A canary like me is afraid of nothing and gets used to everything. Besides I was born in a cage and in a cage I have continued to live. Peacefully. There are canaries that complain all day long about their cage. What annoys me is that they sing like me and no one will ever know that the same song does not arise from the same causes: I am happy, they aren't. An intelligent canary like me dies where it has lived: in its cage. My cage is my natural environment and a congenial one into the bargain. If by misfortune one leaves the cage and gets lost one dies much sooner: not so much for lack of bird-seed as through home-sickness for one's dwelling-place. They wanted to persuade me to try to escape, poor fools, that then let themselves fall into space, resigned and old before their time. And it is this that makes me sing for happiness: the fact that I know all the bitter ups and downs of the rebel canaries who fled from their masters' cage because they were fickle and megalomaniac, all the ups and downs of concepts like 'intensity' and 'quality' and 'liberty' without having had to experience them personally. I have the advantage of having suffered the experiences of beings like myself, let's put it that way, of which I can talk with knowledge of the subject and with elegance, but here in the warmth, a darling of men, with my bird-seed, my lettuce-leaf, my little basin of water which is always renewed, always within reach of my beak. And my song is a clear melody offered to this order that reigns in the world as it is, a song which I perfect from hour to hour and which I have made into the goal of my life.'

'You are a darling. But promise me that one day you will take me to Venice. The gondolas, the pigeons, the high tides.'

'Milk up to the knees –'

'What?'

'It's an Italian expression: to have milk up to one's knees. And I can tell you – Freud doesn't come into it: it means to be bored to death.'

To lie down beside Arlette now will be a torture; she has the face of someone who means to make a night of it. I am better than any comic opera. Maybe the Colonel is already packing, shall I be in time? The last time I saw my mother and Lucia was exactly a year ago in Rimini. I persuaded Lofty to give up the idea of Capri and go to Rimini because my mother had gone there – to work for the season. It was the first time she had seen the sea and the first time she had left home, to be among strangers, to work: the last inn had turned out to be a fiasco too. My father agreed; the important thing was that someone brought money into the house, how didn't matter. Lofty went on to Rimini; I stopped at Montichiari and brought my sister with me, paying for the trip. At Rimini I found my mother in the hotel kitchen, all alone; she was weeping in silence. Not only because of the onions. And because they hadn't told her we were there, she knew nothing, we wanted to give her a surprise. And what a surprise! I hadn't seen her for five months and she seemed to me to have got ten years older. We asked her what she was crying for, she said: Nothing, the onions of course. But you are crying for some other reason. She had come to the end of her energies, notable though they were, that was why: for two months up from six in the morning till eleven at night. Without an hour's rest in the afternoon, without an hour to put her bad leg in the warm sand. Damn these people in Rimini. I swung round, went to the proprietor and told him exactly what I thought with her behind me saying not to do it, that she would lose the job, that I was stupid, that all bosses are the same. But she didn't lose her job and for the week we stayed there she could go out for two hours every afternoon; she sat in the deck-chair under the big umbrella, incredulous, timorous, scarcely raising the long overall so that the rays of the sun could warm her phlebitis, and the two of us – the three of us, rather with Lofty, sitting round her listening to her talking about the hundreds of chickens she had plucked, to the rooms that had to be done, the floors to scrub; each day she said the same things, but we were unfair when we looked at each other as if to say 'what a bore!': for her the hundreds of chickens were always new. I already had some experience, knew something about the cruelty of hotel work, all ex-waiters or peasants

197

who had got rich and were dying to treat others as they had been treated themselves, doubling the dose if possible. And no insurance, nothing for accidents, nothing at all. And now to sit and listen to her had become boring. Ah, well, she would say, how shall we manage this winter, Dario changes jobs every month and he spends more than he earns and with three little children he's always asking for more, never giving anything. Dolfo, oh him, however much he earns, she eats it up, the bitch, and that other one, *the good-looker*, has no wish to work, never had, it will be up to me: a mother can manage to keep twelve children and a husband, but twelve children –' and she contemplated the enormity of her damnably true proverbs.

'What are you thinking about?' asks Arlette turning towards me. I'd like to say: what do you think of that portrait of Madame d'Orian, why do you think Geneviève put it in the bathroom?

'Nothing, I was dozing off. I was listening to the sound of the rain.'

'I exist so little for you –'

'Come on, don't start, I don't want to quarrel.'

'If we don't quarrel, what's left?' she says bitterly. She has learnt from me the rhetorical technique of throwing out words at random without having any idea in her head and then finishing the sentences on the basis of what was unreflectingly said to begin with: usually this gives birth to lines which are not altogether idiotic, which make one think. But for me, unlike her, words, even the most ephemeral ones are facts, as heavy as fetters, they leave deep marks. For example, to transform the name of that painter using Dürer's private symbolism – signing his name backwards – from 8₂9₁ ɘlqɒjoD to Dojaple 1958 (May?) and from there on – there would be no end to stimulating one's imagination. But not her: she ventures but subsides at once. Take my little stories: which I invent (at least the first time) on the spot: she hears only the sound, but I, while I am saying it, am already exploring the other side of the mirror, like archaeological zones one has always had in front of one's eyes which unexpectedly come to light anew and offer treasure all still to be catalogued. If it were only a question of keeping her amused somehow I wouldn't make this trifling effort. And I am the first to be amused by it. From the moment no one ever said anything to me, I say to myself all I'd like to have said to me as well as all I wouldn't like. And I start up again with a rush. Pretext: love.

'I love you. Like a viper which has turned good after the peasants have left, I make my tongue go here and there in search of the enemy, Miss Weasel, to make peace, now that the countryside belongs to us alone and the Christian Democrats are in the government for ever. I love you as the steps love the dance, words the voice, caresses the skin, armpits to be tickled, the moon its well, Jean d'Arc his little bit of a pyre. I love you. For the unknown life that you make vault over the mere sensation of existing . . . Pattern of mute words laid out on the territory – it is unauthentically and unnecessarily large – over which we constantly stumble. To want to say something that tastes of the prohibited loves of adolescence in cellars on trucks in garages, in unfinished houses. To talk about Giacomino as if it were yesterday, to see him again. Today, day of a day, what remains of me? The impossibility of sleeping, a bellyfull of rain-water, a sense of nausea, and empty and without real pain. All the clocks have stopped and I have never myself known the sun. I have gone to live in cold countries and have sought in vain to win enough time to live to some advantage. The mists shrivelled one's breath and, like an empty bubble, I arrived here, where I have women friends who dream of *Allgold* not even being Jews and where Saint Fleming is celebrated. In the remote fjords there remains the spectral music that enchants the pines and the white whales and the head that has risen to the surface of the water encloses in its eyes the melancholy of the ices which have never met a current of warm water. By night I go out and put into my flute all the lament the days have imprisoned. I touch barks into which are cut pierced hearts to find my way back to the road that leads to the lair of the white bear –'

Arlette says excitedly: 'Let's give it a title.'

'Yes. *A wandering non-Jew arrives at Animal Farm* and it has got nothing to do with all this, Arlette. It doesn't even help me to unveil the mystery of Geneviève.'

'What mystery?' she asks in a tone which does not admit of rejoinder. 'You are hypersensitive. What if the mystery consists simply in the lack of one?'

There: she is copying me, she is saying the things which up to now I have only heard myself say. She draws nearer to the truth by moving away from it on purpose, distancing herself from the words. But there is a touch of new cunning in her, necessity sharpens the wits.

'All right, now I'd like to sleep, if I have to listen to myself even

199

when you are talking, one might as well sleep.'

'But you don't really want to go to sleep now, at ten!'

'Look and see if my eyes aren't weeping with fatigue. And tomorrow I have to have the analysis and again in the evening I have to go to college and I still haven't done all the exercises.'

'There are still all the dishes to wash and this lavatory needs a good clean. And you haven't even had a bath.'

'And you tell me now, when we are in bed? Don't you think it's a bit much?'

'Have you looked to see if you have crabs?'

'OK then.'

I go into the bathroom and obviously don't even look to see if I have crabs. I am still thinking of Geneviève. I lock the door and set to work. The thought of which had so upset me when I was about to go on stage at the Folies-Bergère. I begin with the pubic region, first of all without a lather and with the scissors, then with lather and the razor. But what strange dexterity in my fingertips! the feeling of having done it daily for years. And I continue with the chest, under the armpits, I go down over the hips. Whistling. That's it done. Then I look at myself in the mirror, my eyes are really red. I go under the shower, I soap myself with a sulphurated liquid, let it dry for ten minutes, I became totally white, then I rinse myself. And have wakened myself up completely.

'Is that OK now?' I say presenting myself naked to Arlette. She bursts into a loud laugh:

'Heavens, how funny you are like that, all plucked, you look just like –' and she stops suddenly as if thunderstruck.

'Who?' I asked as if nothing had happened, continuing to dry my hair. Geneviève?

'Pablo. He didn't have a single hair,' she says, looking away.

'Well, hair or not, you're not even getting a nibble tonight. Goodnight.' I put on underpants and pyjamas.

'You're vulgar. As if I were interested.'

'Who knows what interests you! Who knows what you have in that little head of yours. Do you really believe that if someone comes and tells me that this morning you robbed a bank or initiated ten immigrants into love in the second-class carriage, I won't believe it!'

'Come on. Tell me the one about the Greco-Roman wrestler and then we'll sleep. Tomorrow I'll ask the concierge to clean the flat.'

'But these are stories I've told you dozens of times and they never really end!'

'But this one is an exception. This time there's an ending. And I beg you not to change it.'

'Ah, this mad desire for an ending! It's the story of the mother of the Greco-Roman wrestler who played it very free and easy, and was often disqualified because, for example, he was too good at punches in the pit of the stomach and, when he looked at his adversary's eyes, instead of punching him with a clenched fist he let fly with open fingers and blinded them all. I know a bit about that. But thanks to his curly blond hair with its long ringlets, to his fine presence and what I might call his physical beauty, he always managed to be let back into the ring to popular acclaim and he had such success with the Norwegian public that the television was forced to follow him in his continual moves from place to place and to cover live all his extravagant performances. Even if Norwegian television would have preferred to film nothing but reindeer feeding all the time, because the camera movements are easy and it's not so essential for the shooting to be live. His mum, an English widow who had been transplanted ages ago to Oslo or maybe Stockholm, settled in her armchair, the teapot at her side, wholemeal biscuits, brown sugar, and turned on the television. Up to a year before she had managed to do it without getting up, simply by stretching out her right foot and pressing the button with her big toe which was very large and dirty with nicotine. But for a year she had become too old and heavy, her leg was always tired, she couldn't manage to lift it any longer and the other wasn't trained at all to change channels – where sometimes there were a few less reindeer, sometimes a few more. She vaguely watched her son bounce into the air for a very long time – as only true illusionists know how – and calmly sipped her tea, without making mental comments, without saying a word to herself. Besides she was alone in the house and she hated animals. Maybe she would have wanted to have one, being English, a puppy, a cat, a budgie maybe, but they dirty things all over the place, you have to feed them, continually let them out and in, otherwise they complain and budgies in general never come back. No, better not. Perhaps if she had been given one, she would have kept it and looked after it properly, simply out of courtesy. But she did not know anyone apart from the postman who brought her her pension once every two months and postmen never give presents. When the match was finishing – and the wrestler's mother was even more tired than before from trying to follow the plot of that soap opera about reindeer – there came to her mind the good old days in Johannesburg when niggers were niggers and that was that. Her leg no longer obeyed her, it was necessary to get up again to put off the set, she shook the teapot, which was empty by now, she filled it up again with water, put in the plug and looking in front of her thought of things about which a wrestler's mother rarely thinks. But she didn't forget a single one. The son came home late, accompanied by applause right up to the door. She had been sleeping for a while, with her teapot and the wholemeal biscuits and the brown sugar on her little bedside table, the light turned very low. He threw himself on her still dressed in that dressing gown with 'Barby's' in dazzling letters on the back, and set about taking the curlers out of her hair so as not to pull off the wig, he took her by her enormous big toe and twisting it with all his strength punched her with his head between the tits and whispered to her so as not to wake her: "I hope you are in form tonight, mummy, the last training session wasn't much use".'

'What a model story, darling. I'd never get tired of hearing it. In that punch with the head between the breasts I feel all the virulence of my sublimated breast-feeding. What's this – sleeping already? perhaps you need a coffee, I'll make a coffee.'

'No, please – I don't want any coffee, I only want –'

'I didn't ask whether you want a coffee, I said I was going to make a coffee. You're at liberty not to drink it, but you'd have some cheek to have me make a coffee and then not drink it... Put on some Chopin meantime, get out the cups... No, not like that – with saucers and two teaspoons, the sugar-bowl. Look, it's going at 45 rpm. Freshen yourself up again, it's only two, maybe we can go out, let's go to Les Halles, you look like a mummy. Sleep is a waste of life.'

'One day I'll kill you, Arlette.'

'You can't. Done it already. There, that's it – a coffee like that deserves a reward, come on, please – it's even nicer with Chopin.'

'Well, are you coming or not? I can't put it off any longer,' says Colonel Dreyfus at the other end of the line.

'Have patience for another day or two, I'm in a confused situation,

I have to wait for my monthly pay and it'll soon be the twenty-seventh.'

'Well, this year I feel so little like going that I prefer to wait rather than go alone. And I warn you – there's nothing to do except stay in the mountain-hut and climb up to the sanatorium. And we're a long way from the centre and there's no bus. The only male about the place is a wolf-hound in the hotel.'

'But do you want me to come or are you going back on your word?'

'Of course I want you to come!'

'Then why are you telling me all this? It looks as if you want to put me off.' But I couldn't be put off, I have a mad desire within me when I think of seeing my mother and Lucia again.

'But you mustn't think it's a place for skiers with après-ski punch. It's an interval in *Traviata*. When can you give me a definite answer?'

'The day after tomorrow.'

'If that's what you want,' says Arlette, 'I'll come to Italy with you. I'll stay in the hotel, I'll give you as little trouble as possible. There's bound to be an hotel in this blessed place you keep talking about.'

'There's no point even in talking about it. I have to go to Monti-chiari alone, I wouldn't have time for you, then I have to see some people in Milan, move about. And then I want to sleep, to sleep, maybe I don't make it clear, I'm worn out by these sleepless nights. Oh, how simple it would be to screw you a couple of times and finally turn the other way and sleep in peace.'

'There, you've said it.'

'Ah b...,' and I think that she's really not very pretty, and that she doesn't take off her glasses even when she is sleeping and that women with glasses only make an impression when they bump into someone. I am astonished at this substratum of vulgarity, worthy of a provincial Don Juan, in my calculations.

'And since you don't do it you are forced to be my minstrel,' she adds with peremptory simplicity, 'Not that I mind, perhaps I am getting used to your stories. You put so much into them!'

'And at least they don't cause abortions.'

'Well, that's not a reason. Today I could even keep a baby.'

I get a lump in my throat and when it clears I have already fled headlong from the stable without turning back to give any caress to any Nanda.

Five o'clock. Dawn. We have left the curtains open for fear of not waking! A rosy, silky light spreads over Geneviève's cage.

'Listen, Arlette. Evidently it is difficult for me to talk about myself because I am never the same piece of lettuce but am changed every day and sometimes even twice. Since I am dependent on the hand that inserts me and the beak that eats me, I have to make some effort to pursue my identity through time, being like this between hammer and anvil. I am undoubtedly green but not always fresh. And the important thing is not to be wet. While still remaining a leaf the kind of vegetation changes: I am never the same leaf of the same salad. Mostly it is *radicchio* and lettuce but I've seen myself at other times got up as savoy, cauliflower, when a blackbird came to peck at me recently. A blackbird which incidentally came to a curious end, throttling itself while it was pushing its neck through two bars of the cage. A leaf of salad prefers to talk about others rather than itself but I am not able to adhere to this natural inclination, I am different from my companion vine leaves, apple leaves, melon leaves. I am aware of my sweetness and of my succulence and I like to talk about it. Because there is only one thing that redeems my destiny and renews my sap once it has been cut: to talk about myself until the last peck comes. Autobiography is the extreme form of life considered as *quid*. Pecked and tortured by a stupid canary which feeds and amuses itself at my cost, I have no other pleasure than to delve down again into my past, when I was still a seed and was part of a tuft of green. Leaves love each other, call each other sister and are immortal. I, for instance, am only apparently renewed. For this reason I can invent for myself any past I like, to grow in a garden or at the side of a road. What matters is not the so-called cause and the so-called effect, but the nervous texture of the capillaries which, by dilating the field of action of the sap, succeed in creating a transmissible reflex of metempsychosis. That is why a leaf is always a leaf, whether we are talking about a case of different plants for each type of leaf, or whether this true leaf is eaten right down to the stalk. In reality I am always myself, the same as before.'

'I don't take off my glasses when I am sleeping because in fact I never sleep. I stay watching you till the morning,' says Arlette, making her own kind of comment on my instalment of storytelling, as if she had read my thoughts.

'Don't tell lies, Arlette. What about the way you wake up every five minutes to tell me the latest shit that comes into your mind! When has there ever been such a thing as "till the morning" since I have been living with you? Only when you go to your people in the country and not always even then. And it's a bit much.'

'Then I keep on my glasses because I have to get up every five minutes and if I didn't have them on I'd stumble, is that all right? do you think it isn't hard on me too? that insomnia is good for me? ...to love you without the minimum of...No, keep quiet. Is that how it is? all right, let's go on like that. But don't preach at me.'

'I told you everything right from the start, I was clear, wasn't I? If it had been up to me we'd still be saying "vous" to each other. Do you remember the first weeks? I said "vous" to you and slept on the floor to disturb you as little as possible. I had terrible aches and pains but it was better than now, here, in your bed as soft as a powder-puff where you never let me sleep for ten minutes on end.'

'Sleep then, who's stopping you? Your conscience. Not me.'

I let it pass. It's odd how, meaning to strike in the opposite direction, this word *conscience* goes straight to the mark: I don't sleep because my conscience is burdened with uncommitted crimes, of hatreds not fully developed, of vendettas not carried out, of loves not responded to. And with one sole rebellion, carried out against a weak person like Gina of Cortina, a memory of which I am ashamed and which by itself is the equivalent of having a *guilty conscience*. But Arlette doesn't know this story, she's a stupid thing who hits out blindly.

'Will you take me to Italy with you?'

'No, I won't take you to Italy with me. There would be no justification for your presence where I was born. I don't want you to walk in with your little shrunken geisha's feet. For you it means something too much like a final consecration. No. And besides you're not pretty enough. If it has to be a useless journey then at least let it tickle my vanity.'

'Thank you,' she says stifling a sob; but what is the point of treating her badly? Certainly not to make her see reason: the more I attempt to make her aware of the impossibility of establishing a relationship between the two of us different from the one already existing the more the hole in the net of possibilities grows and the more everything goes through it, even the most impossible things. 'And here was I hoping at least in your affection...'

'What affection do you mean! You want something else, hen, you want me, and by *me* I don't mean goodness knows what...' and I get dressed and leave banging the door. As if in the end I had not acceded to the ritual and sacrificial desires of the old squinter as well. I felt all the stasis of this situation, this coming and going and the very dynamic of what we say, which is blocked by the circumstance that she is made 'of flesh and blood'; and every so often I have the clear, poisonous impression that Arlette is bluffing shamelessly, is doing everything, one might say, to express feelings which she does not feel and to pursue through me things which go over my head. If I were to come home and catch her stirring into a cauldron toads and bats and human marrow and nettles and she were an old woman, as leathery as parchment, preparing the philtre of youth for another day for herself and her two friends, I wouldn't be surprised. Arlette is normal.

I set out for a bench in the Tuileries, in any case it is almost day and I don't feel like waking the Colonel; then I go to the bank, draw my wage, the usual moan to M. Rigot about my mum not being well, I go to Dr Chang with the envelope with the new analyses, a distinct improvement, look in at home since Arlette is certain to be in the office and take the two suitcases – but I leave a good deal of stuff there so that she doesn't think I have disappeared entirely, and go to the Colonel's *hôtel particulier* to leave the suitcases there.

'Oh, at last! we'll take the train tonight and tomorrow morning we're there. Nougatine has never stopped phoning me, she has a part in *Antigone* and at all costs wants me not to miss the performance. She knows you're coming too. There's only one thing I ask you to remember – Nougatine knows nothing, you understand... we've known each other for more than forty years. Don't spoil the question marks. It's the only thing she knows about me, a good job that I didn't go there before! She was no doubt counting on making me stay for another two weeks, the excuse being *Antigone*.'

'All right, don't worry. Forty years that you've known each other and, I mean to say, she is still wondering how one thing doesn't square with another? Funny. But I mean to say, did she never lose her head over you? It's so difficult to have a woman who's just a friend pure and simple.'

'Once we were on a lake in the north of Madagascar; it feels like going back to before the Flood; what were we doing there? The usual things – putting down rebellions, inflicting wounds on behalf of the government and then bandaging things up. A camp. Well, on a landing-stage, I don't know how it was, I – or perhaps it was her – in short we kissed each other on the mouth. The first and last. I had no special feelings for her, friendship, respect; we never spoke of it again,' and from the couchette above mine I hear him once again unscrew his little iron bottle, the water-bottle that accompanies him everywhere.

'And yet after forty years you still see each other. It's a very odd story. Another of the ones that have never begun, never developed, with any sort of end.'

'You've put it very well. They are the only bearable ones. Either to live them or to tell them. The only ones that come close to a possible idea of *reality*. She'd like me to go and live with her, she has a house on the Atlantic at Mimizan, she's from there; she stays there six months of the year and when it begins to get too hot she goes up into the mountains. It's not ruled out that one day I won't decide to go there. It's a welcoming house, very clean. But you know, it's one thing to go there two or three times a year and another to live there,' the bottle is unscrewed and screwed up again more and more frenetically.

'It might come out that I owe her explanations, how do I know what is floating about in Nougatine's head? I don't feel very much like it. At our age women invent unending regrets. And I don't feel like it. You obviously got syphilis going with women. A little bit of an act, but in any case she doesn't ask questions.'

And before he begins to mutter in that increasingly incomprehensible manner, he says again, but almost to himself:

'The real gratuitous act is never to have committed one. It doesn't exist. For me these two were in agreement in a Gide-like way... And then, in any case, today...on these modern trains...little automatic windows, automatic doors. Impossible. Ballocks, ballocks.'

And here she is, Nougatine who comes towards us gaily, rising from the divan in the hall of the Kurhotel; a little butterfly, even smaller than Arlette, thirty years older, but you wouldn't think so, she could be her small elder sister witch, so light, with round her head a scarf of white silk, dressed in an extremely light suit of beige linen, and old green brooch, picked out with little red drops, worn high on her left shoulder. She dances towards us, but before she has gone five metres stops and coughs once and smiles to us, almost as if apologizing for the fact that the scene of welcome had not been as perfect as she had hoped. And the kisses and embraces – the Colonel lifts her from the ground and twirls her round in his arms. What a hypocrite. And what suffering, truth and sincerity there is in that hypocrisy. How well I know this destructive masquerade of 'now we'll never part again' and one is already in one's mind at one's next goal, alone at last.

'Oh my poor head,' says Nougatine in a self-mocking tone, giving me her hand. 'How nice! Oh heavens, how jealous they will all be! Two gentlemen all for me! thank you, thank you for being here.' Maybe her dream was to play the supporting role to the Duse. And it was nothing but chatter between the two of them, and embracing each other and removing non-existent hairs from each other's clothes and walking to and fro, paying no attention to me, with her gesticulating as she dances, the dramatic movements of her arms which always describe an arc, the rotundity of the memories at the far end of the infinite corridor before turning towards me, the good times together, the road that lay before them.... And the Colonel who keeps saying 'Yes, yes' and is cut off to his great relief in mid-sentence, the adrenalin of the old which is transformed into wax in their ears and in ten minutes everything has become the deafness of an exultant and mechanical repertory that is always the same. And she who is now going all round the hall carrying out an inspection and makes brief gestures to this or that divan, ladies sitting alone, one reading the white spaces of a book, another looking out at the pine-covered precipice, yet another doing her nails this morning as well. No one knitting. If my mother arrived here they would all shortly be knitting together straight from a flock of sheep. And the two of them a few yards from me, Nougatine gives me a refined smile of welcome and then both turn on their heels again, in a slightly military way, and once more start pacing the corridor in the other direction, always a little less excited and a little more deaf.

An extremely beautiful woman appears in a door and gazes at me for an instant: black trousers, a very low-cut clinging red blouse, an enormous mass of raven hair and two eyes burning with direct, impatient, brutal desire. She gives me a sign, tells me to come into her room. I pretend I haven't noticed and go up to Nougatine and the Colonel, shaken by this sudden and desperate invitation, like a sentence against which there is no appeal. The woman has disappeared. I hope no one has noticed her gesture, I feel an instinct to protect her; but I feel on me the eyes of dozens of single women, some of them very young, all with an uneasy look in their eyes, some of disgust, some of entreaty. Nougatine runs quickly to her room to fetch something.

'You were right. They seem all to have been let loose. Let's leave, I feel as if I were dying of embarrassment,' I say in a low voice to Jacques.

'Now we are going to lunch with Nougatine at the pensione.'

The air is fresh in spite of the sun, the little snow that had fallen during the night is soft underfoot and Nougatine has thrown over her shoulders a white woollen shawl shot with gold lamé and in between us takes both our arms.

'When do we begin the injections?' she asks with a smile.

'This very day, in fact, right away, after lunch, if you don't mind.'

'Do you like it here?' and she answers herself. 'A marvellous place. A little isolated. Oh but we have a little cinema with a huge stage, a real little theatre. You'll see, a darling of a theatre.'

'Don't talk so fast – you know it's not good for you,' says the Colonel.

'Oh, on the contrary, it does me so much good. Here we don't talk a lot. Fortunately the play has been an excuse and we've had to communicate otherwise each one would stay in her shell. And then ... all they talk about is men.'

'And you don't like that? Don't tell fibs!' says the Colonel winking.

'Oh, you!' she exclaims very flirtatiously, wrapping herself in her shawl, 'I've never done more than talk about them.'

The Colonel makes a sudden gesture with his little gloved hand which from under Nougatine's arm opens up like the teeth of a little crane and shuts again like a vice.

'Even in the camp, do you remember?' Nougatine goes on undeterred, 'They courted me but because they all felt obliged to do so: sometimes I was the only white woman to be seen within a radius of a hundred kilometres or more, they courted me to apologize for going with the coloured women. And the regulation was clear: by paying court to me they didn't run any risk. And after a while in any case, they treated me like a comrade. No one ever noticed that I was a woman. No one.'

'Good times though, eh?' interrupts Jacques who is still playing the daft laddie. 'We were young then.'

The Colonel doesn't believe a single word of what he is saying, he has no regrets, only feelings of guilt. It is as if he wished in a secret way to carry out a lobotomy on her, cutting into her with harmless banalities. Nougatine, after a moment of reflection, withdraws her arm from his and, stopping, asks:

'And you, Jacques, what did you do with your youth?'

We are coming up to the pensione, ten rooms in all, embroidered curtains on the windows, double beds (unfortunately too narrow) – I and the Colonel have a double room. Jacques is no longer at ease. Nougatine is awaiting a response. It is even probable that my presence has unleashed in the elderly woman a desire to present herself in an unexpected light so as to demolish at one blow whatever expectations I might have had of her. Or perhaps, without making any effort to throw off ways of behaving agreed for decades, she has suddenly found a new gold-bearing vein. Down there an unexpected mine is gleaming; it is no longer possible to pretend to be deaf.

These are all suppositions on my part but in fact it doesn't look to me as if the Colonel, now standing in front of her – she is looking at him questioningly, both of them motionless on the pathway with its mossy sides – is very enthusiastic about these fuses inserted into his certainties by a woman he has known for forty years without knowing her at all. Or only in part; or else he is annoyed at having told me that she has no more mysteries for him, presents no problems of any kind, and knows hardly anything and that if by chance she has question marks, she keeps them to herself. Jacques opens the little wooden gate at the entrance, lets Nougatine and myself go in first.

'Jacques, I asked you something, my dear. What did you do with your youth?'

'But, Nougatine, darling, what sort of questions are these? How can one reply to things of that kind? What was I supposed to do with it? Ballocks, ballocks.'

'Well, I' she goes on, stopping when she has barely entered, 'as you see, have ended up here.'

210

'But you're not young any more, you're at your sunset, like me. Long live sunsets!' he exclaims, trying to shunt the discussion along the somewhat discredited lines of the old gay dog confronting death serenely.

'Long live, yes, if there has been a dawn,' continues Nougatine, who seems to have taken root in the gravel. The Colonel's little maroon-coloured hand begins to cut the air, but not a sound comes from his mouth. He is cursing mentally.

'Even twenty years ago, when I began to come here, maybe I could still have been in time to see a dawn break at last. But then I felt as if I were shutting myself up in a convent, day after day. And now you talk about a sunset and how I should be happy. My sunset has lasted since . . oh, never mind. I still remember the impression that building made on me,' she says, turning back, 'but not right away, after a week. Then, of course, it wasn't as modern as it is now, but for those days it was luxurious, the best of its kind. I had the sensation of having entered to become part of a museum. That something was finished for ever, without having ever begun.'

Then she looks at me, grasps my hand and the Colonel goes on alone towards the door. Nougatine raises her voice slightly. 'I became aware, here, that my youth had never begun, that all my tomorrows had always been the same and that those still to come would be even more so –' and there follows a volley of coughs and she timidly takes refuge behind a tiny handkerchief she holds in her hand.

'You exert yourself too much, keep calm. Oh, here we are at last.' And the proprietress, a big woman with stumpy hands like a wood-cutter and a little face like a subliminal hamster compared to the bulk of her body, comes forward masticating little words of welcome, and makes us sit at a table already set for three. The wolf-dog comes wagging his tail behind her and she shouts at it lovingly, 'You've come back, eh? wandering about all night,' she says, turning to us, 'Every night he goes down to the village, to his mother. He smells the scent and he reappears now. This time the puppies will really have to be killed. Dear Demoiselle, you see that our dear Colonel came? and you kept saying this time he won't come any more, this time he won't come any more. Do you see he's come?' the two women go on exchanging compliments, Nougatine assumes once more the airs of the supporting actress addressing an usher in

211

a theatre, she makes good-natured signs of assent with her little head and in the end sighs. We sit down at table.

'Oh, wine! but please only a drop, that's it! that's enough! you know I can't drink wine. But now there are more things I can't do than the other kind. Your healths, my dears, and thank you, thank you for coming.'

I don't have the courage to remind her about the injection, by now the vegetable broth is on the table. I don't follow what they are saying at all, which is now centred on the *applications* of the treatment, but I can't shake off what the big woman said – about the dog, the scent, the scent of... Pregnant, the puppies. But whose?

'Excuse me,' I say in a perplexed way, 'what does it mean that the dog goes down to the village to his mother every night?' I ask, already foreseeing something terrible, which will contaminate the world for ever.

The two old people look at each other in an amused way and a little surprised and then the Colonel says flatly:

'He goes down to cover her.'

'Who? his mother?'

'All animals – didn't you know?'

'No.'

'And she calls him, ululà, lets him know she is... on heat with the scent from her sex-glands,' adds Nougatine.

'I really didn't know. I... Mother and son,' and they burst out laughing and immediately begin to talk about something else. But I can't cope with the stimulus of my pitiless imagination. A feeling of nausea grips me violently: my mother has her legs open and I am on top, she has a spasm and comes and says: 'Go on, let's make a son, let's make you.'

'Excuse me,' and I rush out, in the open air I try to breathe deep into my lungs, but by now it is too late. I came back in again when I have vomited up everything including my guts.

'What's happening to you, my dear, don't you feel well? Is it the height?' Nougatine asks full of attention and concern, putting an arm round my shoulders.

'Go on – say "tu" to each other and let's get it over with. There really are people who learn *Une saison en enfer* by heart and then are in the dark about the most natural things in this world. It does happen. Is that right?'

212

'Right, Jacques, right.'

'Come then, now eat; you've dirtied your sweater,' says Nougatine and immediately rubs it off with her napkin. I pass mine over my brow, still overwhelmed with what I have learned only today, when I am over twenty-one. I who began my sexual career at four and not even in a very infantile manner.

We dip long two-pronged forks in a common earthenware pot hanging over a tripod and heated by an oil flame, we let the pieces of meat cook and then dip then in various sauces and pay the big woman repeated compliments.

'Won't you come to my place this winter either? Your little room is waiting for you, Colonel.'

'Yes, maybe the moment has come. We've had enough of this rhetoric about dawns and sunsets,' says the Colonel, licking his thick moustaches: he said it very impersonally but one can already feel the effect of the wine, which he quaffs repeatedly.

'It was you that brought it up,' says Nougatine in a low voice. And then, triumphantly: 'But what a time this is! we'll have tremendous fun! we'll go for long walks on the beach, we can even go to Bilbao to see the corridas. It's not by any means the antechamber to –'

'Oh ballocks, ballocks,' says he, thinking of all the joints he has licked with his cracked lips to persuade the young boys to let themselves be sucked off. 'It's not the antechamber to anything else either. It is an antechamber and that's all . . . No one knows the real chamber.'

'You're wrong, I,' says Nougatine without lowering her gaze from the Colonel's drawn face. For a little, absolute silence. Only the wolf-dog makes a rustling noise with its tail as it goes round the big woman's skirt. I wouldn't be surprised if . . . (I've already said so . . . often).

'But do you think that everyone feels what we felt at our age?' Nougatine goes on; in my view, she is overdoing things and if she goes on like this it will end up with the Colonel deciding to leave right away.

'Everybody,' he'd like to add: what do you know about what I feel? But he doesn't dare.

'Even those who have . . . lived?' her question must somehow have a scandalous resonance, the Colonel pops his eyes, takes his glass and empties it at one gulp. And I adore Nougatine. I could cover her with kisses. I am sure that the Colonel is on the point of getting up from the table and is making an effort to behave and stay where he is. These questions, with forty years of complicity which comes crashing down unexpectedly, must have a shattering effect. Two people drag along behind them forty years of half-questions and half-answers until there comes a guest who doesn't belong here and suddenly out pops a complete question which demands a complete answer, the need to decide on a definitive version rather than to put off once more till another more rounded and perfect but increasingly improbable and remote comes along. The crashing noise of the avalanche has no effect on Nougatine, who waits: her lips painted a gleaming orange, her brow stretched tight, the nostrils of her little potato of a nose, all seem to quiver with simple inexorable pleasure.

'Everyone, yes, everyone,' says the Colonel, summoning up his own energies. 'At our age we have all lived in the same way, we were all born on the same day and we will all die at the same instant. Happy?'

'No, not at all. I'm not everyone, and neither are you. I can say, in fact, I'd like to shout it that –' and she bangs a little fist covered with wrinkles and purplish veins on the table and a tear makes its way from the corner of her eyes,' that – that –'

'That you feel you haven't lived?' I ask her, while the Colonel looks daggers at me.

'That's it, thank you. And I can't resign myself, do you see? do you see how unpleasant that is? Oh, it's damnably unpleasant, it's a thorn here, in my head, every minute of the day and often of the night as well. I have not been –' and once more she pulls out of her sleeve the handkerchief embroidered with initials.

'Do you remember that little marching song that went "Ah, Monsieur le Capitaine, j'en ai marre des noix de coco"?' and they begin to sing and Nougatine laughs through her tears. Her voice is strong and her hand mechanically caresses the Colonel's arm; the two old people begin to sway slightly. The big woman claps her hands and joins in the chorus – undoubtedly she too has learned this little march over all these years. There is no one there but us and the mother of the big woman sitting by the fire peeling potatoes. Then the door flies open: raincoat tightly fastened at the waist, black trousers – the little that one can see – a black scarf round her chin, dark glasses. The voice says:

'A coffee, please,' I feel the glance from behind the dark lenses resting on us, perhaps on me. Nougatine makes a slight gesture with her hand to which the unknown woman replies with a similar gesture. But Nougatine does not make any invitation to the figure to come closer. But she remains as if turned to stone or bewitched, all her thoughts seem to have been sucked away.

'Shall we go upstairs for that business?' she says to me, 'we can have coffee later. Are you coming too, Jacques?'

'No, I'll wait for you here,' says the Colonel, who by now is totally absent, hidden behind the impenetrable curtain of the sensations liberated and then gagged by the wine. As I get up I notice out of the corner of my eye a piece of material flying through the air and then another: and she appears with the cascade of jet-black hair spread over her naked shoulders while she takes off raincoat and the glasses as well and, staring at me, smiles to me in a shameless manner, in spite of Nougatine, who has not missed the arrogance of that look. The eyes are grey, a long grey wing-case lines them right to the end of the eyebrows, the mouth bright red, like the blouse with the shoulder-straps she wore this morning. Her breast swells with unnatural breaths as if it wished to exhibit itself rather than perform its normal respiratory function.

'Good day,' I say to her, trying to be merely polite.

'Welcome,' she says in a hoarse voice.

'He came to see me – not you,' says Nougatine with no half-measures as she opens the door to the floor above, and taking me by the hand.

'That remains to be seen, he doesn't belong to you,' says the woman scornfully. 'I am young and I am beautiful.'

'That's enough, Marie, I don't want trouble when I have clients, you know how to behave. Otherwise go and take a walk till you have calmed down,' the big woman intervenes. 'And now drink your coffee and then go home. You know you shouldn't go out dressed like that, it's not allowed.'

'Fucking hell,' I manage to hear and the front door banging. I don't know whether the Colonel had that mocking little smile because of the scene he witnessed or other scenes which were going round in his head heedlessly after his three bottles of wine.

'Who is it?' I ask her as I enter the bedroom, seeing that Nougatine, contrary to what I had expected, made no comment. She lets there be a pause as if the time taken for a reply were all time stolen from her personally, the protagonist of our visit. It doesn't even occur to her that – at least as far as I am concerned – other protagonists have been designated. But I am not unhappy to be here for a variety of reasons, not least because I have learned something new about so-called *nature*: that it is promiscuous and pays no attention to the degrees of kinship before having *instincts* and that a living being is the more desirable the more it is desired by another, an antagonist, an *enemy* – the neighbouring dog from the valley.

Nougatine allows a sigh of resignation to escape: 'If you really want to know.' She is trying to find a way of telling me what she thinks while damping down from the start the effect it might have on me: she has no intention of making of Marie a disturbing, interesting personage, and for this reason she seeks to temper the negativity of the remarks she is about to make: 'A poor crazy thing, abandoned by every one –'

'A nymphomaniac?' I exclaim, without being very clear what this extremely crude word means.

'There, you've said it. Does she interest you?' she asks, waving the syringe, and squirting out a little penicillin.

'Well, you can't say that you come across types like that every day.'

'Keep away from her, she only causes trouble. And the sort of thing you have to be cured of now,' and she looks at me as if she wanted to put her whole little arm into me. 'A wrecker of families, even her own people can't stand her. No one ever comes to see her. Apart from –'

'Apart from?'

'Apart from a crowd of men down in the village. You'll see what a noisy pack there'll be this evening. Tonight is the new moon and it goes on like that for all the first week of every month. Among the pines, not even in a car: on the snow, the moss, a rug and that's it. If only the administration could find another place to take her. A shame, a dishonour for the institute. But they don't want her any more anywhere. Because of the male staff,' and she begins to cough and her hand shakes a little, 'there – that's done.'

'She's very young –'

'Very young, very young! Much less young than she looks. More or less my age when I arrived here – She hasn't lost any time. Not even beforehand, I mean.'

216

'Thank you,' and I throw the wad of cotton-wool into the waste-paper basket.

'No, it's better not to do that. And not the container either; give me them and I'll take them away. It's better if the proprietress doesn't see them –' and then, starting up again, because she can't contain it. 'Ten days in a row, with everyone, without sleeping, menstruating or not, and the other twenty in bed, ill, phlebotomies, antibiograms. She's already had twenty-seven abortions and she's proud of it, the mad thing. All these days she doesn't sleep, she becomes a hyena: oh, she's mad. She doesn't resign herself. I –' she looks at me, as if asking herself whether what she'd like to tell me about herself might interest me as much as what she is telling me about Marie. 'Never mind – Was I good?'

'Marvellous' and Nougatine stands up on tiptoe and gives me a little kiss on the cheek and I return it on both of hers. 'You could be my son – no – my grandson. Ah, how proud I would be to have brought in to the world something like you,' but she adds 'like you' out of expediency, because I am there – not out of conviction.

'Let's go down now. At three there's the dress rehearsal. A pity that strangers aren't allowed in. It will be a surprise. The first night is the day after tomorrow. They come up from the village in a bus: the people from the library, the mayor, the doctors with their wives. It will be such an exciting evening.'

I am dying to know whether Marie acts too and what part she has, but I am not allowed to ask, I don't want to hurt Nougatine.

'What part do you have?'

A ray of sun strikes the brooch which sizzles with beams stained with red.

'Tiresias! Oh, a very very small part! I foretell the fate of the others –' she makes a pause – 'perhaps when one doesn't have one of one's own – And then,' she goes on smiling maliciously as she opens the door to the restaurant, 'I had no choice: either Tiresias or Eurydice. Because of my cough, you know.'

The Colonel is lavishing thunderous noises and mighty whistles on the empty room and on the dog curled up by the fire: he is snoring with his arms crossed on his stomach.

'My God, he snores!' I cry in disgust, thinking of the double room to be shared with him, with that deafening mass in the bed which is already so much smaller than normal.

217

'Didn't you know?' asks Nougatine.

'No – and so the clattering of the train was – But I need to sleep!' I find myself shouting. 'Oh, I shall ask for another room immediately. I won't shut an eye. My God! let's hope they have one.'

Nougatine has seen my sudden pallor, she must have noted the sincerity of my desperation, she says:

'And I thought that –'

I understand.

'Oh heavens, half past three already, I must rush.' She gives me a kiss on the cheek and one to the Colonel, who mutters something and makes a gesture with his little maroon-coloured hand as if to chase away a fly.

Poor Colonel Dreyfus: apart from the fact that it doesn't seem accurate that Nougatine is 'a woman who doesn't ask questions', I am also profoundly convinced that she doesn't need to, that she never did, because she is one of those women of the old breed who are never ignorant of what is kept quiet. Even for forty years on end. Obviously the Colonel has to wonder if, when it comes to it, she perhaps knew or guessed, but it seems to me to be a delusion if he gave himself a definite answer so as to pigeonhole Nougatine solely on the basis of something as unconvincing as silence. He has perpetuated this childish attitude to Nougatine for dozens of years, falling finally into senescence at the very moment – who knows how long ago – when he accepted this comfortable and official interpretation of her silence and began constantly scuttling away from the sense of guilt which deals increasingly heavy blows, a fugue of blows which in the end are as deadly as a trap, assuaged by the beauty of a few adolescents scattered here and there like shining milestones on a muddy road, the one that leads to no maturity of any kind. A spoilt child, that is what the Colonel is, a muddy cul-de-sac, who has dragged behind him a pram with Nougatine in it, who had not enough autonomous energy to break loose alone and to carry on till she emerged from that quagmire that held her captive and find some other direction. Nougatine, at some distant point in time, by chance and through the obstinacy which chance injects into its victims (until they are persuaded, given the lack of anything better or of a better explanation, to transform the casual experiences of being bogged down into a choice or a *destiny*) had been sucked into the Colonel's shifting sands like a fly on to flypaper, and had begun to spin round uselessly without ever noticing the lack of movement, year after year, and as for him, he had never had the courage or the commonsense or the generosity or the sense of humour to throw her off altogether or to bring her alongside himself or to make her turn back. He had simply let her sink there and now they were like two Siamese twins who hate each other to death without being able to say it right out, because the death of the one would mean the death of the other. 'I foretell the destiny of the others,' said Nougatine sighing, 'because when one doesn't have one of one's own –': and she is by now sucked so far into the Colonel's shifting sands that she looks back with great indulgence, only so as not to see what her vision, her second-sight cannot allow her to see: that she too has had a destiny.

'Oh, done already?' asks the Colonel a good hour later, rubbing his eyes and smoothing his thick reddish-grey beard.

'I've asked for another room. I didn't know you gave these concerts. Come on, let's get on with it,' I say moving to the settle near the table and putting in front of him Sophocles' *Antigone*, which we began to read together on the train at my insistence.

'Forget it, I've other things to think about,' he says in a rough voice.

'For example?'

'Oh ballocks, ballocks – It's the first time I've heard her speak like that. She wanted to make an impression on you, on the telephone I dinned into her about your culture! Well, if she wanted to impress you she's succeeded.'

'Me? Only me? Sometimes a person begins by pretending to be in Tiresias' shoes and ends up seeing a lot of things – outside of the tragedy, I mean –'

'Now you're getting into it too? and what is there to see? when did she say she was coming back?' he asks, rising.

'Later, towards evening, towards suppertime, I imagine. I hope you don't mind about the room.'

'Not at all, it was a good idea, the hotel is empty, off-season prices. And then they are special for me. Ah, what a pity, what a pity.'

'What?' Perhaps he too needs to get things off his chest a little and can't make up his mind whether to stay or go off and sleep again, I imagine. Perhaps in the next five minutes he might do what he hasn't done all his life – change route or, better still, set himself one. Run to Nougatine, talk to her openheartedly, tell her, that is, what she knows already. The pram would break free, he and she could find a way out of some kind, *they would be rejuvenated.* 'To think that there isn't even some little chap with tuberculosis. Did you see how that woman looked at you?' he whispers in my ear, bending down and beginning to sneer, and he goes up the stairs leading to the bedroom.

I woke up suddenly, leaping up in bed. The first thing I think is: open–the–window–what–time–is–it? – why this dream? this particular one, which in a sense is out of place here because if anything I could have dreamt about the corpses of the two brothers who killed each other or of Marie naked in the snow calling on me and meantime, perhaps, being mounted by the wolf-dog and maybe she is a kind of wolf-mother (but that could never correspond to Marie) instead this unexpected and horrifying dream I have had, that little blazing heart on the girl's hip... Her – Geneviève – Madame Bonsants and a little girl: Madame Bonsants with that wave of hair standing up and that purposely rebel lock and the gold brooch and a suit of pale blue of many years ago; the little girl is like one of Degas' dancers: smaller than normal, a little white dress with shoulder straps, a pinkish ribbon somewhere and open lacework in the tulle, with her left hand she manages a hoop bigger than herself but at every revolution the hoop gives a jump which lifts the child up for a moment because two horns are attached to the hoop. Geneviève is wrapped in a black cloak. I see nothing of the faces of the three women who are holding each other's hands, I know it is them walking along with their backs to me – Geneviève's phosphorescent mane stands out against the black collar of the cloak; the girl is certanly Madame Bonsants' daughter and has two tresses of blond hair which form at the nape of her neck something between a pigtail and a plait. They continue to walk and I, invisible to myself, somehow manage to follow, I keep behind them, I am not tracking them, I am simply there, that's all. They quicken their pace. The girl stumbles on the horns of the hoop which becomes white and her little dress of white tulle falls down. Underneath she is naked, and she is losing something from her little hip: reddish liquid of some sort. There's a little heart on it, a kind of transfer which is becoming more and more red. On the transfer letters are stamped, they are the musical notes, doh–re–mi–ple–soh… PLE? Then the sudden flutter of the cloak; Geneviève all of a sudden turns towards me and Madame Bonsants' decomposed face leers, it is a skull veiled with flesh, the two dental arcs rise up, the skin begins to run. With shrunken hands she throws open the cloak and a solar light blinds me. The hoop escapes from the girl's hand, rolls towards me, a clatter of hooves, but it is Geneviève's dream that is charging at me and raising the dust. It has red eyes which dazzle me while it charges furiously at me and I avoid it by a hair's-breadth. The white bull has disappeared behind me where I can't see. The girl is playing with Nougatine's brooch-clip, distracted and indifferent, and begins to sing 'ay, trece de mayo'. Now it is Geneviève's sarcastic eyes that stare at mine and I am unable to break through the light they emit and fix mine on the open cloak. And I wake up with a start while Madame Bonsants, waving a rod of rusty iron with on the end of it a little semi-incandescent arc, advances towards me determined to blind me and says lazily 'Happy now?' and Suzanne too who goes past me leading Jean d'Arc behind her by a horn says 'Happy now?' And suddenly it begins to rain. Urine. Cow's?

Happy with what? I think, I had no wish to attack them from behind and was not moved by the curiosity which an entomologist can have for an insect not yet catalogued which has the misfortune to come within his range; probably I only wanted to join them in their walk and say good-day to them, with complete respect for their relationship; perhaps I actually wanted to share with them my unconditional sympathy; that is to say, I wasn't there to be inquisitive and *report*; perhaps I was catching up with them to offer an ice to little Arlette. But that Geneviève without even seeing me should plan with the other two to let loose the bull like this and should wish to have me removed or my eyes branded, seems to me oneirologically exaggerated. 'Happy now?' I continue to repeat to myself while I rinse my face and obliterate that refulgence of her body which instead of revealing it obliterated it. No, I am not at all happy. On the contrary: I have the feeling that there is more, something else, and that Madame Bonsants and this daughter-Arlette-girl (who pops up from another century) and Suzanne, stamping on my supposedly vulgar and destructive curiosity that 'Happy now?', have merely made me persevere with that curiosity, which might well have a reason to exist. But had I not wakened I would not have known what it was: because I was falling from the window-sill at the bank and would have ended up by transfixing myself down on the street, cleaning rags and window-cleaner in my hand, on that strange piece of iron carried by Madame Bonsants. And Geneviève seemed to me to be a dead woman, dead and with the sneer of her mother's portrait, a sneer of mad and farsighted cruelty. Probably her cruelty has something forced and bitter about it, it is the cruelty of someone to whom it is not granted to turn her love into love... And these eyes: red with two vertical incandescent slits in the middle, are opened wide more in an effort to block my gaze than in an attempt to strike me with lightning – and yet nothing that emanates from Geneviève can have an object in focus: it is so only momentarily. So, while the girl and Madame Bonsants turned exclusively to me, Geneviève showed herself naked and splendid to me and to everything behind me: the rest of the world. And I am sure she was going to piss on it.

But after a few seconds, I no longer remember anything: I remember only interpretations, and they do not interest me, and discarding them one after the other, I try to recall those moving beautiful colours, those pictorial scenes. But things, without the interpretations which keep them alive, vanish too.

At first, when I woke up unexpectedly – I was dreaming, I was falling from a height, I don't know any longer – it occurred to me: why didn't I dream about Marie instead, a sort of wolf-woman, a lycanthrope, no – a wolf-mother, that's it! But that could never correspond to anything real: Marie cannot be the originator of anything, she gives birth to nothing; in her obstinate sterility she is undefeated, she offers only pure pleasure, the obscene sex of the female who perhaps experiences pleasure, perhaps not, but in her mind is always turned towards the West of an impossible dawn so that everything will consume itself with desire and nothing ever be born. Marie, the one and only, with her desire for unassuaged and unassuageable love – the least human being that can exist and the most desirable: the monster – my God, I am getting excited, I shut my eyes again in the dark and see that open wound which sucks me in once more little by little and back into time; I manage to concentrate my thoughts for a second and to put to flight the conditioned reflex of a Male Minotaur in hot pursuit, there, I begin to enter gently, to descend into Marie, 'Come, Polynices, come, *my brother*,' whispers Marie-Lucia and I awake completely from my rapture, I run to the window, throw it open, the blood flows back into the usual pockets scattered through the rest of my body and I rinse my face again. The light is still exactly the same as it was, as when I lay down on the bed, I can see from here the disc of the moon and that of the sun – the former has passed the third quarter. The men of the valley are surely preparing for the evening, passing the word to each other. I shall go down, perhaps Nougatine wants to have a chat with me, let's leave the Colonel to snore off his drunken stupor.

A slight knock on the door followed by another. Slept it off already. 'I'm ready,' I say to the Colonel, 'come in.'

And the door is thrown wide open and Marie comes through it like a gust of red wind, shuts it behind her and leans on it and gives a deep sigh and closes her eyes. Now, not to ruin everything, I shall not ask for explanations, and won't even speak. I shall not reduce her to a *human* being, because I desire Marie, I desire her madly and moderately at one and the same time. And I undress her slowly and she looks out of the window, looks at the moon. I make her lie on the bed delicately, as if I was afraid I might break her in two: the monster, the marvellous creature I find useful on the one hand and the woman, humanly unhappy, ill, alone with herself, on the other. And I want both parts. With gentleness and force she thrusts her pelvis against me, I contemplate the sinuosity of her full and slim body, my finger-tips are avid and knowing and my eyes full to the brim with dense waves of sweet flesh. Marie entwines herself on me and fastens her silvery nails in my back, her wide-open pupils, like mine, wander frenetically over screens on which I have only a small part. Who knows if she feels the potency of my reserve, of how I am courteous so as not to wound her. She begins to abandon herself in alarm at my symmetrical thrusts, which wait for the impetus of her pelvis before increasing in intensity, which pause when she seems lost in some gulf and has that look of supplication to which I reply with a gesture which was always mine when I was Barbino: I planted a kiss wherever I could reach on anyone who gave me a caress or offered me a sweet and with time that kiss was always placed there: on the tip of the elbow, that is to say, where I could reach. And Marie has a vague smile of childish gaiety: and who has ever given her a kiss on an elbow there in the snow? she must be thinking. And, as she thinks, her transport becomes more animal, her abandon becomes cruder and more demanding and she begins to kiss me on the neck and to bite me (something I don't like at all) and I, who am controlling myself and letting her do what she likes, determined to make her come as much and more than a multitude of males, begin to feel the pleasure of losing control, of reaching an accord so perfect with her that I abandon her to herself and to her inappropriate East and concentrate calmly on my pulsating desire. Our pleasures, although so different and distant in terms of rhythms and sexual habits, are immensely close, they send each other signals of understanding, they overtake each other and stop and wait for each other, setting off again suddenly, giving each other chances, taking delight in placing a distance between each other, in hiding, in bursting out unexpectedly. Disconcertingly easy. When she has dressed again and has put on her raincoat, I say to her in a low voice:

'Can I ask you a favour?' and I grip one of her hands tightly so that she can understand that it means a lot to me and that I am asking an enormous sacrifice of her, perhaps, and that yet I don't want her to think how crude I am to dedicate to something of the kind my first thought after making love as we have done.

'Yes,' she says, at the door by now, ready to open it, as if she were in her own house, as if she at least had nothing to fear from anybody.

'Don't tell Nougatine. Do you promise me?'

'Why?' says Marie, actually a little surprised and disappointed.

'Because it is something that must make us happy and not make anyone else unhappy,' I say lying to her with promptness.

Marie seems to regain her serenity but still somewhat against her will.

'All right then, as you like,' she says at last, sighing.

'I'll go out and see if there's anyone there.'

'And I'll go through the little door at the back then,' says Marie, her face a little clouded.

I wouldn't like to give her the impression just at this moment of being in a hurry: but there is no request in her glance, which seems to have been extinguished, which no longer seems to remember. Perhaps it really is like this: perhaps behind that sudden coldness and lack of feeling there is all the involuntary adaptation to a destiny which one cannot and must never ask to prolong the fleeting moments, together with the destructive desire to obliterate them each time – that habit which then becomes transformed into the conditioned reflex of the grim, dull suffering of the animal sunk in lethargy, which does not know it has been wounded and which continues to bleed even in its sleep.

'Are you coming down?' asks Jacques' voice from the corridor.

'Right away, Jacques.'

'Is there someone there?' asks the Colonel, always so terribly inquisitive so apt to get on one's tits when he shouldn't and so full of tact and a thousand attentions when it isn't necessary. My God, what a heap!

'Yes, of course, the wolf-hound,' and I hear his little laugh and footsteps going away, padded ones.

Marie opens her eyes wide: a good idea that about the wolf-hound but she has a gleam of disquiet in her eyes and I am not at all sure that the obscene hint which caused the Colonel to give that little laugh has completely escaped her.

'What part are you playing in *Antigone*?' I ask her, having followed the noise of feet down the stairs, standing now in front of her in the door but without touching her.

'None. I made the masks,' she says proudly, staring at me and pressing a thigh against the crotch of my trousers. I reply to the thrust; I feel as if I had done nothing else all my life.

Next day the Colonel has once more become more laconic, locked in a state of pedantic lack of interest, and Nougatine, who is always so full of solicitude, so visibly disturbed, has to make infinite changes of tack to bring him back to the old, agreed reality. 'I should never have begun talking like that yesterday. Here's the result. After forty years I rebelled like any stupid woman, and there you have it: I feel I have lost him' is how she suddenly opened up in my room, while she sucks the liquid from the little bottle and her hand trembles more than usual. 'And to think that he is as lonely as I am. What a stupid woman, how shall I make things up now? why did I have to rake it all up? out of vanity, that's why!... What will he do alone in Paris?' she asks herself, it wasn't me who asked the question: I could tell her that the Colonel does three thousand things every hour and she would still shake her head as a sign of forbearance: it is she, the

225

Siamese twin, who controls his innards. 'He'll do what he did in the camp.'

Nougatine is truly talking to herself and has no need of an interlocutor. I am here and it is as if I were not here, yet she touches me and looks at me.

'Did you see that disgusting exhibition last night?' she asks, shaking herself a little. I remain silent. In fact I didn't sleep a wink all night. My door remained open in vain. I kept going to the window and looking down, around, and did not see anything. Every so often a leather coat that came and went and disappeared. 'But it is her, that virago downstairs, that protects her. If only because it is the only meeting place outside – Marie gets off with everyone – even with her,' and with her index finger she makes signs on her little belly, low down. I feel I have been too delicate in my dealings with Nougatine: her nastiness towards Marie – mixed undoubtedly with a hate much deeper than jealousy – wounds me.

'Ah,' I say, in passing, jokingly, 'on the poster for tomorrow evening I saw a big white mask –'

'A silly idea of that woman's,' says Nougatine and suddenly plunges once more into her narrative solitude of a little while ago, I mean that she has begun in silence to go over to herself the story of the Colonel without giving me more than a few little wry smiles and a few sighs. Then the silence becomes definitely concrete, comes to the surface again in the form of words:

'He was called *the rude angel* just as I was called *Nougatine* – because of the little kids in Morocco and Algeria who the moment they saw me ran after me, I always had little bits of chocolate with me, and shouted: *nougatine! nougatine!* and stretched out their arms. He was a good-looking man, a bit like Jesus of Nazareth: his hair a little longer than officers had ever allowed themselves to wear it, a beard and whiskers and all that blondness round his head which has become reddish now. And he was nice: he swore, of course, but in the end if he could he went to all sorts of lengths for everybody. He is a distant sort of person, who neither gave nor received confidences. He was the first person to wonder about the naked servants in the camp: they were all adolescents, Berbers, mulattos, Negroes, they took messages from one part of the city or the camps to another or stayed around the officers to clean their boots, that sort of thing. I don't for a moment think it was from moral scruples; there were so many kinds of infection, and he began to give them boots through at the toes, then along with the boots came shorts as well, made from old trousers thrown away by the soldiers. In short, it was always something. Once Jacques had, as you might say, clothed all the little servants in the camp and no one was running about naked any more, I noticed how he began to look at them differently, his glance had become avid, as if he lost himself looking at those half-dressed bodies to which, I feel, he had never paid any attention or who knows – certainly rumours soon get about among the other ranks. In the camp they knew about officers who got off with these urchins; I was in the sick bay, one soon draws one's conclusions, and there were no women about except me in the sick-bay, and an old woman, veteran of the First World War, all dried up, who looked exactly like any soldier. They were still inventing penicillin, one never knew when drugs would arrive, blennorhagias were treated as best one could, and then after a little started up again. The fact of the little servants was totally accepted by everyone, even by the generals who came and went, I think; no one talked about it, obviously, but everyone did it. Sometimes children of eight came to me bleeding, terrified, but they never said who it had been. And even if they had said nothing would have happened, and I kept quiet about it, what could I do? The veteran said in a matter-of-fact way: "Let's have a look at this, let's have a look" as if it was a case of a thorn or a nail stuck into the heel. I think too that most of the soldiers ill-treated these children. Venereal diseases, according to the soldiers, were their fault, the fault of the children, of whom they said: "These people, they have pox in their blood": we had to ship soldiers back to the General Hospital in Marseilles who looked like walking lepers, the ones that had weak blood, more exposed too. But they had not imported the illnesses from Europe. Naturally I had never expressed an opinion of that kind, probably I never even thought about it. Well, to get back to the Colonel: he was, what shall I say? the most distinguished, the most *man*, the one who never took part in debauchery, the one who kept himself apart, in his tent. He knew how to make himself respected, he was unyielding. He gave people three days field punishment without bread or water. After which, if they didn't die first, he was as nice as before and his niceness, even towards those whom he had punished, was unchanged, as if nothing had happened, as if by magic the law had applied itself, without his

227

personal intervention. He was a soldier, but – what shall I say? – a man at the same time. All that was needed was a look from him, for a dispute or an argument to be settled immediately; after which he gave a smile all round – never a clap on the shoulder, never a word too many: this smile, which in a kind of a way was as terrible and implacable as it was serene and at peace with itself and the world – and he would withdraw into his tent. He used to read. He had all the new volumes of the Pléiade edition sent straight from the publishers, no less. It was in this way that I could come into slightly more personal contact with him: I said to myself, read? why not? He was very jealous of these books – so much so that when one was finished he wrapped it in paper and as soon as possible sent it off to an address back home. Well, there were these books going to and fro from his tent to miné, then the first comments on certain works which, in the nature of things, we had both read. Oh, he was a mine of culture. I hadn't even finished secondary school. Then there was a kiss, then nothing more. Almost nothing. That is to say, more books, more comments – but it was as if that kiss had been buried and continued to live only for me. To begin with this waiting was very exciting for a woman – it was for fifteen years, for all that time during which we moved about here and there, to Africa and to the Middle East and to Madagascar. Well, one evening – I know, it was a bit late, I could never have permitted myself to hand the book back at that time of night but I was a bit alarmed about myself. That kiss was there, huge, overwhelming in that desert, I wanted to force his hand – I kept saying to myself, always having that veteran under my eyes: I shall become like her, *a soldier* and the thought appalled me, even if I believed blindly in what I was doing: do something *for yourself*, I said to myself: I was twenty and had enlisted at seventeen and although I had dreamt a bit about a blue-eyed lieutenant like everyone else – well, I get close to his tent, the petrol lamp was feebly lit, hardly at all. I peep in through a gap in the fastenings and the first thing I see is the cone of light from a torch which opens out on the narrow chest and ends on the terrified eyes of a Berber servant, an adolescent, and the sudden glint of a blade which appears in the other hand as it rises up from his groin, yellow against the brown of the body; the hand clasps a razor, the blade reaches the nipples, I see the arm up to the elbow while the blade begins to caress the skin of the little motionless body. And the Colonel's voice commenting with stifled anger on what was going on below the torso and which I could not see. He was saying terrible things, I get goose-flesh just to think of them –'

'What was he saying, Nougatine?' I ask her taking one of her small wrinkled hands in mine, both sitting on the edge of my bed. Not even with my hand pressing on hers does she seem to notice me. Her eyes are calm, they express no dismay: the dismay has been left behind, pushed down to the bottom of the pram, is totally gone from sight, could no longer have the energy to manifest itself.

'He was saying to him: "You get it up even with the razor, you get it up, you get it up, little black piece of shit," he went on repeating and his voice became cavernous, remote; I could not take my eye away from the hole and my desire to start to shout was such that I was paralysed, gripping the book with all my strength. Then the boy gave a groan and I heard the Colonel making noises with his tongue and in his throat. Then silence, the boy begins to put his shorts on again slowly and I know I must go, flee with my secret and this kiss, this horrifying kiss on *my* mouth and *for ever*.'

'Did you go back to the tent any more? I mean, at night, at what time?'

'Yes – often. Until I began to notice certain elementary things: that the Colonel was impotent and that the little servant was hardened to it. That is to say, that he simulated his terror, and that Jacques, in return, continued to be a generous person, with an odd habit or two, but nothing compared to what went on in the other tents. And I, I don't know how to put it, became more and more attached to him, I wasn't able to get him out of my head and when I talked to him I had got into the habit of not making the least reference to anything, to anything that wasn't routine administration. Until one night I reach the tent, it was a fixation, it was two or three in the morning, his tent was a little apart from the others, it was near the lines for the mules and horses, you didn't have to go through the others to get there; following the stockade made up of carcasses of jeeps, of tarpaulins, of petrol-tins, of wire, one could get there quite unseen, and there wasn't a breath of wind, and suddenly, a gust of sand hits me full in the face and I heard the light footfall of a cautious gallop – unusual, heavier than normal, that's what I mean – which disappears ahead of me and loses itself in the desert. From the silhouette I could see that it was him, the tent was dark and I went in; I lit my torch and at once saw the bloodstains. I followed them, they led to the fence. Instinctively I covered them with more sand, going about at random because I had had to put out my torch and besides the night was so starry that you could see for miles. I went back into the tent; the razor was there on the ground, there was no need to look for it. I took it and cleaned it well with my handkerchief and let it fall where it was before. So that he would know only that someone knew. That handkerchief, I still have it. But now, as soon as I get back, I shall burn it. It doesn't mean anything any longer.'

'What about him?' I ask with my hair standing on end at the lack of any emotion.

'Oh, him! As if nothing had happened; no one notices the disappearance of the boy and he makes a vague reference to it as if to say, he'll have gone off with his caravan; and meantime three more days and three nights pass; in three days the ravens and the hyenas have time to devour the results of Herod's massacre, never mind a child. They look for him everywhere. Finally, I make an effort and take the book back to the Colonel and I too ask about the child. He looks me straight in the eye and says his usual catchword: ballocks! And there am I with the handkerchief in my pocket and I squeeze it tightly in my fist and I feel I am bursting and I want to do too many things all at once and in the end don't do anything, I turn round suddenly and go away. If you think about it, in a certain sense, away for ever. But not from him, from myself – only then I didn't put things in that way. We moved to somewhere else; we were always together; he always stopped me from going anywhere else, even when once I decided to – break things off... He stopped me.'

'How?'

'You can easily imagine how. By kissing me for the second time after fifteen years. Or perhaps I invented this second kiss myself. I don't remember.'

And she looks at me and realizes she has been telling these things to a stranger and she doesn't mind: neither about my reaction nor what I might do, nor the fact that I might tell the Colonel about the conversation and put him on the spot. Nor the possibility that I might not believe a word and might decide to make them confront each other without their expecting it, this evening at table; she doesn't care about anything. All this time she has even forgotten to cough.

'Then there was the accident, the grenade that exploded in his hand, he was repatriated, shortly afterwards I took my pension too, I began to come here. They managed to save it, in part. A hand-grenade that went off in the hand of a French colonel! That certainly wasn't the official version – He has never wanted to explain how on earth it happened.'

'You know, Nougatine, I like your brooch very much, what is it?' I say to her getting up from the edge of the bed.

'Oh nothing, but for the setting it wouldn't be worth a thing. A very ordinary chalcedony. An old present from Jacques. Do you like it? Do you want it?'

'Oh, what are you saying? I wouldn't dream of it!' I had started to talk about the brooch because I felt like saying something that was on the tip of my tongue: that hand-grenade – he made it explode in his murderous hand himself, intentionally. But I say nothing, it is too romantic an interpretation. Quite capable of really doing it, but so as to come home as a disabled person and get a bigger pension than usual, no question of handing out justice to himself.

Let them deal with it, that's it.

I have closed the door, but I don't sleep a wink. I keep turning in my hands the poster for the play, with gilt capital letters, the white mask in the centre, the names of the players, the director etc. 'All the characters except Antigone have fixed roles. They cannot be anything other than they are. We know all about them from the moment they appear on the set: what they will do, if not precisely how they will justify it. Hence the idea of covering them with white masks which are the same for everyone. Great holes to emit sounds they are forced to make, great holes for not seeing. Antigone has no mask, she is the only one. Why? A debate follows. You are kindly requested to remain in the hall.'

The handle moves loudly. It is her. I have decided not to open. I know she is out there. I even hold my breath. The handle again falls softly and stops. The key is in here, she can look through and understand. It doesn't matter. A piece of paper is slipped under the door. I stare at it from the bed – a little boat grounded on an island on which I shall never land again. I pick it up: 'Why? Because Antigone loves. She is unpredictable.'

Thinking about it on the train home I am astounded that the aura which has remained in me of love with Marie is so devoid of passion: nothing apocalyptic, no unexpected longing. Of Marie I begin to see that grimace at the sides of the mouth while she was making love and which appeared in all the other expressions of her face. A kind of permanent scar beneath the skin which in the end levelled out the qualities of that extremely beautiful intense face which is however irredeemably condemned to the fixity of a pleasure manifested always in the wanton parting of the lips, the dead weight of a habit of relationships experienced as *dirty*, very exciting but equally contemptible, even the one with me, so full of conscious abandon. One of those persons who for many reasons end up too soon by making all males into men, and when they would like to be still able to distinguish between them, no longer know how and, yes, separate a man from the pack but inevitably call on him with the name of God – and a real man finds this unpleasant.

Or perhaps I am disappointed in my love precisely because Marie, that evening too and on the following one, went off along the path, and those four men in the inn knocked back a double *grappa* each and then in secret complicity went out one after the other? and did the others turn up again? because she loves and is *predictable*? or only because, having come to orgasm with a woman, I too have become a little more *human* and now the figure of Marie superimposes itself on that of Lucia and that of Lucia on that of my mother and that of my mother on that of Carolina and that of Carolina on that of Nanda and, in the end, at the bottom down there, there opens up the despairing banality of a man's life while I climb up through the years with tremendous efforts and reach Marie, and then, all that remains of that journey is the *impartial* twist of these red lips, the mechanical quality of that grimace of *nature qua nature*? a shadow of irremovable disgust? which controls your thoughts and channels them unknown to you in a direction laid down once and for ever?

And Nougatine, who was giving me the third injection and spent the whole morning trying to excuse the fact that the people from the library hadn't arrived or the doctors with their wives; the little hall desolately empty and those women, tremendously good even in the characters of Creon and of the Guard, who acted for themselves, within themselves, because they knew in any case that at the last moment the healthy people would invent a headache? And those white masks, overwhelmed by the official nature of the roles they

232

had to play, which instead of having holes had oral whirlpools, out of all proportion to what they were saying because, would they, in any case, have found other words impossible? And this intuition of Marie's that one needs huge and monstrous apparatuses to shout nothing whatsoever? All this worries me and looking out of the window there come towards me little cages with stuffed white canaries in them. So out loud I shall tell myself the last tale I intended to tell Arlette before running away four days ago.

'I am a cage like lots of others, neither particularly beautiful nor particularly ugly. A silly canary lives in me and he neither loves nor hates me, I am indifferent to him. But the others try to escape at every opportunity. Hung from the ceiling of a modest flat I too have a dream: to become infinite and to enclose within my bars the whole universe, God included. Sometimes I think about it and thus I pass the time making myself feel giddy. My nail is out of all proportion to the weight it has to bear. I do not know myself very well, a cage can never circumnavigate itself, know of how many little struts and how many metres of wire it is made. Whoever lives in me is always someone less important than me, and they wrongly bear me a grudge for it, because I don't imprison anyone intentionally. I happen to exist. I am myself even when empty, I have no need of a presence to feel more or less of a cage. The air comes in and goes out and the wind makes me sway. What can it matter to me if it is a thrush, a canary or a budgerigar that lives in me? they all die sooner or later, only I am immortal. I shall always be there, here or elsewhere. I believe so strongly in my function, my *necessity* that if I could express a desire it would be this: to be a cage in a cage. *Pour L'Eternité.*'

MORE SWAMPS

I have brought with me stuff for my sister, my sisters-in-law, my nieces every time I have come back from a journey of any length; at the end of the season, for example, when the customers gave a tip to the personnel I asked them if they had things they wouldn't wear any more – probably they were all so amazed that they didn't even have time to reflect and got down on their knees along the corridors to search in suitcases already packed. I even found dresses, so-called casuals, which even my mother could get into. The ones for her I brought back from as far away as Lille – one day I had gone to a private show and had met the painter who was showing her work: a tall robust woman with her hair in a pony-tail and very beautiful too, a languorous look framed by eyes heavily lined with black and extended with ash-grey powder. The day after I was in her studio she was already there looking in the cupboard and running her hands along the hangers. I have even brought home unusual things: Indian dressing-gowns, Lebanese tunics, wraps, camel-wool scarves, alpaca gloves, blazers for ladies who go on cruises. And purses big and little. My relatives always wore everything, often just as it was. It isn't always easy to make presents of things which are clearly other people's presents, so I have always let these things fall into their hands as if I were apologizing for their not being first-hand and explicitly asking my relations to accept them as things *which had cost me nothing*. They always took me at my word. Sometimes they quarrelled quietly over some dress, apparently pure silk established effective hierarchies and cotton mixed with linen unrecognized orders of precedence (I accept only the most choice stuff, sometimes I force their hands with a particularly polite phrase or one that displays muted arrogance so that it will be quite clear that in these days one cannot permit oneself to give charity casually, ridding oneself only of what is superfluous or worn or threadbare, and that beggars are very touchy and critical and violent persons) and that those made-to-measure suits of pure virgin wool were there only because I had merely bent down to pick them up, scattered as they were in bedrooms, bathrooms, corridors, lifts. While they gave me these clothes, often with a pang, these women also transmitted to me the precarious equilibrium of their humours, which then faded in a nonchalant gesture precisely because I contrived to make my pimping go down the scale from 'good nature' to a political eulogy on 'the apartheid of clothing' and, thus surrounded, it was too late for them to give me a slap in the face and put everything back.

And not even my brothers and my father have ever asked themselves where it was those tweed jackets or these gaberdine coats or those flannel trousers *(too big for me)* which I went about collecting for them came from. Nothing I can bring home has ever any value – partly because I make them believe it, partly because they think that mine is a life of debauchery, dedicated only to sensual pleasures, not the least of which being that of elegance (of *ambition* as they say). There it was and that was that – it had no origins, behind them there was not a single, classical drop of sweat of my brow. And they who think it immoral to change their underpants in under ten days and that suits are money thrown away, give themselves airs with this high-class manna which I make appear from the suitcases like a conjurer, from *zero*.

I arrived home when it was raining. I threw open the door and made my entrance balancing between the over-full suitcases and an umbrella found in the train.

I took a taxi at the station in Brescia because I arrived at ten o'clock and after ten there are no more buses for Montichiari until the morning. Money thrown away.

My mother will have been alerted by the motor humming outside in the completely empty little square which is soaking after the early summer storm and her eyes will have been fixed on the threshold even before I entered. The other houses round about are all uninhabited or are being rebuilt. If anyone stops there with the bus, his obligatory goal can only be her inn.

235

Now her eyes seemed to be motionless, exposed in the void like two fragments of bottle-glass, although I am already before her and am bending over the suitcases, accompanying them centimetre by centimetre towards the ground.

She utters an imperceptible cry. She is alone in the inn and is crochetting.

'Hey there!' I cry exultantly. And in this greeting there is the desperate joy of joy that is forbidden.

It must be a while since she had her hair dyed; her forehead above the light eyes – none of us has eyes of that pale green – reveals the furrow caused by a constant state of being half awake, half asleep, which nothing can get rid of.

'What are you doing here?'

I turned round almost abruptly, wounded by this touching question, trying to gain a few seconds by arranging the tottering suitcases and taking off the thin cotton jacket presented to me by Brother Fox – discarded, two sizes too big for me. 'I was passing,' I reply, attempting a passably jokey tone. 'Are you well?'

We embrace in silence, without excessive warmth. The effort we have to use to make this gesture, which is so unusual but obligatory, embarrasses us both. There have never been spontaneous performances of this kind in the family, there was never any occasion for them or when one presented itself it always found everyone unprepared. Muscles tense and perplexed. Total lack of practice for taps on the cheeks, pinches on the bottom, claps on the shoulder. Never mind an entire embrace. When a member of the family meets another in the street he is seized with panic: we don't even know how to greet each other or whether we should, we saw each other twenty seconds ago; not that we bear grudges or not only because we do; it is that we don't have the formula – and that 'ciao', that 'hey there' feels a torture to us, so much so that, by tacit consent, we all end up pretending not to see each other or we take another street.

The joy which we foresaw by letter for our meeting – I, she, Lucia – joy which in the lines I wrote I kept on saying was imminent, remained entangled in the words with which I wanted to capture it so as to study it, take it apart, articulate it for when the right moment would come – to put it into practice – and now it no longer has room for any of those impulses long suppressed, meditated, perfected from afar. In short, between one cheek and another there is an invisible thin sheet, the unfortunate presence of a lack of precedents, of any formal point of reference.

Keeping my arm on her shoulder like a dead branch hanging over a pond, we spill out words which we do not grasp, names of little girls, traffic accidents, hospital, insurance, pension stamps, pension, how to get by, the boat; and already we are confessing that we are together again and, tacitly, as every other time, already a little more distant. And so she, not knowing it, not understanding properly, had brought into the world a kind of abnormal thing, a – sick person? in short, someone who – not like us, that was it, and she had never really understood about this thing with men, nor what it meant in practice. And one day, inadvertently, she discovered she had given birth to a monster, a 'homosexual', they said you called it, and, deeply upset, something had cracked in her, a grave offence had been done to her for ever, to her, who had gone through so much, who had never hurt anyone. And these slimy thoughts within her I still inhale them, I feel these pernicious tadpoles darting about in her brain: even if she had the instinct to embrace me there is a kind of supreme veto – *people* – and in the long run, being contaminated, she must feel any physical contact with me as something more contaminating still, something to be avoided without giving it more weight than necessary: after all I am *her son*. And this attitude, I noticed exactly a year ago, had begun to affect Lucia too – her look had become more inquisitive and at the same time more impartial, she too avoided any manifestation of tenderness to which I had accustomed her over the years, when she was my only refuge after my father and my brothers and my mother had beaten me till I bled. In fact, there, at the seaside, was the first time that, when we were walking on the beach or I took her dancing (Lofty didn't want to come with me, he stayed waiting for me in the hotel) her hand lay listlessly in mine – and then we simply began to walk side by side and our discussions became less frequent. Only her letters maintained a halo of the ancient – suddenly ancient, a dead language – tenderness.

As for my mother, here you have Maria's generous breast! It has done her no good to be a wet-nurse, nor to open restaurants, nor to run an hotel, nor to go into service, nor to knit night and day nor to rear white rabbits under the stairs, nor to dig every little square of available earth and then lower and lower still until this inn, where the customers can be counted on your fingers and they come only if they see that my father is not behind the bar.

My father must have been a wizard who not only doesn't explain the trick to you but doesn't even show you what conjuring tricks he is capable of, because she, somehow and for some reason, every time contrived to desire to find a way of restoring the economic situation of the family, where she was the only one to contribute the necessary hard work. Dario was smashing up motorbikes and leaving farewell letters on the pillow. Dolfo had left home after his military service.

We could be up to the neck in shit and there were terrifying scenes over some promissory note that fell due the day after tomorrow, but, in the end, *he* always had starched collars, was looked after and shaved and handsome and *his own man*. Once the usual hints were sown in her mind about the activities of her husband and a widow in the parish, and she raises her eyes from her crochetting and says to the bearer of the gossip: 'If other women like him it means he's good-looking, certainly that sort of thing doesn't happen to your husband.'

My brothers got married as hastily as possible just so that they didn't have to hand over their pay to their father, I went off at the age of thirteen and a half (according to Dolfo 'fled' in a cowardly way, he thinks he is better than anyone with his modesty and resignation), Lucia works, yes, but she has to pay for her evening classes – and I, wretched creature that I am, put a thing like that into her head, pff, *to study*, something for *high-ups* and a woman besides who in any case should get married and that's that. Lucia doesn't come home even in the evening because she lives with the nuns in Brescia, in the institute for the deaf and dumb where she often works seven days out of seven.

And my father: he was exemplary out of the house. Clear political ideas, a defender of Democratic and Christian justice, a certain pretension to elegance, devoted to Montanelli and the *Corriere della Sera*, friend of good solid people, all lawyers, doctors, teachers: never worked all his life however hard the village tries to remember. He had had a narrow escape when he came back from *the front*. They wanted to lynch him, they had lynched so many others in those days of the Liberation. And my mother: it was out of respect for her that they didn't kill him and let him out of the cell where he had been shut up waiting for the noose (and when every so often she would say in her moments of anger: 'I'd have done better to leave him there' one knew right away what that *there* was, where he had once found himself).

When anyone offered him manual work, to him, who already had enough (that is to say, various businesses carried on by my mother and of which he looked after only the *administrative* side – that is pocketing the money at the end of the day and, indeed yes, paying the suppliers but inexplicably making the rest disappear), how could they take the liberty? he should mind his own business, he should go and be a labourer himself. In fact I think he was ashamed of manual work, which he did not think to be worthy of him: a diabolical piece of impertinence, that was what it was. Yet he doesn't come from a land-owning family, he had always been a share-cropper, that's true, then (or maybe before this) they had also had land, but everything had gone wrong, someone had started to drink, another to bring home the whores from the Carmen – from the name of the Carmelite convent in Brescia – then idiots, usurers, partnerships – but, be that as it may, he must have dirtied his hands too, seeing that once he let out that when he drove the cart with the dung or took the milk to town as a young man every morning 'he had three of them for half a lira'.

But after settling in the village, however, after having experienced the intoxication of lifting little cups of ice with black cherries in them instead of bundles of hay and pails, something about work must have struck him as pleasurable: if one could live lifting less it was undoubtedly possible to live lifting less still – in the end, only watermarked paper.

His infallible political instinct led him to take sides only with the victors, with the *bosses* and he who is not a boss of anything except us, feels he has the right to keep company only with them: imitating his father – old Angelo who ended his life in our house ten years ago and has left behind him patriarchal traces scraped away for many years after his decease: from the backs of chairs, in the straw of the seats, on the mattresses, the blankets, the corners of the wooden trunks – he plays the landlord with us instead of going to the factory or on to the new agricultural machines or on to the roofs of the building sites and, if at all, pours with contempt a little marsala, a grappa, a glass of claret: and from us he has always demanded our

239

pay and accounts of every smallest piece of personal expenditure (and both my brothers and my mother kept their heads down and swallowed it; I got to the other side of the table and began to enumerate my *rights* and his *wrongs* until he became purple and then one of my parental jailers seized me and dragged me to him). So somehow he felt himself to be a boss too – he was very particular about his hands, which were very well kept, always so beautiful, big, muscular, bronzed. He cuts his nails so that they finish in an arrowhead – I remember them well: they are very hard, they can go into your skin and tear away a strip of flesh. I imagine his satisfaction, his pleasure, when after the snack, the picnics with his friends, the insurance agents, car salesmen, chairmen of municipal bands, of hospitals, banks, the lawyers, he was afforded the occasion to display these hands, like theirs, on the table at a game of *briscola*. Everyone cansee that they are the hands of a gentleman, not of a labourer, not of a peasant. But when years ago he was in the restaurant or the bar or in some other hotel and those hands had to condescend to pour something for a dustman or a workman or some ordinary person he flared up: his infallible instinct for self-preservation must have warned him that something alien had been sent to impair his patriarchal aesthetic integrity. All of a sudden on some pretext or other he would begin to bully him, usually tripping him up in political discussion or because he had made a salacious remark about women – woe betide anyone who allowed himself the slightest vulgarity in his presence; clearly his reference to the 'three for half a lira' had been a weak move to try to put up a brave front to the verbal obscenity with which I challenged his respectability by simply asking direct questions which he had to show he could deal with (probably because we were at that moment the only ones in the house and I, unfortunately for him, was on the wrong side of the table; like the time I asked him if he had ever gone with a man and he, without even changing colour, said to me: 'What do you think they did at the front? only there's no need to flaunt it all over the place like you'). And woe betide anyone who spoke badly of the *bosses* in front of him! It was not allowed even in the abstract, not even with the resigned weariness of the poor devils who say something that amounts to *because in any case it's always been like that and always will be*. He began to roar, it was like an invitation to a wedding where the present, apart from anything else, is taken, not given. You could hear him a hundred metres away – there was always someone who came running to listen; he loved to have a public, haranguing made him elated – he and his father had heard so much of it in real life, they ran along to all the Fascist rallies; they were *the three from the Mill*, and it was best to keep clear of them, hadn't old Angelo strangled a bull? And when *He* spoke at Brescia, with the Piazza Vittoria almost full, Angelo was there on the balcony among the chosen few, and his sons still full of *sharn* and *strae* would be able to salute Him. 'And I beg you,' he had said to them, 'bright eyes because the Duce likes that but if you shed a tear I'll kill the lot of you.' *He* had really known how to speak. And fortunately today we have our Fanfani's and Andreotti's – they speak well and Gronchi, Gronchi, what an upright man, and Almirante! he's a spell-binder...!

And a glass of claret on top of a glass of white wine, tripe after tripe, the places for 'refreshment' in which my mother had laboured like a mule, ended up deserted because of my father – and had to be closed, without his getting upset about it, because of the goodwill: half to him, gone for ever, half to my mother so that by getting together with her foster-children she could set about opening up another business as quickly as possible. And the removals!

Even now, here, in front of my mother: she is nothing but a pretext for thinking about my father, to evoke him as if he were a figure from times gone for ever. And instead he is maybe in there or already in bed and my efforts to give a patina of the past to everything are already crumbling in the face of the immediate reality of a hatred which is deep and viscid and pullulating, like the ferment of vinegar in a bottle of wine that has gone off and yet one can't throw away. I look at her sideways while our cheeks rub without having touched each other: a piece that has got lost through being moved here and there within the fixed perimeter of a vicious circle.

In spite of the two litre bottles of eau de Cologne which I gave her at Rimini she has kept the same smell of garlic and parsley which stays in bread cut with a knife put away without being cleaned. We never had a bath or a shower – not even in the so-called hotel: the better rooms were those with the better water jugs and basins and that was that. I used to go into the courtyard and spray myself with the rubber hose. Even in winter – sometimes it was in revenge but almost always because I didn't want to smell like them. And in any case she would never have had time to take a bath, she *had no time*

241

to lose, she would have said to explain away the fact that between her and her man it was a question of smell and darkness (because he had said to Dario – who has become my internal spy now that he has enough beating to do in his own house – that our mother has never once seen him naked nor he her and that it would be unthinkable). My mother sat up even at night, with the lamp lit under its shade, crochetting, even if she had to be up and about at six.

I, for the occasion, had put a drop of perfume on my chin, partly because I have noticed that it helps me to restrain the mad desire to scratch everywhere because of the skin which is growing again, partly to give me the courage to be different even in my smell, different from that smell of something scaly and rancid which one day coagulated in me, on the outside of an unbuttoned overall, and which I always had under my nose when I was in Cortina already, then in Limone on Lake Garda, and then in Milan. Above all I thought that this drop of perfume, presented to me by Nougatine before leaving, would allow me to set up a certain distance where my father was concerned, when he began to ask me the usual things and how long did I intend to stay and what did I intend to do and how much money had I saved – that is, the same things as my mother: and why had I never sent home a single lira? Did I think I hadn't cost anything either? But now, I said to myself in the train, unscrewing the stopper of the bottle, he won't dare to submit me to the same interrogation; above all because I am not staying more than three days, and then because I am *my own master* and can even allow myself the gesture, a degrading one for him, of handing over to my mother those savings I shall end up giving her from my pay. To her and not to him, at the cost of making a tremendous quarrel break out. He is capable of turning into a beast in the space of a second if he is wounded in his male pride, he is like his father: a violent, legitimate guardian of the public good (my grandfather drove about, he and his other son, the blind one, at the behest of the Fascist Mayor to make troublemakers, *reds*, drink castor-oil), he foams a little, on purpose, and knows exactly how to control himself when he has to put on the act of the offended deity in a furious rage, and that axe and that knife so often dreamt of but never in fact brought down more than necessary – that is to say, never, naturally, otherwise neither I nor my mother would be here now, with this close feeling of suffocation, with this nostalgia for a nostalgia which is not there

242

away and I was there too on holiday and said to him please make it up. But it was as if I wasn't there. You know how he is when someone shows they are afraid, he begins to laugh behind his moustaches as if to say cry, cry, you won't do this to me. But she, even if she was crying, didn't give in and when he saw that she meant it, that she really meant to keep half the money for herself, he said to her and here you've cost me more in hospital fees. The man who had maybe brought her a little packet of sugar or one of grated cheese, because we and the insurance saw to the rest. She said what a shit-face. And there was pandemonium. And now when she goes to work on Fridays in the market with Galizzi or up the hill with Albina, she keeps the money. And she has a bank account. And she sends him you know where.'

'You've got a nice perfume. Expensive stuff, eh?' and she smiles biting her lip.

'You could wear perfume too.'

'Ah, that's night closes again at nine instead of at midnight – he says it cuts down the costs. Everyone says that there is never anyone there.' Then: 'They have operated on her, it's still difficult for her to walk, she has to stay in bed, but on the whole she is well. She has been home for two days. He goes on as if nothing had happened, as if she were completely restored to health and had no need to stay in bed. He goes off and away so that she has hardly had a day in bed and stands there serving the customers with all these bandages.' And the latest: 'Something nasty happened: they quarrelled and she said somethinng awful to him, the same thing as she said to him that time you were wandering about in the fields for two days without coming home and then Dario caught you by the river and went right at you with the motor-bike to corner you and gave you a hiding and then loaded you on to the bike in front of him and handed you over to papa. She said he was a loafer and that even you do something nowadays. He was blind with rage. He chased her round the square with the pruning-hook, then the mechanic stopped him. She fell too and even scratched all the leg just where she had been operated, it seems like fate. The business began when she gave him only half the money she earned at Rimini working for the season. So long as she was in hospital he pretended not to notice; she had taken the money with her and kept it in her bra with a pin. Then at home she gave him the exact half. And he said, aren't you even ashamed? She reacted, she began to tell him what he had done to her all her life and what he had not done. She began to cry right away and I was there too on holiday and said to him please make it up. But it was as if I wasn't there. You know how he is when someone shows they are afraid, he begins to laugh behind his moustaches as if to say cry, cry, you won't do this to me. But she, even if she was crying, didn't give in and when he saw that she meant it, that she really meant to keep half the money for herself, he said to her and here you've cost me more in hospital fees. The man who had maybe brought her a little packet of sugar or one of grated cheese, because we and the insurance saw to the rest. She said what a shit-face. And there was pandemonium. And now when she goes to work on Fridays in the market with Galizzi or up the hill with Albina, she keeps the money. And she has a bank account. And she sends him you know where.'

'You've got a nice perfume. Expensive stuff, eh?' and she smiles biting her lip.

'You could wear perfume too.'

'Ah, that's not for me, to go where? They've even raised the rent and . . .'

I know that when she begins to count the polyhedrical and firmly fixed sides of *poverty* (the infinite possibilities leading to shame and dishonour), she can go on for hours, full of high spirits again, with her fatigue forgotten; after a little she would pass from laments to curses, would rediscover the leonine fury of years gone by, she would give me no peace: everything would take second place: the mystery of life and death would become a trifle compared to the gas and electricity bills; out of the confusion of the first ten minutes of my return there would reappear the threat of another mouth to feed; I know the repertory of her outburst against things that go wrong although she works furiously night and day, this poverty which is the most bitter enemy of her existence, centre of her invective-charged soliloquies, the insomniac rage of her nights, the lacerating effort not to leave an hour of her day idle: with her looking for jumpers and shawls to knit even for pennies, weddings and baptisms and communions in the farms where she goes to cook, grape-harvests, mountains of radishes to peel, home-made *agnolotti* and *lasagne* for some glutton, and the sails to be hemmed with the sewing machine for the toy factory, and, over and above that, the business. And him waking up naturally because he can't sleep any longer and staying in the inn only if there is a game of cards or to lay down the law about

244

international politics to some local unemployed.

I let her boil over and don't grasp a single word of what she is shouting. I go upstairs: the two bottles of eau de Colgone are on the window-sill, intact, as knick-knacks. But I know why they are there: because she will try to sell them and for that reason keeps them handy.

I run down again and look at my mother shaking my head. 'Always the same! The bottles of eau de Cologne are like your dowry, still wrapped up in the chest after thirty years.'

'It doesn't get spoiled. And it will come in handy for Lucia. With what things cost today. Even bread...'

'And your leg?' I cut her short. Her right leg, swollen with elephantiasis, sticks out of her overall, gray like a verminous root by the side of a puddle.

'It's there, my leg,' she says, leaning forward, stroking it.

'But do you do anything for it or not?'

'Yes, of course, even if...'

'You won't do anything, you don't look after it, you want to be paralysed.'

'But I do, I've told you I look after it, that's enough.'

'You wrote me that you'd been to the specialist, that you had to go to the specialist and that in any case you had begun...'

'For you everything's no sooner said than done, as if people can allow themselves to go to the specialist like that. It's not free.'

She always has this power to make me feel guilty about all the things I have not committed and about all the things I could not prevent. This drop of perfume, here, confronted by her leg, has become a thorn which penetrates through my nostrils and implants itself somewhere in the brain, vexatious and gigantic, like my sense of disarmed cowardice, of nullity which she always succeeds in drumming into my head.

She keeps her eyes down and stares at my almost new shoes – I bought them in the flea market.

'You have nice shoes – goodness knows how much they cost. You always were crazy about clothes. As for me my old pair of shoes it's been –'

'And where is he?'

She seems to become more animated at this question, she gesticulates, it's what she expected.

245

'Oh him! what do you expect! always together with these three idiots, talking about politics. Only these others have put their backs into it and have got a house and we after thirty years have got lice. Always out, always in other people's inns instead of drawing a few customers to his own. Then he comes home at three in the morning and says he earns a day's wages himself, playing *morra* and making pasta and leaving everything all over the place! And there's me who can't sleep, five, three, seven, trumps, until the dawn. But sooner or later they will fine him, you'll see. All we need is a fine. For these three layabouts there. And there he is winning and losing like all the others, always the first to sit down at the table when there's a game of cards or a game of *morra*. He says he earns enough for himself, and that the others should look after themselves. Ah, if it comes to that, we have looked after ourselves, that's for sure! But he isn't...'

I have already climbed to the top of the stairs with the suitcases. In my room there are the same pieces of furniture which I have known since I was a boy, coming apart everywhere, the same immensely high beds, the glass in the window is still the same with the crack through which in winter the moon used to come and warm itself in the warmth of my breath and of my nocturnal miasmas. On my bed the mattress is turned back against the head of the bed. But the walls have been whitewashed and there's more order: everything is in order and dead.

I always slept here with Lucia since Dolfo got married. Before Lucia slept in the corridor which leads to the attic. Lucia is very pretty, she resembles my mother as a young woman, all the relations say. Pretty and headstrong, a grown woman already but sweet as a child. She has managed to change the gifts of the intellect into the gifts of the heart. Then this kind of monastic asceticism, which is very strict, work–study–work and surrounded by nuns, has hardened her, even where I am concerned. And her letters, seeing that by now the mistakes in grammar have become fewer, have become fewer too. When she was sleeping I used to get up out of my bed and stroke her hair – everyone said 'curly hair for the boys, straight hair for the girl' – because I loved her and because without her I would not have known how to love. In the darkness I felt myself tremble: the contact of her brow under my hand gave me the feeling that I was entering to become part of her dreams because to possess her thoughts only by day no longer sufficed for me. I dreamt that she must be dreaming about castles, round tables festively decked with so much food for everyone, white roses, talking dolls, princes radiant with beauty, the same ones as in my dreams had put on the monstrous sneer of beasts lying in ambush. When I began to shout in my sleep she used to waken me, she calmed me and her eyes were full of tears – perhaps I had frightened her, perhaps in some way she breathed in my terror and she was sorry.

The thought that anything bad could happen to her drove me mad: it was for her above all that I collected the cast-offs. Once, many years ago, I gave her a slap: I think that of all those I *got* it was the one that hurt me most.

From the stairs my mother asks me if I want something warm. Her voice, weary when she happens to forget *poverty* for a moment and limpid when she manages for a little to resign herself to it, is now very different from the timbre I remember, a *guardsman's* voice, vibrant and strong, when there was still a going business to get on with.

No trace of my books in the wardrobe, the half-shelf has disappeared to make room for Lucia's clothes.

'Where are my books?' I yell.

'Your books! Your books! What a mania! they're in the attic your books! here!'

And she lays the bowl of milky coffee on the bedside table.

'Lucia needed room. Drink it – it's getting cold. And in any case what are they doing here, you've read them all... Your books! always the same craze. What about how much do you make it come to for me?'

When she asks 'How much do you make it come to for me?' she is referring to money, a subject which is already too long delayed. What am I supposed *to make it come to* I'd like to reply, the number of holes in my behind? I tell her about the bank, about the classes. It's always like this: maybe I do have a little money to give her, but I have learned to wait till the last minute. Before I used to give her it at once, thus annulling any relationship between me and her based on force, and it was as if I had stolen it. She took it and put it in her pocket. My money has never had any value for her – she has always thought: if he gives me so much it means that he keeps twice as much for himself, so he's cheating me.

'The bank, the bank! If it's true why did you shout about your books? Like the time when I had burnt them all. Your books. What do your books matter if you have a job? Damn your books! And damn whoever invented them! Look how much time you've lost! And there am I cooking my guts in front of the ranges in other people's restaurants and you reading your books there and buying magazines! And they've been the ruination of you, your damned books. All excuses for not putting your back into other things, for not working, far from it. If you had gone with Dolfo to lay floors then you would have earned some money and wouldn't need anyone. Are you staying? Are you going off again?'

'You know I'm leaving, don't you?'

'I'm old. You've all made me old before my time. I'll end up like my mother, dead of heart-break.'

'But didn't she die an alcoholic?' I asked, just to gain time, to keep her on tenterhooks.

'You getting her mixed up with your father's. She drank to drown her sorrows and she drank, ah your grandfather was a great whore-monger, he brought them into the house and then it was off with sacks of flour, poultry. He even tried it with me, when your father was at the war. But what are you making me say?'

'I don't have much. With this you can go to the specialist and buy yourself ten pairs of shoes. It's French money, you have to go to the bank, they'll change it for you,' I say all in one breath.

'Are they really all right? I don't want anything from you I'd just like to see you settle down. Have you a girl-friend?'

'Come on, don't get on my tits, put it away and that's an end of it.'

'I don't want anything from you, nothing,' she repeats putting the money in her pocket after having a good look at it, 'only for you to settle down.'

'Put the syringe to boil as soon as you get down.'

'Are we back at that? another of these things?'

'Things that happen,' I say, struggling with the suitcases.

'Goodness knows where you come from.'

'You made me, you didn't find me at the church-door.'

'It would have been better, my heart would be more at peace,' she says as she goes out. If Lucia at least, just to pretend, had opened one of the two bottles. I think of the tufts of hair which Whisky left each night at the bottom of my bed, and wonder if I'll ever find the time to tame another cat. Down below, in the little kitchen, I open the phial and she gives me the injection.

'And to think that from the outside you seem so strong and instead obviously you really have weak blood. Your father, can you imagine, made me put up with all sorts of things with the ones from the brothel and from the music-hall but he never brought anything like this home. And are you saying they weren't infected? say I. At least one of them will have been, won't she? But no. Just because he has strong blood, he does.'

'Of course, he sucks it out of you.'

'And to think that there was even the chemist from Castenedolo who came courting me. But he was as ugly as could be. Now that's how we are: until he goes to the cemetery I have him on my back. Pull up your trousers, you didn't even feel it. And now let's go and make up the bed. If he's not here in half an hour I'll shut up shop and go to bed.'

She never said 'go to sleep' always 'I'm going to bed'. Meanwhile she tucks in the sheets, I think I'll have to go still further away, make my return more and more difficult, force myself to stay away for ever.

'It's nippy tonight, don't sleep naked, put something on. And if you stay let's hope you find a job quickly. Now they're taking everyone on, they even bring them from Sardinia because labour is scarce.'

'But I told you I'm going to stay for two days at the most.' But she isn't listening to me, she continues undeterred with a speech, the one from last year – from two, three, four, five years ago.

'And let's hope you don't start writing again and using up the electricity, because if not I don't know how you'll get on with your father. I'm going downstairs, maybe someone will come. I haven't sold a glass all evening.'

Far from here, far from this poverty which would make everything more difficult, not so much life as a probable suicide, everything could finish some night, after a cigarette and, why not, after putting a drop of scent on my ear-lobes. Here everything is stuck and eternal and impossible. And she never talks to me, she talks always and only to herself. For her I am always thirteen, I haven't grown up, I will never grow up. All of us have betrayed her once and for all, we have taken everything from this woman without ever

249

asking ourselves where she found the strength to give and give continually as she has done, until she grew tired of him and of the lot of us. And she has begun to ignore us, to be with us remembering us even when we are standing in front of her.

But I'm not listening to her any more and there's nothing that I have to tell her. The first bus for Brescia is at half past five, in less than five hours. I pull out a few drawers, I am looking for old notebooks, to see what I used to write. Probably things crammed full of little symbols with some meaning only for me, the doodles of my sensual and erotomanic adolescence. But I find nothing. Lucia in fact wrote to me in a letter 'to be brave', that mamma had made another big bonfire 'with all the papers she found about the place.' But in truth she never *found* anything about the place: she always looked, she always sniffed it out.

The outside door creaks. My mother is putting up the chain and leaves the key on the window.

'Aren't you sleeping? Aren't you getting undressed?' she says entering the room suddenly. 'You haven't drunk your coffee. Do you want me to heat it up for you?'

'No, I'll drink it cold.'

'And if you're not sleeping don't go turning everything upside down. See about the suitcases tomorrow. Goodnight then. How much is it in lire?'

'Ciao, I'm not sure. Mamma...'

'What is it?'

She looks at me and waits: do you remember when you said to your sister Rina my oddest son has gone off and I don't know when I'll see him again, the son who troubles my heart most has gone away and my blood rebels day and night, I don't know whether he has enough to eat, a place to sleep in, if he looks after himself: he's an original but he's not bad, in fact, he's the best of them.

'Nothing. I wanted a blanket but then I thought it's going to be so warm in any case. These things are for you,' and I pull out of the suitcase the cast-off dress from Lille and a silk shirt.

'How lovely! I'm going to try them on right away. Ciao then.'

It's not true, she doesn't try them on. Standing outside her bedroom door I listened: in ten minutes she was already fast asleep, like an old animal which no longer has a single reason to keep up the light defensive sleep of young animals on the alert.

250

My father must have smelt me, because when he comes in, if his card-playing mates are not there, he makes straight for the stairs and never puts on the light and can't have seen my jacket hanging on the clothes rack. He opened the door of my room and put on the light: it wasn't long till the alarum would ring, at five. He said with a smile:

'Ciao, you're back.'

'Ciao.'

'Are you all right?'

'Yes.'

'Not bad.'

'Right, ciao,' I said to him and I put out the light. He went to his room and began to talk away to her, and to ask her what he couldn't ask me. With muffled movements I finished doing up the suitcase and then went out by the back door with only one suitcase and the umbrella too. In London they say it is always raining.

The last time I saw Lucia – Lofty had left Rimini alone and I had travelled back with her – was here in Brescia a year ago. We got out here in this station and she said:

'Goodbye then.'

'I'm going home to get the suitcase and then tonight I'm taking the train to Lille. I have to change in Paris,' I was trying to gain time, I'd have liked to go back with her to the Institute for the deaf and dumb and thought she would have asked me to. Instead she was saying goodbye under the platform roof. She was going off alone with the bus. 'I have lots of time, I can come with you, if you like.'

'Oh, don't bother,' and while I hadn't even finished what I was saying a girl with chestnut hair and a somewhat oblong face had come rushing up to Lucia and embraced her and asked how she was and then her questioning glance fell on me.

'It's my brother,' Lucia had said with a weary voice: she hated introductions. 'A colleague of mine from the Institute.'

'Which brother? Obviously not the father of your nieces.'

'No, the one who's in France.'

'Ah you never told me about him,' said the girl, slightly puzzled.

'I thought I had,' Lucia had said with a distracted air.

'I swear you didn't,' said the other and then changing the subject:

251

'You look great.'

It was the kind of comment that could get my sister's temper up.

'You're the same as ever; come on, are you going to the Institute too? then let's go.'

We kissed each other on the cheek and the two of them disappeared behind the parking-lot.

So Lucia didn't talk about me, she didn't make me live in the things she said. Perhaps she was ashamed of the way I publicly asserted myself and aimed to put everyone in a state of crisis and make them face up to themselves before anyone took the liberty of trying the same thing on me. For her it was exhibitionism, for me a form of moral rigour, of existential method, a refusal to delegate power, responsibility and... And I didn't insist on accompanying her, I took the bus and went home, to leave almost at once after the usual argument with my father.

And now I am at the station in Brescia and it is only ten past six; there wasn't much traffic on the streets and a radiant light. I stroll about a little and keep on saying to myself to phone her at least, wait till it is a decent time to phone her. And suppose some inquisitive teacher answers? And suppose she has once again to make a sad reference to that brother of hers *who's in France*?

I dialled the number twice leaving out the last figure. Then I intentionally miss the train and take the half past nine so that I don't have to change in Milan.

MADAME THE MINOTAUR

The Colonel is still sleeping, he can be heard from the end of the corridor. I asked the hamster-woman how he was.

'Last night he got very tight. It was a good idea to phone before coming back. There was talk of going immediately after you left. Nougatine, I mean. Mademoiselle was so insistent. You almost missed him, you know.'

I don't wake him and go to my room. I have no desire any longer to spend the other three days here before starting work again on Monday. It's better if the Colonel wants to leave too, in that way we'll leave as soon as possible, maybe as soon as he wakes up. And I have no desire to see Nougatine again far less Marie. Let them get on with it. I'm already so depressed myself.

'So are we going to do this injection or not?' asks Nougatine, throwing open the door which I have left ajar.

'Ciao Nougatine, your perfume was a knockout!' I say and she gives me the usual little kiss, rising up on the tip of her shoes.

'You know,' she says to me in a conspiratorial tone, 'he has promised that in September he's coming to spend the autumn in Mimizan. Isn't it marvellous?' and she's already busying herself with the file and the tube. 'Will you come and visit us?'

'Oh, the moment there's a chance.'

'I cook very well, you know, oriental too,' she says in a garrulous little voice. 'And to think that he wanted to leave me here right away. You know what I said to him? He would never have expected it. I said to him, and I hope you don't mind if I used you as a guinea-pig – I know that there's only a platonic friendship between you two – I asked him if you had passed it on to him – like that, just to see how he reacted. He said that tubercular is OK but mad no and gave me a push and went up to pack. My God, what a scene. He was lying on the bed scarcely breathing. That's it, I thought, a paralysis, a thrombosis. A cerebral disturbance. For so little. That's enough, I've tested the terrain. There are too many mines. It's a swamp. I won't go any further.'

'Good day to you both,' says the Colonel looking in at the door. Nougatine runs and kisses him. 'You're back already, I see. So much the better. We'll leave right away. And Nougatine will let us go, won't you Nougatine and not make a fuss.'

The two old people go up to each other again and hug each other sweetly.

'I've already been invited to Mimizan, Jacques. A pity that I'll be in London, otherwise I'd have gone with you.'

'Meantime come with me to Paris, it's better than nothing. If we put a move on we'll manage to catch the express at half-past five and at eleven we are in Paris. You have buttocks that look as if birds had been pecking at them.'

We have supper served a little early and at five a hired car arrives in front of the little courtyard. Marie is running down from the sanatorium out of breath.

'She never misses a thing,' says Nougatine with annoyance. 'Look how she is running, thoughtless thing. She won't last long if she goes on like this.' She is carrying in her hands a square package wrapped in maroon paper and, while she opens the little gate, I see that there is string round it.

Marie's hair is streaming in the wind, she regains her breath and never ceases to gaze at me.

'I saw from the window that you had arrived. But what are you doing?' she asks, breathing with difficulty. Now little waves of moisture heavy with make-up pour from her brow and cheeks.

'They're leaving,' answers Nougatine and with slightly theatrical promptness adds, slightly distorting the facts, not to mention my intentions. 'We'll all see each other again in three months' time at Mimizan, won't we?'

'I wanted to give you this,' says Marie, holding the parcel out to me.

'Oh, Marie, I ... What have you done, why?' to be given a present, especially in front of other people, brings me out in a cold sweat.

And I hadn't even thought of it! I wish I could sink into the ground.

'Please take it. But don't open it now,' she turns her eyes on to Jacques, then fixes them on Nougatine. 'Open it when you are alone, promise me.'

'All right, Marie, thank you.'

'Thank you,' she says too.

She stands there looking at me while the cases are loaded into the boot. I know she would like to talk to me, to tell me something, and I take great care not to go into the pensione or to find myself alone with her at all in the few minutes that remain before leaving. Marie has now lost much of her boldness even where Nougatine is concerned, for the latter's reproving glance at her intrusion allows no alternative. They are leaving *her*, no one else. And now a flock of women is coming down from the clinic to drink tea here. The confusion makes it easier for the car to set off. Among all the hands, their two as well, side by side, waving.

'Jacques, now you are coming with me and you're going to shut your eyes to some things. We're going to the sauna. There are Americans in Paris now.'

'Oh my God, and what am I going to do among all these old men?'

'Yes, I know, they're almost all eighteen at least and are beautiful and ardent and know what they want and there's no need to corrupt them. It means you'll simply shut your eyes to some things.'

'All right.'

Seeing that I am getting back so soon I might as well enjoy myself a little more before confronting Arlette. And the sauna is also an excuse for Jacques to let me sleep at his place, in the next door room, on the divan.

And so we pass every day until Sunday together, sauna and dinner every day – and his beard is streaked with the furtive encrusted trails of snails and beads of spunk without his ever losing his bearing – head up chest out. He's all ruddy with his towel laid over the little ungloved hand, like an old butler; he says it's because of the steam, instead it is because in the intervals of his voracious impotence, he goes to the bar and knocks back a bottle of Bordeaux on his own. Never a word about the past nor about Nougatine nor about Mimizan; we talk about the Americans and how Hollywoodishly piggish they are where sex is concerned, just because they are puritans and respectable. He is in ecstasy over the fact – which he seems to be

255

discovering for the first time – of how many eighteen-year-olds there are in the world who are exclusively gerontophiles and who can't manage an erection if they aren't faced by an extremely mature shuddering jelly, a survivor from the Excelsior Ball, a little old grandfather from *Les Misérables*.

Among the hundreds of volumes of the *Pléiade* on the Colonel's bookshelves there is also a Larousse encyclopedia of medicine. But I'm no wiser than before:

'(from the Latin *albus*, white. – A normal state which manifests itself from birth and is caused by the complete or partial absence of pigment: 1) in the *skin*, which is pale white and covered with white or whitish yellow hair; 2) in the *iris*, which is pale pink; 3) in the *choroid*, which gives the pupil a red colour' and that's all right as far as it goes.

'*True albinoism, generalised* is hereditary with a simple recessive character . . .' that is, to be brief, it's not found in their direct descendants.

'Often there are other anomalies: low stature' and that's no good: Geneviève is at least a metre seventy-five in her stocking feet; 'rather delicate' no good either: she has a strong slender physique, very taut, except when she must be very tired from work; 'sweetness of character' – don't let's exaggerate; 'mentally slow' – poor Larousse! 'congenital cataract' – very slight, almost invisible: 'lower expectation of life' and that remains to be seen. In fact the only thing that I wanted to know and even I don't know why, was whether an albino woman is more *sexual* than others and since this is a case of a lesbian who grew up on a stud-farm and who is professionally dedicated to artificial insemination, if it is normal for her to amuse herself by branding her lovers on the hips, abetted by her mother, claiming to secure the property in perpetuity even once it has been abandoned. And what kind of threat might she make if anyone dared to default on this transaction of buying-and-selling. And then if I could get perhaps a science-fiction description of what it sees and how it sees, this eye like that of an angora rabbit ('see eye, disorders of refraction').

Then I also find a volume with coloured illustrations on *Minerals and Rocks* and I lose myself in it because it makes kind of anthropological history out of stones. Of Nougatine's chalcedony, for instance, it says something sensational, that it makes one turn automatically towards another beam of light – à propos of the Colonel and his age-old premeditation in all things, which is more psychic than merely malignant, even when it comes to making a present of a brooch.

In the evening, in the Colonel's kitchen living-room, my eye falls on Marie's square package which I really have no desire to open; everything concerning her strikes me as tremendously true and un-authentic at the same time, a little story full of pathos, but ruined by the fact that it has been told too often – or not told – only in a workingmen's club.

I ought to get rid of this parcel which runs the risk of turning Marie, the first and last woman in my life, into a being that is merely human, weak, in need of affection, as perhaps not even she imagines herself to be. And this bridge which she throws with this gift – to make it collapse immediately while I am still in time now that the thought of not recrossing it would not cost me anything. But there is this fear of regret, so I prefer to register its existence, to catalogue it along with the shirts and socks and put it away somewhere but not here. Certainly at the mere thought of how happy I would make her if one day I visited her, once Nougatine has gone to Mimizan, I feel a shiver which is a mixture of vanity, of madness, of sensual pleasure and irony, run over my face where once there must have been the paths traced by neuralgia of the trigeminal nerve. My God, this package; and all the conjectures I make about the accompanying letter: 'I am sending you them all so that you can have Antigone's, the one that isn't there' or again: 'one must take off all those we have to put on the one that doesn't exist' or: 'the only way to put it on is to take it off' and so on, mask after mask.

It is just like when I got a letter from the family: sometimes it stays there for days and days before I make up my mind to open it. I refuse it the right to have anything urgent to communicate to me; nothing must come from that direction to disturb my own directions and distract me from them. In this way she will get lost and I shall forget her totally. Who knows that the same won't happen to this light package, in which nothing moves, from which there seems to emanate only a sad and slightly senseless Hellenic silence – too exag-gerated for what it contains.

Home, with suitcase and umbrella and package – which I immediately place in the bottom of the suitcase, pulling out the first bundle of things that comes to hand – a pair of letters for me, a few hundred francs under a glass and a note: 'It would be very nice if you came at the usual time to fetch me from the station with a flower. I have written to my friends in Middlesex, the same family I was with *au pair*: they will be able to find you a job in time. Nothing else except – but I will say it to you. I miss you.' A note from Domenico, certainly put into the letter-box by the concierge: 'My dear, no sign of you. On my side a long tranquil desolation, like *the Waste Land*. I'd like to see you again; listen, before you go off leave me your address in Italy. Ciao, days of wine and roses.' What a bore. One from Lucia, very short – she isn't going to become a nun any more, she has fallen in love. When am I coming to Montichiari?

I tear everything up and lie down on the bed. Hoping that Arlette's train has a breakdown and that she arrives as late as possible – but the usual time is close, I should already be on my way. I don't want to think of the sort of reaction I shall have with Arlette after all the silly stories she has told me, well, not all of them, but I certainly don't understand why she should be so ashamed of having had Geneviève too besides Pablo-Pablito. And probably of continuing to see her on Mondays or on Saturday evenings or on Sundays unknown to Suzanne. What a lot of stories! And perhaps a game has been being played between the girls *ex-en-fleur*, a little pact of blood on the right or left buttock, a tattoo, that's it, D'Orian-Jarre-Arlette. *Pour L'Èternité*. DOJAPLE. And there would be a brand for Suzanne too. *Dorsple* and one for Madame Bonsants, *Dob.ple*, whose first name I don't know. The games of my childhood or adolescence were so much more interesting than theirs, the games of these bisexual and discreetly sabbatical and esoteric dykes.

I think of Gina at Cortina d'Ampezzo, who at nine o'clock at night was at the station, dressed in black from head to foot, beautiful smiling eyes, full of extremely minute solidified tears. Then at half past nine the station door was shut and I prepared myself for my third night of camping out with my cardboard suitcase and she behind me, the last – evidently whoever she was expecting hadn't arrived. She looked at me and came towards me saying:

'You look terrible. Have you missed the train?' She was just over forty and looked twenty years younger.

'No, I've caught too many,' I threw out, perhaps with a certain rancour. But she must have seen that I had a burden of shivering fits and suffering, that I wasn't normal.

'Well,' she said with a sigh, 'she hasn't come, if you want to sleep at my house there's a bed.'

I didn't believe my ears and followed her. She lived in a basement but her little flat was comfortable, two small rooms, a tiny kitchen as wide as a ribbon, a wash-basin with hot water, a toilet. I slept for a whole day under a mountain of old blankets and patched quilts and never had time to say a word to her. I turned over and slept for another day. At the end of the second day she arrived with a roast chicken which she had bought as soon as she left the dry-cleaner's where she did the ironing; she called me, we ate together. Without ever speaking. Then I started off once more to look for some sort of job; it was very difficult, the season had begun some time ago, they were all full up. Exhausted from walking and going into hotels like a stray dog, I threw myself on to the bed until the next morning – she began to buy extra milk and bread and sugar. Exactly on the fourth day she said: 'Well, I'm going to see if she's going to come this evening at least. If she comes you'll go into the corridor.'

Then she came back and said:

'She didn't come. If only she'd show up.'

Then one evening she came back and began to tell my fortune with the tarot cards: I didn't want to, I didn't like having the cards read, but I agreed out of pure politeness.

It wasn't that Gina was an unbalanced woman and nourished excessive faith in the way the cards fell and went to the station in her mind even when she didn't go there: these were episodes in her week which were well defined, completely isolated, which did not impinge at all on the rest of her day, far less on the efficiency of her work. I mean, if Lisetta had been there, in the cemetery at Cortina instead of in the one at Treviso, she would have gone there instead of going to the station. She was a woman full of energy and spirit – only that every three days, coming home again with those tears a tiny bit less liquefied than normal, she began to read the tarot cards. Two years before her sixteen-year-old daughter had been mangled along with her fiancé on a Vespa by a lorry and Gina went to the station to see if by any chance the train that arrived from Treviso at ten past, a quarter past nine, would bring her dead daughter once and for all. I began to suffer desperately with her and hoped to free myself soon from this situation, I no longer slept in the basement where I felt bound to play from morning to evening the part of compassion, of discretion, of desperation alleviated by faith in the resurrection of the body of the young girls who arrive fully dressed from the beyond with the last train at ten past nine from Treviso. And to pretend into the bargain to be superstitious. And however did I manage to fly off the handle one evening and shout in her face that Lisetta was dead, dead for ever, that it was time to stop, that she would never get off that damned ten past nine train nor any other, have you got that? have you got that?

Why did I do it? Why have I never been able to play a part to the end? And now where will Gina be, who turned her head slowly and, as if nothing had happened, threw on her black shawl and went as usual to the usual appointment. And why, when, having returned, she appeared at the door with the tarot cards in her hand, did I once again throw in her face – the face of the woman who had picked me up out of the ice and illness and sleep – all her madness which I could not but breathe in moment by moment? And why did these tears instead of melting altogether after the jolt I had given her harden for ever? And the next day something happened at the dry-cleaner's and a woman came to get a dressing-gown from the bedroom and underwear and a few other things and said: 'They're taking her away.'

'Where?'

'Poor thing, Poor woman,' and she went away refusing to answer my questions; I got there and Gina was gone and since then I have perhaps done nothing but try to expiate for having preferred the concrete rationality of selfishness to the abstract and sad unreason of someone who had built dams to her grief as best she might.

Arlette opens the door and hasn't time to open it properly before I assail her with my excuses:

'Oh, I'm so sorry, I've just arrived and just had time to read your note' but she throws her arms round my neck, drops everything, panting and says:

'It's good that you're here. I can't bear it any longer. My God, what a lot has happened all at once. And not to have anyone to tell it to. Suzanne – but how are you how are you?' and she nestles in my arms and I feel that she is sobbing, sobs of the kind that come before weeping. Only now do I notice that the castanets and the fan have disappeared and in the little cage there is a white, living canary which I have never seen or heard.

'But Arlette, come on! I'm here now. Tell me everything, what is it, what's wrong?' But it's not true that I am here, suddenly this situation is of no importance to me.

'Meantime if you give me a hand we'll cook a slap-up supper. And we don't even know who it was, do you understand? She – she never saw anyone but the two of us. Geneviève and me: one simply can't believe it. Pregnant. Suzanne, do you understand? Pregnant. Oh no, look, just clean the vegetables for me, I'll see to the cooking. You can clean up later.'

'And how did Geneviève take it?'

'Who knows, we were all stunned. I'd like to know what our Madame Bonsants thinks of it. We can't take it in. She's not exactly young, I mean! A child at that age! at forty-three.'

'What about her?'

'Her? you'd think nothing had happened. She turns up with her little tummy and one can feel that she will defend it tooth and nail; no question of having it aborted, she's never been so jolly. But me, of course they made me have an abortion,' says Arlette with a certain rancour. That's her business.

'All lilies and a little nanny-goat and rainbows, I imagine. And roses.'

'Of course *she* wants the child! But whose is it? who made her pregnant?' She asks questions and begins to smile to herself. 'She doesn't want to say. She smiles and changes the subject. Her gynae-cologist? the head of the office himself? he courted her as a young man, I mean twenty years ago. Suzanne has had no other jobs except the present one; always the same firm. But the head of the office, who is also secretly the boss – you should have seen his face when Suzanne without a word of warning to anyone arrived for the first time in a maternity dress. I said to her, you know, because of the fashion that has everything hanging loose everywhere: so you're being a hippy now, Suzanne? you look pregnant. "That's right!" said she. That's right.'

'And what do the Bradleys say?' I ask just to change the subject and to resist the temptation of putting my cards on the table: who knows how happy she will be now to be able to have Geneviève all to herself if, because of the sudden affront, she leaves Suzanne.

'Well, they'll give you a hand if they can. My God, one doesn't know where to begin. And how was it at home? did you see the new canary? You, going away like that like a thief. I phoned the bank, they told me you had gone home because your mother was ill, but that you would be coming back as soon as possible, that you would do your best to start work again tomorrow. You know it's not easy to find a legal job in London. You'll have to take whatever turns up.'

'Now that's really something new.'

'It's a chicken, my mother stuffed it and everything, this time she put in almond kernels as well as you said. Then Suzanne said – what did she say? ah yes, "I am", and that was all. I said, I said to myself, don't say anything to her, don't ask questions, hold back and she'll tell it all herself. I've learned from you. Well, not a word. Nothing, and Geneviève, I'm sure she learned the same day as me, or that, anyway, she grasped the whole thing only in the evening, when we met, because we had a date at Geneviève's. She went pale, she didn't say anything all evening that could give a hint of her real state of mind.'

So they discovered after all these years of friendship that they really knew nothing about each other: Geneviève that Suzanne had a male lover, a real one, not like that Hippolyte of hers, and Suzanne doesn't know that Arlette is still seeing Geneviève. But the truth is always different and I won't cudgel my brains about it. I am leaving for London shortly, my 'births' are different.

'Oh, such an oppressive evening: and Suzanne in intimate conversation with her child, paying no attention to us, quite indifferent and as amiable as ever; and prepared to leave Geneviève if she...'

'You can take a breath, Arlette.'

'It's that I am terribly agitated, you can understand. You wanting to go away to London, Suzanne going on maternity leave in a few months and goodness knows who will take her place and who knows how long I shall have to stay here alone. Geneviève who, poor thing, never talked much, now she is so traumatised that she seems to me on the brink of suicide. And all this in a week.'

'But I'm not going away now. I wouldn't even have the money. I'll take another month.'

'Oh, listen don't let's start. If you want a loan, I'll give it to you. And the Bradleys will be at hand as long as it takes you to settle down. You can eat with them, I mean, if you're prepared to live in Middlesex. Close by there's the same school as I went to and which Madame Bonsants' daughter is going to. It doesn't cost much, a trifle, it's run by the council, for foreigners. You'll sleep at a friend of theirs, Fritzi whom I know too, she rents rooms, and only to Italians, Spaniards, Greeks and Turks. I feel like going sick at the thought of having to face Suzanne's serenity tomorrow morning. But with whom, I wonder, with the porter? with a messenger? with a gigolo? Set the table. A child! now!'

'But now is the right age! soon she'll go on pension and will be able to stay with it all the time. She will have no regrets, not for the theatre, nor for the holidays, nor because she has to sit at home while others go out. She will feel privileged. A little frolicsome kid for her middle age and old age. Someone to talk to about flowers and dawns and sunsets. And about the old witch, Madame Bonsants –' I throw in and wait. Nothing happens.

'Yes, and the father? and she'll lose Geneviève's friendship, I feel it. It's as if she had turned into ice – her friend for ten years, do you understand?'

'Well, she has a boy-friend too.' What's the point of telling her now what I think? She wants to be like the Colonel with Nougatine. Let her.

'Yes, in a manner of speaking. I'll cut my throat if they've ever been – Geneviève isn't the kind of person to have a foot in two camps,' says Arlette with the most natural air in the world; my view is that Geneviève is the kind to have her feet all over the place.

'Yes, I think so too. Mutual social cover. Yet,' I say, supportively, 'the important thing now is to stand by Suzanne if she needs it, don't you think?'

'Yes, you're right, it's the only thing that counts. Oh, I'd like to do something for Geneviève too – but what?'

'If *you* don't know –' I say. No unusual reaction. 'Would you like me to speak to her?'

'No question of it.'

'To tell her that it would be a good idea if she accepts things as they are without eating herself up? That she could – why not? – think of Suzanne's child as theirs and they could bring it up together?

What do you say? That this is exactly what Suzanne had in mind?

'Oh, it's not possible. Too sensible. Geneviève isn't the type to accept advice. She has a head as hard as the Pyrenees and she's a lawyer. Advice with her is all one way: she gives it to other people!'

'In that sense she's a real dyke. She doesn't allow discussions, she's dogmatic, she doesn't talk about certain things. To tell the truth, she never speaks about any woman...'

'Don't be vulgar.'

And the conversation continues even when our eyes can no longer take it, what with balancing in the air half-truths, half-admissions, half-lies. I think of London, of the train and the ferry, of the double-decker buses I have never seen. Arlette slips heedlessly towards me and puts a hand on my chest and lays her little head shamefacedly against my shoulders.

During the last three weeks a progressive paresis has disfigured all the left side of the Colonel's face. His eye keeps weeping and I have told him that I have a job too and can't always be with him. He lives in terror of total paralysis. I didn't want it to be me who mentioned Mimizan, but he must have been thinking of it. It will have been largely the result of auto-suggestion, but he cannot manage to pronounce the whole sentence. He snorts, only snorts. Now he no longer even bothers to make all the empty bottles in the flat disappear, it has been transformed into a boring glassware shop. I have sworn that I won't do him the favour of interpreting his silences, which are full of entreaties, he will find the way himself to get down from the pedestal of such life as remains to him. Since he can't even make up his mind to call Nougatine, he looks at me with an incredulous and honey-sweet air: perhaps he didn't think that there existed a condition worse than the one in which he found himself up to yesterday. He no longer says 'ballocks', it must be serious. I look at him and continually send him the message: 'Make up your mind – leave Paris or go into a home or leave for Mimizan', but without saying a word and he does not react.

'Call Nougatine, explain to her,' he says at last, one day when he came in after falling because of a sudden cramp. 'You'll come with me, won't you? I'll give you a tip, garçon.'

'It would come in useful. I wouldn't refuse it.'

'I know, in London it will come in useful. Old Dreyfus has saved enough to afford it,' he says sticking out his chest. His mouth has contracted in a grimace which disfigures him right up to the left ear: it has become tight, even words have difficulty in passing through it. I think it should be a case for a not inconsiderable tip. The fact is that he really won't know how to spend it – all that money – walking on the beach in autumn with Nougatine – assuming that for the time being he still manages to walk. Nougatine on the telephone, doesn't seem surprised, she says that five years ago he had had a hint of this paresis and that then it had partly healed and that she is a bit alarmed at having to go home so soon, in mid-summer, which for her is half way to suicide, but what else can she do? So I take everything on in my spare time. I pack the books – five wooden chests to send to the removal agency – the clothes, the shoes, various white boxes full of indefinable objects. Not a letter, not a postcard: things like pencil sharpeners, corkscrews, corks, plastic corks, metal ones, automatics, boot horns, brushes, combs, scissors of all sizes, a notable collection of owls of all shapes and sizes, an old razor with what is maybe an ivory handle I think. Now I shall make a little parcel and at Mimizan, before saying goodbye, I'll give it him as a present and inside I'll put a note: 'Try to remember.' But for Nougatine I would do it; this unpunished crime annoys me, above all when I think that it is maybe imaginary – something I personally don't believe – and that one will never be able to know anything about it. He lies stretched on the bed while I put things away, with the usual bottle of red wine on the bedside table. He vaguely resembles Hemingway.

Then the men from the removal agency come to load everything.

When I come home, Arlette tells me she has decided to go away on Sunday, as she does more and more often – so I don't even tell her where I am going, seeing that I'll be back on the same day.

We talk about London, of this parting which is drawing closer. The Bradleys have even sent me a note in French... Actually it is Mrs Bradley who writes to me, then greetings from her husband and the adolescent son (another case of an interesting condition round about forty-four).

'And so you'll go to London, you'll learn English. It was really worthwhile finding you a job in a bank and then for you not to stay even four months...' says Arlette, who if she could, simply to make me stay here, would transplant me into that zone of her brain where she keeps her 'just a moment please'. 'Of course when one is so young a year is nothing. I'll be waiting for you. When you come back we'll move house, we'll go and live in a bigger one. We'll live together. Oh, please, be quiet: each one will have their freedom. With a couple of foreign languages you're certain to get a good job, maybe in a left-wing paper. Geneviève only finds it difficult to arrange jobs as messengers and waiters, the further up you go the easier it is for her, and I – Well, the same can always happen to me as happened to Suzanne... No, not with you, you'd only bring it up. Wouldn't you like that?'

'My God, what questions, what subjects, Arlette! I have the impression that you are repeating a lesson you've learnt by heart. It is a speech prepared by your fear of being left alone. And with this fear you really will be. I'm sorry to have reduced you to this. I'm deeply sorry. Was it Suzanne and Geneviève that put these things in your head?' I would like to add: to salvage your social responsibility? so now Suzanne's man pops up, Geneviève has her Hippolyte and I would be the third for you! All topics I can't bring into my conversation because even if I think that a bit of lesbianism can naturally enrich femininity, as far as I can see, Arlette seems to me to be boringly heterosexual and I really cannot imagine her in the arms of Geneviève or any other woman. I have the feeling that I am continually circling round a stronghold which is walled up alive from the inside: no real breach so that I can get in and put an end to these suppositions. And Arlette, here in front of me, seems the speaking image of eternal love.

'How can you love me like this, in a void?' I throw out, merely following the feeling that is uppermost in me. 'I don't feel anything for you. Maybe I would throw myself into the water to save you if you couldn't swim, but that doesn't mean love, love is...' I'd like to say 'unexpected' and 'doesn't save anyone' but I'd have to tell her about the Colonel and the story of Marie and I stop there.

'What is it?'

'Ballocks.'

'Don't talk nonsense. In any case I don't love you, you imagine it. How could a woman love you? What would she get out of it?' she says, asks herself: these are all rhetorical questions which always stop short and she by now is in a vicious circle that is entirely her own, hers and her friends', in which she never manages to include me; as she extends to the utmost this mysterious compass with which she surrounds existence, I make a little jump and am always outside the line she traces; by a hair's breadth but it is enough.

'Exactly, she would get nothing out of it. You are using my own words to affirm my own arguments, as if I wanted to use other ones to affirm other things. I don't know whether you realize that you are distressing yourself over a false problem, Arlette.'

'Set the table, take the lace table-cloth, the silver cutlery, the crystal glasses. I have the feeling that I am losing you for ever. And I don't want to think about it.' In this case too she uses empty words, because it is abstract to say 'not to think about it'. 'For me you are not a man, you're a Martian. You have a heart of stone. You have no heart. You can't even pretend a little. It's a great lack. You're asocial. Come on, pretend!'

She too! I seem to be hearing Macigna and Brother Fox once more saying to me: 'All you need to do is pretend to be a little nice', but they said it referring to third persons whom I was supposed to get something out of. Here the business of getting something out of somebody is straightforward: I'm suppose to pretend to myself to get something out of myself.

'Arlette, I feel like death. I'm exhausted. There's no hope for our relationship as you see it. Don't blame me for it. I can't help it.'

'My God, but why do I feel alive with you as never before and like with no one else for ten years?'

'Your caresses disgust me. I have always tolerated them, smiling because I was exhausted and well brought-up. But I can't go on pretending. They disgust me: I feel them to be profanations, emotional rather than sexual rapes, that's it, I could slap your face for every caress you give me. At night, when I could sleep at last I can't because I think: now she'll put her hands on me, will I manage to remove them without wounding her more than necessary? And it is a continual nightmare. It wasn't in the terms we agreed. Weren't we to stay good friends?' But I throw in this absurd phrase more to take a short cut, to leave the main road of cruelty, which is not essential to me, which I find so tiresome and out of place with her. But Arlette won't let me off and won't let herself off: she takes things literally.

'The terms we agreed! Your terms! But I am made of flesh and blood, I'm a human being, I don't amuse myself like you by making laws and imposing them on others, to keep them at a distance when it would be your own turn to give. It's you that lay down certain formalities, because you are arid of feelings, because there is no play in your sexuality, there's no evolution.'

'Thank heaven there isn't. I like it fine as it is, Ptolemaic, flat and circumscribed.'

'I haven't had a physical relationship with a man for ten years. Since the last abortion they all disgust me. And then you arrive with your false attentiveness, your false scientific courtesy, your little stories with their verbal diarrhoea. And I fell for it. And besides do you remember how diffident you were when you said that ours would be a pure and disinterested friendship? They all say that, how could I take you seriously?'

'But with me it's true, I was frank without being brutal.'

'Right. You could have made yourself clearer.'

Arlette sobs and the white canary emits groans too. I'd like to ask her: and with a woman?

She doesn't want my hand on her shoulder, which is only a gesture of brotherly feeling, precisely something of which, unlike me, she has always had less need.

'If you keep crying over them the meat-balls will taste of tears and I'll end up crying too,' I say to her, hoping to make her smile.

'For five months I've been waiting for something to happen, for you to make me feel a woman . . .' She has always used clichés like that 'to feel a woman', 'to feel oneself a man' and good luck to anyone who knows what that means. 'You can't understand what these ten years of loneliness have been . . . in this flat, without any experience of the city to begin with. And then suddenly embittered, disgusted, isolated. I haven't been lucky. First the Spaniard, now you. But he at least . . .'

In fact Arlette is like the cunning old man with the squint perennially in search of his own lost assassin. But I don't have to stay here much longer, with the tip the Colonel will give me and my pay for the month I could even leave within the fortnight perhaps within the week. If only it wasn't she who maintained the contact with the Bradleys.

'Paris-London is less than an hour's flight; I could come on Friday and go back on Sunday evening. I want to make up again before sitting down at table. I shall be very beautiful, yes, very beautiful.

268

And desirable. For the canary there. And uncork that other blessed bottle of champagne. We'll drink to my failures.'

'Do you want me to tell a story?'

'Your stories! I see now that they were only stories and that was all. Without even an ending. Have I ever had to take in anything more literary and squalid than your stories?'

'Why? what did you think they were? I invented them for me, for you, for us. And listen who's talking about reality! I want reality too! You want certainties, to come to a conclusion, to make things add up, the opposite of any reality!'

By chance, *en passant*, full of resentment, that night I made love to Arlette. I gave in. I was too curious to know where my finger-tips would find the tiny obstacle in the texture of her buttocks.

And before opening the door, when she, ready to start over again, was begging me not to go away, where was I going, my God, at this time of day, I said to her:

'And Arlette, no stories about abortions with me. No one ever got pregnant that way.'

In the train, next day, or rather late in the morning of the same day, the Colonel and I and two huge military canvas suitcases take the train for Mimizan. I simply hope he doesn't forget the tip.

'What was in that parcel from Marie then?' he asks without curiosity, simply for something to say.

'A razor with an ivory handle like yours, and a towelling dressing-gown.'

'What an idea,' he says thinking of something else.

'Perhaps she didn't manage to find anything else down in the village. Or perhaps she wanted to tell me I could cut it off,' I bring out, having to invent something quickly, seeing that the package passed into his hands too between Chamonix and Paris. As if it could contain anything other than the white paper masks of *Antigone* and some figure of speech about love, the drooping little piece of theatre about *feelings* etc.

'The brooch you gave Nougatine is very nice, what stone is it?' I say trying to get on to the subject while pretending to change it.

'I don't remember, chalcedony, I think, nothing special,' and he begins to doze again and then to snore. There's no one in our first-class compartment. It's so much better without people packed together producing omelettes and greasy packages as in the second class in Italy. I leave the Colonel finally to his own fate, Nougatine to hers – Nougatine insisted on giving me her heliotrope, which I was most unwilling to accept – and I take the first train back to Paris.

These two hundred pounds – equivalent to more than a month's work – given to me by the Colonel have set my feet itching. Every hour passed with Arlette feels like an eternity. I want to leave, to go away as soon as possible and to leave as many fates as I can to their fate. Busy myself with the luxurious lack of my own. Tomorrow, Tuesday, Wednesday at the latest, I need give no notice, work is falling off, a lot of people are on holiday already, I'll lose the insurance money for the penicillin, but never mind. A letter from Lucia: greetings – she doesn't ask why I didn't come to see her, why I didn't even phone her – and seeing Carolina is dead don't I want to send a telegram of condolences. That they shouldn't have kept her in plaster so long. That she suffered, that almost nothing was left inside the plaster. Then I take a sheet of paper and an envelope and begin. I find I don't know what to say and feel nothing: neither sorrow, nor nostalgia, nor *indifference*. I make some efforts of memory: the eve of Santa Lucia, me on the stairs of the block of government-subsidised houses where I lived and she who knew it and promptly at five came to take me out of the freezing cold of the night and gave me a tray of cakes and a toy; my mother telling the story of Carolina when the Allies arrived: 'They had put them in a cart drawn by two donkeys and had shaved their heads and got up like that they took them through the village, every part of it, because they had gone with the Germans. There was the girl from Asti, The Quiet One, the Good-for-Nothing and Carolina. She was the only one who answered back when the people spat on them and everyone shouted 'Coooows! Whooores!' and pails of piss coming down from the windows. And then when the Americans came, Carolina and the Good-for-Nothing, to get their own back, what do they do? they jump on to the first jeep and whoops! they're there with their arses sticking out of the windows. And when the Americans with the truck went about handing stuff out, they were always on it and said: this one yes, that one no – in Eng-lish! depending on who had called them whores and had thrown down the piss. And when you were scarcely born she came out from Montichiari and took you home as if you were hers. She was quite mad. You took after her.' But nothing about the innumerable days spent with her among the ditches and fields looking for snails and mushrooms and gleaning, cutting grass for the rabbits, stealing heads of maize. I remember nothing, that is, they evoke no nostalgia. And to that daughter of hers and her few relations I don't know what to say: the love I felt I no longer feel and my memories seem to me neither pleasant nor unpleasant: they are part of the ordinary manure of the earth, they are useless in my mind, they no longer belong to me. And after half an hour over the white page, finally, I feel my eyes grow wet by dint of concentration, so as to have some idea of the words someone utters who imposes on himself a sorrow that has nothing to do with him. I am desperately sorry not to feel anything at this news, my sorrow is more grief at having suddenly nothing to say, nothing I can transmit to anyone else. Death leaves me dry. I have never understood the cult of the dead, the funerals, the wakes, the wreaths, the need for ceremony to bury another human animal, another so little loved and respected in life. In any case, usually, when someone dies old, they rarely die without having long been dead in all those who remain. So now I write a couple of formal sentences where, as a child, the breadth of an epic poem would not have been enough for me. My love for Carolina was a happy and perfect love, recipro- cal, full of tenderness and of joy, a love which experienced all the fullness it deserved: perhaps it is for this reason that it has left no trace in me, and probably, not in her either. It was not cut short or violated in any way: it burnt out to the last spark, day after day, and then nothing more was left, because true things never leave anything behind them.

Arlette makes her entry on her return from the office and says: 'Suzanne and Geneviève want to know the day and the exact time of your departure, they want to come to the train, to make you promise to come back.'

'How nice of them! with all the hot potatoes they have in their heads, their necks, their groins and various orifices, they still have time to think about me. But of course I'll come back, where am I supposed to go, seeing that all you need is a couple of lies to make you happy. After England I'll go to Germany, Arlette, and then to Spain. Tomorrow I'm going to the bank to get paid off, I'll leave the day after tomorrow.'

'Your usual vulgar self. And tomorrow evening we're going to Saint Germain to eat couscous.'

'Of course, if there are no difficulties at the bank I could leave tomorrow evening.'

'Tomorrow you can't, you have to tell Suzanne and Geneviève at least a week beforehand when you are going. They have presents for you. But hadn't you best wait till the treatment...'

'My blood has cleared up very nicely and the treatment isn't a problem any more. I'm trying to learn to do the injections myself. Today, at the third attempt, I managed to get the needle in.'

'I've bought a present for the Bradleys, a plate of Sèvres china with another smaller one on top, it can be put together as a fruit dish. You'll have to be careful how you put it in your suitcase.'

'Why not a rock crystal carafe! This mania for presents – and fragile ones too.'

'But my dear, the Bradleys might wonder where you came from if you arrived empty-handed. It isn't done and that's that. In any case it's well wrapped up in straw, it doesn't take up much room. You're very nice in your new dressing-gown. Have you a story to tell me? Seeing that you don't ask about me, about what I did in the country –'

'I think so, I have the very story for you, I feel cheerful tonight. I'll have nothing to stop me from telling you all the stories you want. But nothing to titillate my innate egoism as an exorcist, all right? I am a prince transformed into a migrating pigeon by What-a-Life, a very ordinary witch. Migrant pigeon, prince of an extinct dynasty, my fate is to fly aimlessly from one country to another without ever becoming snared by the tourists' enforced goals. My peers keep apart from me, they feel that I am of a different breed and I do nothing to hide it and they have all kinds of suspicions about my resemblance to themselves. And solitary, I come and go, following the first wind that comes my way, alone and aimless like me. I have neither nest nor cranny, neither father nor mother nor brothers nor lovers nor offspring. I fly. And when I no longer know what to do I fly on, and I spread the rumour that something exists that is an end in itself but that you can reach it only after resigning yourself to the fact that everything is a function of something else. My aristocratic nature is nothing compared to my far-sighted demo-cracy, because I have never made use of it. And a Prince Charming transformed into a pigeon is not very different from a pigeon nor from a pigeon transformed into a Prince Charming in blue: we are

272

animal dimensions in various degrees of blue, but nothing else. My wings are sturdy and can take me anywhere and I never rest. Neither on roofs nor on main-masts. Between here and there I use up my life as if in a reality, waiting to wake up or fall asleep. Nothing frightens me: neither fires, nor storms, nor hunger, nor fatigue. Once I tried to kill myself, deliberately, with the smoke from a chimney, because the uniformity of my dimension had frightened me to death. I have such incongruous moments, perilously sentimental ones. And perhaps I am really dead, I don't know, I don't remember. Flying over Venice, the night is bitter and the dawn a red carcass, an albino foctus.'

'Venice,' Arlette repeats to herself. 'Is it true that it's sinking?'

'You're not a good feed, you always give me the least appropriate lines. With you it is impossible to reach a climax of even average range.'

'What are you saying? What do you mean?'

'Nothing.'

In fact I was about to say something to her: that the mystery is still where it was and that the fact, a commonplace one after all, of Suzanne's interesting condition and of her mysterious lover no longer has the power to distract me from the focal point of my original intuition: Geneviève. And that is why I'd like to avoid meeting them at the station, reconciled now, Geneviève resigned to her paternal role, Suzanne with the same air which is now decidedly maternal and celestial, somehow cruel towards her friend of ten years who finds herself betrayed in the most brutal way, I think, for a lesbian, 'take it or leave it'. To avoid them, to avoid Geneviève, because now I have taken over her personality and find myself, without knowing it, following its internal contours, searching for their original matrix, and I try to recapture her voice, her look when I chanced to be with her, when she felt so good, so safe, that she could trust. And something says to me: don't do anything more, stay as you are, you already are Geneviève. When I think of the photo of Geneviève! on the window ledge *cleaning the panes*! Maybe whistling, going out and in, without even worrying about where she was putting her feet. With some maid inside begging her to come down and her reassuring everyone, saying she didn't understand, that someone had to do it after all. She must have an extra sense, it's not surprising given her physiognomy, her physical constitution.

273

She thinks that if she falls, she'll fall right on her paws and won't hurt herself. From the sixth floor. Like a cat. But if she was not cleaning the windows what the devil was she doing there, displaying herself on the window sill with her legs apart?

'Why have you never asked me any more about Suzanne and Geneviève?' Arlette asks me, overcoming her natural reluctance to bring up her godmother-guardians and who knows what else, if one thinks of the strange violence with which she snatched from my hands her precious relics. The only thing I would like to ask her is this sort of thing: what colour is the underwear of an albino with an apartment as showy as hers? Arlette must have taken the photograph of Geneviève either with her agreement or for some motive that cannot be confessed: to fix on the roll of film the ruinous shattering of a secret, the white shadow under the billowing dressing-gown. Her friend, with her legs apart on the window-still, was wearing *nothing* underneath. And from below, for Arlette it must have been like measuring an upside-down well, an aerial well in all its remote magnificence.

'Do you feel you gave me answer when I did?' But now I am too taken up with my departure, now I have no more psychological time. Now, when I think of them, I see myself in front of a kind of temple made by priestesses where no man can enter and where even the king is received on the threshold. And where silence reigns. And which they rejoice in, they have created it for themselves. Do they want invisibility? let them have it. Artificial insemination? social cover? Let them experiment if they like, now it has nothing to do with me. I am leaving.

The next day it is clear that Arlette has not made the slightest mention of my departure to Suzanne and Geneviève because when we are back from the Moroccan restaurant in Saint Michel she suddenly says:

'I have a big surprise for you: the journalist, Geneviève's botanist friend, will try to fix an appointment for you with Montherlant.'

'Am I supposed to believe that? He sees no one, he is too taken up with looking inside his blindness, can you imagine him receiving me. Besides, I'm afraid that as a man he doesn't interest me at all. It would be the first time that an interesting artist was also an interesting man. It's better to stay with one's illusions.'

'What I mean is you just have to stay another week and he'll try to arrange it. He's not the ogre people say.'

'Arlette, forget it, come on. You know that if I stay in Paris any longer I'll end up not having any money for London and will have to work another month and one can't resign from a job and be taken on again the next day. Why do you lay all these traps? I must leave and I'll do so tomorrow. At half past eleven at night.'

Arlette goes to the bathroom, I hear the noise of the water in the bath. She won't expect me to repeat the *tour de force* of last week! Oh, if only I could leave now, go to a place I know.

In the semi-darkness of the room – it was almost dawn, we had forgotten to draw the big curtain – I took her breasts in my hands, as I had seen people do in films, I twisted them delicately in a clockwise direction and then, to my great amazement, began to run my thumb, moistened with saliva round the nipples, which were crowned with tips as big as rosary beads which turned hard; I felt the skin getting tight all round and the zone became firmer and I began to kiss them, without knowing why and to nibble at them as well – it seemed to me to be the right thing to do, that something like this was expected. I kissed her on the mouth, but she doesn't know how to kiss, unlike Marie's mouth, which is bigger and generous and damp, and sucks more. To begin with she has such a little mouth, and then she kept her teeth too close together, as if she were afraid they would fall out, and you could feel only the sharp and strong tip of her little tongue, and it felt to me like the kiss of a stubborn little girl, but a viperish one taking her first amorous steps. I tried to resist turning her roughly round to get a good look at her buttocks. I smiled to her, without understanding in fact what I was doing and hoped she would come as soon as possible because I knew that my erection was fortuitous (she had wakened me after I don't know how long, she had taken off my drawers in my sleep, she had grasped my cock in her little well-cared-for hands and had made me come on her, turning me round bodily and trying to insert it herself; and when I sleep I am always excited: my excitement wouldn't last long because it had nothing to do with her, she was merely making it hers, stealing it from my oneiric bottoms and pricks). I looked at her face damp with sweat, so tiny and hot, suavely perfect, and I said to myself, a pity about those eyes so small and impassioned, passion doesn't entirely suit them, those lips which are so cutting a pity it is her and not Marie and not Giacomino. But as I made up

275

my mind finally to slip my hands over her hips, the fact that she was she and no one else began to excite me, I abandoned the mechanical business of thrusting; she whispers my name – no other one than mine, I even felt pleased – and I, not knowing what to say in what was for me an unusual case, said; 'I'm here', embarrassedly, but more than anything else to convince myself wholly. On the left buttock, finally, by dint of cautious palpation, I felt a hollow, she kept sighing things like 'again, again' etc. I stopped and asked her:

'What's this hole here?' pressing on her buttock.

'I cut myself on a gate when I was a child.'

'Oh yes?'

And when, in spite of my efforts and also of that little initial feeling of languor I began to feel on my foreskin (a nervous termination unlike any other, never felt before and very pleasing), the erection is over and I haven't even come, she had had an orgasm and I don't know what took me and, perhaps hoping to excite myself, I slipped down there where the smell of the overall was immediate. And I said to myself, now I'll do you properly and then we'll give over for ever. It was when I raised her legs as men do and began to go down on her that she raised that agonizing cry which echoed in the deserted Place de la Bastille.

'Oh, yes, please!'

Now I don't know much about female parts in front: I would not be able to tell a virgin from a whore in a brothel or a lady. But as for the posterior well, I know at once and perfectly what I can deduce from the tension or the relaxed state of the tissues offered. With Arlette it was not worth while taking any precaution. The passage could be described as very fresh, a matter of a couple of days before: no friction was any longer possible. She twisted about, it was incredible how she performed with that little somewhat pear-like bottom of hers, but I felt I was on the other side of a black hole. Out of curiosity I came out and said to her:

'Arlette, take a breather.'

'Do you like it?'

'Beyond anything. Can I put on the light?'

'Be quiet. No,' she said firmly.

A Minotaur had indeed passed that way.

'Why are you looking at me like that?' asks Arlette a moment after she comes out of the bathroom. And to think that at twelve I still had the problem of walking like a duck with my feet turned out and that I forced myself to turn in the toes of my shoes and to walk was a torture, each step a violence to the tendons and now, almost ten years on, I am here, pondering to myself on *cunnilingus* and sodomy practised on women by other women with goodness knows what apparatus and I don't even walk flat-footed any more.

'I was looking at you.'

'That's what it looked like to me. What were you thinking about?'

'I couldn't say. Aren't you sleepy? Do you know what time it is?'

'Sleep then, I'll read a little, do you like my new nightdress? When I was at it I bought a real pair of pyjamas for you too, not that rag there. And a pair of flannel shirts. It's cold even in summer you know, the London climate. Oh, yes, you wanted to sleep.'

'If you go on chattering I certainly won't be able to.'

'You know what Suzanne declared in front of me and Geneviève? That she knows perfectly well what we are thinking, but we mustn't give it a thought: when the time comes the father will pop out because he must recognize his child, willy-nilly. You know, the law on paternity. Aren't you interested?'

'It's not that it isn't interesting. But what need does Suzanne have to give her son a father? Above all it's not money she lacks.'

'Oh she's not without means. But money – there's never enough money. I think she even gets a percentage on deals successfully completed.'

'Or perhaps it is because of this mad desire to conform, to return to the bosom of normality and of the conventions. An amoral question nevertheless. Well, goodnight,' I throw out in the improbable hope of fishing four hours' sleep from an inexhaustible reserve of words.

'You haven't even noticed that I have had my eyebrows plucked. And the parting in my hair is on the left instead of on the right.'

'You know I pay no attention to such things.' But it's not true: I know perfectly well why a woman wears a certain dress and puts on a certain kind of rouge and combs her hair like that, there is never anything that leaves me indifferent in a woman; if she wears open sandals I run my eyes over the nails to see if they are varnished and am always fascinated by Sicilian widows who at funerals wear mourning that is very tight over the breasts and the thighs. 'A woman

277

with a body like yours shouldn't waste it on homosexuals. And, my God, there are masses of you. The moment you catch the scent of a homosexual you feel it your duty to find something there and end up by losing your heads. And when you kiss,' I say yawning, 'you must open your mouth more, you keep it too shut, you must part your teeth, let your tongue move about.'

'Like this?'

'More or less – that's better already. And now goodnight, don't pester me. And don't waken me again.'

'I don't know how to kiss because Pablo gave me the last kiss. You know I won't kiss anyone else for another ten years. For me there is only you. And I will wait all the time you need to repeat last night.'

'But what do lesbians use with each other, besides the tongue? Wooden or rubber phalluses: do they fasten them to their bellies with straps?'

Arlette looks at me out of the corner of her eye.

'You promised not to speculate about our friends? Why don't you ask them directly? Do you know what risks you run if it came out, don't you? You'd really find yourself in pieces in the Seine. They'd do away with you. I'm not being dramatic.'

'I think so too, I understand your fear now. But why is a woman like Geneviève so afraid of people knowing she's lesbian?'

'Geneviève is a political woman. Hundreds of thousands of francs are involved in her researches. She can't allow herself to take any risks. Well, it's better that way,' says Arlette with relief.

'What is?'

'I was just saying.'

So there's more to it. What, for heaven's sake? Besides it is not possible that her rivals don't know about her women, including Arlette. So if they don't make use of it it's because it isn't a sufficient reason. So what is Geneviève defending? What is she hiding that is so counterproductive? Probably nothing.

'If you were to say to me: leave with me, tomorrow I'll give notice and leave with you. Don't you believe me? put me to the test. What will I do here with this double and triple life and no one.'

'But I would never give you an invitation of that kind, you have too much need to be protected every minute. And you who demand reality from others, you get too much fun out of changing the cards on the table. Let's go our own ways. Arlette, I can't deceive you, say things to you I don't feel. There, now all I need to do is to make you cry.'

'Why don't you learn to lie sometimes? It is as if you stabbed me each time.'

'So it's best to say nothing. Goodnight.'

She is waiting for something, keeps sitting against the end of the bed and turns over in her mind everything a wounded, desperate and overburdened woman can turn over. And what about leaving! And what would Geneviève and Suzanne think? Would they let her? Perhaps Arlette is the depository of some secret, I don't know, a military one or something like that. At certain moments she releases terror and fear from her body. And in the end, after whole nights spent sleeplessly explaining, lacerating her spirit to escape from clichés, cleaving her heart in two to look for some possible sincerity, lo and behold the usual idea triumphs:

'But aren't there cures, treatments? There must be some therapy! Why don't you talk to Geneviève?'

I feel that under all this there is a fairly obvious trap, even if it is not altogether clear to me. I turn round and without more ado with one hand take her chin and with the other give her a hard slap and then another.

'Cow, nasty shitty cow. Pervert. Fascist. Why don't you get treatment yourself along with your two friends?'

And I go off at four in the morning in a taxi as far as the Trocadero, deserted and lit as bright as day, foaming with rage.

At ten, time for the office for Arlette, I go home determined to leave alone with my two suitcases, without the Bradleys' fruit-dish.

'Arlette, where are the suitcases?' I ask her on the phone, trying to keep calm.

'They're at the Gare du Nord. I have the ticket. Before leaving we must make peace. What do you have in that brown box? I hadn't seen it before.'

'It's two bath-towels, my sister gave me them along with the dressing-gown. I had completely forgotten about them.'

'And did you have to put string round it?'

'What the fuck do you want from me? what do I know. All right, let's make a peace. But I want to leave today.'

'Tomorrow.'

279

'All right, tomorrow.'

And at the Gare du Nord on Saturday, too many days later with the excuse that 'there was no room on the train', Arlette, Geneviève, Suzanne and I have a good half-hour before my departure. Yet, with the excuse that there was 'a matinée one shouldn't miss' they tried even today to postpone it: but thanks to the final combustion of *Jeanne d'Arc au bûcher* by Honegger we made it – at least I have. The last interval never came and, full of resentment, peevish, with wings on my feet already, so that I wouldn't notice I ended up remaining awake and attentive until the cremation of that untimely paladin.

Geneviève, while she handed me a white felt case, looked at me from another world.

'Oh, cuff-links,' and I immediately recognized, besides the platinum, the green heliotrope speckled with red that Nougatine wore on the lapel of her jacket; in ancient times it was thought that this stone had the power to make one invisible. 'What stone is it?'

'Oh, a kind of chalcedony. Do you like them?' says Suzanne instead of Geneviève. My glance is devoid of any trace of gratitude, and has a new gleam for Geneviève.

Arlette, since we got into the taxi, has not let go of my hand for a moment under the rotundly maternal glance of Suzanne, who peach-skinned, milky-voiced, has a real belly. Geneviève, wrapped in a white and yellow and black two-piece, trousers very wide at the top and narrow at the ankles, allows one to guess at a beauty of incomparable forms, even if her breasts must be very small and flat and perhaps not even her own. She has painted her lips brick-red in that completely white face, with a light down that trembles beneath her pink nostrils. Men stop in amazement to look at her, thunderstruck by the strange creature who could hold up dozens of English trains that were about to leave if, while thinking of something else, she were to raise the lance of her glance towards the rails. Yet this ostentation of hers has something defensive which conceals her.

Suzanne, more chaste and relaxed in her linen dress which falls over and covers her belly, has words of comfort for everyone and is very grateful to me for not having asked her any questions during these last weeks. It is the same placid Suzanne as ever, fecund from a fecundation which seems not even hers or anyone else's, something which she *alone* has assumed the burden of carrying to its termination for a higher cause. They all try to make me believe it to the full.

Each one is scrupulous to say something to fill up the wait for the train – which is already standing at the platform – and we say forcedly witty things to each other under the lights of the dome as if nothing had changed since that first dinner organized by the Alliance Française for *this* Alliance Française. Geneviève stands erect in front of me with her hand in front of her in a vaguely obscene gesture, her feet planted firmly on the ground, her legs apart: all she needs to do is to pull out the bottle of cleaning fluid and to wave her red pants in the other hand. She looks at me in a way that is uneasy and insolent at the same time: the same look of insolent alarm with which Madame Bonsanta received me in the restaurant at the bank. Then I didn't know and now that I *know* nothing is changed.

'How the yellow and white and black suits you, Geneviève, you look ten years younger, as if you needed to. Jeanne d'Arc, if she had dressed like that instead of in a very boring cuirass, would have routed the enemy sitting on a terrace taking a pastis. I hope my compliments don't bore you.'

Geneviève has a profoundly embarrassed expression and looks fixedly at Arlette, who looks away and stares at Suzanne. The dear girls – so jealous of their dark places which have now been torn open, still so united against me, who am making myself scarce.

'Geneviève,' I continue undeterred: it certainly won't be me who shows her the book of her *infamies*, she will go to the pyre by herself; I must simply think how to betray myself a little at least if I want to save myself entirely – in twenty-seven minutes exactly – 'you have the finest bearing in Paris. You could be described as France's white angel. Gène d'Arc,' I venture. The important thing is to say certain things with determination.

In any case they deserve it: it was they who made me sit in the theatre for five hours gasping and tense. A prologue and eleven, *eleven* scenes. It's no wonder if I still seem to hear the extremely nasal celestial voice calling 'Jeanne! Jeanne!'

'Have you seen how you stop everyone in their tracks?' I say, hastening to blush a little, just enough to be forgiven if it should sound rude. But Geneviève is quick to spot that my target is a different one and that I can not only pronounce precisely *jeune, jaune, gêne, gène* and *Geneviève d'Arc* but am also capable of distinguishing between a Jean with an *arc* and a Jeanne with an arrow. I want to reassure her somehow that I will keep her secret to myself, red pants and all.

'Oh, assez avec votre charme! You are the only one to believe these things, mon petit. Anyone would stop to look at an elephant on a bicycle or a woman who looks like a cone of whipped cream with a preserved cherry on top. Vous reviendrez, n'est-ce pas?' she asks, bringing into focus her glance which is by its nature absent.

'Oh, but of course he will come back. He and Arlette have got to be godparents, have you forgotten?' says Suzanne anticipating my habitual and increasingly feeble Yes. 'We will stay faithful to you and you to us, won't you, dear? And with English I have a marvellous job ready for you at four hundred thousand francs a month. Can godparents ever be poor?'

'Which you will spend all on us and only on us, won't you?' adds Arlette, forcing herself to be funny, her pathetic and rapacious little hand is clutching mine. 'How long is there to go?' she asks then, pursuing her most desolate thoughts, far from our conventional chatter, which is both allusive and disturbing.

'There's time, ma petite. Let's sit in the bar while Geneviève goes and buys magazines for the journey: come on, Arlette, you'll break his hand if you hold it like that!' And all three begin to laugh; a second and the laughter has already died. What else can one invent?

'Geneviève, I'll come too,' I say, getting up from the table and following her. These links must cost a fortune and, in their turn, buy one. But I wouldn't let myself be made invisible.

We go up to the kiosk, we look at some magazines. Geneviève every so often looks up and stares at me. Who must begin first? And is it necessary? And all I want, now, is to prevent her, because of me, from making some false step, I'd merely like to make her understand that nothing will come from me to disturb her equilibrium and that I too will continue to believe that the kind of cover M. Hippolyte affords her is merely social. But it is difficult. Besides I have the feeling that she knows that she no longer belongs only to the late Madame d'Orian, at whose hands she suffered the first and definitive violence, to Madame Bonsants, and to Suzanne and to Arlette and to the venereal gardener on whom she has imposed her bewitching and generous rule but to me as well, who am defined not in terms of a flight but of a simple deparfure. She, who if she had been a man could have aspired to be accepted among France's

Immortals, whether she did it on purpose or not, has become entangled with one of her albino hairs in the spectrum of my sensibility, and a reflection of her existence today depends on me.

'Geneviève, we haven't much time. And to tell the truth I don't want to talk about anything you don't want. I only want to say this: that I have not and never will say anything to anyone, and that Arlette is faithful to you and not a word has come from her mouth and that she is perfect. But I dreamed a dream: the white bull was charging at me and suddenly I understood everything, that is the little that is essential to me. I like you and want you to believe that I am your friend. From the bottom of my heart. I so much hope that everything can continue better than before, now, and that you will all be happy.'

Geneviève did not say: how did he get there? Fearing that if I got there her secret is therefore discoverable and can be discovered by others. She knows it is not like that, that losses of identity like mine are not so common and that the breach is not in her (something which, if I didn't tell her, would certainly lead her to make false steps, that is to say awaken suspicions because for the first time since she was born she might put herself on the defensive, the most fatal of errors, and change some aspects of her behaviour or dress) but in me, in this natural inclination of mine to immerse myself in the personality of others.

'Thank you. I knew I could trust you. But now let's go back.'

With some magazines and arm in arm – one can't imagine a more formal 'arm-in-arm' – Geneviève and I return to the table and since I have been told not to buy the ticket now it is Suzanne's turn.

'Take this meanwhile. It's my little present. It's so uncomfortable, travelling in a couchette. And don't worry we'll look after Arlette in the meantime. In love age means nothing,' says Suzanne with her hands crossed peacefully in her lap; she is the most authoritative witness to that assertion. But is it possible that they really think I'm in love with Arlette? Isn't there perhaps another invitation for a cherished victim on its way to the secretariat of the Alliance Française already?

'One day,' says Geneviève, pointing at the links which I am turning over in my hands, 'you will wear only silk shirts with our links and they will look very good. You'll never wear any others – promise. You won't forget your friends, mon petit?' and she is right back in her role of Geneviève-Geneviève.

'How could I?' I say screwing up my eyes, this time as a sign of gratitude, and I can see myself already in a T-shirt in Chelsea in the company of some Jamaican with a prick as big as a tobacco leaf.

'Oh,' exclaims Suzanne, 'But you've got a sexy magazine there too! Since May '68 that's all anyone reads! Well, let's drink a toast in our mints.'

'To our minds?!' I reply.

We raise our glasses of green water and whisper wishes for good luck, happiness, female children, while the departure is being announced over the loudspeaker. Suzanne and Geneviève wanted us to have some gin in us.

'Au revoir!'

'Au revoir!'

And Arlette and I go off along the platform. Her hand annoys me more than ever; another three minutes, I keep repeating to myself, and I shall be free for ever from this tentacle. I won't even write her a postcard to say I have arrived safely, that her porcelain fruit-dish gave the Bradleys great pleasure.

'Write as soon as you get there. But right away, promise! Don't make me worry.'

I feel like telling her: Arlette aren't the things that happened to you in May '58 a bit much? And who was Pablo-Pablito really? The most linear version to avoid too many superimpositions of time-space?

'A promise. Come, don't cry. You should be glad to be rid of me for a while.'

'Now it will all be as nasty as before. I'll go home and won't even feel like cooking myself an egg. I'll sit in front of the television-set I have ordered and will wait till Friday evening to go to mass with my mother on Sunday. Tell me the moment you have settled in, I'll come and see you. If you have money problems...'

'I've told you I have plenty of money' I say, thinking that if I have money problems I shall immediately go and sell these links which feel like red-hot handcuffs in my pocket.

'Well I don't have much but I wouldn't think of asking Suzanne or Geneviève for it.'

'But have you told them I am in love with you?'

'What I am obliged to tell them is none of your business. Do you

284

want to wound me even now. *If it isn't true* it shouldn't matter to you what I have or haven't told them.'

She won't even cook herself an egg, she'll watch the colour television and she'll wait till her turn comes and she finally makes it, before or after or between Suzanne and Hippolyte. In short, the mystery of Suzanne made fecund could really exist, I mean it could really have been a *message-boy* unless five months ago she decided to put her back to the wall and say: 'Geneviève, *mon cher*, either this way or it's all over between us.'

'Arlette, try to take up with someone else. Try to get into your head once and for all that there's no future for us two, that it's unlikely that I'll come back to you in Paris, because I never go back twice to the same place and if I do I have to escape at once because it is always a guaranteed failure. I don't like seeing someone I know through and through. I wouldn't be able to keep silent.'

'You're like an assassin, you,' says Arlette, trying to find refuge in the usual cliché.

'Yes, you're right. Where I pass, I sow corpses and depression, if you want to put it that way. But I have never been one of the many last drops that make the glass overflow. I have never filled anything from the bottom up, I have always found everything already on the point of brimming over. Everything belongs already. Even with you. Even in other cases. I wouldn't have either the energy or the patience or the time to invent more and more new sufferings for myself, Arlette, it is so difficult and unrewarding that task of *always* making people suffer. It's leaving, go back to Suzanne and Geneviève. Goodbye. And let the canary go.'

'You can always have me near you even if you never love me. We could have a bigger house, I could ask for a loan from the family, we could...'

And from the end of the platform Suzanne and Geneviève wave a white handkerchief and I wave one too, while Arlette walks towards her guardians in a way that allows one to forecast only good: without turning round. Suzanne and Geneviève receive her one on each side. In the light of dawn I leave my wagon-lit and go on board the ferry-boat. I look at the sea before me. My God, how alive I am. I take the links from my pocket and throw them into the Channel. Goodbye, Madame Geneviève, the Minotaur.

The customs inspection is done right there in Victoria Station. They form us into a queue along the pavement which a cordon separates from the rest of the right of way. Everyone gets past the barrier without difficulty. The officer I get asks how much money I have. I say three hundred pounds. He puts on a fairly amiable face. And what do I have in that big bag? Personal things. English grammars.

'Open up.' As he says this three other officers, among them a woman come round me. I open the suitcase, I open the bag.

'Do you know anyone in London?'

'Yes.'

'Who? Do you by any chance have a letter to show us?'

I show the very bureaucratic letter written by Mrs Bradley with a view to this customs formality.

'And what is in that paper?'

'A fruit-dish. A present.'

And I open it. From the paper and the straw emerge the two layers of porcelain with blue and white convolvululses and the brass stem. A really fine object.

'And in that package?' he says pointing to Marie's box which is still untouched by scissors.

'Oh that! Masks, a memento.'

'What kind of masks?'

'Masks, cardboard cut and painted. In white.'

'Open it.'

So trying to keep calm (I am not at all the kind of person who thinks: it had to happen to me. Things happen to me and amen.) I begin to pull at the string at the corners so that it will slips down. But the string is too tight, then a hand reaches out a pair of scissors. Then I take off the brown paper and begin to hate England.

'*You* look,' I say a little resentfully, still in French. Meanwhile my passport has been examined by at least five guardians of their law and order. He lifts the lid and in the same instant with the other hand pushes back the peak of his cap. They all come running. The policewoman looks elsewhere.

'Masks, eh? Follow me.'

'But may I know why?'

'Get along, get along,' says another digging his elbow in my liver. 'Shut your cases and come with us.'

As best I can I get suitcase and bag together and drag them with

286

me, always being careful not to let Arlette's fruit-dish fall.

'Sit down,' says the first official, he opens a desk drawer and takes out a file. 'You shitty Italians!' I am dumbfounded, speechless.

'So this is supposed to be a mask, eh?' he says taking a rag and sticking his hand with his fingers spread wide into Marie's box, and into the air, like a jack-in-the-box, jumps an enormous black rubber phallus. 'Traffic in pornography. You can get two weeks in prison for a thing like that. Masks! A rubber phallus.'

In the box, after it has been shaken by the hand for a moment that is an eternity, I see the cube of foam rubber into which the black thing had been perfectly fitted.

'What shall we say then?'

'I really don't understand. I didn't...' I venture timidly.

'You all say that. Dirty Italian sex maniacs.'

'What can I do?' I ask, humiliated by this nasty trick pinned on me by my painful romanticism.

'First and foremost immediate confiscation and destruction of the article. Then: a fine of two hundred pounds and the cancellation of the offence and the right to step onto Her Majesty's territory, or else two months' prison and expulsion for five years from Her Majesty's territory. Choose!'

'Choose,' I mutter without the least tinge of anger in my voice. Marie said that anyone who loves is unpredictable. Well, this is. 'Couldn't one do a week in prison, let's say, and pay a hundred pound fine and then set foot on Her Majesty's territory.' I've never yet had the experience of prison and a week would still come under the heading of *souvenirs de voyage*.

'No,' he says puffing, 'such a possibility is not contemplated.'

'All right then.' I pull out the two hundred pounds and from afar I seem to hear the sneer and a clipped 'ballocks, ballocks'. However while I am counting them I feel that life is beginning to go my way, I say 'May I?' and empty the foam rubber from the box and then put the bull's prick back in it. In fact underneath there is a white envelope, the shape of a visiting-card:

>Who was in life an enemy, does not in death
>   become a friend.

Obviously some quotation from *Antigone*.

Damn it, this is a story which *is going to end* – even if I have to begin

287

from the beginning again, two hundred pounds lighter, asking for alms outside the city walls and leading a beggar's life. And tomorrow or the day after tomorrow or whenever it is and whatever time it is in the course of a couple of seconds I shall have forgotten everything again. There are more explanations that lead nowhere and are definitive than there are others which lead somewhere but remain open. And so, what remains of all the pain I thought to have suffered? Nothing, only counterfeited reminiscences, apocryphal tales.